21.80

Hollywood Boulevard

Janyce Stefan-Cole

UNBRIDLED BOOKS

Hollywood Boulevard

This is a work of fiction. The names, characters, places and incidents are either
the product of the author's imagination or are used fictitiously, and any
resemblance to actual persons living or dead, business establishments,
events, or locales is entirely coincidental.

Unbridled Books

Copyright © 2012 by Janyce Stefan-Cole

Library of Congress Cataloging-in-Publication Data

Stefan-Cole, Janyce.
Hollywood Boulevard / Janyce Stefan-Cole.
p. cm.
ISBN 978-1-60953-075-4
1. Actresses—Fiction.   2. Hotels—California—Los Angeles—Fiction.
3. Hollywood (Los Angeles, Calif.)—Fiction.   4. Psychological fiction.
I. Title.
PS3619.T4455H65 2012
813'.6—dc23
2011043886

1   3   5   7   9   10   8   6   4   2

Book Design by SH • CV

First Printing

For Brandon

Come, come, whoever you are

Wonderer, worshipper, wanderer, lover of leaving,
whatever you are.
This is no caravan of despair.

Come—even if you have failed
and dropped out dozens of times—

Come on, try again, come.

—Jalal ad-Din ar-Rumi

Part One

But his own mind was helpless against every moment's headline. He did nothing but leap into the mass of changes and explore them and all the tiny facets so that eventually he was almost completely governed by fears of certainty.

—Michael Ondaatje,
Coming Through Slaughter

1

Leaving Joe

used to think about quitting all the time. Then I quit, and now I still think about it. Maybe the dream slipped away, or got sullied into something no longer recognizable, or came at too high a price—as in be careful what you wish for. So I float between a sleeping dream and real life. At the moment I'm holed up at the hotel swimming pool, a terraced affair set below a pricey Japanese restaurant, with narrow gardens guests can visit via little golden keys that open short red gates to various paths. It's off-season, the unheated pool is glacial; leaves fall in, float a while, and sink. A Shinto gate sits importantly on the pool's south side, like offspring of the restaurant above. The landscaping is uneven: artificial waterfalls, a miniature pomegranate tree, the Shinto gate aligned with a chain-link fence facing nondescript Hollywood back streets below; calm and common all at once.

The maid cleaning my room is the reason I am lying low, wrapped in layers against the early-spring chill. What does the staff think of me in my suite—with kitchen—so much of the time? The awkwardness of having to get out of the maid's way so my mess can be cleaned, though I like not having to do it myself and have mostly not had to. Her arrival threatens my days. Today the interruption came near noon; tomorrow it could be three P.M. or ten thirty A.M. Maid or no maid, I prefer my mornings. A day that ends badly may have begun with sunlit, wide-awake eyes. It doesn't take much to tip the scales; my mornings do not inform my nights, they never have.

Too persistently the question arises just what the maid is interrupting. The answer is always a big nothing. I was an actor until I quit, walked away, some said with my best work in front of me, but that sort of talk comes cheap; quitting does not. Can the maid, Zaneda—I think that's what she said her name is—imagine my life as I can so easily imagine hers? What does she think I am doing at the pool, noticing the haphazard landscaping while the sweet Chicana makes my very tossed bed? Does she wonder that there are no signs of sex on the sheets? Her prettiness is homey, eyes behind wire glasses gentle. She treats me as if I am special.

"El Señor is a director of movies, no?" she asked when I first arrived. She meant my husband, Andre Lucerne.

"Señor is a director of movies, *sí*," I replied, cutting the conversation short. El Señor insisted I come, which explains in a nutshell my presence at the Hotel Muse. My having agreed, my being back in Hollywood while he shoots his film, could spell trouble, like a recovering junkie camped out in the poppy fields.

He said he needed me by his side. That's not how Andre expresses himself. He expresses himself through his work, so I was surprised by his words and, I admit, a little suspicious, and I don't know why I agreed to come.

I'm not sure how much English Zaneda understands. I try to speak to her in Spanish. I did learn that she has four children, aged sixteen to three. She works long, hard hours, traveling who knows how far to get to the hotel, by car or bus or metro, to support those many kids. Yet her smile is uncompromised by exploitation. I think she said the other day that she'd seen me in a movie once. Possibly I misunderstood. It hasn't been that long since I quit, but Hollywood develops amnesia faster than a corpse forgets to breathe. I don't *have* to escape my room and Zaneda's enduring reality against my—what?—ethereal existence, but if explanations begin to be required, of how I spend my days and why I stopped acting, then I have no choice but to flee. Imagined conversations can be worse than actual ones.

I shifted my chaise three times just now. The sun was warm, out of the breeze. I looked up, hearing voices above me in the outdoor grill area that has been vacant each time I've come here before. I closed my eyes to wish the intruders away.

I dozed a few minutes, and now the voices have gone. It was probably safe to go back to my rooms, but I began rearranging the deck chairs instead. I walked the perimeter and found four wasted beer bottles tossed in a corner next to a blooming bird-of-paradise. Three days ago I walked the Japanese garden paths for the first time. Past stunted sculpted trees and little waterfalls and pools with timid goldfish that skittered away at my approach. Directly below the restaurant is a small pavilion with steep steps leading to it and two red benches under a peaked roof, a spot for viewing sunsets. Precisely below, a matter of inches from the pavilion, I noticed a bubblegum-blue used condom. I examined the red bench where the event had probably taken place. Maybe the couple had been drunk or in a hurry, the condom tossed in the dark. The next day it was still there. The find was solid gold, treasure a secret observer lives for—I've become a kind of hotel spy in my endless spare time. The restaurant has a reputation, so I was surprised to see the prophylactic lying there, but it's off-season and we are in a recession; cleanups might not be what they have been. Still.

I kicked the beer bottles next to the chain-link fence. I ought to have resisted the desire to arrange the pool deck but didn't. Having to arrange, *needing* to, possibly reflects something wrong with me. But I'm not interested; what good would it do if I learned I was a compulsive this or that, a so-and-such unable to reveal myself except through gestures like rearranging furniture, an utterly failed communicator—for an actor? I enjoy few things better than creating order out of chaos, yet my life is a study in disorder. Lurking is the awareness, faint and intermittent, occasionally urgent, that something *is* wrong and does need fixing. Or maybe the pool area looking a lot better now is explanation enough.

Husband number one said I only played at house. This was around the time I signed with Harry and Hollywood. That would be Harry Machin, Big Time Agent and proprietor of the very exclusive Machin Talent. Apparently with issues of his own—I mean the ex, a writer, he once hid out in a broom closet. I'd taken him to a party, not an A-list deal but sufficiently who's who. I didn't notice him missing until the hostess found him among the cleaning products and whispered in my ear to ask what was wrong with my guy. Back then I thought we would be a comfort to each other in social situations. I thought that's what couples did. Social outings are knotty anyway, on a guy's arm or flying solo. At the time of the closet incident I was better at taking cues and holding up my end, though I'd wilt at the smallest off-key passage: a casually unkind word, the bon mot landing flat. Still, I had a solid sense of what I wanted to be when I grew up, and nothing was going to stop me; I'd run over anyone who tried. I'm not saying I don't savvy the parley, flirting just enough to raise an eyebrow, playing the provocateur until my energy saps and I collapse like a diseased lung, sagging under the weight of human contact. Which, considering the assumed largeness of ego expected in my former profession, and the supposed need of an audience, makes me a candidate for problems from the start.

At a recent party here in Hollywood—no, Silver Lake, to be precise—where I knew enough people well enough to indulge in conversational back-and-forth, I left the crowd to play with the family's five-year-old, Ella. She proudly exhibited her many fairy dolls. All showy dresses, translucent wings, and long luscious hair, blond and thick like hers. After oohing and aahing appropriately, I began checking for underwear, lifting gossamer gowns, cotton pinafores, and tulip minis. "Let's see if she's wearing underpants," I said, peering at one doll's lower parts. Soon the dear little girl was checking too. "Underpants!" she'd say. "Underpants," we'd say, examining each doll. "No underpants!" she gasped. "Let's see!" I said, pulling the delinquent figurine from her small hand. Seeing the naked, rubbery flesh-colored blank where genitals ought to be, it occurred to me that I'd taught this lovely child something her parents might not appreciate. What was I thinking? Children are so unselfconsciously sexual as it is, and she was just at that Freudian cusp, five, the postphallic stage, on the verge of the superego. I've perused a few pages of Freud, and he's a pessimist, if you ask me, and all wrong about penis envy. My grandmother used to say men start wars to match the heroics of women producing babies. Who knows, maybe *they* have the envy. That's a thorny topic, though, starting with Adam trying to shift blame onto a wily snake, quite possibly the beginning of blaming the victim, and certainly the genesis of men getting all the good lines in movies while the actresses get the great clothes. And I'm not certain there really is a victim, though I read somewhere that, according to Victorian mores, a "lady lies still" during the sex act. And what, studies the ceiling? I know it's a mixed-up ball of wax if the lady is taking it passively on her tummy or handing it out on top. Sex could be simple, lovely fun, but somehow there are always complications.

Anyhow, another guest (at the party), who happens to be a good-looking dwarf, poked his head through the doorway. "Are you hiding out in here?" he asked.

"Hiding out, yes," I said softly (trying, I think, for an effect. Why? Because he was born condensed?), realizing a split second later that he meant the little girl. He abruptly left.

There is some truth to what my ex said about how I play house. I spent time and some money nesting in the current suite. Which means I think I'll stay, though I threaten Andre from day to day to clear out back to our loft in New York. I've lived countless days and months in hotels, and I've learned it's important to claim the place, leave my mark like a dog peeing on a pole. But my ex implied it's all pretense, that things are not so clean under appealing surfaces. Dirt's not the point, I once tried to explain, but the way a space *feels*: harmonious or not, high or low contrast, and lighting—lighting is of utmost importance. He scoffed, "Spoken like a true actress." He told me I see things as others would, like a performance. As if light and color don't have real effect. "What's wrong with considering the effect?" I asked, apparently missing the point.

"Life," he said, "my pretty-pretty, is not an effect." (You know, I *knew* that.)

"Then you can be my resident reality check," I said, trying to disarm a potential fight. He frowned—set to object—but I jumped in: "Actors require reality checks; didn't that come with my instructions?"

Harry—this was back then—told me to cut "the hubby" loose.

"Get him off the nipple; he's nothing. You're a great actress, the next Kate Hepburn."

"Harry, you know I can't stand Hepburn."

"I meant you're classy, not flimflam in a costume. Never a cheap shot from Ardennes Thrush."

That sounded like a line he might have used before. I didn't have a comeback, so I just sat there, opposite Harry at his very wide, bleached-birch desk, so wide it seemed like the deck of a small ship.

"I see what he is," Harry said to my silence. "That—what's his name again?"

"Joe?"

"Joe. Perfect. Joe Schmo. He's a moper. He'll never let you succeed. He'll tear down anything you do. Trust me on this. Guys like that prey on a woman's weakness."

I thought, isn't that what producers and the other money men do? There was an iota of truth to Harry's words, though; Joe did seem at times to debunk my growing success. What surprised me was Harry picking up on that part of Joe after at most two very brief meetings. I wondered how a deal-making manipulator like Harry Machin could have such insights. Maybe it was because Harry truly enjoyed what he did, was in it up to his elbows with all his heart.

"He doesn't have an agent, does he?" Harry added, watching me from under those heavy eyelids of his.

He didn't. I kept quiet again. Harry's phone rang. He said, "Okay," into the receiver, which meant he'd take the call. Which meant it was someone important because when Harry called you into the office he meant business and had his calls held. Harry was always telling me what to do and I was always trying to sort out for myself what I should do. Which is not to imply I knew back then what was best for me, but when I didn't know, I had my ready fallback position, which was to hold out. I was named after the Ardennes Forest, where what is called the Battle of the Bulge took place in the bitter winter of 1944. My father was a boy of twenty and he made it out alive when something on the order of 81,000 GIs were wounded, died or went missing in the last merciless thrust of the Nazis. I wasn't born then, not even close. My mother wanted to name me Autumn, after her favorite season, when she and my dad married. He was a good deal older than his second wife, just as my half-brother and -sister were to me. My mother said it wasn't a good idea to name a child, a girl no less, after a World War II battle, but I'd had a rough go of it and wasn't expected to live because of a problem in my tiny heart, a valve that they were able to reroute or something, and my dad told her I was a fighter and a survivor, like him. Maybe he figured he might not be around for me as long as most dads and wanted me to remember the young soldier who'd made it through the Ardennes Offensive. Anyhow, my mother agreed, and if I don't tell people the origin they think my name is exotically French or that I made it up as a stage name. I don't usually bother to explain.

It was probably just as well he wasn't around when I quit acting. How could I tell my dad it was the thought of quitting that kept me going? That the idea was a relief, like death, if you try to look into death's positive light, its silver lining. I don't mean to be morbid; in fact, I think it's morbid to want life to go on forever. There'd be no edge, just a soppy on and on. Maybe deep down inside everyone dreams of quitting, of being free of the task each of us supposedly has in life. I picked up that idea—about the task each of us has— from reading Sufi wisdom, the catch being, I suppose, finding the destined path. I sometimes wonder if Joe would have celebrated my quitting. We'd have made a normal life together; I'd have cooked dinner and been home to ask how his day had been. I once told

Harry I gave my best performances on the days I was sure I would drop out. He wept the day I told him I was through; honest-to-goodness tears, nose honking, hanky and all.

"This is a crime against God," he said when he could finally speak.

His extreme reaction surprised me. "Against God, Harry?"

"Why? Tell me how your kind of talent quits, throws itself into the toilet and flushes. How?"

"It's not as if I was single-handedly making you rich," I said, trying for levity. I think I thought he'd get mad, yell, insult me, anything but that pained expression as he slowly shook his oversized head. He spent the next hour telling me what was wrong with my decision. He barked at his secretary to hold everything: "*Everything*, even if it's the president of the United States on the line!" I just remember being thirsty as he carried on. The longer he went on, the thirstier I got. This is where the Battle of The Ardennes comes in: I can hold out against just about anybody's verbal barrage to get me to change my mind. The more they try, the more I dig in. The truth is, I can black out the whole world, blacker than the blackest cave two miles into the bowels of the earth. I can go to a place so dark it's as if the world was never created. So Harry couldn't squeeze out of me why I quit, try as he did. He couldn't blame Joe either; it was too late for that. And by the way, Harry had nothing to do with Joe and me busting up. He did practically dance a jig on his desktop when he found out, but that was before I called it quits.

It took me a long time to shake Joe, considering the rough ride we'd had almost from day one. I'm not sure I ever did shake him. I've always been attracted to writers and this one was no slouch, though he could barely earn a dime on his work the whole while we were together. He had socialist ideas too, so that if I did bring in a nice check from time to time, a part in a pet-food commercial, say, that went national—with hefty residuals—it was right away suspect, like Chairman Mao or Lenin would get wind of Joe having had dealings with the capitalist devil.

Joe had a lot of anger. Not because the world had been unjust to him but because it's an unjust place. For me, the world's too big to be angry at all in a gulp. Joe scolded old friends too, if they betrayed the code. He would go on for days about the crime of getting a book published for a sum that had to be corrupt. *What kind of whore game did he play to get that advance? Christ!* But the lapsed friend was only a pawn of the society that had wrought him, a culture of which Joe disapproved and felt punished living in. Joe's basic premise was if people at the top would only wise up and take less, things could even out.

Happily, not even Joe could contemplate the distribution of wealth every day, and if he didn't bother too much about saving the world, he was just the guy I wanted. Basically, he lived simply, wanting most of all to read and write and think. The two of us, side by side reading in bed, Joe charming me with a passage of Yeats or Wordsworth pulled out of the air. Knowing when I was lost in my lines rehearsing for an off-off-Broadway play, a cold-water, firetrap stage. Showing up at late-night rehearsals, walking me home after midnight, streets solitary and slick, maybe one of those cat-sized rats running out from behind a trash can, Joe saying there were worse rats than them living in penthouse apartments. Giving me notes, really, really wanting me to soar; that was where I wanted my world to be.

He kept me guessing too, not a dull bone to him; there was always a new corner to turn with Joe. I never got all the way inside. Then again, Joe didn't think it was possible for an actor to get truly close. Or did he mean that about me only? All those emotions, he'd say, faking it with a part, how would anyone know if the tears at home weren't just more of the same?

Finally exasperated, I said, "Maybe they aren't ever an act."

"That only proves it, even you don't know," he shot back.

Worse than that was the time he said I was empty when no one was looking. It was only years later that the rejoinder came to me: How would you know? How could you possibly know, Joe? Was he knowing or only passing judgment? He'd get me all confused. Partly because I needed him to be right and partly because I needed him so much that I'd get muddled and couldn't think what to say, maybe couldn't think at all.

It was moving to L.A. that finally did the marriage in. Harry was after me to settle out west from the first big job he landed me: four scenes in a star-cast movie, thirty lines. My character—Laurel, early twenties—was not a hooker but available to wealthy men with fetishes like foot sucking or egg rolling. My first scene had me in a slinky summer dress: I walk into a darkened hotel room, balcony shutters closed to the tropical sea beyond, strips of sunlight piercing through the slats. A thug slips out of the shadows.

Thug: "What are you doing here?"

Laurel, frightened but keeping her cool: "I left my hat."

Thug: "Who let you in?"

Laurel: "I'm a friend of Abe's."

Thug, looking Laurel over like she's quick lunch: "Nobody's a friend of Abe's. Whaddaya, servicing his spanking needs?"

CUT!

It would be my one and only megamovie role. After that the studios made some overtures, smelled young blood in the water, but I wasn't interested. It wasn't as if Paramount was breaking down the door, but if Harry had his way I'd have cultivated myself, played along. Harry's line was that you have to wade through a little garbage to get to the high road you're meant to be on; that nothing good comes pure. Joe helped me steer clear of what he saw as Harry's hype. Some said Joe's steering might have ruined me. Anyhow, I got noticed in the medium-budget and indie-film worlds. Joe was okay with that. He'd ranted when I took the mega job, paragraphs' worth, and promised not to touch one penny of the filthy lucre I was paid, going so far as to set up a separate account for himself. He did live by his word.

I began flying back and forth between New York and Los Angeles. With the bigger parts I had to stay out for longer spells, and the parts *were* getting bigger. I made a few friends and stopped making so much fun of the too-friendly Angelinos. There's too much space is the problem, that's why they're so eager to connect. I once had a woman start a chat from underneath the next toilet stall. That was technically not in L.A. but at a stop for date shakes at Hadley's on the 10 Freeway, the San Bernardino route to Palm Springs, out past the wind farm that took my breath away every time I saw those thousand arms circling crazily over the arid earth. But people talk to strangers in elevators, other customers in a store, standing at a stop light, all friendly and open. I never got used to it.

I did get Los Angeles itself, a tactile place with big light and lots of texture where nature hasn't been conquered. Earthquakes lie in wait, full-blown desert only a hard drought away. Rub the surface of anyone who's been there long enough and you'll find a seeker. It doesn't much matter after what—L.A. is cult nirvana—some sort of god quest over the rainbow, born of that light and an underlying sense that all this gorgeousness can't last. The only thing people in New York City seek, my singer friend Dottie once let me know, is a way out. Dottie did her time in the Big Apple, but she was from

Kansas and wide-open space was home to her and that translated into Los Angeles. In her case, her cabaret career faltered. We sort of reversed each other: I was always glad to get back to New York and Joe. I was never going to put down roots in that shallow western soil.

My time in Hollywood—especially my first serious movie—was more like a prolonged in-passing friendship. Mostly I was holding my emotional breath. Joe and me having phone sex, trying hard to keep it real over long distance. Harry giving me no peace, making threats, saying I was hurting my career by not making myself available to the machinery, that I wasn't hungry enough and was being passed over. He said if I wanted things to happen I had to get out there and get dirty.

"You're a Hollywood dame," he harangued. "Look at you, you blossom in the sunlight."

I'll never forget that conversation. It was winter, it was cold and wet. I was wrapping up a part, my ticket home already purchased. "It's been raining in L.A. for three days, Harry."

"Ardennes, Ardennes, Ardennes, when will you come to your senses?"

"I'm a New York–based actor. For the umpteenth time: I'll come out anytime a good part calls, but home is—"

He cut me off with a grunt and a half wave of his left hand, temporarily lifted off its perch on his belly. "Home! With Joe and the two cats, a dark, roach-infested apartment. Are the cats helpful there? Listen to me: What makes a rose more beautiful?" I lifted my hands to say, tell me. "Manure, that's what. Cow shit in the soil. See my point? You gotta taste it, Ardennes, you gotta sacrifice to it morning, noon, and night; you gotta *want* the prize, and you gotta make the journey *to* the prize."

What Harry didn't see was that, different as we were, Joe and

I overlapped in crucial ways. He could pick up a false note in my work and excise it like a surgeon. And I loved those two cats, Molly and Corot, and our too-small West Side flat. The dark streets of New York were like the veins along my hands, avenues and boulevards in my blood. I held New York close in my heart. "Success at what price, Harry?"

He looked at me from below those heavy lids, scanning my interior, a stone Buddha, arms across his large front. "You think I talk of crass success? Dollar bills falling out of your brassiere, manse in the hills with the saline pool, ego billing on the marquee? You think I don't know you? Craft, Ardennes—A-R-T—is not going to settle for trysts and one-night stands, rendezvous in a bus station. A-R-T wants all of you! And all of you is all I want you to be."

It sounded so enlightened.

"Poetic, Harry," I said. I looked at my watch. "I gotta run, a night shoot today. I'm due on set at four." I stood up, reaching for my purse. I still didn't know why Harry had called me in that day. I was hoping for a month off, time with Joe.

He barely stirred, ever so slightly lifted that left hand again. "You got the part."

"What? You mean *Separation and Rain*? The *lead*?"

Harry nodded sagely. "You start one hour before this part ends. No time to go home and feed the cats."

I whooped, I spun, I clapped my hands. I was young enough to whoop and spin. I was big-eyed, all goals, virgin territory; I was all the places I would never get to that I would strive for until the last breath was out of me. This was big, colossal, this would move the earth: a plum part I knew I was right for, that I wanted badly, that would give me the chance to really show what I knew I had untapped inside me. This was my shot to breathe life into a character half alive on paper; this was my Michelangelo: Adam reaching out to touch the hand of God. Okay, I was not about to be God to some Adam, but I would make that character live. I would! Wouldn't I? I flashed on a memory of Joe and me stretched out on a blanket on the rolling grass of the Sheep Meadow in Central Park. Joe poured wine into a thermos so we wouldn't be caught drinking out in the open. We had a baguette and cheese, and grapes, I think. We were having a what-if-one-of-us-makes-it conversation we had a lot in those days, and Joe said I wouldn't be able to take it anyway if I did make it big. He was tender about it. He knew how uncomfortable strange surroundings can make me, and that too many demands send me into a confused tailspin so I lose my bearings and need to run away. "I should have been a librarian," I told him that day. Joe said, "Nah, not with that face; none of the boys would get any homework done." I smiled at him from my toes up to my heart. "Your home is with me," he said. That was a good moment, the kind that can make up for so much, that ought to be the real essence of being alive but somehow never is.

"Harry, don't fool with me."

Harry's eyelids widened a fraction. "I never fool," he said with mild indignation.

"Then this is real!" I felt my breath catch. "The lead . . ." I sat down. This was a twenty-million-dollar budget with a solid script and a superior director. (I didn't know that day—and it was a few years off—that I would one day be married to Andre Lucerne, perhaps the most demanding director in Hollywood.) "You're sure? Andre Lucerne cast *me*?" I remember the doubts starting to creep in, that a mistake had been made, a mix-up in head shots or the audition tapes. I even suspected Harry might have bribed the producer, used blackmail, called in a life-and-death favor owed and I would be found out and dismissed as a fraud. I was working up to full-fledged panic when I heard Harry moving.

He lifted his cumbersome frame out of the plush leather desk chair and waddled to a small fridge you wouldn't know was there, tucked beneath some shelves in the well-appointed, screaming-success office. He leaned down heavily and pulled out a split of champagne, and from a nearby cabinet two flutes. "If you didn't have work tonight, we'd celebrate properly at Spago, on the Strip. Will this do for now?" He held up a bottle of Cristal. Spago was the place to be seen; the Cristal cost about what a New York City immigrant garment worker made in a week. He popped the cork and poured out wine and fizz.

I reached blindly for the glass Harry pushed toward me. I'd had my small victories; some—plenty of—actors would say I was in a good place even without this bit of luck, but I suddenly didn't know what to do, didn't know how to handle getting what I wanted. Harry was always saying luck had nothing to do with it, but that's not so; luck is either at work in a person's life or it's not. I sagged backward into the thick cushions of Harry's buffalo-hide sofa and put the flute down on the coffee table. Harry chuckled. I looked up; tears filled my eyes, ready to spill over. "Thank you, Harry," I whispered.

"Don't thank me. All I did was make a few calls, let the world know an angel had descended. You did the rest."

That snapped me back to my senses. I never knew if Harry bought his own lines or not. I jumped up, pointing to the phone on his desk. "I have to tell Joe!"

Harry snorted. "Go ahead, call that chump. You're halfway up the mountain; see if he can't find a way to drag you back down."

I smiled. "Don't ruin it, Harry," I said, reaching for the flute with my right hand as I punched in the numbers with my left. I raised the glass to Harry and took the bubbly down in one swallow. I listened impatiently to Joe's ring tone but hung up when the leave-a-message voice came on. I didn't leave one. I canceled the call and saw what I'd just done register on Harry's face. I looked at him as I chewed on my lower lip.

"This is a game changer, Ardennes," Harry said. "Nothing will be the same after today." And nothing ever was.

So here I am in L.A., climbing a mountain of remembering, killing a day piled high with the past. I should give Proust another try. I walked idly up to the pavilion to check on the condom before heading back to my freshly cleaned rooms. *Remembrance of Things Past*—I never got through it. Joe did; all seven volumes in one year, ten pages a night. Joe, what's he up to now? I miss his ironclad discipline. I've read all his books, four so far. Remembrance of Joe . . . There it is! Dropped a foot farther down toward the parking lot, lying in the dirt; sunshine has baked the rubber hard, the semen into crisp mica crusts. Do the lovers remember their fallen condom; is it part of *their* meaningful past?

Where did I see that rosemary the other day, along one of the paths? I wanted to pick a few stems on the off chance I'd grow ambitious in the little kitchen and maybe cook a chicken.

I gave up on the rosemary and turned toward the stairs that led down to my suite. That was when I spotted a cat walking behind a man. They were on one of the footbridges connecting the top tier of rooms, in back. Some suites are permanent apartments with tatty screen doors and potted plants and other domestic touches along the balconies. The man was pale—hair, skin, voice, stooped posture, he looked to be a full-time renter with a noticeable Californianess about him, a certain stratum of weed smoker with few ambitions.

When you've haunted as many hotels as I have you spot the underlying characters, the tensions, the esprit de corps—or lack of it—among the workers, the essence of an establishment by the quirks encountered. The cat was striped rust and black, with splashes of white. Pale Guy said yes when I asked if the cat was with him. I said, "Hey, Kitty," in a high-pitched, girlish voice. "Hi, Kitty," I repeated quietly, remembering Joe and my long-gone sister cats. I thought of telling Pale Guy I loved cats but moved around too much to keep them—though that was more my former working self. Thankfully, I held my tongue. I did say, "He doesn't run away?"

"Not when he's hungry."

" 'Bye, Kitty," I said, half wishing the cat would follow me instead. I'd put out a saucer of milk, buy a can of tuna, make a little bed in the corner. Pale Guy continued on his way, Kitty in tow, tail hoisted high. I guess they've seen enough guests come and go not to bother. Pale Guy and Kitty were nuggets, though, not gold, but solid pieces of the texture of the hotel. I looked down and saw the rosemary right there at my feet. I bent to pinch a stem, thinking, as I always do when I pilfer flowers, if everyone did this there would be none left.

The Hotel Muse is old by Hollywood measure, a nightclub originally, from the late '40s, featuring acts better suited to a circus sideshow. The hotel was added later. Halfway up the hill is the upper part where we are situated—modest cousin to the main hotel on the avenue. It's the director's whim that his wife and principal crew (mostly imports from the East Coast) be installed up top, forming a kind of colony. Andre likes the availability of his people grouped together, but there are fewer amenities up top. Below, the pool is heated; Turkish bathrobes, wireless, DVDs, and cable are provided—perks for those who prefer sanitized luxury. With us scruffier sorts above, services are hit-and-miss; no DVDs or wireless. Internet and breakfast are had by trekking downhill to the main lobby area, laptop in tow. The lobby is small so most mornings Internet users from uphill gather around the pool, rain or shine, chill or warm, huddling under patio umbrellas. I've noticed a number of German film types at breakfast. They talked loudly on Skype as they pace, necks swathed in scarves, woolen caps pulled low.

Andre's quirks usually pay off. I like his crew, and the arty types up here, for once inheriting the earth—or the spectacular view, any-how. Our outsized, east-facing balcony overlooks a coral tree where wild green parrots squawk and screech each morning among the bright red flower petals. The landscape reminds me of the south of France, houses and villas tumbling steeply down the hills in a hodgepodge of styles, an architectural balancing act. The view to the right veers neurotically into L.A.'s urban sprawl and the sudden verticality of downtown. Straight ahead I can see the gray dome of the Griffith Observatory. On mornings when fog or the yellow-brown curtain of smog lifts, the San Gabriel Mountains are visible, snow-capped and reassuring in the distance. Brown-dotted hills segue into mountains in snow, urban and wild in the same snapshot. I hear there are lions in those mountains. I look out each day and imagine the city living on borrowed time, that the earth under Hollywood will someday shift and shrug houses and people, the ob-servatory, trees, birds, coyotes, squirrels, cats, snakes, and everyone's dreams off the hills into the yawning abyss.

Another day has passed—faded meaninglessly into evening. I went outside for the sunset. The wind and chill were sharp up at the benched pavilion. Someone had taken a rake to the grounds; the condom was gone, and the narrative seemed lost without it. Over my shoulder a stream of distant planes flowed silently from the east, into LAX. To the west a slip of the Pacific Ocean shone like a piece of broken plate under a limpid sky. When the earth finally does shake the hills loose, the ocean will flood the coast and slimy sea monsters will roam the earth, lapping at the fallen city's face.

That's what I was imagining when I saw that the old gray man and his dog were back. He's been there every evening I've come up. He stood below the condom pavilion, at the top of the restaurant parking lot. His dog, an ugly black-and-brown pit bull, stared up at me. The grizzled man never turned my way, if he knew I was there. I made a friendly little click toward the dog, who continued to stare. I thought the old man had libation with him, a jar with purple remnants, communion with the setting sun. He was not a guest but arrived by a narrow path through the undergrowth outside the chain-link fence, past the pool. I'd thought of disguising scotch in a coffee mug to carry with me as I bade the day adieu but had decided I'd reward myself when I returned to the rooms, chilled from my own sunset homage.

Walking back toward the pool I heard voices, customers from the restaurant, the cocktail hour officially on. Asian tourists held cameras, peered toward the west, murmuring their pleasure; a night out on the town, living it up, spending plenty of yen. I wanted to slip out of sight (tricky since they were above me with a clear advantage), feeling like the old man, pretending I was alone to keep the moment to myself. I had a friend once—no, he was a writer pal of Joe's, a lanky poetic type who said I was a hoarder of moments. Maybe that's true. As I turned at the waterfall at the top of the stairs, heading down to my rooms, the kitty ran out in front of me.

"Where did you come from?" I said, bending to pet him. His purr was a minor roar. He sidled along my legs, rubbing around and back again. "Want to come home with me?" I asked, kneading my fingers through his thick fur. He followed as I veered back to the pool, then ran up a squat tree with perpetually shedding purple flowers, showing off. I watched for a few minutes, but he didn't follow when I turned to go.

Back at the rooms I poured myself a proper scotch—two ice cubes—into one of the glasses I'd purchased for the purpose. I went out to the balcony, the cashmere shawl Andre had given me the previous Christmas over my shoulders, Mexican-serape style. The last orange traces of sun were leaving the tops of the hills, the houses below already deep in shadow. The observatory held the golden glow longest, and then it too dimmed to a colorless form. I saw, across the hill, that the man was there in his garden.

I have been watching the man. I call him White Shirt because white seems to be his preference. His house is perched on the hill pretty much dead opposite my balcony, on the other side of a steep arroyo. It's French country style with a blue front door. I'd trade a toe for my binoculars back in New York. I could buy a pair here but that seems as if it would be cheating. My method of hotel discovery is slow, hints here and there, bits of life: an outdoor umbrella shifted, soft illumination from a nighttime window, the glow of a television or computer screen flickering in the middle of the night. I tried to drive up White Shirt's hill yesterday but got lost winding my way, ending up on Mulholland, at the top of Runyon Canyon. I parked the car in the small unpaved lot. A sign at the entrance warned of rattlesnakes. I walked alone along a dirt trail in the baking-hot sun until I came to one of the pinnacles. I could have been anywhere; the view shifted from angle to angle and felt foreign. Nothing was clarified, but I'm in no hurry. Things reveal themselves in their own time, time being a commodity I currently have to spare.

White Shirt was the first sign of life on that side of the hill. There is another house, a large two-family Spanish style. I look down on its backyard, where a lollipop-shaped tree is lit up each night with white lights. There was a cocktail party one evening on the patio, which I enjoyed watching, but the people in that house don't interest me. There is a chewable normalcy to the "Spanish Heights" house, something too obvious. White Shirt does interest me. His house is on the other side of the street from the Spanish Heights, and his yard is a square, grassy plot on top of his garage. One of the garage doors— white flap-downs—is broken; a dim light stays on all night over a white sports car.

White Shirt is home a lot. So am I. I watch him as David watched Bathsheba, though so far I am not lusting. Without binoculars I can see only that he is tall and slim with a full head of light brown hair. He must know he faces a hotel with large balconies; he must know he can be seen. In the Bible story David was supposed to be at war with his men; it was spring, *the time kings went to war.* Full stop. Why would kings, as a matter of course, go to war in the spring? Anyway, David was up on his roof prowling in the wee hours, and Bathsheba was up on hers having a late-night bath. Did a full moon illuminate her wet alabaster skin? Why was she bathing at that hour? Were they both insomniacs? Her husband, Uriah the Hittite, was at war, where David ought to have been instead of spying on bathing women. He sent one of his servants to invite her over. He was king, so his was probably an invitation one literally could not refuse. What did he want? Come lie with me, Mrs., we will have a grand old time.

The Bible doesn't bother with her take on the situation, other than mentioning that Bathsheba cleaned herself after the act. We are not told if she tried to beg off with a headache or if she was flattered; after all, this was David who slew the giant, handsome, powerful King David. Did she love her husband? Uriah was a dedicated warrior; perhaps she felt neglected. Soon after David lay with her, Bathsheba let him know she was with child. David hadn't thought of that, apparently, but he figured he'd bring Uriah back from battle and pin the child on him. Go to your house, he told Uriah after faking a query about how the war was going. But loyal Uriah slept outside the palace doors that night. His men were in harm's way; his king and liege had spoken to him, quite the honor; this was no time to be dallying with the wife in the comforts of home. The same thing happened for two more nights, even after David got him drunk. Uriah was loyal to a fault. His wife might have thought so even before David seduced her. The story soon took a bad turn: David saw to it that Uriah died in battle, and then God killed David and Bathsheba's newborn as punishment. Bathsheba paid, but we don't know exactly for what: the unsanctioned dalliance with David or her infidelity to Uriah. The God of the Old Testament didn't seem to finesse the details when demanding his pound of flesh. Things eventually worked out for David and Bathsheba—

Andre! He came in just now, all a flurry of breathless, manly purpose, surprising me on the balcony. White Shirt had just gone inside his house.

"Let's have a drink," Andre announced.

"I'm ahead of you," I said, walking inside, drink in hand. I turned on the news, trying to mask the flutter in my stomach—a signal of any number of reactions to this unscheduled arrival of the director for a drink with his wife. Did he have time off the set during a complicated lighting shift . . . or was something wrong that he could leave, or had he said he'd have an early night and I'd forgotten?

It was a hurried drink. A drink should never be hurried. "How you grace me with your presence!" I spoke to his back as the door closed. He left with the bottle. He'd come for the bottle, the drink a nickel's worth of his time bestowed. Was his leading lady thirsty?

They are shooting close by, close enough for me to drop in, which he said I should do. But I won't. I would be treated on set like the general's wife. There would be curious stares and fawning over his onetime lead, the actress who took best prize at Cannes under his direction. The unanswered question always hovering: Why did she retire early, still in her prime, when the full blossoming of her breasts tantalizes most and she begins to understand her craft and to take bigger risks—why? Were the producers already casting about for less ripe, more malleable girls with dreams of stardom; was that it? Andre insists the lead is in me yet. Ha! I walked away of my own free will. Why would I walk back into that insecure cesspool of chattering facades called acting?

Andre doesn't like that word, *insecure*. He says it's overused, a catchall excuse for lack of discipline.

"Wobbly, then," I said back. "People are wobbly in who they are. You might try to be more sympathetic."

"Rubbish." It could almost have been Joe talking. But Joe would have qualified the retort by saying that the system of civilization discourages personal strengths, the better to control a populace.

I stopped myself from throwing my drink at the door behind Andre. Wasted! I am wasted on peasants. If I came at you, dear audience, full force, you couldn't withstand me, yet Andre can crush me with a glance, like a rose petal under heavy boots.

Between Joe and Andre there were others. Once Joe and I bled dry, were wrung out, twisting in the winds of our failure, others entered the void. I was all alone in L.A. We didn't want to split up a pair of sisters, so Joe kept the cats, old by then but missed terribly, and I would not replace them. Harry kept me busy. He bent over backward to make the physical part of my move painless. It wasn't. He secured invitations to the important parties. That was hell. It was all I could do to keep from finding the broom closet until enough time passed to head for the door, get into my car, and drive home. I'd bought a brand-new compact to spirit me across the vastness of Los Angeles. I sublet a furnished bungalow on Gardiner Street, up in the hills—not too far from where I am now—and hunkered down among the chintz upholstery, shades drawn. I napped a lot, like a three-year-old, or I paced the small, secluded garden draped with intoxicating jasmine, surrounded by tall eucalyptus trees. I went for walks and absorbed the stares of the locals for doing the unthinkable, using my feet on the pavement. I detested L.A. at that point with all the strength my newly single sorry soul had available.

Dottie was my one solid friend. We were an odd mix. She was much older and very overt. Singers are a different sort of showman than actors. She started out doing radio jingles in Wichita, then went east, played the Rainbow Room, other high-end New York nightspots. Dottie was auditory color; she'd made a brief splash in a tough town. She told me she was born with perfect pitch. "That was God's gift," she declared. "I had not a thing to do with it." It was her Plains modesty talking; Dottie's no-nonsense values didn't always fit with her bright outfits and flamboyant theatrics. We had in common a shyness hidden by what we did for a living. With Dottie it was Kansas proper—no one out in all that open likes a show-off, she'd say—though she could ham it up pretty good at the piano. I was shy at the bone. If you scratched Dottie, you scratched dirt, where corn or soy or wheat comes from: solid earth, simple and clean and probably conservative in ways I might not tolerate if Dottie wasn't a chanteuse. Scratch my surface and you get blood, guts, darkness, and dumb hope.

She sang Noël Coward ballads and old show tunes with flare but not a whole lot of depth—the material didn't encourage it. She worked sporadically. A well-off husband died, leaving her comfortably placed. About Joe she said, sensibly, "Ard, honey, the boy who'll follow a girl around the world hasn't been invented yet. They'll calve before that happens. You had no choice. Or yes, you did: It was you for yourself or him." Why'd I have to choose at all? Joe hadn't given me an ultimatum, and I hadn't given him one. I was wracked with doubt. Should I have moved out west, put my career ahead of Joe? Was Dottie right: Woman follows man? Was I doomed to die alone?

I hit bottom, started turning down jobs, refusing phone calls. Harry was ready to work me over with a whip. He called to tell me Andre Lucerne was looking to direct another feature; he wouldn't cast me in the lead this time but was offering a strong supporting role that was mine for the taking. I said no, thanks.

"You're turning down Andre Lucerne?" Harry said. "Help me here, Ardennes."

"I'm not turning down Lucerne. I'm turning down the location. Stockholm in winter, Harry? It's too far away. I'm just not ready." Harry snorted his disbelief. "Okay, I don't like the part either."

"You're wrong; that part is a perfect vehicle for you. And Stockholm is glorious in winter. Lucerne *himself* called." This time

I snorted a so-what. "Never mind." Harry said all calm business. "I'm giving you one month to finish suffering and then I'm dropping you."

"Harry . . ."

Dottie said what did I expect; Harry wasn't my uncle. She didn't let on how worried she was about me hanging around the house all day with a bad case of the guilty blues. She'd take me shopping or come over and make us cocktails, sing ditties until I'd smile, which was about all I could manage, and that was mostly polite. "Dear girl, that sea is loaded with fish, you just have to dive in and pull. And for heaven's sake climb out of those tired old pj's and get outside. Go back to work!"

I wasn't sure if Harry was bluffing or if he'd really drop me. I also genuinely did not know if I'd ever stand in front of a camera again. I wanted so badly to call Joe, tell him that I'd made a terrible mistake, that I wanted to come home; I'd go back to stage acting and our life together, forget all about Hollywood. But he didn't call either and I think that was what hurt the most, that he could just do without me. He'd had a lot of practice, Dottie pointed out, all those absences, me out here working among the fleshpots of Southern California. But Joe didn't doubt me in that way; he was the surest guy I ever met. In the end I think he just didn't want to be married to a movie actress.

Dottie said it was not what she had in mind when I started going around with a friend of hers, a steadily employed character actor in big movies. We met at one of Dottie's rare singing dates. For a couple of weeks she was the closing act at a club that specialized in after-hours drinkers, well-off layabouts, a crowd that ate up her songs, was never loaded to the point of clamor, and by closing time would be singing along, adoring Dottie and their carefree lives.

Like me, Fits (that's all anyone ever called him except in movie credits, where "Matthew Fitzgerald" scrolled across the screen) didn't fit the cabaret scene. He didn't know the lyrics to Dottie's numbers and flat-out hated show tunes. We were there for her, and maybe the generous drinks. Fits was not my type. He was heavyset with sandy, graying hair scattered like buckshot over his head, and a good number of years older. His small eyes had an ironic twinkle belying the rough kindness of his nature. He was unexpectedly light on his feet and sexy and, at that particular moment, the best shoulder in the world for me to cry on. Like Joe, he had radar for injustice and a healthy sense of outrage. And, like most actors I know, he was on the lookout for injury, his ego on his sleeve, finding slights where none was intended. His main complaint, besides rarely getting the lead, was not enough camera time. I've never met an actor who didn't have that particular complaint. But it wasn't something he got ugly about, or only fleetingly, and not a true disappointment. When I met him he was cleaning up. He said he'd wake up not knowing if it was the booze or the coke from the night before that made him feel like slow death each morning; he'd decided he did not want to live that way anymore. He was divorced—twice—who isn't in Hollywood—and the father of a kid living problematically with her mother, which added worry and increased the booze-or-cocaine or cocaine-or-booze routine—whichever it was. He wanted to be able to account for his nights and learn to let things be: his acquired wisdom; very L.A.

He teased me that night for being so young and pathetic, and for being Dottie's friend. I pointed out that he was her friend too, but he said that was different and went on calling me a child and so on until I finally asked him to dance with me just to get him to shut up. His elegant dancing took me very much by surprise. I mean, Fits could waltz. I'm a closet dancer. I respond to music; even dumb, sentimental twaddle wafts its way into my skin and my hips begin to sway. Joe mocked dancing unless it was exotic, by which he meant Indian or Indonesian, not lap. Dancing was a bourgeois pastime meant to allow repressed people to touch, he said. He did learn to watch me improvise at home, to jazz mostly, saying it was probably necessary for an actor to be connected to the body in that way. Once in a while we played at striptease. Ah, Joe.

Anyhow, Dottie was singing a Gershwin tune that night I'd forgotten requesting. She didn't know all the lyrics and said so, sticking the blame of her attempt on me. The song was "Someone to Watch over Me," and I hummed along in Fits's ear as we danced, fighting down tears. He chuckled, his loose frame wobbling in my arms. "Don't laugh at me," I murmured.

He pulled back to look into my face. "I would never laugh at you," he said. "At the song maybe, but not you."

I looked back to see if he was fooling with me. He wasn't. I moved to the music, not even needing a partner. "Who's leading?" I asked.

"I always lead," Fits replied.

It was a Hollywood moment.

He took me home that night. Dottie had insisted I take a car service to the club, though it was not far, down on Fountain, I think. I didn't drink that much anyway and could have driven even if it was three A.M. and I was weary. So Fits took me home in his beat-up Beemer and came in and made himself a pot of coffee, and we sat up in the bungalow for what was left of the night and talked. He was contrary and proud and not easy, but he was the right guy that night. Underneath a fair amount of armor, my soul was safe with Fits.

He was full of stories, having arrived on the scene just ahead of AIDS slowing down the Hollywood sex-press. He'd been skinny—believe it, he insisted—fresh, raw meat. "This one time I was invited to this A-list actress's house [he wouldn't name names, but I guessed] about a part in a movie. She'd lead *and* produce, so it was kind of an audition. I wanted the work bad—not a great part but solidly supporting: a dumped lover she keeps around for play. Got the idea?"

I did.

"So I arrive at her Brentwood manor house and I mean castle and the butler or assistant, whatever they were called then, asked me to wait and this monster dog runs up and pins me to the foyer wall. I mean paws up on my shoulders, standing taller than me and he could make lunch out of my arms, steamy dog breath all over my face. The servant comes back and leads me (and the dog) to the 'spa,' meaning the bathroom—big enough for a New York studio apartment. And she's in the tub under a blanket of bubbles and I sit on a little fluffy chair thing and the dog sits too and soon she wants me to hand her her towel. I begin to wrap it around her and the dog goes into protection-mode pacing and I'm scared to shitting and she says, *Good dog.* And I'm thinking I don't want to die for this part or be maimed either. Next thing she opens a door off the spa and we're outside in a garden overlooking L.A., spread like jewelry before us, and she sits on a chaise naked as Christmas and her legs are open. She pulls me down, I trip, the chair topples, and the dog goes into a crouch, ready to spring. She calls me a klutz and shoves me off and I figure that's it, I blew it, I can go now, only she goes into another door which is to the bedroom. I stand there until she asks what I'm waiting for. The dog is looking at me like with the same question and in we go. She's on the bed and there can't be much doubt why. *Some audition*, she says, and I'm, *Okay I get it now*, and I'm in that fast.

Just as I get the rhythm going the dog jumps on the bed and begins to lick my ass. And he's heading underneath. I don't do animals, so I'm done, my rod wilts and I'm outta there. She calls me a queer as I pull on my pants fast as I can. I slam the bedroom door on the dog and find my own way to the exit." He took a breath.

"Did you get the part?" I asked.

Fits sipped his coffee and grinned. "It was a wild town back then." The sky was beginning to give up the night; wan morning light filtered into the comfy living room. Fits lay back in his deep-cushioned armchair. "So you want to be an actor," he said just as I sat up straight on the couch.

"What's the big idea? I *am* an actor! I just wrecked my marriage for acting. Jeez."

"Okay, take it easy. So you have some creds, that's nice, but you're only at the beginning of the journey."

I didn't think that was true but saw no point in going into it, digging up the past. I won Cannes; didn't he know that? Did he expect an argument, a defense? But Fits was a tester of waters. He said things to jolt, to get a person to reveal herself, pokes here and there until an opening appeared into which he'd shove little mind swords to see the stuff a person had inside. "So what if I was only starting out?" I said, chin forward. "Which I am not."

"So nothing,"

"Okay. All right, Mr. Seasoned Movie Man, what is acting?"

He grimaced, leaned forward, his overly full top lip briefly curling upward. "What is fucking?"

I thought a minute. "Fucking is listening."

"So is acting."

It didn't start that night, but before long I was listening closely to Fits. I don't know how much he listened to me. We were not in love. Well, Fits was in love with the idea of love, his head turning at every pretty girl. I was briefly jealous, only because I was so bruised and Fits was the life jacket I'd been thrown. He would not let me cling, though. He would not let me betray myself that way in him; he was too honest for that. The world really doesn't forgive a broken heart, or at least not the mourning of it. In a way Fits was just the tonic. There was something about a guy with more experience under his belt that allowed me some perspective, even to laugh at myself. If I was moving in the direction of success, all that seemed to be required was my heart. Fits may have been my life jacket, but I didn't have to take us too seriously. That was an education. I don't think I would have pulled out of that funk without him; I'm not suggesting I ever could have done it alone, but he showed me how to let things be what they were. Good old Fits.

Quickies have checked into the room below—one- or two-nighters—joyriders, boisterous and looking to party. Heavy-metal rock vibrates through the floor with a pounding refrain: *Let it rock, let it rock*, over and over. Is someone being pounded on the bed in time to the pulsing beat? I'm guessing a dusting of cocaine residue on the nightstand. It might be a good time to hit the hotel laundry downstairs, make a dent in the pile of dirty clothes mushrooming in the closet, but, nah, the mess can wait till morning. My grandmother used to say never do wash at night; you can't see the dirt.

The lovers must have gone out around midnight because I was kept awake until then and was asleep when Andre came in from his night location. I heard him climb into bed and held very still, careful to keep my breathing even. I don't know if we are going to make it, he and I. I'm a grass widow anyway. Andre is entwined in the undergrowth of a movie set, the miniature universe, the womb and birth and life of filmmaking. I know it firsthand. He's faithless anyway. Usually not when he's directing; the film is Andre's mistress then. But he's a director; actresses fling themselves in his path. Casual cupcakes of an afternoon, dalliances, the poor starlets: paper peeled off, icing licked, maybe a walk-on part.

As I lay pretending to be asleep, I thought maybe my dad had named me wrong. I should have been called Retreat. Or did I desert—as in abandoned my post? A retreater finds safety to gear up and return to battle. Deserters are shot. How *did* my dad get out of the Ardennes alive? He was awarded the Silver Star, which is given for gallantry in battle. Gallantry? I don't even know what that word means. They didn't call it gallantry in 1945. It was simply heroism. Why the change? He was twenty and promoted to captain because they were running out of captains by the hour. He told the few men left under his young command that no one had ordered them to die in the frigid winter woods, so they aimed at anything in gray and scrammed out of there. It was a retreat; he got them out alive. If they'd planned to desert, presumably they wouldn't have gone back to whatever base camp there was. Were they gallant men? Am I a deserter?

Andre was out cold next me. He'd throw a pillow over his head and that was that. I wondered how he could handle all the pressures and energy and concentration of directing a movie and just crash like that as soon as his head hit the pillow. He hasn't an ounce of nervous energy. I, on the other side of the California king, was wide awake, a jangle of free-floating brain waves trying to pass themselves off as thoughts.

After I turned down the part he offered me, I learned—back when Fits and I were briefly an item—that Andre had been intrigued by my refusal to work with him a second time. He doesn't direct many movies. Producers despise what they think of as his arrogance, but his films reach a steady audience, an arty following here and in Europe and Japan, and the classier critics love him, so he gets his financing. Word is he'll do *anything* to get a movie the way he wants it. He's co-written two of his films but is not a writer; Joe wouldn't say so, and I would agree. He's visually brilliant, his characters never less than vivid. He's been called the poet in Godard combined with the bite of Clouzot and the careful structure of Lumet. As a director he is exacting and manipulating and doesn't allow his actors to run loose, even undermining their control over their characters—which scares most actors pantless. Anyhow, I heard through an actress who had a small part in *Separation and Rain* that Andre was amused. "It just doesn't happen," the other actor, Mindy Scott, told me. We'd met for coffee at a place near the Beverly Center. "Is it because it's not the lead? I have to ask, I mean, are you all right? I personally would do any part of Andre Lucerne to work with him again. I'd do it even as an extra. I mean, Andre Lucerne's the greatest director alive right now."

"You really think so?" I asked. Word on set had been that she'd couch-auditioned her part. I smiled, and suddenly Mindy's eye contact wasn't so steady.

I called Harry the next day. "Did I kill it with Lucerne by declining?"

"Interestingly, no," Harry said. "But you can't change your mind now."

I was biting my nails. "But I blew up that bridge, huh?" I was getting pretty good at blowing up bridges.

"That's not the way I hear it. Are you ready to go to work?"

"Soon, Harry . . ."

Fits laughed when I told him. "Good for you; these directors can get to thinking they're gods," he said. "Be careful, though, not to turn saying no into a self-destructive pattern."

He had just wrapped a movie and had time on his hands. He said we should go to Mexico. There was a place, San Quintín, about a third of the way down Baja; he'd go fishing and I could ride horses on the beach. I'd never been to Mexico so I said okay, and we took off that night. Fits drove straight through to Ensenada, where we spent two days in a hotel on the harbor. He taught me how to drink tequila; he'd watch, buying the rounds as I downed one after the other. I discovered real Mexican food and fell for tacos, stopping at every taqueria we passed. Things didn't go so well in San Quintín. The place was beautiful but empty. We had the off-season hotel almost to ourselves. I felt far away and panicky. I felt far away all the time, but this was worse. When the divorce papers came through I felt far away, detached, unmoored and scared. They cited abandonment, meaning I had done the abandoning. I called Joe, my voice weak and drained. He felt lousy too, but I said he at least had the advantage of being at home with the cats. He said the place was full of the ghosts of us, and I cried into the phone. I'd begun to forget what I was so far from as Los Angeles asserted itself, but that open, lonely, windy beach with the seagulls screeching mournfully was too far too fast. I told Fits I had to go back, I'd freak if I didn't get to someplace familiar. He said to quit carrying on like a bad acid trip but agreed to take me back to L.A. the next day.

That time in Mexico was the beginning of the end of me and Fits being physical together. We did become good friends. Fits is basically a loner; he just let me borrow his world at a time when mine was crumbling around me. Once I got back into the swirl, once I let the business take me over, figuring, finally, the thread between me and Joe was truly snapped, and my heart got a nice big scab over it, there were lovers. Some I remember their names but not much else. At least one turned stormy—on his part. One almost got to me. None were ever as kind as Fits.

The morning after I got back from Mexico, I picked up the phone to hear Andre Lucerne's voice on the other end. I was still undressed at eleven, probably hadn't brushed my teeth, sipping tea in the kitchen, my stomach wrenched from too many tacos and tequilas. I thought maybe it was Fits fooling around, but he'd made it pretty clear we should let a few days pass without seeing each other. I told Andre I was sorry for turning down the part and was about to drift into the untouchable topic of my recent divorce, but he wasn't interested. He asked me to dinner.

"Dinner?" I repeated, biting my tongue from adding, *why?* He'd hardly given me a second glance when I'd been his lead. He'd gotten the performance he wanted and hadn't bothered with the on-set nice-nice-let's-get-to-know-each-other groove. All the actors were terrified of Andre, though he was never genuinely mean or bullying. He was not so much distant as preoccupied, as if each day was profoundly itself and there was only time and energy enough to make it brilliant; all else was distraction and waste. You felt you had to please him, to try to break through and capture his approval, which usually came in the form of a nod and, if really pleased, a nod and slight raising of his eyebrows. If the eyebrows dipped and he fell silent you knew you were miles off course.

Why was he bothering with me now? Besides the fact that he was married and twelve years older—a very attractive twelve years— and I'd said no to his movie.

"Dinner, yes. You do eat dinner?" he said.

"I do, but . . ."

"Free tonight?"

As a bird, but there was my stomach and . . . and did I want to have dinner with Andre Lucerne? "I was in Mexico for a few days," I said, "I—I'm a little out of sorts."

"Ah, the tourista. Drink some tequila—hair of the dog—and swallow raw garlic cloves; you will live."

We set a date for the following week and met at a little Moroccan place in Los Feliz, a café, very relaxed. I nearly got lost finding the place. Andre had lamb. I hate lamb, so I ate a tabouli dish with hummus, baba ghanoush, and some sort of spicy fish. He did nearly all the talking. He told me his theories on film, which were vast and contradictory. I started thinking, at heart he's an anarchist—if he isn't nuts—all the while picturing Joe making faces behind his back, as in *Who is this guy?* Possibly he noticed my concentration wandering and got off theory and told a very funny story of the making of his first film and how he hadn't really intended to be a filmmaker. "I think I would have preferred to be a painter," he said, as if the idea had just come to him and I was not seated opposite, listening. "If only because with painting one can erase. One is freer. There are too many details that can barely be controlled in making films."

"Like the actors?" I ventured.

If he heard me he didn't react. The café sold Moroccan items: pointed leather slippers, clay tagines, spices, even clothing and mother-of-pearl combs. As we were sipping our mint tea and coffee after dinner, Andre abruptly walked over to an armoire that had a sumptuous gold-threaded white caftan hanging on the open door. He brought it to the table and told me to stand and hold it up. "This would fit you perfectly," he said. I couldn't help noticing the three-hundred-fifty-dollar price tag. Calling for the check, he told the waiter to add the caftan and wrap it up. He gave me the package out on the sidewalk.

"For me?" I was embarrassed by his extravagance and what it might imply for the rest of the night, but all he did was kiss my hand.

"Thank you for your silence; it's a rare gift these days. I enjoyed our dinner."

(I have a gift for silence?)

That was it. Assured I knew my way back to Hollywood, he said good-night. I didn't see him again for nearly two years. He was right about the caftan; it fit as if it had been custom-made. That café became a favorite of mine, but not sentimentally; I had no idea what to make of the evening or why Andre wanted to have dinner with me. As far as I knew, he went home to wife number two, an actress, that night.

In the morning I got up whisper-quiet, not to waken Andre. I made a pot of tea to drink on the balcony as I idly watched for signs of White Shirt. There were none. The day was bright, clear, and almost cold. I could see snow on the mountains. Without the sun, now well over the San Gabriels, I would have frozen stiff. The caftan is here with me, in L.A., and I look for excuses to wear it. I wonder sometimes if in his mind that Moroccan dinner was the start of Andre's courting me. The next time we met he referred to the evening as if it had taken place the week before. The caftan is meant for a Park Avenue apartment with a cascading marble staircase, for descending à la Loretta Young, swishing to greet guests for cocktails or late-morning confidential chats in the boudoir. I have neither cascading stairs nor a bedroom fit for an heiress, and no Fred Astaire type arrives of an evening, the butler showing him in. The garment is of another era. Joan Crawford comes to mind.

Too bad it wasn't with me when I won best actress at Cannes. Andre was up too, for best director, for *Separation and Rain*. He didn't win, but his leading lady did. The French adored Andre, and Cannes had already awarded him best director, so he was relaxed either way. I nearly threw up when they announced my name. I didn't even have a new dress but an old filmy thing I'd had around forever that I wore to every event. I jazzed it up with a silk shawl I'd seen in a shop window along the Croisette, which Harry surprised me by buying. Mindy Scott showed up in Cannes, scraped the money together, she said, to fly over for the festival and was hanging on to me like skin on bone. She'd had all of three lines in the movie. She must have told Harry about the shawl, and I figured he must have paid her way over, probably to keep tabs on me, though Mindy was not his client. He'd wanted to buy me a new dress, but I'd refused. I told him to forget it; I was not going to win and not to waste his money. I shocked him by getting my hair cut très short. I walked cold into a salon and said, "Take it off." It looked great, if I do say so myself. Harry of course pooh-poohed the style. "Eurotrash!" he called it.

Cannes was a disappointment; the town, the film festival, even the fabled beach was a letdown. Beneath a glamorous veneer the festival was a flesh factory for selling cans of movies and careers. We had press nearly every day; Andre and the producers, the principal actors, interviews and photo ops to keep the excitement revved up. Andre was very nice, helped me handle the glare and field some of the numbingly inane questions the press threw at me. Mindy was practically my Siamese twin, so she made some press appearances too. I didn't fault her pushiness. I held on to her in the street, where we were trailed by a band of bored-looking paparazzi. Until I won; then it was a wolf pack of international camera snappers in my face, all part of the star machinery.

Joe flew over after I called to say I'd been nominated, making it to Cannes one hour before the ceremonies began. At least he wore a black sports coat over his jeans. He loved the hair. "Very gamine," he said in my ear. Cannes disgusted him as much as it did me. The water off Nice looked polluted from the plane, he said, like a milky stream of sewage pouring in next to the bathers. The road from Nice to Cannes was littered with an obnoxious string of minimalls—not Big Mac and Burger King but *pan, pizza, poulet* joints—fast food French style. The Ritz, where Harry had put me up, was over the top. Even the coffee shop was a four-star deal; luckily the room came with breakfast of croissant and bowls of café au lait. Joe asked if they didn't have a Motel 8 or something like it near the airport. I was worrying about how he was going to take all the after-ceremony parties I'd have to attend—de rigueur—just because I'd been nominated, so I didn't hear when they announced my name. Joe nudged me. "It'll be all right," I said. "We'll pop in, say hello, and scram to the next party, ten minutes each, max."

"What are you talking about? You won, silly goose." He held and kissed the palm of my hand. I stared at him. They said my name again, and I felt myself stand up among the audience as if I were being lifted on an ocean wave, my stomach bucking. Suddenly Andre was there, kissing both my cheeks, his hands on my shoulders, nearly knocking off the mauve shawl. Harry was squashed into a seat two rows behind me; he pushed himself up to come embrace me, his breath wet in my ear. An usher appeared to guide me to the stage. My legs were rubber doll's legs. I faced Joe with a get-me-outta-here look. But he was applauding along with everyone else. I didn't figure I'd have a snowball's chance in hell of winning so I had nothing prepared to say. One of my idols, Giulietta Masina, won best actress at Cannes—for *Nights of Cabiria*—was I worthy of her? Some genie moved my hands for me, tossing the shawl gamely over one shoulder, leaving the other bare, the strap of my dress slipping ever so slightly. Joe said later the hair and subdued sexiness of the shawl worked magic. The French papers next day exclaimed over my chicly original sense of style. Ha.

I stumbled through a thank-you. I felt I wasn't breathing. I kept my eyes down and spoke just above a whisper, thanking Andre and the cast and Harry and the producers and, oh, the French, *"Viva La France!"* popped out of my mouth, eliciting a puff of laughter from the crowd. I felt the surge of their energy: an almost out-of-body sensation. I paused and looked out at all those faces, just for a second. It was like firecrackers lit just for me, ten thousand fireworks and I was the Fourth of July; a thousand flaming torches—all for me. It was madness. Finally, I thanked the writer Joe Finn.

He was furious. We were up all night arguing after the parties Harry dragged us to in rapid succession. Joe had steadily downed the drinks, whatever the waiters were passing around. I watched him nervously; Joe wasn't much of a drinker. Back at the room I burst into tears. At one A.M. Andre called: Where was I? The big *Separation and Rain* celebration was just warming up and the star was missing. He sent up a bottle of champagne. I had the waiter open it, though Joe stood there glaring like poison. I went down to the party alone, a study in misery. Once again Andre stepped in, was gentlemanly and solicitous, guiding me through the night.

The next day Cannes was dead, a ghost town. Everybody was either in bed hungover or on a plane home now that no one would pick up their tab if they stayed on. Outside, sweepers were at work as the locals reclaimed their town. Harry woke me up with a phone call at noon: Why wasn't I at the airport?

My head was splitting, my mouth like old chewing gum and

sawdust. "Can you change my ticket to a few days from now, please, Harry, and please don't ask me any questions."

"It's that moper, isn't it?"

"That's a question, Harry. Just please work some deal with my first-class ticket, cash it in for two coach fares back to New York in, say, four days. I'm begging you, Harry." I hung up.

We rented a car and drove up to Aix en Provence, stopping at a roadside stand selling cherries—*cerise*—that were the plumpest, sweetest we'd ever tasted. "These aren't cherries," Joe said, holding one up. "These are tree-grown orgasms." He turned the car around and we bought another half kilo. We drank Pernod at the café Des Deux Garçons, where Cézanne used to hang out. We visited his studio, up past a housing-project slum outside Aix. Inside were the painter's props and his straw field hat and black all-weather coat hung on a hook by the door, as if he'd only just gone out. The very same leggy germaniums, still-life jars and vases; only fresh pears and apples were missing. We had the place to ourselves until a small troop of tourists filed in, cameras like appendages hanging off their necks. Even Joe thought we'd stood on something like hallowed ground that day.

We went to the market for fresh goat cheese, bread, fruit, wine, tomatoes, and olives for a picnic at the base of Mont St. Victoire. I recall stopping the car to pee in the woods, and the glassy light in the forest, the reddish tree trunks and a wash of silver in the air. I remember thinking Cézanne had seen that light and captured it on canvas. We laughed out loud arriving at the view he'd painted so many times, the tumbledown boulders of St. Victoire. I said to Joe, "That's it, that's cubism right there; he painted what he saw!"

"Good old crotchety Cézanne. And Hortense, his wife: the ball and chain," Joe said with a wink.

"Hey!" I shot back. "What about 'Theory shits,' what he said to his painter pals in Paris, Monet and Pissarro and the others, before he took off for the south, never to look back."

"A man who knew what he wanted and wasn't afraid to go after it," Joe said.

We worked to patch things up under that pale Provençal sky that seemed as if it could cleanse any human sin. I thought Joe was angry at me for thanking Andre and everyone else first at the ceremony, but he sneered at that. "Andre?" he said, exaggerating the name (*Ahhhhhndray*). "All right, the man has talent, but all Andre does is Andre."

I decided I'd skip that part. "Is this about you taking that electrical work? You don't have to."

"Really? You took an apartment in Los Angeles; now we have two rents to pay."

"It's just temporary, and I can handle both, Joe; it's way cheaper than a hotel." I made my voice small because money talk could cause an avalanche.

"Do you think about what you're doing, Ardennes?"

"Taking the apartment? I'll get more work if I'm out there. . . . I wish so much you'd come, just for a little while. The cats could fly out too."

"I'm saying: Is this what you *want*?" His tone was like a clamp on my throat.

"It's what I *do*, Joe; I'm an actor. It's just, I—what do you want me to do, act in documentaries?" I'd done everything in my life to be doing what I was doing; what was I supposed to make of Joe's question? Was I any different than Cézanne going after his art? "I don't see your writing saving the world from hunger—"

"—Just forget it!" he cut in. (That was *his* fallback position.)

After a tense silence I said, "I couldn't have done the award without you. I can't do anything without you."

He dismissed that idea. "Ah, cut it out. *You* won all by yourself. Just keep me out of the cheesy stuff is all I ask. I'll boost my own career."

Oh, I said to myself, I shouldn't have called him a writer. He *is* a writer! I felt so helplessly sad. It was impossible to keep guessing at what was going to work with Joe. It seemed like I was wrong seventy-five percent of the time. I must have looked like unhappiness incarnate, my face falling like a car wreck. Joe put his arms around me. "It's all right, don't fret, Ardennes."

I brightened like a dumb flower that can't help itself when the sun peeks out from behind a cloud. I muttered the word *cerise* into his warm shoulder. We finished our picnic in peace and that night had magnificent *c'est ci bon* French sex. The next morning I was briefly recognized for my prize—it was all over the newspapers that week. I was afraid Joe would get mad again, but he was quiet as I thanked the concierge of the inn for congratulating me. He presented us with a bottle of Châteauneuf du Pape, asking first if I preferred red or white. Then he asked us to wait one moment while he ran back inside to present us with a bottle of white as well, kissing first me and then Joe on each of our cheeks.

Joe beamed. "Looks like pretty good wine," he said, holding up the Châteauneuf.

We returned home to a pile of scripts for me to read. All I wanted was to bask in springtime New York, rest up and be normal again, cook us dinner, walk the city, visit friends. Instead I picked up walking pneumonia. "At least I get to be here for longer," I told Joe. "No one would hire me now. I look like an old sock." He nursed me with teas and soups and antibiotics. I slept while he wrote, the cats keeping vigil at the foot of the bed. I weeded through the pile of mostly junk scripts as spring outside heated up toward summer. By the end of July I was back at work, on location in New Orleans, a supporting role again. Whatever cachet I'd gained from the Cannes win had little currency across the Atlantic. Harry blamed the haircut.

I finished my bowl of cereal and, tiptoeing, took a shower and dressed. It was ten o'clock. No signs of life from Andre under his pillow. His cell phone, on vibrate, rock-'n'-rolled on the dining table. I looped the MAID *Please Make Up This Room* sign, on the side that showed a sleeping, smiling quarter moon and a *Do Not Disturb* message, over the door and went out. One of the maids I'd seen before down at the main hotel greeted me in Spanish. The others spoke to me in Spanish first too. I have picked up a blush of sun on my naturally pale olive skin, but do I look Latin? Andre tells me I am secretly Ethiopian, calling me his dark mistress. I am occasionally taken for Mediterranean but never for a great beauty, though my grandmother would have had me believe otherwise. "Striking" has been used to describe me in reviews. Godard's Anna Karina comes to mind: unassumingly sexual, but look closely and the nose is just the wrong side of big, the teeth a disappointment, the mouth wide for her angular chin, yet so intriguing on camera, even into her sixties. Or take Anouk Aimée: Is she beautiful? Is she in a class with the gold heat of Bardot or Grace Kelly's burnished radiance? What is beauty anyway? I mean, what does it mean? Joe always said beauty had to be earned. Good thing the camera liked me because in person I think I'm funny-looking, with big light brown hair and faded blue eyes, large teeth—none of it quite going with my skin tone. I don't know about all this supposed darkness either. Andre says it comes from the inside. Does he mean that I am dark, as a metaphor?

"A metaphor, yes," he once said. "But, more, you are not white."

I look white to me, in the mirror. Maybe the darkness metaphor is why I was offered so few leads.

Annoyed, Andre told me I knew perfectly well the camera ate me alive and served me up to a responsive audience. I didn't respond that I knew nothing perfectly well. And he didn't add that I couldn't expect the lead if I quit.

Leaving him to his sleep, I walked down the steep hill, out the heavy security gate and on down to the avenue, pulling my new magenta silk scarf closer around my neck. The verdigris cotton sweater I'd tossed on was not sufficient against the morning chill so I walked faster. At least the jeans and sneakers made sense as I practically trotted to Hollywood Boulevard. When I lived and worked here I never walked the Walk of Fame. I tried not to step directly on the actors' names. I've never heard of half the immortalized stars; why, for example, did Dolores Hope merit a star?

I moved along in my usual interior way, taking in the street while trying to remain invisible. "What?" I said, sensing someone pushing through my barrier. It's not unusual for me to be mentally miles away.

"Excuse me," said a youngish man. I think it might have been for the third time. "Would you agree to be interviewed for television?"

"*What?*" Luckily my sunglasses were large and dark.

"It's for the Style Network."

I thought, sure, Hollywood Boulevard: Jason from *Friday the 13th*, Elvis, Batman, Darth Vader, Tinker Bell out trolling for tourists dumb enough to pay to have their photos taken with them; why not a pseudo TV shoot? I assumed I was supposed to be impressed, flattered, the tourist rube from Podunk suddenly on TV. "Why me?" I said, sarcastic. "Do I *look* stylish?"

"Yes," he said, "as a matter of fact, you do." And, pronto, a camera was thrust in my face, and a miniboom. Out of nowhere the personnel appeared, including the babe who would interview me, made up to seduce: coiffed, petite, pretty and perky. The director took over, telling me what questions I'd be asked. "It's about a new perfume," he explained, upbeat and positive, as if he were making an important feature, not a grade-B infomercial. Another fellow held high a smoky-glassed bottle of perfume, reached for my wrist, and sprayed two clouds of an organic, peaty, nighttime scent.

The camera started to roll. "No!" I said palms up to protect my face. *"No, no, no!"*

The camera stopped. The operator peered out from behind his giant lens. "Hang on a minute," he said, "isn't that—" He turned to the director. "Isn't she—"

"I'm sorry. I have to go."

I hurried away, past the pretend made incarnate: Darth and Elvis, Edward Scissorhands, Freddy Krueger, Dorothy complete with a stuffed Toto. I walked on. I stopped when I came to Frederick's of Hollywood, still selling sexpot lingerie after all these years. I looked in the window, remembering seeing a Frederick's catalog as a child, but where? Whose? My long-widowed grandmother? My *mother*? I remembered a sense of arousal, looking at the pointy brassieres and revealing nighties at a time when I was only just becoming aware of arousal. Busty women with blond, bouffant dos; breasts pushed into bra cups, nearly spilling out; pasties and G-strings and see-through panties—it got my attention then and now. I moved on when a guy sidled up to me and I saw us reflected in the window, him too close. I pictured the unsheathed penis-under-a-raincoat cliché and moved on, past other sex boutiques with names like For Play and Naughty, and bong shops and cheap eateries, the seedier part of the boulevard where you might not want to be immortalized with a star. Here stains and chewing gum marred the pink stars trimmed in gold. If they ever get around to giving me a place on the Walk of Fame it'll be in this unglamorous, stagnant stretch: punishment for quitting. I didn't slow down again until I was at the corner of Vine.

I was just walking. I had nowhere to be and was in no hurry to get there. I stopped in front of a kiosk of postcards, two for fifty cents. They were not the most up-to-date and they'd been out on the rack a while, curling in on themselves and sun-faded. I picked out four. I asked the man inside who took my dollar what else he sold. "Posters," he said. "Pictures of the stars, gen-U-ine *autographs*," he added, emphasizing the last word as if letting me in on a steamy secret. Would he have an autographed image of me lying about somewhere, on the off chance? There *were* photos of me in existence, even posters, but I doubted this fellow had any.

"A real Hollywood store," I said, peering briefly over my glasses, letting him think I believed him. Plenty of suckers would.

"Yup," he said; a friendly schlump in his dump of a shop. I'd bet an arm he didn't have a single original autograph, but a truckload of fakes. The whole concept was sickening anyway: a sorry, sad public willing to play along, to be photographed with an actor posing as a character from a movie, twice-removed-from-reality Tinsel Town. And the fans: praying to touch the magic, shamelessly begging for a glance, a smile, the contact of a handshake equaling bliss, waiting hours along the ropes for their favorite star to stroll by in a tux or sequined gown, roaring as the limo doors opened. An old Kinks song came to me—the name wouldn't—I used to sing it at parties. This was after Fits, some other, forgettable guy on my arm. I was working again, staying busy and dumb and distracted. I'd developed a post-Joe ironic tongue, as if I were channeling him to make up for what I'd become. I took most of the parts Harry sent my way, auditioned, returned calls; wore my hair long and done up by the right salon, fitted dresses when I had to, slouchy on my own, though, the real me sometimes having trouble making it out of the house, in horror of being seen.

I drew the line at nudity. I was probably too skinny anyhow. Harry feigned horror: Nudity is not what Ardennes Thrush is about. Wasn't he kind not to say no director had asked? My sexiness, about which I was confident even back then, was not of the silver-screen style. Dumb, extravagantly good-looking guys don't usually day-dream my type. I'm a touch independent, a shade intimidating. Pro-ducers tend to be fairly predictable guys that way. Not that I'm offering excuses. Hepburn, for example, was about as sexy as a per-fect piece of furniture. If you want sexuality that looks you in the eye, I'm your girl. That's what I think they meant by striking.

I had an on-set conversation once with one of those knockout boys, an obviously handsome, not-my-type lead who'd send some women into spasms merely walking into a room. The film was a quirky whodunit. The actress opposite Knockout was having trou-ble lying flat on an expensive carpet, in a swoon—or maybe she'd been hit over the head, I forget. Fifteen minutes were called. Knock-out and I sat down to wait. We'd be on camera once the starlet got it right. I was playing a tough lawyer sucked into my client's (Knockout's) involvement with a murder. Of course he and his love-girl turn out to be innocent while I provide the juicier dark content. The director was having a tête-à-tête with his crew, and Knock-out turned to me, out of the blue blue of his eyes, and said, "Can't she even play dead? I mean, those lips could stop a train. . . ." He shrugged.

I nodded without cozying. Well, Einstein, she was hired for those lips; the acting's up to us. He surprised me by continuing, "You get a chick like that home and there's nothing there. I've seen it enough times. Knock, knock: a hollow door."

I turned to look into the face of this unexpected wisdom. He smiled. "I bet that's not true of you." Was he hitting on me or offering a consolation prize to the supporting role? (At the time I was involved with a musician, if "involved" is the right term.) The first AD called places: take in three minutes. Makeup came over and did touch-ups on us. A costumer adjusted my skirt, hair did a quick check, and we were ready to go.

QUIET ON THE SET . . . CAMERAS ROLLING . . . AND . . . ACTION:

Knockout and I push in the partially open apartment door. We see his girlfriend lying on the Persian rug. Knockout's character (Eric) rushes in, kneels: "Katie!"

My character (Laura) sits on a white-upholstered armchair, crossing her legs: "This doesn't look too promising."

Eric: "Laura! Get help!"

Laura takes a lace handkerchief out of her purse, reaches for the phone, picks up the receiver, using the hanky. To Eric: "I'd be careful of fingerprints."

Katie opens her eyes, blinks: "Eric?"

Laura replaces the receiver: "Cancel the cavalry?"

CUT!

I've done love scenes. Close-ups can be as awkward as dying with your underpants down, pulling off a conventional movie love scene. Stay in character, I'd repeat to myself like a mantra, stay in character. The actors stepped up to the plate, kissed and held me like they meant it, breath cool mint vapors, hand grasping a breast, my full mouth bruised. Go for it. The crew polite, supportive, respectful even, but it was all crap and nonsense. I was living it then, and I couldn't smell it on me because I was making a huge effort to go along. I brought everything I could to whatever I was handed: tramp, schoolteacher, victim of violent crime, even a wayward cop who ended up shot dead. Word went out: Ardennes Thrush delivers; finds her character and gives it all she's got. All the while I kept thinking right around the corner I'd get a handle on things again. I'd remember what I meant, why I chose acting in the first place, where and what I wanted my work to be. Underneath me flowed a miserable stream, a kind of leak: That was me dripping slowly away from myself, terrified I was nothing, a big zero; that Joe had been right all along about me, about actors—we were nothing but shells playing at being people, a pack of counterfeiters. I started catching on to all the cocaine and booze and bad behavior surrounding me; none of us was grounded, none of us was real. "Celluloid Heroes"—that's the name of the Kinks song!

I'd go to the parties and shine and show off and make funny, bitter little jokes, and I'd sing, a few drinks in me to loosen my tongue, my voice gravelly: ". . . Everybody's a dreamer . . ." I'd go for a cheap laugh with a Swedish accent. They put Greta on a throne, looking small and fragile, until the burden drove her to be alone. Garbo, by the way, didn't say she wanted to be alone. She said she wanted to be left alone, pointing out, to anyone who cared to listen, that there was a difference.

Director George Cukor supposedly once asked Garbo why she would allow no visitors on her sets, why she minded people looking at her. "When people are watching, I'm just a woman making faces for the camera. It destroys the illusion," was her supposed reply.

Sure, the illusion . . .

Born-again freaks were out on the Boulevard as I headed back to the hotel. I'd remembered Andre talking about throwing a cocktail party for the crew if he could free up time, so I'd gone into a Bed Bath and Beyond that I came across between Vine and Sunset and ordered an inexpensive outdoor glass garden table for our sitting room because there are never enough surfaces in hotels for books and drinks. A party was not something I looked forward to, though some of the crew were smart and bright, not looking over their financial shoulders every other minute. One of the actors reminded me of a younger Fits. We'd had a funny conversation about life and death just before Andre and I left the party in Silver Lake, after Ella and I had done examining her dolls' bottoms.

A gaggle of Jehovah's Witnesses was congregated at the courtyard of the Kodak Theater Mall, looking defeated. How could they compete with the hustlers, the fans and dreamers, the shoppers, tourists, souvenir hunters—a few shops sold gold plastic Oscars, so you could go home with your own—and morning liquor-store patrons? Even Ripley's looked abandoned. At Grauman's Chinese Theatre a Jesus wannabe prophet-type crazy let a small crowd know the Lord loved them, making it sound like a threat. He was perched on a box, barefoot, wearing nothing but a white loincloth, long blond hair flowing, ginger beard down to his breast as he bellowed about perdition. "*You*, sir, have borne false witness, lied to the Lord!" he let a passerby know. I walked briskly between him and the crowd, head lowered. I should have crossed to the other side of the street. "*You*, madam, have sinned!"

Was he talking to me? Without stopping I gave him the thumbs-up. You bet I've sinned. This town would be nothing without lies and transgression. He called out to me. "Dear lady, is your heart pure?" I turned, and I think I saw him wink.

Well, is my heart pure? No time to ponder the question: My cell phone rang.

It was Andre. Where was I? Out shopping, I told him. He said I didn't need any more shoes. I could have mentioned ordering the table for his proposed cocktail party but didn't. "I thought you had a thing for shoes," I said, acting the pervert. He laughed slightly, said I should stop by the set later for dinner. "Ah, honey-wagon food. How can I resist?"

"We have a pretty good caterer this time around." He'd call later, he promised, repeating that I should come to the set. Those involved have no idea how boring movie sets are to those who are not. Well, the grips do, and makeup, costumers, and the PAs. Plenty of hurry-up-and-wait, like watching snails cross the road. If only the fans knew what a glued-together patchwork movie acting really is, so much of it manufactured in the editing. Is that still magical?

Waiting for the light to change, I overheard a creamy hustler lure two chubby female Midwesterners onto a double-decker bus tour of celebrity homes. The ladies at first wisely declined. He seemed to accept their turndown, no aggression from him, only nat-ural, oily charm: Take a look at that wide-open, sun-kissed face, a gander at those defined pecs. The trap's maw widened: "Where you pretty ladies from?" A titter. Watch out, girls.

I'd heard about a football-field-sized discount shoe store on Sunset and decided I would go ahead and buy myself a pair of shoes, now that Andre had put the idea into my head. Not that I needed shoes any more than those gals needed to have a gawk at the movie-star mansions. Does the audience know an actor gets to keep all

those Prada shoes and Armani suits? Yup, thousands of dollars'
worth of cell phones and wines and clothing, lists of product-
placement goodies. If a star pulls out a BlackBerry in public, who
benefits? Not you, dear audience, springing ten or twelve for a
movie seat. Nope. Just another perk in the lives of those needing it
least. Joe pointed that out to me, and he was right. I cut down Orange and swung a right onto Sunset.

It was hours before I made it back to the rooms, dispirited, fed up
and hungry. There was a fresh bouquet of lilies on the side table where
I usually dropped my keys. My sleeve brushed a stamen, leaving an
orange streak on the verdigris sweater. I swore instead of appreciating
Andre's gesture and the heady scent of lilies filling the room. I was
furious at myself for wasting hours at the discount store. I don't
know why I was so cranky. What difference did it make if I demol-
ished time in a shoe store or popping bonbons on the hotel couch?

I can easily afford full price, but everybody loves a bargain, I kept
telling myself as minutes in the store melted into hours. I'd searched
and searched for something between sexy and smart. A minor break-
down held me, going over and over the same rows long after I knew
there was nothing there for me. I blame Alesso Lorenzo, Andre's set
designer; spry Alesso who notices a woman's shoes first, before breasts
or eyes. Before "hello," he'll say, "What shoe do you wear today?"
He's from a fishing village in Italy, near Brindisi, toward the heel of
the boot; what does he know of shoes? "I am Italian!" he protested
before I raised my leg to display an expensively sneakered foot. "Ah,
this is the first time with those," he said. He hated the burgundy
leather running shoes. One afternoon I returned to the hotel to find
Andre and Alesso in the walk-in closet, all the shoes I'd brought
with me from New York spread out on the floor, Alesso evaluating
each pair. They were supposed to be having a budget meeting.

I'd worn suede ballet flats the evening we were introduced. That was two days after I arrived in L.A., at a party given by the producer, out near Venice Beach. It was too cold with the sea breezes, but I'd stood out on the deck as long as I could, the wind off the Pacific blowing through my hair, shaking out the plane ride and any remnants of New York. Alesso admired my shoes to Andre, whispering that my small feet were *tesoro*, a treasure. My feet are small for my height, something my father was weirdly proud of. "He would like to put them in his mouth," Andre suggested in the car on the way back to the hotel. "The foot or the shoe?" I asked. Andre shrugged: Maybe Alesso had a shoe fetish, but he was good at what he did; his habits were only an amusement. "Good thing he's not into panties," I observed.

What do I care for Alesso's ecstasies? Shoes don't mean that much to me—they could, yes, I see that they could. I prefer hats. Hats are good street costume, a way to hide in plain sight. And scarves, bits of fabric tossed gamely around the neck. What sort of female am I, though, walking out of a shoe store empty-handed? And that poor, bulked-up sales guy. He tailed me no matter how politely I tried to shake him. It wasn't even that kind of store; you're lucky to find a clerk to pay, never mind one to find you a size. I was considering two pairs and caved, asking the clerk which shoe looked better, guessing he'd go for the sluttier heels. He did. The undercurrent of sexuality in a shoe (ask Alesso): By soliciting his opinion I had opened the door. Well, there were only foot mirrors, and too few of those; I needed a second opinion. I turned my ankle this way and that, argued for the Joan and David backless pointed loafer with a senseless silver buckle that I knew Andre would insist I return as too American bourgeois. The clerk tried to backtrack. He let me know I have fantastic legs, "but, I mean, if the need is for a more formal shoe . . ." No, I told him, I would not take either pair after all.

He followed me to the exit, saying he recognized me but couldn't think from which movie. So that was why he'd been so attentive. Out of the corner of my eye I saw what seemed like the store manager look over at us from behind the checkout counter. I tucked my head into my neck; the clerk must be confusing me with someone else. "Would I be shopping here if I was in the movies?" (Well, yes, if I was washed up; a girl still needs something on her feet.) He was an actor, he said. Of course he was. I stuck the card he handed me, listing his measurements among other vitals, into my pocket. Maybe I could help him, you never know. Wasn't I married to a director? Andre, I knew, would throw the card into the trash. Find something better than shoes, I wanted to say to the clerk; it's gonna be a long life. He said he was from Cincinnati, Ohio.

I threw the lily-stained sweater on the couch and looked into the fridge. Nothing of the nearly nothing in there interested me, so I wandered foodless into the bedroom to lie down, to ready myself for another hotel evening alone. My eyes were shut and I was drifting off on the novel I was reading when the house phone rang—the hot phone, I call it, which hardly ever rang and seemed to portend trouble when it did.

"Hello?" A mechanized voice told me to wait one moment, please, and then I heard Harry Machin's unmistakable voice on the other end. "Harry!"

He'd had some sort of massive coronary event a year ago. I'd heard he'd lost seventy pounds. He still owned the agency but for now personally handled only a couple of clients, working mainly out of his house. The famous lone wolf Harry Machin had taken a partner into his once solitary lair. That must have hurt.

"You've been in town how long, I don't hear from you?"

"I'm not sure I'm actually here myself, Harry,"

He let out a breath and said I should come to lunch. "Come tomorrow. I'm betting you're not busy. The cook will prepare us flavorless poached fish with stunningly bland rice. I'll have a nice pinot to go with it, though."

Harry lived way the hell up in Beverly Hills. You had to get there and then climb the winding, narrow roads full of houses in varying levels of overdone, squeezed onto lots meant to feel like estates. He was literally on the top, the last house on a street you needed a GPS and luck to find. But he was right; I wasn't busy. My rented car was just sitting outside unused and running up a bill. I might as well say yes. "Good," Harry said. "You remember the address?"

It was sudden, but I had no excuse, not even a plausible white lie handy. Harry'd been there for me, and I hadn't even sent him a get-well card when he was convalescing. The thing about abandoning a former life is everything goes with it, every shred of evidence, the symbols and trappings, the friends. That was what made my being here with Andre the one wound left to close. Now I'd be seeing Harry, another wound opening up.

My cell phone rang as soon as I hung up the house phone. The night was turning busy. I stood up to close the curtains as I talked.

It was one of the PAs. He was on his way—Andre's orders—to pick me up for dinner on the set. "Can you put him on the phone?" I asked.

"Can't do, I'm on the stairs to your room now. I'm sorry, Ms. Thrush; Mr. Lucerne said not to call any sooner than that." And, true to his threat, he knocked on my door.

I was talking to him on my phone as I answered the door, in jeans, t-shirt, bare feet, with the magenta scarf still around my neck. He was a cute kid. They all are. Skinny and self-possessed and full of some secret certain purpose that most likely doesn't really exist or will not be fulfilled in an increasingly blurry future. He looked straight into my eyes, unnerving me for a second, but he was so clearly just an open face that I looked back and smiled. "Wow, you really are beautiful," he said. "I mean, wow, I shouldn't have said that."

"Especially since it isn't so."

"No, it is, but not like obvious, not like, you know, magazines. I don't know, just awesome." His jeans hung perilously low over a pair of narrow hips.

I shook my head, pulled the door open and indicated for him to come in. "There's beer in the fridge," I said as I speed-dialed Andre's cell. He didn't pick up, and I canceled the call. "Are they shooting right now—sorry, what's your name?"

"Jarrad. Yeah, they're on the twelfth take of the lead guy walking toward a door. The lighting's all f—screwed up or something."

"Well, Jarrad, you came, you saw, you didn't conquer. Not that you couldn't. Please tell Mr. Lucerne his wife thanks him but is not able to come to the set tonight." He didn't move. "Were you told to kidnap me, take me down at gunpoint?"

"I was told not to come back without you."

"No beer?" He shook his head. "It was a fool's errand, Jarrad. I don't take orders so easily. You tell the director I appreciate the message and the messenger and be on your way." Jarrad nodded and turned to go. "You eat my dinner for me, okay?" I called after him. He looked like he could use a meal.

"I don't really eat," he called back.

I opened up a carton of Trader Joe's pumpkin soup, ate it with a glass of wine, washed the pot and bowl, and wondered what next. I killed some time going over neglected bank statements. I changed into a nightgown and was watching an old Bette Davis movie about a rich girl fooling around with mobster types, *Fog over Frisco*, when Andre came in at midnight. I think he must have been early. He slapped his phone down on the table and headed for the bottle of vodka in the freezer and one of the frozen glasses next to it. It must have been a bruising night.

"Get the shot you needed?" I called from the couch.

"Just," he said downing the vodka and pouring out another, still standing. "Dammit. The lighting people were going at it, taking all night. A simple shot. Dammit."

I was deciding whether I should shut the movie off, which I did not want to do; I was enjoying Bette. "But it came out all right?" I didn't care if it did or not. I'm supposed to care, or at least act the part.

I knew he knew I was only being polite and would hate the cheapness of it. "Oh, stuff it," he said, coming over to the couch. "Why didn't you come down to the set?"

Things were turning foul; a squall was in the air. "I'm not ready for cameras . . . for that whole scene."

"The camera would not be on *you*. . . ." he said, not finishing his thought. A look of disgust surfaced and passed. "What is it you do all day?"

The question was out of bounds, and he knew it. What I did all day was an accounting that led inevitably back to what I had once done all day, and that led back to why I didn't do it anymore. It was a question always hovering that we'd been dancing around for a long while; it was the DMZ we tacitly agreed to steer clear of at all costs. "I am going to bed," he said to my silence. He shut the bedroom doors.

I turned off the television. "Good-night, Bette," I said softly.

After his light went out I poured myself a brandy and went out onto the balcony, into the cold night air. The light was on in White Shirt's garage; otherwise his house was dark. Most of the houses were dark. The hills looked like a village asleep. To the right, L.A. was eternally on: neon patches and low dark in-betweens, downtown lit up but not as much as New York's downtown at night. A plane crawled silently across the sky.

Andre was never one for a good, meaty argument, not like Joe and I could go at it. He's too aloof for that, or controlled. His passion is reserved for his work. I noticed our arguments were of shorter duration these days. They don't resolve so much as peter out. Are we running out of ammo, the knives and darts growing dull, or are we tired or bored with the same old hurt? What is the same old hurt anyway between a man and a woman that the penis and vagina connecting does not bridge come the light of day or, better, lightless night? Some brief moment of tenderness soothing the ache?

I was wide awake. I already regretted agreeing to see Harry. Dammit! It was cold. Silver moonlight shone along the balcony rail. I leaned out to greet her majesty the moon, lying leisurely on her side, owning the night. I think it a form of sin to fail to greet the heavenly bodies when we encounter them. But what's this? Leaning further out, bare feet and shoulders in my nightgown, the chill boring into my bones, my eyes glanced down to see a woman lift herself out of a large bed. I nearly gasped. The bed light shone on white-on-white linen, the same white sheets and white down quilt as on our bed. Flesh on white. I stood, rapt by the vision. Assuming the nymph had gone to the bathroom, I waited. After a minute I trotted soundlessly back inside for my cashmere shawl. "Naked girl exiting bed in still of night," I told myself. I held my breath. But wait, that was one of our rooms, that was one of Andre's people—the pretty little she returned to the bed. Lo! Another body! More white flesh on white sheeting.

Was the bedmate male or female, youthful, smooth androgyny from where I stood, looking down. The back windows in the rear of that small unit, below and across the drive from us, are below grade—at about car level. Most units have frosted louvered windows in back, squat rectangles above the beds. This window was clear. Could the lovers imagine being seen? Imagine another guest wide awake with a bird's-eye view of their nakedness? Would they have dreamed that an accidental witness would stay and stare, her breath nearly taken away as the two young bodies briefly intertwined when the girl climbed back into bed? And would they suspect her delight when the other person got up to use the toilet, his maleness now on view? Oh, happy view.

Alone and under the quilt, the woman wiggled her hips. I knew the movement well. But was it a contented or an anticipatory wiggle? Had I witnessed the preamble or the postcoital moment? Oh, delicious moment to see the unconscious nakedness of lovers. The bathroom light went out. He returned, she sat up, and, legs tucked beneath her (I couldn't quite see her breasts), leaned in his direction. She seemed exultant, alive at every pore. Did I sense a slight hesitation or unresponsiveness on his part? This would have been sensing a filament, a quiver in the air surrounding the lovers. Ah, she reached over and turned out the light.

I stood alone on the balcony, the aura of the scene stilling me, the intimacy of it. A mockingbird in mating was singing somewhere out to my left, the repertoire recited over and over. I walked quietly inside. What a gift this night had given me. Why did this delight me so? Voyeur, you will be punished!

This brings me back to White Shirt. I can no longer locate the Provençal blue door. Did I imagine it? From the pool the other day, seated in a different corner, while hiding out from the maid—and the searing sun—I had a very different view of his house. There is a muddy sea-green door to the flat, boxy part of the house and a long brick stair leading up to it. Also, there is a door below the stairs, to the right, I think. I can be certain of very little. For example, I thought I saw a stroller in the yard last weekend. There was a woman, the first female I've seen with White Shirt and I assumed since she was acting with propriety that she was related in some way—sister, ex? And I thought a child sat in the stroller. An hour later, however, when I checked, the stroller was still in place and the afternoon had grown chilly. The light had changed too. Was it a cripple instead, in a wheelchair? Toward evening I had to conclude I was wrong on both counts. Who would leave an invalid or a child out all day into the evening, the heat evaporating fast as the sun went down? The car seemed to be gone from the garage too. How much do I make up; how much do I see only to correct later on? There was, as it turned out, no stroller, no child or cripple. I don't know what I'd seen—a lawn chair, a table? Whatever it was, it was gone.

I have not seen the woman again. I did see a tall balding man one day. He and White Shirt were walking on the lawn in a friendly, familiar way. I thought that day that White Shirt might be gay. The gay theory held until there were no further sightings of the balding man, or any other man. But that leaves the sheets. White Shirt hangs an inordinate number of sheets out on his line for someone who appears to live alone. The question is: Am I bothered by the idea that White Shirt might be gay? Just how far are my musings willing to go?

Okay, I admit, I want clues, a never-ending supply of clues.

I want to know what goes on, but from the safety of distance. I want to feel good somehow in my discreet peering into others' lives. And I do mean discreet. And to feel good, not sensually but more that things are harmoniously in their place and all is as it should be and, and, and what? What? I don't know. A wash of good feeling— what's wrong with that? Nothing, except I want the dark corners too, the shadows created by thick bougainvilleas on a sunny day, the soft light at night, the person awake when they should not be; I want all to be well and yet—mysterious. I am not interested in the normal and well-rounded, the life of overt purpose and presumptions.

I sense no such purposefulness with White Shirt. For one thing, like me, he has too much time on his hands. He hangs out the sheets nearly every day. No intimate apparel or shorts or shirts. A single male who hangs out his wash, is home a lot, and putters. Divorced? He's not old. Not middle-aged; late thirties or early forties? I don't see other clotheslines on the hills; maybe they are there, but I don't see them. How much would a cheap pair of binoculars cost? Is that too much of a commitment? Have I committed myself to spying on White Shirt? He has a sports car, but he hangs his sheets out to dry. Thinking about it, White Shirt is the only one there for me *to* observe. Where are all the people? Is he a watcher like me? A furtive slinker into corners?

I glanced up the other day—that's not true—I stood up from the couch, where I was reading that endless novel, feigning interest, and walked to the large window just in time to catch a glimpse of White Shirt before he slipped behind the very tall pine tree that hides much of his yard. Of course he didn't *slip* behind the tree. He moved behind a tree on his property in the service of some gesture or other, perfectly natural; a chore, or working in the garden— perfectly in order. It only *seemed* that he slipped into the shadow of the tree. Possibly it wasn't even him. I looked again, this time from the large bedroom window. No one there. Had I only imagined someone slipping out of sight? The car was in the garage—I checked, so I knew he was at home.

He could be a self-conscious observer, possibly a writer. He could feel illegitimate some of the time, he could work and then not work, he could feel he has purpose and then feel he has none. He could dwell on a fringe, not fully embraced or embracing. He could be a perpetual outsider, a criminal of the soul, so to speak, a person slightly out of tune with others while possibly, if unevenly, attuned to his society of one.

It was nearly two A.M., time for bed. All in all it had been a very rich night.

We slept in the next morning. Thank goodness Harry scheduled for two o'clock. He had a client coming and would lunch late. We awoke at eleven. Andre was surprised to see me lying next to him. He was perfectly gleeful when I said I'd be having lunch with Harry. "That's excellent," he said, watching me as I got up to shower. He said it at least three more times over the course of the morning. I smiled, biting down the question: What was so excellent about me lunching with Harry Machin?

We ate breakfast. I made tea; Andre made the Wolfgang Puck coffee the hotel provided. He cooked us eggs and toast and insisted we eat outside at the round balcony table. It felt like a little holiday with our plates of breakfast in the sunny morning. Jam and butter and an orange shared. "There's a man out there," Andre said, not pointing. He meant White Shirt. "There, across the way, looking." He looked at me. "Do you see?"

"Yes," I said, keeping my eyes on Andre, "I've noticed the man."

We said good-bye at our cars. I headed for Beverly Hills, Andre to the day's location. We agreed to phone each other later. "Excellent," he said again as I lowered myself into my car. I set Harry's address in the GPS and pulled out. Andre waited for me to go first. He pulled over when one of the PAs drove up behind him and tooted, not Jarrad. I sped off. I continued straight for as long as I could before cutting over to Sunset. I passed Gardiner Street and thought of the bungalow I had once lived in, the big floral upholstery I'd once cried into.

It took a long time to reach Harry's. The Los Angeles streets were achingly familiar as I drove. I knew the minute I pulled up to his house I'd made a mistake. Harry opened the door, his housekeeper, an Englishwoman of stout proportions, at his side. He looked as if he'd been to the grave and back and there was something else, a fierceness I'd not seen in him before. I sensed Harry had a different hold on things and that every gesture counted. His pallor was waxy gray, and he was not so much thin as loose. Poor old Harry. He was tired just walking out to the garden. "It's polluted today," he said. The view of L.A. smeared below us was dim, as if a Vaseline glaze had been rubbed on the camera lens. Even this high up the air was not inviting to breathe, and the day was suddenly very warm.

"We'll eat in the dining room," Harry told Lundy, the housekeeper, who would have to reset the table. The house was hushed and impersonal. Harry kept photos of some of his more famous clients hanging in a large downstairs powder room. The living room was comfortably decorated. Not by Harry. There were overstuffed couches and big-leg chairs in spacious rooms, a low, sprawling house. I think Harry'd always been more at home in his office. The grounds appeared extensive, but that was the typical illusion created by pricy gardening contractors. I looked out of a large bay window, and I could have been on a ranch, a small farm or a suburb. L.A.: It's all smoke and mirrors.

Harry groused some about the client who'd come up to see him earlier. An actor on the way up who couldn't accept the smaller parts Harry was bringing in for him. "I'm getting him regular work to build on; he threatens to fire me? He should do me the favor."

No, he answered me: He only got down to the office maybe twice a week. He missed it, but so much was done online now, and the actors were willing to come up to the house, so he managed. "Harry still has it," he said, coming as close to smiling as he ever did.

We sat down to lunch, and I was desperate what we'd talk about. The phone rang and the housekeeper told him who it was and Harry said he'd take the call. The food was as flavorless as promised. I ate while he talked. It was the actor from earlier, apologizing for being a hothead. The conversation went on a bit, with Harry saying okay, he'd get back to the producer today and see if he could audition for a bigger part and so on, all of it sounding painfully familiar.

"I guess nothing's changed in movieland," I said.

Harry looked at me. "Everything's changed. The whole damn studio system is on the way out. That whole approach. Streaming videos, animation, 'straight to DVD' . . . The star system is dying, Ardennes."

I took a sip of wine.

"I liked it better in the old days, but I guess every old fart says the same damn thing." He waved his hand dismissively, with more energy than he had ever shown before, no protruding belly now to tuck his arm back onto. I felt sudden compassion for Harry. Not because he'd been so sick or because the times were changing and some of the light had gone out of his once-upon-a-time sharp eyes but because of that once-upon-a-time itself. A time when Harry Machin called the shots, was mother hen, pissed-off daddy, and fighting superagent who could make me feel anxious or secure, who'd shaped so much of my and others' lives. Maybe it was a wave of compassion for my own past too. I pictured Harry walking heavily down the Croisette, at Cannes, after a press conference, telling me I'd done well. Telling me the plan if I won Cannes, how we'd take the whole world. Harry was going to see to it that I arrived and that I got there in style. That was the day he tried to buy me a new dress for the award ceremony.

The table was cleared and tea brought out, green for Harry, black for me. I asked for milk. Harry was scanning me, that old Buddha scan, quiet and penetrating. "What?" I said, knowing what was coming.

"I could work you. Goddammit, you still have it. You have it more than you ever did. You're just approaching peak. Don't you know that? This is a crime."

Was I a horse? Place your bets? "Harry . . ."

"What are you doing these days? Writing haiku, flower-arranging classes? Ah, a memoir, perhaps?" The sarcasm came with a kind of bluing of his lips. His eyes were dark underneath.

I started to stand. "I should probably go."

Harry held up his hand. "I'm going to stay calm, though I'd like to slap you around, to make you come to your senses. Do you think life gives you a choice?"

"I don't know what you mean." I felt heavy and tired and sank back into my chair.

"If you have something to give the world, it is your duty, your

God-given duty, to take that something—talent—and make it live, push it to the limit, and bring it home." As he spoke his left hand tapped each word out on the table.

"Don't, Harry. This isn't necessary."

"Not necessary?" That fierceness I'd sensed when I'd arrived was piercing now, like a knife blade in the sun, a hawk about to dive at its prey. "Then give me a reason; tell me what you would not tell me before."

I shook my head slowly.

"WHY DID YOU QUIT?" he thundered, banging his hand on the table.

I flinched. The housekeeper came running into the dining room. "Mr. Machin! Mr. Machin? You mustn't upset yourself." She gave me a dirty look.

Harry waved her away. He stood up, hands grabbing the edge of the table. To me he said—his eyes boring into my smallest, most curled-up corner—almost in a whisper: *"Why?"*

2

Hotel Fire

The blush is off the rose. I have no wish to see the setting sun or snow-capped San Gabriels, the pomegranate ripening in the tree that I'm only guessing is a pomegranate, the squawking green parrots; all the charming fragments that held my fragments together. I did venture up the other day, forced myself. The old man was there with his jar of wine and unassuming dog with the appealingly ugly face, faithfully witnessing another day sink into the graveyard of spent time as another Hollywood night approached: beauty, brilliance, power, the desire to outshine the sun. Does it all boil down to power? Not for the old man and his dog.

Joe used to say greed was the only deadly sin and that all the others fit neatly under that banner. If you gave in to greed, you gave in to lust and envy, wrath, gluttony, sloth, and most of all pride, wanting it all for yourself. "Rapaciousness rules," he'd say. Joe believed the growing corporate plutocracy was ruining us and pretty soon the neo–robber barons would be broke too because they'd broken the buying public, who in turn could no longer purchase their junk. Joe's solution? Simple: Find a better motivation than making money. He didn't mean the wage-earners, of course.

Harry's been dead nearly a week. No more deals and percentages for him, no more raking it in, no more power. No more tomorrows, no sunsets: no Harry. A monument thrown into the dust, he just toppled over. Lundy stood there and screamed her British head off. "What have you done? You've killed Mr. Machin!" she shouted at me.

Why was she shouting? was my first thought. Well, my second. The first was that Harry wasn't breathing. He seemed to rear up; the chair toppled over behind him as he clawed his chest, and then he dropped to the dining room floor like a sack of potatoes. That fast.

"Harry?" I said, and for some reason I thought of my father.

She wouldn't stop yelling. What happened to the English stiff upper lip and all that proper proper? She was verging on hysteria. "We need 911," I said, pulling out my phone.

"*She* did it!" she told the police when they arrived, about a minute after the ambulance. I wondered how they'd made it up the winding hills so fast. She pointed a stubby finger at me, housekeeping hands blotchy red. "That woman killed Mr. Machin."

The emergency technician kneeled over Harry and shook his head toward the police officers: "Looks like standard heart attack to me."

"She did it!"

"Ma'am, I'm going to have to ask you to calm down," one officer told Lundy. The other cop took me into the living room, where we could still hear her carrying on as they covered Harry with a sheet. I briefly wondered where the sheet had come from. Did emergency workers carry them around like those ubiquitous latex gloves?

"Can you tell me what happened in there?"

"We had lunch; he got upset. His heart was bad. . . ."

"What is your relation?"

"I was his client."

"You're an actress?"

"Not anymore."

"You had a dispute?" I shook my head. "All right," he said, pulling out a pad, "name and address." We did the formalities, and the officer said they'd be in touch; I was free to go. "You'll stay in Los Angeles, not go back to New York, correct." He wasn't asking. I nodded my head.

Lundy yelled as I walked to the door: Why wasn't I being arrested; why was I allowed to go free? "She's a murderer!"

They wheeled Harry out as I got into my car. I'd stood a few minutes catching my breath. The ambulance was blocking me in anyway. I thought of calling Andre but didn't. I drove back to the hotel, a zombie behind the wheel. It was bad enough about Harry, but why'd that woman accuse me? I drove over that little crest on Sunset Boulevard, where on rare days the snow can be seen on the distant mountains, but not today. Today I saw the dry hills to my left and thought what I always used to think when I lived here: This place looks like dinosaur country; they're hiding up there. There's oil under L.A. How can a huge metropolis have oil rigs pumping, and how can there be tar pits in the middle of a city? Any day now the dinosaurs will come clomping down, scattering all the people. It'll be like King Kong in New York, when he grabs the elevated subway car in his fist and all the little people inside fall over, screaming in terror.

I pulled over and called Carola, Andre's first assistant director, to find out if they were shooting anywhere near the hotel. They weren't far, she said, an interior at a bar in Los Feliz. I plugged the address into the GPS and found myself on the 101 heading south-east, which didn't seem right, but it got me there and I found a meter and fed it and then saw the trucks and vans and the usual milling-around crew and wondered what I was doing and turned and started back down toward the car when someone called to me: "Ms. Thrush? Ms. Thrush!" Louder the second time. It was Jarrad, the same jeans hanging perilously low atop skinny hips, a soft smile warming his face. All of a sudden I wanted to sob. It was seeing Harry fall like that; he was supposed to go on being Harry forever, a monument.

"Hello, Jarrad. How's it going on set?"

"Good. Well, I'm out here, but I haven't heard of any trouble so far."

"Is it a big scene right now, between the leads?"

"Nah, establishing shot in the bar; the shithead—oh, sorry— the bad guy and the girl come on later, probably after dinner break. It'll be another late night, probably."

If the leads were not up I wouldn't be too much of a disruption, showing up like this. "You think it would be all right for me to go in?"

Jarrad puffed importantly for the briefest second, got on his walkie-talkie to say there was a visitor and would it be okay to bring her in now. I smiled at his cool assessment, and at his not using my name. "Thank you, Jarrad," I said as he led me inside. He nodded and took off.

The scene had just broken up. The gaffers got going on the lights for the next shot. I walked along the back of the humming activity, a ways behind the monitor, where Andre was talking with Carola and Renny, his cameraman. Carola spotted me first. This was her second film with Andre; she was a New York import too, via Lisbon, and so was staying at the hotel. I liked Carola. She was quick and smart and serious. "Ardennes," she called out in that not-shouting shout a good assistant director learns how to do.

Andre turned around. He cocked his head to the side. It was probably not a good idea for me to just show up on his set. For the director, it's nearly never a good time. He finished his consult with Renny, nodded to Carola, and turned. I walked toward him as he walked toward me. A musical score should have played as we advanced, signaling the emotions, informing the audience what to feel about the key characters approaching each other as if time would stop as their energies meshed like violent destiny—as if the actors might not succeed in doing that without a musical cue.

We'd done this before, walked toward each other on a movie set; uncertain on my part, masterful on his. It was the set of *Separation and Rain*, and my big scene was up, my crescendo moment. As usual with movies, the denouement was scheduled at the start of the shoot. It was six A.M.; I had just arrived and was very anxious. We were toward the end of the first week. Everyone was well tuned in at that point, but no big scenes had been shot yet. I hadn't felt satisfied— far from it—at rehearsal, but Andre had been fine. With typically little to say, he'd said okay, called it a night and walked away. Even if he hadn't walked away I'm not sure I would have been able to say to him, I need more time, I need to get this right, I'm not sure of a thing. So a troop of tap dancers was practicing on my gut; I was jumpy and jittery as a bird. I pretty much wanted out. I'd called Joe in New York after rehearsal. He said I'd be great, to forget everything, especially the meaning of the words, and just go with it. Sure. Just go with it. Of course he was right.

Andre looked at me that day as we closed in and I understood

I was exactly where he wanted me to be: full of doubt. For a split second I looked away, unwilling to be manipulated without so much as a nod. But his confidence won out; he was certain of me even if I wasn't. I clicked to the correct interpretation, shut down the rebellion raging inside and got the scene in three takes. When it was over I stormed off to the dressing room. He may have been right, but I loathed Andre Lucerne at that moment with all my heart.

So here were Andre and I walking toward each other on a movie set once again, and the tap dancers were suddenly practicing inside me again and I had a bad feeling all over, a déjà vu of massive proportions, a dream coming at me that I'd dreamed before, only this time it was daylight and I was wide awake.

"Something is wrong?" he asked.

I'm generally unaware of Andre's accent, but today I realized, as if for the first time: He has an accent. His mother was American, so his Swiss French is tempered, though at his father's insistence he grew up speaking no English. His mother read to him in her language, their little secret to keep her identity alive in her son. Andre and his mother had a world of their own, out of his father's domineering gaze. I pictured him hearing "Hansel and Gretel" in English, sequestered with his mother in his corner bedroom, snow outside the window, a low lamp on the table, a triangle of light illuminating the conspirators. I mentally corrected him: *Is something wrong?* or the old movie standard, *Are you all right?* But that formal, stiff *Something is wrong?* the word *wrong* coming out all wrong, almost made me laugh.

"I should have called first," I said. We were inches apart now.

"No. It is good you came." Had he forgotten I was lunching with Harry? I was about to tell him the news, but the head gaffer, Quinn, came over about the lights. Carola followed. She kissed my cheeks, said how good it was to see me. She explained the day was going well so far after the horrors of last night, when everything possible had seemed to go wrong.

"Give me a minute," Andre said to me, and he and Quinn went off to talk to the electrical crew.

"There's coffee and stuff; unfortunately it's outside today . . . the small space in here," Carola said, her hand sweeping the air.

I was in the way. I thanked Carola and slipped into the background, the part of the bar that would not be seen on camera, stepped over electrical cables as thick as my arms, black drapes over anything that might cast unintended light, a makeup table to one side, the extras in a clutch doing what extras mostly did: wait around. One of them caught my eye, and I quickly turned to go.

"Okay to open the door?" I asked the PA guarding it. He nodded and I hurried outside.

I drove back to the Muse, speeding on the freeway like a pro who'd never left L.A. I parked and went up to the freshly made-up room, fell on the bed and cried into my pillow. Harry had been a force, a man who'd cried when I quit, who'd stood by me—in his way—when I suffered, and who most of all had always believed in me. Harry Machin: half actor, half god; part fake, part sage. He was a limb lopped off an ancient tree. My tears fell into an anonymous hotel pillow. How many others' tears of woe, of joy or ecstasy, and how much loneliness had this pillow already absorbed? Harry Machin booked actors, fed the movie machine with their flesh and blood and demanded high prices in return and ten percent for himself. He used us and we used him and we all went like little piggies off to the bank. I was crying my eyes out into a hotel pillow for one of Hollywood's biggest deal-makers. There was something ironic in that, but for the moment it was lost on me.

I have always bounced back after darkness, found my way to the light, but this time, this darkness that has descended since Harry died on me like that, on top of my being back here in Hollywood, has knocked the light right out of me. Should I go outside later to see if the old man is there, reassuringly blessing the end of the day? I could introduce myself, fall at his feet seeking wisdom. Maybe Kitty will show up and rub along gates and trees and corners, inviting me to rub his thick coat in unconditional, sensuous love. No, I could not greet man or beast today. Is it the interrupted sleep since Harry? Was it the suddenness of his going and the bleakness of seeing myself now as a hopeless misfit, a piece in the wrong jigsaw puzzle? His death seemed to cut me off once and for all from all that I once was.

Naturally, there was press coverage. Harry was a big deal. Heart attack, the papers and blogs said; a former client was with him, *Ardennes Thrush, once nominated for an Oscar for her part in Mark Wirlach's haunting film,* Darkness During Daylight. *The actress retired,* one piece said; *rumor has it she was ready to sign up again with Machin, return to the silver screen.* That would be a rumor the writer made up. The *New York* and *Los Angeles Times* kept the obit simple and respectful, with my name out of it. Only *Variety* intimated funny doings. Lundy let it be known—to anyone who'd listen—that Harry and I had argued and it had grown violent. "We did not argue," I told the *Variety* reporter who called me at the hotel. But Lundy's version won out. A freelancer called to ask if it was true I was going back to work, and could she have the scoop. No scoop, I told her; she had it all wrong.

I'd had to drive to the Beverly Hills police precinct for questioning, way over on Rexford. To get there I drove past Doheny, in

West Hollywood, where I used to get my hair done (and would need to again soon). I asked the detective interviewing me if I was up on an involuntary manslaughter charge—criminally negligent or otherwise—or perhaps some other evil offense.

"You find the death funny?" Detective Collins asked, his expression a study in neutral.

I wanted to ask him if he didn't secretly long to be a movie star. He had the looks. Detective Collins was a solid, tight William Holden à la *Sunset Boulevard*—I was thinking the scene where Gloria Swanson towels him off at the pool. I also sensed interiority, which I might not have expected in a cop, though that was probably too much Hollywood talking. What did I know about real cops, inside or outside? "I wasn't laughing," I replied, trying on my own version of tonal beige.

"The housekeeper says you and Mr. Machin argued."

"Wasn't she in the kitchen?"

"Did you argue?"

"No."

"She said there was shouting."

"Yes, but not me. Harry got overexcited."

"Over what?"

"Over me no longer acting."

"He was your agent?"

I nodded. We were quiet in the drab little interview room of the not-very-busy upstairs detective quarters, a setup involving mostly too many cluttered desks for the space. The Detective looked to be sizing things up. For a second I was afraid he was going to say something about me as a "personality." But he asked, "Any idea why Mrs. Lundy would say you killed Mr. Machin?"

"She overreacted."

"People seem to overstimulate themselves around you. I suppose that's a good thing in an actor."

"I no longer am an actor."

"Did you know of the heart condition?"

"I knew he'd been sick."

"Tough to prove, even if you did knowingly push him over the edge."

"I'm assuming that's in the realm of fantasy?" If I was playing a part, I was doing a good job because I wasn't at all comfortable sitting in the precinct opposite the handsome detective. That was about when I started getting the bad feeling I haven't been able to shake since.

Detective Collins stood up. "Thanks for coming in, Miss Thrush." I stood up too, and he escorted me to the top of the stairs, handing me his card, "On the off chance you think of something related to Mr. Machin's death." I stuffed the card into my pocket without looking at it. "You were a good actress," he tossed over his shoulder after I said good-bye.

I turned around on the stairs. "Cops go to the movies?" I said.

He turned around too. The smallest suggestion of a smile played across his mouth like a breeze over the surface of a mountain lake. "They're allowed to," he said.

He hadn't officially said I was not a person of interest, and part of me wondered if I *hadn't* killed Harry, involuntarily. That was not a good thing to be wondering, even if I knew the idea was mostly madness.

The next morning Andre said it was just coincidence it had been me there at lunch. It could have been anyone; it could have been the Lundy woman he'd dropped dead on. I'd wanted to ask why he'd been so happy that day about my having lunch with

Harry, but Andre put a stop to any further Harry Machin speculation. He was probably right, but that didn't stop my brain from repeatedly raking over those last few minutes: I should have left when I'd said I should leave, or Harry saying he was going to stay calm and then losing it. All he wanted to know was why I quit acting . . . I'd never even had a chance to answer the million-dollar question. All the seconds that might have turned out differently . . . if only . . . If only I'd had a flat tire, if only I'd said no to lunch, if only I hadn't picked up the house phone, if only I had gone to the set with Jarrad the night before . . . who knows, I might have canceled the lunch and Harry might still be alive . . . If only.

As I was spinning on that mental carousel, the house phone rang, almost like a joke. I stared at it as if it were a live, dangerous animal trapped in my house. It wouldn't be the police; they had my cell number. If it was a reporter I'd hang up, but I didn't think it would be. Harry's story was dying of inertia, his obituary yesterday's news. I waited for the mechanical voice to put the human one on, looking out toward White Shirt's house as I did. My time of spying on him now seemed a bygone, innocent era.

"Ard, honey? I see by the papers you're back in town." Not the smallest suggestion of resentment in her voice that I hadn't called her. Dear old Dottie.

"Dottie! Oh, Dottie, Harry died."

"I read all about it. I'm surprised you're not in front of a firing squad by now."

"I am so glad to hear your voice, Dot." She sounded close and familiar, as if we'd just had dinner the other night. It must have been a couple of years since we'd spoken.

"Why not come see me? I'm right down the street."

"Where?"

"I sold that old Pasadena house a year ago. I'm doing my own version of assisted living right here on Hollywood Boulevard, tenth floor of the Roosevelt. They have a new music bar downstairs, and room service sends up the driest martinis in the neighborhood. Why not come take a sample this afternoon?"

"Four o'clock okay?"

"I'll keep a lookout."

I checked the clock: two-thirty. Dottie may have just saved me. I killed some time changing my clothes and wrote out a couple of the curly old postcards I'd bought to send to friends in New York, but I had no stamps. When I first arrived I'd made calls back east, but that stopped. I was here; they were there. Dottie's call shamed me into writing absent but not forgotten greetings. By then it was time to drive down the hill.

Dottie looked older, thinner, drier—like a stick—but she still wore those snazzy Chanel suits, her ash-blond hair pulled back, sparkling diamond earrings catching the light, and she still had that breathless vitality into her midseventies. She performed privately now, in the homes of die-hard rich fans, all of whom apparently owned baby grand pianos.

We spent two martinis together. Dottie's suite had an upright, and she nibbled at the keys with her long fingers after we'd hit a lull in things to say. There wasn't much to catch up on, on my end. Dottie knew not to push. She did say, sitting on the piano bench with her rod-straight posture, that that was where she proposed to end her days. "Ard, honey, I just don't know what I'd do if I stopped playing. They'll pull me off the keys in rigor mortis before I let go." I guess I knew what she meant but had nothing to say except that maybe acting was a different saddle to try to die in.

We discussed poor old Harry, and she pretty much felt as Andre did that there was no point in dwelling on it. "Everybody in town knew he wasn't well," she said, adding, "I s'pose it's the end of an era, Harry's passing."

"I suppose so too," I said, thinking how close Dottie might be to that fading era herself. Hollywood is so unkind to the elderly, as if age were an affront to the sunshine and swimming pools, the gym-and-yoga culture. She was right, though; if she kept at her playing, she'd beat the system, or play it her way.

The martinis settled down with the hors d'oeuvres Dottie put out, and I said I'd better head back up to the hotel. It was going on seven. Andre was on days and would be back by nine.

"How are you two?" Dottie asked, walking me to the elevator.

"I don't know," I said truthfully.

"He still chase the ladies?"

"The other way around: They chase him."

"He could run a little faster."

The elevator came; I kissed Dottie's powdery cheeks and slid down to the lobby in the cushioned conveyance and walked out to the car valet.

Forty minutes later I was stranded in the lobby of the Hotel Muse. My door pass had demagnetized again. I was locked out for the second time that week. As I waited, I overheard the desk flirt, Sharif, saying something to another guest about it being the anniversary of the fire. I had to pee from Dottie's hefty martinis but didn't want to walk all the way out to the bathroom servicing the pool area. I felt a wave of irritation at having to wait, but what was all this about a fire? Sharif was busy regaling a heavy woman in a too-bright sports outfit. I heard him again say, "The hotel fire." Finally she left for her room.

"I'm so sorry, Ms. Thrush, a new guest. We like to give them all a warm welcome . . . not your key again? I nodded. "I'm so sorry. Give me one second." He quickly did whatever they do to reactivate the key and came back to the front. "I apologize again," he said, handing me the plastic card.

"What's all this about a fire, Sharif?"

"A fire?"

"Just now . . ." (I couldn't say, "that Teutonic matron you were just toying with" . . .) "the other guest," I said, pointing to the poolside room she'd walked toward before I'd lost sight of her.

"Oh, the *hotel* fire. It's just a story. I mean, there *was* a fire, small, more smoke than flame, still . . . Every hotel has its little ghost stories. . . ." He showed a row of tiny teeth as he smiled.

"A fire in one of the rooms?"

"Yes, but not big."

"What room? Here or above?"

Sharif laughed, but I wasn't fooled. "I think it was 304. Yes, that was it, room 304." He tried to sound casual, but his foot was in his mouth up to his kneecap. He must be a liability to the management. Anyone that talkative inevitably becomes a loose cannon.

"Up top? Wouldn't that be next to me, room 304?" That would be Sylvia Vernon's apartment, the full-timer next door with her ubiquitous teacup poodle, Mucho, and her wide-brimmed hats.

"Come to think of it, that is next to you."

"Who died?"

Sharif's eyes went big. He tried that phony laugh again. "No one died."

"Of smoke inhalation, I'm guessing?"

"Yes, that was it, smoke inhalation. An actress . . . your typical Hollywood tabloid news," he said, leaning back on his heels as he does when he's satisfactorily had his say. He just couldn't help himself. He looked at me and his eyes seemed to shrink. He prob-ably remembered the little to-do with Harry and my shadowy involvement.

"When did all this take place, Sharif?" I had him now.

"Oh, ancient history; not long after the hotel was built . . . The '50s, Hollywood in its prime, a great era . . . well, the '30s and '40s were the truly great eras of glamour."

Sharif is ages too young to know old Hollywood. He's not even a native; English is his second language. But he knows the hotel in-side out. I suspect there's not much going on with Sharif outside work. The way he greets guests with all he's got, hooks into their little habits, anticipates needs. A born lackey, though not resentful (as I would be) of comfortably-off guests or arty movie types—some with plenty of attitude. I sense no secret dark corner in Sharif har-boring little social hatreds. I've only seen him once out of uniform. Embarrassing in his street clothes, a figureless man in loose jeans, lost out of the smart white oxford shirt and dark navy serge trousers and hotel blazer. It is as if Sharif—deskman extraordinaire, role player and implied bon vivant—isn't quite real outside of the hotel.

"Tell me—the fire, Sharif; what do you know?"

"I don't want to upset you."

I smiled sweetly. "I don't upset that easy. What was the ac-tress's name?"

"You know, I don't remember, but you can go to the websites for Hollywood crime pages. I'm sure it's there." He pressed his hands to his chest, lowered his voice. "So many crimes! One actress jumped to her death from the H in the Hollywood sign. I always wondered how she got up there; did she have help?" He paused to consider. "Plenty of starlet suicides, one little actress murdered right here in the Hills by a handyman who tried to go too far. Bludgeoned . . ."

"Go on . . ."

"This is long ago: first Prohibition, then the postwar boom; narcotics arrests, prostitution. As recently as the '90s too, right over in West Hollywood a high-class brothel at a la-di-da address." He moved in toward me. I was glad of the desk between us. "Did you know Gary Cooper was arrested for speeding? And there was the Errol Flynn scandal, with a fourteen-year-old if you can imagine . . ." He leaned back on his heels. "Excuse me." The hotel phone was ringing. Sharif answered in his well-greased voice, naming the hotel, then himself, and asking how he could be of assistance.

I mouthed I'd be on my way, held up my room pass in a salute. Sharif smiled, all courtesy, happy in spite of himself for our private little tête-à-tête. I raced to the car, sped up the hill to the room, the bathroom, and blessed silence.

There was barely a trace of sunset toward the east. No lights on in White Shirt's house. I turned on a lamp in the sitting room and one by the bed, and then the little lamp on the desk in the bedroom, where I kept my computer and where there was a printer that belonged to the film that Andre had given me to use. Seeing Dottie had cheered me some, but I didn't intend a repeat. I closed the glass doors to the bedroom and lay down on the couch. It was eight o'clock. Andre would be—I wanted to say *home* soon—but we're in a hotel.

The next morning it was Fits's turn to call. Old friends were crawling out of the woodwork now that Harry had walked out of the daylight and I'd found my way back into the Hollywood headlines. The house phone stirred. I stared at it, this time as if it were a rodent, unwanted, dirty, and full of bad luck. Hearing Fits on the other end of the line after all this time was both comforting and not.

I got the sinking feeling I was being sucked back to where I was before I decided I didn't want to be there anymore. And, worse, what did I possibly have to say to Fits?

"I hear you're up on a murder rap?" he said, jolliness warming his voice.

"Dear Fits. How *are* you?"

"Never mind me. What are you working on these days?"

"You know I—"

"Yeah, yeah, but that quitting thing was just a ploy, right?"

I laughed by way of not answering.

"You free later today? How about a hookup at Musso's?"

"Musso and Frank's? On Hollywood? I thought you hated that place?"

"I do, but it's easy. I moved up to Hidden Hills. My daughter's mother wouldn't let her visit the old Echo Park dive anymore, so it's convenient."

"Isn't she grown up by now?"

"Missy's sixteen; hard to believe."

"You're gentry now, Fits."

Fits, though his paychecks were big and regular, had lived like a bum on a back street in Echo Park with a parrot, a cat and a collection of silver buckles. I'd gone there twice, then told him he'd have to meet me at my bungalow or a neutral location. I got hiccups and sneezes if I went near his place. Dottie had given me the dirt on his recent move. I couldn't see him in Hidden Hills, though, even with its country feel for a place so close to Hollywood. He owned a little land with a million eucalyptus trees on it and the regulation swimming pool. It seemed Fits might be settling down.

I said okay to Musso and Frank's, and we closed the call. The idea of seeing Fits later gave some shape to my day. I put the do-not-disturb sleeping-moon tag over the door so I could do a little research while the time passed. I was stuck on Sharif's tale of fire and mayhem next door. I wanted to find out about the actress who'd died. Andre had made a fuss and hotel management found a way to bring Internet service up the hill to our suite and to Carola's room, a few of the others in his crew. It was an improvement that came with higher rates, but Andre didn't care. I kind of missed the poolside down below in the mornings, especially if I got there early enough to grab one of the fresh-delivered croissants. Anyhow, I sat down and started Googling old Hollywood crime sites. At least my mind was off Harry.

Andre, on days, was up at dawn and would be in at a civilized hour tonight if he didn't go to dailies. Last night after seeing Dottie, I'd cooked a red snapper in butter, garlic, sun-dried tomatoes, and red wine, sautéed some bok choi, tossed a salad, and we'd managed to sit down to a nearly normal meal in between his getting one phone call after another. I hadn't gone to Harry's funeral. Some family had been dug up somewhere in New Jersey, and a rabbi showed up and they put him in the ground as soon as the medical examiner declared the death natural causes. I didn't hear anything further about Lundy and her crazy accusations. Detective Collins hadn't called, so I assumed I was free of suspicion and clean—even if I did feel dirtied by the death. Dottie had asked if Lundy might not press a civil wrongful-death suit, but I said I thought, based on gut feeling, that the estate had settled her and she'd gone quietly back to wherever she'd crawled out of when Harry found her. They'd seemed okay together, so my guess was Harry had taken care of her in his will.

I told Andre I had no choice but to steer clear of the funeral. The event was a who's who of Hollywood fame, for all the clients Harry had shaped over the years. Andre agreed with me and for once didn't give me the song and dance about me hiding out on life. I'd enjoyed throwing the meal together and sitting down with him. I even lit a couple of candles, and there was nighttime L.A. outside, and what was not to like, but we seemed to be two people searching for a conversation more than anything intimate, and anyway his phone kept on right up to the last mouthful. He thanked me and said the meal was excellent, which it wasn't, but I think he meant it was a break from the hectic eating on set, but not much of one with the phone going every two minutes. We were becoming as formal as a count and countess; I said he was welcome and cleared the table. He was almost asleep by the time I washed up.

I changed my clothes to meet Fits at Musso's. Before I left the hotel I called Andre to let him know I'd be having a drink with Fits. He didn't pick up, so I left a message.

Fits looked pretty much the same, grayer but no heavier and no more serious-seeming than he'd ever been. That was my first impression. He was seated in the once-upon-a-time coveted corner leather booth in the back room, with a commanding view of whoever came and went and the bar that always had a handful of drinkers hanging on. There wasn't much coming and going these days. Musso's felt like yesteryear, but in a good way; the era of cocktail gowns and sizzling affairs spoken of in whispers just loud enough to hear—in other words, old Hollywood glamour. I slid into the booth next to him, and Fits leaned in to give me a kiss and pass a hand down my back, glancing off my derriere.

"You're looking better than ever," he said appreciatively, just shy of a leer. "And you always looked good."

I smiled. The waiter came over, and I pointed to Fits's wide lake of a glass and little extras pitcher next to it and said I'd have the same, only vodka, in case Fits was having a gin martini.

"So?" he said. "What'd you do to Harry?"

I shrugged. "We had lunch."

Fits shook his head slowly. The gesture was about as solemn as I'd ever seen in him. I expected his high-wattage grin to break out but it didn't. "This town is all about relationships—pure bullshit the majority—but it was Harry's town and relationships were his lifeline and you broke it."

"I'm a coldhearted killer," I said, trying for coy, but Fits wasn't buying any.

My drink came. I lifted the glass in salutation, hoping to change the subject. I wanted to know what he was doing in Hidden Hills.

He ignored my query. "Why'd the hausfrau tell the cops you did it?"

"You sound like a B movie, Fits."

"I *am* a B movie. So come clean."

"I guess is it's like you said; I broke a life thread." I took a sip of my martini. Musso and Frank's didn't cheat the first drink; they'd probably lasted as long as they had by not cheating, and Musso's was Hollywood's oldest joint, dating back to 1919. Of course the drinks were fourteen bucks apiece. Back when Musso's was *the* place, the bar was famous, or infamous, depending on who was saddled up there. Once you entered Musso and Frank's it was perpetual night-time. The bow-tied bartenders looked more like they belonged in a sleeper-train club car than on the Boulevard of Fame, and they *never* saw daylight. "I didn't get it that Harry was such a passionate guy, but I guess he was," I said, starting to feel bad all over again.

Fits looked me over. "Why'd you quit?"

"That's what Harry wanted to know just before he keeled over."

Fits looked briefly as if a spider had been thrown down his shirt front. He reached into the beat-up leather shoulder bag he still dragged around with him, holding scripts and who knew what else, and pulled out an equally beat-up paperback novel that he slapped down on the table. It was a dog-eared copy of *Franny and Zooey*.

"Salinger?" I said, eyebrows up. "They're making a movie of it?" I asked, pointing to the book between us, next to the condiment shakers and a bottle of Texas Pete Hot Sauce.

Fits shook his head. He opened the book to a page he'd marked, and put his finger on the text to hold his place.

I wanted to laugh. Was Fits going to give me a sermon now? "What?"

"This is about desire, your wanting to act. Probably not even free choice. Salinger writes it like it's a finger of karma or something, Zooey telling his sister she can't drop out, she *has* to act: No choice in the matter. You walk away from this and you're killing more than just performing. You see where I'm going?"

"Fits, hold on. . . ."

"No, listen, if you were a hack, Ardennes Thrush, a canned bit of hot looks with a smear of talent, I'd say, go ahead and quit; sell real estate, buy jewelry. But that's not you, never was, never will be. And you *are* stuck."

I took a gulp of martini; a lame attempt to feel tough.

He closed the book and began to recite from it. I'd read the book years ago, and the passage made me want to weep. I lowered my head as I listened.

"That was quite a performance, Fits," I said after a pause.

"That's what you have to say? A performance?"

I was already on my extras pitcher; Fits had hardly touched his drink. I remember him cleaning out the substances about the time we met; I guess he'd stuck to it. Why bother to order the drink? I was feeling fidgety and uncomfortable; how come the martini hadn't deadened my nerves? I hadn't expected this from Fits. Not the performance or what I guessed he was trying to say with it—or do. He'd blindsided me.

"I found the book in the house. I think it's Missy's. Take it. Read it."

"Did you memorize that passage, Fits?"

He looked around the room. A couple of quiet drunks were leaning along the bar in the early part of their daily tie-ons. There was a woman, too old for her tight dress and the man she was with, and the hairdo, and the whole moment began to look done and sad and what was the point anyway? I saw what Fits saw, and here was this book by J. D. Salinger, whom Joe had once called a writer incapable of a false note. It belonged to Fits's daughter, and what was I supposed to do with it?

"I'm an actor," Fits said. "That's what I do: I work other people's words. I bring them to life if I can; you did that once, remember—very well, as I recall." His tone was almost ugly, his gaze on me as hard as he could muster, which thankfully was not very. "So, *yeah*, I memorized the passage."

"You did that for me?"

"It was a slow night."

"Whaddaya have to go and be all mean about?"

He took maybe the second sip of his drink.

"I'll read the book, Fits."

He stood up, threw a wad of bills on the table and said he had to go. It was pretty clear he loathed me at that moment. Had I broken a lifeline with him too? I looked up. "A person has a right to stop doing something that's slowly killing them."

"Something's slowly killing us all. What's'a matter, burden'a life got you down? If you were at least—what *are* you doing now?"

I faced the tablecloth. I felt like a shattered pile of nothing. "Thanks for the drink," I said, not looking at him.

"Yeah, that's what I thought."

"I suppose you think it's easy," I said, eyes glued on the pepper shaker. I was afraid of any daggers shooting out of his eyes if I looked up.

"How long's it been since you worked?"

I shrugged again. "Two years, I guess." I couldn't get my voice above a hollow whisper.

"Read the book," he said. "And quit blubbering." When I looked up again, he was gone.

I was tempted to sit there and order another vodka martini, to drown my sorrows in a nice clear brew with a salty olive to match the salty tears I refused to shed, nurse myself out of thinking I was the heel Fits had all but said I was. Only this was Hollywood and I had once been a player and I was married to Andre Lucerne, so being found alone at a booth in Musso's with a second knockout martini in my hand—and on top of the Harry mess—just wouldn't do. Luckily for me the waiter came over, the old-time type with radar that reads every short story unfolding at his tables. "Can you bring the check, please?" I asked him. Fits left enough cash for four drinks and I left all of it for the waiter, whose discretion I could maybe count on. And maybe not.

I was back up at the Muse earlier than I'd planned, leaving me with extra, unaccounted-for time that was unaccounted for anyway. I lay down and read the Salinger up to the part where Franny tells her shallow, full-of-himself boyfriend she's quit acting and is having some sort of anorexic episode, a spiritual crisis. She's come to see acting as all about egomania, and she's ashamed. I closed the book, and threw it into the bed-table drawer. There was nothing wrong with *my* appetite. I went out to the sitting room and turned on the TV. Maybe television would dumb my brain down to the mush the martini hadn't.

The house phone rang. I was beginning to hate that thing enough to want to smash it to bits, fling it over the balcony and then run my rented car over it, back and forth a couple of times until the plastic housing was beaten to smithereens. I shouldn't have picked up. It was a guy from the *Hollywood Reporter*. They were planning on doing a piece on Andre Lucerne's new movie, and—

I cut him off. "You'll have to speak to Mr. Lucerne's management to arrange that." They knew that, but they'd just learned his wife—me—was in town, and with my background and all, the paper thought—

You mean you found out I was in town from the lie that maniac Lundy planted in *Variety*, I said to myself. "I'm sorry, I don't give interviews. I'm here with my husband, that's the whole story." He said he'd find an angle. I kept the turndown as polite as I could until he finally let it go. I was not about to agree to a-whatever-happened-to-Ardennes-Thrush feature.

Christ, what a day! I hoped Andre would be in early. I'd suggest Thai takeout, or I could throw some pasta together. Where was he anyhow; he hadn't called all afternoon. He hadn't even returned my call. Okay, he was busy with the film. Sure, he was busy. I was pacing. I stopped at the big window. The sun was nearly gone all the way into night. I hadn't partially closed the glass curtains as I usually do, ahead of the heavy, room-darkening damask drapes I closed each night before bed. I thought I saw White Shirt standing in his yard, facing me. I was staring hard until I remembered if I could see him, he could see me. I nearly jumped a mile when that stinking house phone rang again. Suppose I ripped the damn line right out of the wall? Trouble is there are two extensions, one here, one in the bedroom; I couldn't very well tell the hotel people I'd tripped twice.

I growled a hello as rough as I could; if it was that reporter again—

"Good evening, Ms. Thrush. It's Sharif, at the front desk."

"Oh, Sharif, I'm glad." That sounded insane; why would I be glad it was Sharif?

"Oh . . . well, there is a gentleman down at the desk who says it's urgent he speak with you. Shall I put him on the phone?"

"*No!* No. Listen, Sharif, find out if he's a reporter. Please tell him I'm not talking to the press."

"I understand. Can you give me a moment?" I said yes, and he hung up.

I turned down the lights and closed the glass curtains all the way. I went into the bedroom and did the same, leaving a light on by the bed. The house phone rang again two minutes later. I picked up at the bed. "Ms. Thrush? Sharif again. The gentleman is not a reporter. He said you spoke the other day. His name is Eddie Tompkins."

Eddie Tompkins? Who was Eddie Tompkins? "Did he say what this was about? Never mind, Sharif. Ask him to wait; I'll drive down to the lobby."

I still had on the form-fitting dress I'd worn to meet Fits. I'd wanted to look good for him, for old time's sake, I suppose. I found a baggy, neutral brown cardigan, tossed a wide scarf over that, grabbed the door pass and car keys, and walked outside. The cool evening air hit me like a slap. I needed a slap just then. The road down to the main hotel is high, narrow, and steep. On the right, past the buildings, is an immediate hill with a sprinkler system watering what might be pindo palms and some kind of dusty-looking, maybe Aleppo pines. Creeping purple flowers fill in the hill that drops off sharply to the left. I drove a little too fast on the dark road and had to brake hard for the slow-moving automatic security gate opening out.

I parked in the ten-minute zone and walked quickly into the lobby, still with no idea who Eddie Tompkins might be. I was glad for the small lobby. I would be in sight of Sharif or the other desk personnel. A man stood up, tall, built, and black. It took me a minute or two to recognize the shoe clerk from the discount place on Sunset. I had no idea what to think to explain his presence. Did I drop my wallet at the store? Nothing was missing that I knew of.

"Ms. Thrush, thank you for seeing me on such short notice."

Short or long, what did he want? "What's this about, Mr.—"

"Tompkins." He held out his hand, I didn't take it. "I'm sorry to be so forward; I figured you'd understand, being an actor too. . . ."

I scrunched up my face, genuinely lost.

"Did you give my card to Mr. Lucerne?"

"Your card?"

"Yes, I gave you my card the other day."

"In the shoe store, would that be right? You gave me it in the shoe store where you work, is that correct?"

"Yes . . ."

"Mr. Tompkins, people give each other business cards all the time. Perhaps that's why they are so—I was going to say cheap, but inexpensive will do. Usually nothing comes of the gesture, but I think the understanding is along the lines of don't call us, we'll call you." He really was a nice-looking guy and bigger in the little hotel lobby than I remembered from the sprawling, life-swallowing shoe store. I was actually seeing his face for the first time. He looked all right, pleasant enough. Christ, could I blame him; he wanted a job. Still, coming to my hotel, and at night?

"Is everything all right, Ms. Thrush?" That was good old Sharif behind me at the desk.

"Yes, Sharif, Mr. Tompkins was just leaving."

"Please, call me Eddie."

"No, Mr. Tompkins. And I don't know what became of your card. My husband usually throws them out. You can imagine the demands people make . . . so I'm sorry not to be able to help out. If you'll excuse me . . ."

"I'm the one to apologize, Ms. Thrush. . . ."

He looked as if he had more to say, but I turned and walked to Sharif. "Good night," I said over my shoulder. I was opposite the front desk in a matter of steps. "I don't think I've checked on the mail lately, Sharif." My voice was too loud and cheerful, I fought down a stammer.

Sharif, ever at the ready, smiled wide. "I have your mail right here for you." He looked past me as he handed me a row of white envelopes. The automatic entrance doors facing the front drive whooshed open and then closed. "He's gone, Ms. Thrush."

"Thank you, Sharif."

"Of course. A woman in your position can't be too careful. Would you like a cup of tea, Ms. Thrush?"

I thought a minute. Eddie could still be hanging around the driveway. "You know, I would."

Sharif, about to go off duty, gave me the all clear, and forty minutes later I was in the car on my way back up to the rooms. I'd forgotten my cell phone when I'd gone down to the desk, and it felt like a limb was missing. I drove fast up to the restaurant entrance. The valet stepped out of her booth. I waved when she recognized me and veered left to the computerized gate into the upper hotel grounds. I glanced in the rearview mirror to be certain no one was following and punched in the code numbers; the gate opened, and I drove in. My slot was way at the other end from the hotel units. I saw Andre's car parked below ours as I passed. I glanced at the clock; he was early. I parked and walked toward the stairs, the mail clutched in my left hand. Looking up, I saw the lights go out in our suite. Was Andre leaving again? Dammit, I didn't have my phone. I raced up the stairs and there he was, in the hallway. I thought I heard Sylvia Vernon's voice and then her door close.

"Andre?"

He looked up and nodded. "Come," he said, waving me in.

He closed and locked our door once we were inside, turning on the kitchen light. "Is everything all right?" I pointed to the wall in common between our two units. We both turned when a sudden breeze blew the balcony door open. I'd locked that door and closed the glass curtains, which were now partially open. I always locked the balcony door before going out. Okay. Maybe Andre had stepped out for a minute. Maybe I couldn't be dead certain I'd locked the balcony door, but I was sure I'd seen the lights go out.

Andre strode over and closed the door. I turned on some lights in the sitting room. Knowing without having to ask, he poured me a glass of red wine from an open bottle on the kitchen counter. He poured vodka for himself out of the bottle in the freezer. "Andre?" I said, taking the glass.

He lifted his. "Cheers."

I took a sip, obeying the custom after a toast. "Were you next door?"

"Hmm? Ah, the old crone heard me come in just now and said hello."

"Sylvia Vernon?"

"Is that her name?" His phone vibrated in his pocket. He moved to the dining table and glanced at the caller ID.

"Were you going out again?"

"What? No." He said hello into his phone. To me he said, "Come here. You look lovely." He studied my dress under the sweater and nodded approval. He said into the phone, "No, Carola, my dear, I was talking to my wife." I went to him and he reached for my neck and hair, pulling me gently to him as he continued talking into the phone. I lingered a moment, taking in the scent of deodorant, someone's cigarette smoke, and the faint hint of his body odor underneath. Over his shoulder I saw my cell phone blinking on the couch. I walked over and picked it up; one call: ID BLOCKED. No messages. I turned the phone off.

"So, how is Fits?" Andre asked, finished with his call. "Weren't you having dinner? It must have been quick."

It was a disaster, I thought. "He couldn't stay long," I said, going for bland.

"He is an interesting actor. I ought to use him in one of these films." He seemed to be considering. Andre often seemed to be considering.

"Have you eaten?" I asked. I didn't want to talk about Fits.

"Yes, a bit. I'm not hungry, really." His phone rang again. I walked into the kitchen to see what there was to put out. I decided on bread and cheese and dipping oil and set out a plate. I refreshed Andre's drink. I found a ripe mango I didn't remember buying that I peeled and sliced and put out too. I wanted this sudden domesticity to dispel an uneasiness enveloping me like a leather-gloved hand—a hairy hand—but it wasn't working. Too much was going on all of a sudden and I was feeling tossed like a cork on the sea of that too much.

I sat down at the table, opposite Andre. I didn't mention Eddie Tompkins. I did mention Lucille Trevor—the actress who'd died in the fire next door. When I'd seen Andre standing close to Sylvia's door I'd thought of her, as if she might have been magically alive inside. Andre said he'd heard about the fire.

"Then you knew? When you booked the hotel?"

"Didn't I mention this to you over the phone, in New York?"

"Did you? I think I would have remembered. She was an actress."

"Ah, Hollywood loves a dark tale. Actress-tied-to-the-train-tracks melodrama."

"But it did happen, right next door in Sylvia Vernon's suite."

He looked at me, head angled. "You're not superstitious, are you?"

I wanted to ask why he was home so early, but his phone rang again. He shrugged an apology as he answered. I ate a little as he talked. Between calls I listened, without resentment for once, to him telling me of the day's shoot. I gathered there was trouble brewing with his leading lady, Luce Bouclé.

I'm already forgetting to look at the hills. When I make my morning tea it's possible to pretend I am in Italy: the red-tiled roofs on the hillside and the thick palm trees that sprout out of their serrated trunks like flowers on steroids. There's the Italianate house in pale ocher stucco and the surrounding cypress trees, rigid as sentries with their at-attention compressed arms. I spent three days in Umbria once, on location—that's my reference to Italy. Afternoons the hills are strictly south of France. I've gotten so hunkered down inside myself I have to remind my eyes to stay alert as the hills go brown under an insufficiently rainy spring. Masses of magenta bougainvillea explode here and there. The Russian sage trees don't seem to mind too little water, but the pines look wan and dry. That's the funny thing about this town; a day that starts out moist with weather off the Pacific, heavy dew or fog or thickly clouded skies, can end bone dry by afternoon, zero humidity. I can only guess the foliage sucks the moisture out of the air when it's there to be sucked, and makes do. This morning promises another sunny, moisture-free day. Good for doing laundry.

Andre was up early and gone. I was alone with thoughts that were not making much sense. I watched the parrots gad about, electric green and going loco all over the coral tree. They didn't look like their thoughts made too much sense either. I told myself to make myself useful. With my tea steeping, I ran with the plastic basket of wash down to the laundry room. The sign advises, "Laundry 9 A.M.–9 P.M. ONLY." It was seven thirty. I loaded a machine, put the soap and quarters in and raced back upstairs before anyone saw me in a hooded sweatshirt over my satin nightgown tucked into a pair of gym pants. I microwaved soy milk for my tea, grabbed a peach yogurt out of the fridge, and looked out the large window. Too cold, I decided, to sit outside, so I parked myself at the table, facing out, and took a sip of boiling-hot tea. Sylvia Vernon's door banged shut next door. I was sure I'd heard that same bang last night when I came back up after Eddie Tompkins's creepy visit. She's a habitual door slammer.

We first met in the laundry. I ran smack into her as I was racing out in a fury because I'd put my dollar's worth of quarters into the machine and started it without opening the lid first, which was backward. The water started to flow and *then* I opened the lid to find someone else's wet clothes still in the machine. I had no choice but to pay for a second round. The clothes must have sat there all night, and I suspected they belonged to one Andre's people who'd tossed the wash in and then gone for a beer. I had only two quarters in my pocket, meant for the dryer. I swore out loud as I filled another machine with my clothes. There were only three washing machines, and none of them looked too clean—something I planned to let Sharif know about, though what can a hotel's management do about slobs? How can they prevent a guest from trashing a room or having loud, rock-'n'-roll-fueled sex or doing the wash earlier than the sign says? Anyhow, I turned for the door full speed ahead and that was when I ran into Sylvia Vernon.

She must have been up at the crack because she was there to retrieve her finished wash from the dryer. "Easy, tiger," she said, her voice throaty from years of cigarette smoke. In between apologizing for nearly knocking her down, I spit out boa feathers from the collar of an off-white satin dressing gown. Her hair was the near white, bleached blond of Carol Channing's on a head that was no longer young. I'd steadied her by clutching a pair of slim—not bony—shoulders and felt a surprising current of energy beneath.

Though we shared a common wall and balcony and our front doors were only inches apart, I heard almost no sounds from Sylvia's side other than the door slamming. A guest would have to crane over the balcony parapet and past the partition to catch a glimpse next door. Sylvia had added a wide wooden storage unit to her side of the partition, so we were doubly separate. If she sat on her balcony with her poodle, I certainly was not aware of it. Andre and I were probably more of a noisy presence. I guess she walks the dog—whose cream coloring nearly matches her hair—very early and then very late because I rarely see them outside. Mucho is always with her, tucked under an arm or inside a wide pocketbook, so when I nearly toppled her in the laundry, I nearly squished him.

He didn't bark, only looked up at me with big shiny black eyes and a kind of grin.

Sylvia rang my doorbell later that afternoon, holding a pineapple upside-down cake on a flowered plate. I was immediately fearful that her visit would be the start of repeated familiarity. I'd only been in L.A. about a week at that point and did not want to ooze into becoming one of the hotel lifer set. I also can't stand pineapple upside-down cake. But I had Sylvia pegged all wrong. She wasn't particularly interested in being neighborly. She hadn't even made the cake. I asked her in and offered tea. She sat, declining, setting Mucho down to help himself to a tour and sniff of the rooms, nosing into every corner, doing little to endear himself.

She told me she'd taught dancing, had been a dancer herself. I could see she had the legs. She'd worked Vegas and Reno and Tahoe, the heyday of "good dancing" now gone, she said, to lap dances, poles, and raunchy. "I don't *do* laps," she declared. It took me a minute to understand that by dance she meant striptease.

She asked if she hadn't seen my face in a movie or two, and I confessed I'd been in the business but was out of it now. She peered at me inquisitively, a quick smile passing over her mouth, edging toward a smirk. "What's the matter? Not enough ego?"

I let the remark go, surprised at the tone of it, and explained that I was in L.A. with my husband, Andre Lucerne, who was directing a film. "Ah," she said, "you're with that crowd taking up half the rooms. A nice bunch of kids, couple'a good-looking fellas too."

I said I hoped she wasn't disturbed by the late nights.

"Not me. I like people around, so long as they don't make too many demands. I look at the world, Ar*den*," she said, mispronouncing—hitting the *dennes* too hard. "A peeper in my way. It's how I get my thrills these days." I had the sense she'd had plenty of thrills—maybe not all of them positive—in her time. Mucho trotted back to her, and it looked as if he'd decided it was time for them to go. She picked him up and stroked his head. "Plenty of poking going on; I've seen those kids coming and going at all hours, not always from the rooms they start out in."

Amused, I wondered if she was an insomniac. "Movie sets are short-lived hives; proximity breeds quick partnering."

There was something like disdain in her expression as she said, "Not just movies; all of entertainment, half of it spent in the sack. You see, I've been in the illusion business too." She paused, feeling for something in her pocket that evidently was not there. "This was a more passionate town a few years back. I'm a born Angelina, so I know. There really can't be too much lovemaking in the world, can there?"

I looked at her and laughed the first good, solid laugh since I'd arrived. I thanked her for the cake and neither of us made any polite overtures about a drink or a see-you-later line. The visit had been brief, more a pair of animals sniffing out their terrain, both satisfied to leave it at that. Or I was.

So when I heard her door bang shut just now I was tempted to rush out and waylay her. I went out on the balcony and peeked over the rail. A minute later I saw her put tiny Mucho down on the driveway. He shook his miniature body and headed up the low rise of the roadway at surprising speed, Sylvia following. Wasn't she afraid a car or a cat would kill the runt? One of Andre's crew said he'd seen a coyote near the back entrance to our unit, precisely where the dog was headed. Sylvia must have overslept to be walking him this late. She was attired to be noticed in a leopard-skin-print smock over white capris, and bless her if she didn't have heels on. A wide-brimmed hat and sunglasses finished the look.

I wanted to ask her about the long-ago fire and mysterious death in her apartment. Did she know about it? I wanted her to invite me in so I could see for myself where the event had taken place. From what I'd been able to gather online—which wasn't much—I had the idea this was a cold case and someone had maybe gotten away with murder all those years ago.

I waited but didn't hear Sylvia return. The back entrance was near what I call the troll house, a low bungalow with a slate roof that could have been dropped out of a fairy tale. It was a separate rental and, as far as I knew, empty. From there a narrow path leads sharply up to two levels of wooden stairs, one to the first floor of rooms, one to our floor. All the rooms and suites have more than one way of being reached. The third floor is set back from the second, so I, happily, have no one tramping above me. The entries to the third-floor rooms face west and the pool below. Bridges lead to the doors along an open walkway. It was on one of the bridges that I'd seen Pale Guy and Kitty. I hadn't seen Pale Guy again, and that was fine with me. Sylvia must have walked up to the pool area via the first floor, past the fake waterfall. But it was time for me to throw my clothes into the dryer.

I had an actual mission today, a wifely one at that. I'd forgotten how cool L.A. springs can be, especially at night, and hadn't brought enough sweaters. Andre hadn't either and for once he let his needs be known instead of stoically handling things on his own. I told him I'd pick up a scarf for him and a couple of sweaters for us both. With all the brand-name shops sprung up around the new Kodak Theater, I could walk to my errand. It would put me back on the Boulevard, but this time with the safety of purpose in my step. I wouldn't get trapped in a shoe store.

Dressed and showered, the wash folded and put away, I was

ready for my mission. I'd try to get hold of Sylvia another time. My cell rang as I was heading for the door. It was Fits. I leaned against the kitchen counter to hear what he had to say, glad he'd called and maybe wasn't angry anymore but anxious that maybe he was.

"Did you read the book?"

That was his hello. "You just gave it to me—but yes, up to the part where she tells the loser beau she's quit acting."

"Right. So finish it."

"I will. . . . Fits, I'm sorry I didn't keep up."

"I didn't either."

"But you didn't disappear—"

"Let's not drag out the treacle. You made a mistake. A bad one. I don't care why. Just fix it. All right? I gotta run."

"No, Fits, wait! Does the name Sylvia Vernon mean anything to you?"

"Sounds like a Chandler noir character. An actor?"

"Burlesque dancer, I think, or was."

"Sounds fake."

"Probably is. Did you know there was a fire at the Hotel Muse— in the early '50s—and that an actress died?"

"Right, and Janis Joplin offed herself at the Highland Gardens. There's myths all over this town."

"The actress was *possibly* murdered."

"And?"

"Well."

"You're thinking the burlesque queen did the actress in? You becoming a private dick now?"

I saw how silly everything I'd just said sounded. So what if Sylvia was a contemporary of the deceased and lived in the apartment where she'd been killed (*if* she'd been killed)? "What if she did it?"

"The stripper? What if she did? What do you have for motive, Marlowe? Mind if I call you Marlowe?"

I laughed. "Nothing, I guess." The wind was out of my sails. I felt foolish.

"You said the '50s; that's a long time ago. You need to use that imagination in front of a camera, Ardennes."

"I sound nuts, right?"

"You sound like you have too much loose time. But I *do* have an actual appointment."

"I'll see you soon, I hope, Fits." He said sure, and we hung up.

As I opened my door to go out, I thought I heard Sylvia's door quietly snap shut. "Sylvia?" I called out softly. I pressed up against her door but heard nothing from inside. Maybe I am nuts, or on my way.

Feeling foolish didn't stop me from picking at the mystery of Lucille Trevor. What I'd learned is that she was a bottom-tier, B-movie actress who maybe slept around to supplement rent money, as plenty did—and still do. What was rare for those days was the studio bosses letting her keep her real name. She was pretty with a soft voice, too soft for an actor. She ended up playing background, classy sorts of tarts. The Lucille Trevors of the world make up the working underbelly of Hollywood, actresses whose names are as forgettable as the train tickets that bring them west. She was replaceable the day she died by ten good-looking girls, fresh and eager and newly arrived with hopes and dreams to take over where Garbo left off. It looked as if nobody cared a hang about Lucille Trevor and her sad ending. Wow, Fits was right; I was starting to sound like a dopey private eye.

It was just what Sylvia said that day with the pineapple upside-down cake, about my not having enough ego. Or was it that smirk when she said it? I could see it was the flimsiest of clues, but what is communication if not the unintended little revelations? All right, that was the actor in me picking up the potential false note. I never said I quit *being* an actor; I just quit *doing* it. Why would Sylvia ask if *I* had enough ego? She was a stripper; what's it take to bare it all for a pack of leering, slobbering men in a bar?

That was what I was chewing over as I walked out the gate and down the hill to the avenue. The sun was warm; it felt good. Not hot like that freak heat the day Harry died (maybe *that's* what killed him, together with the lousy air). There wasn't much to look at once I was past the crest and under the trees. I turned left on the avenue, toward the intersection with a stoplight—vehicular deaths to pedestrians are no joking matter in Los Angeles, and the avenue the Muse sat on zoomed with speeding cars heading to or from the nearby 101 ramp. Across the street was a corner park with a few benches and some shade trees, a miserable location for a miserable little park. When I arrived someone was living there in a pup tent, but that has since been corrected, no doubt by concerned citizens and God-fearing cops.

I glanced into the park and froze, then veered sharply left into other end of the Muse driveway. A long row of poplars hides the driveway from the street, and I quickly dropped out of sight. My breath caught in my throat and my heart started to race. I was pretty sure I'd seen Eddie Tompkins standing in the park. I couldn't step out to make certain because if he saw me . . . he'd be coming over now. Quick into the lobby! No one was at the desk, meaning someone was nearby and would appear if I so much as breathed. I continued on to the pool area and sat down at one of the tables that couldn't be seen from the lobby's back entrance, under the shade of a wide umbrella.

Within a minute Sharif stepped outside. "Ms. Thrush, good

morning." He held up two white envelopes. "We just sorted the mail—is everything all right?"

"Oh, Sharif, I think I may have twisted my ankle just now walking down the hill."

He was immediately all doting concern. "Do you need a doctor?"

"No, no. It's just I was going to run an errand, and now I'm not sure I can walk. I mean, I *can* walk, but it's a little uncomfortable."

"What you want is Epsom salts to soak the ankle."

"Do you think someone could drive me up to my room?"

"Of course. I'll have one of the staff take you, and we can send to Long's Pharmacy for salts. Rest here a minute."

"Oh, thank you, Sharif. How good you are. But weren't you busy? Didn't I see someone in the lobby just now?"

Sharif poked his head around the corner. "No, no one there. Just one minute till I round up a driver."

The black hotel SUV was usually parked out front, just before the guests' garage entrance, down from the lobby steps. I'd have to go back out front, but there was no other way. A few minutes later Arturo appeared in his blue maintenance uniform. Sharif insisted on helping me walk. He placed a thick palm around my waist and I had no choice but to lean into his short frame and turn in a star performance of a person limping in pain. Actress that I was, the ankle actually began to ache. Atta girl, I told myself. There were two ways to the hill from the lobby, I asked Arturo to turn right onto the avenue at the light, then right again, up the hill. This was not the obvious or fastest route, but it would take me past the corner park. Arturo gave me a funny look but shrugged and did as I asked.

I smiled and rubbed my ankle. I saw absolutely not a soul in the park unless someone was hidden behind a tree.

Sharif instructed Arturo to help me up the stairs to the room, but I said I'd hang on to the railing and be fine. Arturo was a quiet Mexican who seemed generally distrustful, but it's possible he spoke less English than he understood. I gave him a five-dollar tip to keep him happy and quiet. He waited, and I limped carefully up the stairs and waved that I was okay. I stalled in the room for half an hour before going out again, and then got into my car. I was more certain than ever Eddie Tompkins had been standing across the street from the hotel. Why would he do that?

Before I went out I fished around for his card on the table under Andre's mess of papers. We try to keep the papers to one side of the round table so we can set our plates out to eat, but the mess drifts. I found it under the expense bills Andre would hand in to his producer. The card had a tiny photo of Eddie: height, weight, and a scanty set of utterly unimpressive credits, and even that little bit looked padded. Poor guy, he wanted in, just as Lucille Trevor once had, and maybe he was willing to stalk me to get a shot at it. And I hadn't said a word to Andre about him. Really, there was no point; he wouldn't give Eddie the time of day.

No one was around when I walked to my car. Passing the little corner park again, I looked, but it was empty. I parked the car and took the back way into the Kodak Mall, through the loading lot for the Hollywood tour buses. I hurried through a few clothing stores on Hollywood, assaulted by music so loud and inane I had to fight not to scream. I wondered the salespeople didn't go deaf or mad hearing that racket all day long week after week. I found a scarf and four sweaters that I hoped fit—I didn't even try mine on—paid, and headed back to the car. Shopping makes me anxious; too many choices, I think. Sure, I appreciate nice things, but—There he is again! Doesn't he have a job?

Eddie Tompkins was standing at the top of the stairs to the mall, near where I'd planned to shortcut back to my car, parked on a side street whose name I didn't know. The parking meter would be just about up. I turned left toward Highland—the long way—off Hollywood, moving fast, not sure which I feared more: a parking ticket or that Eddie had shown up for the second time—or the third—and looked to be clearly following me.

How did he know where I was? There were no other pedestrians on Highland, there never are, and the little street I was parked on would be even more deserted. What if he knew where I was parked? Should I leave the car and walk back up to the hotel? Would they tow me if I did? Should I call 911? And report what? As a born New Yorker, the idea of having my car towed was almost as bad as contemplating cancer; a ticket was bad enough. I decided to keep going. There are so few people on the streets in L.A. Suddenly there were hardly any cars either. I forced myself not to break into a run.

I pulled out my cell phone and speed-dialed Andre—the old pretend-you're-not-alone trick. He picked up. "Andre! How is the shoot going?"

He was clearly surprised by my sudden interest. "Not bad—well, very bad . . . the actress . . ."

"Are you okay to talk?"

"I have a minute."

"I bought you a sweater; two, actually." I sounded way too excited. There was a long pause on his end. "Andre?"

"Okay. Good."

He was ready to hang up. Andre cannot abide small talk and

I'm clearly lousy at it too, so we were already out of idle things to say. "Do you think you'll replace her?"

"Who? Oh, not at this moment," he said. Meaning he couldn't talk; his lead must have approached. "I'll give you a call later," he said.

"Don't hang up!" Too late. Okay, but no one knew he'd hung up. Just keep talking, I told myself: good, smile, good. I spoke loudly into the dead phone: "Ha, ha, that's very funny. Yes, I'm getting into the car right now; no, I'm five minutes away. What . . . ?" There's the car, here are my keys, hit the boop boop: locks open, no one near the car, all clear. There he is! On the sidewalk! But he's facing the other way. What do I do now? Oh, a woman walking her dog! Thank God. A huge dog; bigger than she is: *good* dog. Okay, over to the car. He sees me, but the woman is between us. Quick, into the car.

"Miss Thrush! Ardennes! Please, a minute . . . I only want to talk. I'm a good actor—"

I locked the car doors. The woman with the dog looked up when he called out; so did her dog. He was coming toward the car. I had a witness. He used my first name! Ignition, back up—careful—out of the parking space, left blinker on . . . *drive.*

I sped up the hill. I thanked the security gate that shut me in. I parked and ran to the rooms. I was thirsty like the walls of the Grand Canyon. There was a plastic Long's Pharmacy sack hung over the doorknob, with a carton of Epsom salts inside. Good old Sharif. They must have knocked and then seen my car was gone. I'd say I'd had to go to the bank if it came up. It wouldn't come up.

Inside, I dropped the Epsom salts on the kitchen counter, tossed the shopping bag of new clothes onto the couch, and called the desk on the house phone. Sharif was at lunch, but Christy—I think she said—told me the Epsom salts were on the house. "Did anyone ask for me at the desk, a young bla—a nice-looking guy named Black, I mean Eddie?" Now what, unconscious racism? Uh!

"Ah . . ." There was a pause while she looked. "Not that I know of, and there's no note to the effect of a visitor. Is everything all right, Ms. Thrush?"

"Oh, yes, perfect, perfectly all right." I thanked her, adding to please thank Sharif for the salts, and hung up. I was supposed to have a bad ankle. Perfectly all right, huh?

I went to the sink and filled a large glass of water, sucking on it as if I'd just crossed Death Valley. Rumors crept around the back of my mind about how it's not so safe to drink the L.A. water, but I drank anyway. I was calmer now. I was in my hotel with security in place. But he knew my car; he knew my movements. How? I picked my purse up off the side table and looked for Detective Collins's card in my wallet. It wasn't there. Hell! I ran to the closet to find the jacket I'd worn to the Beverly Hills precinct. I found the card in the pocket and ran back to my cell phone, where I'd left it on the table. I tapped the card and flicked the edge, thinking whether I should call or not. Was I overreacting? The phone rang in my hand. I said hello, but whoever it was hung up, the number undisclosed: ID BLOCKED. That was the second blocked-ID call. Reading off the card, I pecked out Detective Collins's number into my keypad. I don't know why I thought of Alice tumbling down the Wonderland rabbit hole, waiting to hit bottom. He didn't pick up.

3

Billy

ndre and I were married in a private villa above Montego Bay, Jamaica. A friend of his owned the place, and we each invited two sets of guests for a week in paradise. Our honeymoon was soaked in coca rum sipped on a terrace overlooking the moonlit bay. A bag of mellow Jamaican pot materialized along with rolling papers, and one night we watched a light show over Cuba as a thunderstorm worked its way slowly from there to where we sat. There was snorkeling in an upside-down Eden: the silently undulating world of crazily colorful fish cruising and darting under the turquoise sea. We ate from papaya, mango, and avocado trees growing on the property. Andre was as relaxed as I'd ever seen him, even dancing with me to a reggae band. When I married Joe there hadn't been a honeymoon at all, only a rushed trip to City Hall and diner dinner later with friends by way of a party.

I watched for hours that week as gigantic, lusty clouds puffed in dialogue with the Caribbean, spread before me like a flat, shiny stone running headlong into the sky. We drove in jeeps up over the mountains along dense Shangri-la-like hills where coffee grew and the people, poor as scratch, had the whitest teeth and readiest smiles. Each day we drank from fresh, machete-cut coconuts, a straw stuck in to sip, spooning out the pudding after the milk was gone. It was peaceful and empty and I got into the rhythm of days that grew progressively hotter and slower, one day much like the next. I began to wonder if that rhythm didn't make more sense than the chaotic passing of days in New York or Los Angeles, especially as days went on movie locations: self-important, chaotically on edge.

Andre had just released a film, and leaving town as the reviews came out was his way of dealing with the outcome. He didn't care much one way or the other what the critics had to say, claiming it was more stylish to let a movie sort itself out (he all but refused to grant promotional interviews, which drove his producers into fits). The wedding had been worked in around the release date. At the time we were living in separate sections of New York. Andre had a huge loft in Soho; I was in a two-bedroom on the upper East Side. I bought the apartment after Joe, figuring there'd be less chance of us running into each other in that neighborhood and feeling like crap all over again. Joe grew Marxist over the moneyed East Side and rarely crossed over from the West Side. I spent hardly any time in my apartment, though I pretended the sparsely furnished rooms were home. I lived mostly in L.A., renting a house in Malibu at the time. Harry kept the jobs coming and my quote went up with each one. He kept advising me to buy property as a tax shelter and for security, but he didn't mean in New York City.

Once I started seeing Andre, I mean once we went from having dinner a couple of times when he was in L.A.—where he'd be on a fishing expedition for financing his next film—and things looked to be turning into something more than casual, I tried to go home more often, managing a whole autumn season at the New York apartment. I'd spend a night here and there with Andre, or he'd come up to what he called my fake European flat. I lived a pleasant walk from the Metropolitan Museum. Joe used to call the museum New York City's cathedral. The few times I went there with Andre I half worried I'd see Joe, but it didn't happen. I'd picture him mocking Andre right to his face, maybe in front of a Rembrandt self-portrait. I didn't picture the other side, what Andre would do with Joe. Both men possessed rock-hard confidence but not much else in common that I could see.

Joe claimed he proposed to me on the IRT number 1 as the subway car careened between stops under Broadway. I don't remember him asking, but I don't remember either how it came to pass that we did decide to marry. I'm not your most romantic female for those sorts of agendas. Andre wasn't much more definitive. He turned to me one evening after hanging up from a call with his producer. We were at his loft and it was late winter and snow was swirling outside the floor-length windows. I was standing in front of one making faces at Andre on the phone, doing a little snow dance, trying to coax him outside, like an excited child, and when he hung up he said we should get married.

"What about the snow?" was all I said in response. Andre stood up and kissed the top of my head, as if to say *good girl*. We bundled scarves over our coats and went out into a hushed city, an inch already sticking, the sky sprinkling powdery flakes. We were inside a bistro after walking for fifteen minutes; everyone in the bar was in good spirits for no better reason than the falling snow, as if we were all happily stranded in a fort far from the real world. We found a table and decided to skip the dinner I'd planned to cook. After the second glass of wine, as the coq au vin arrived, Andre said a friend of his had a place in Jamaica. It was free in two weeks, and we should go down for the wedding.

I asked, "What wedding?"

"You, me. My assistant, Marta, will file for us down there. You will need a birth certificate, and they perform the rite. Is it rite or ritual?"

"Ceremony. How much thought have you given this?"

"None. Or some. Why must we think?"

"Let's see; I would be your third wife and you would be my second husband, for starters."

"What is the connection?"

"We're two- and one-time losers. Why go through all that again?"

"How very practical you are tonight. The snow has gotten harder." He was looking past me out the restaurant's window.

"You're serious, Andre, aren't you?"

He smiled indulgently, shrugged. "We can let it go."

After dinner and dessert, of hot tarte tatin à la mode, we walked all the way to the Hudson River and were soggy in our coats by the time we found a cab to take us back to Andre's. I toyed in the cab with the idea of dropping him off and going back to my place, but my purse was in the loft. Stripping off our wet clothes inside Andre's door, my hair dripping, my scarf like used paper towel, pulling off my boots, I said, "Okay."

"Okay," Andre said back. "Will you make us tea?"

"I meant, okay, I'll go to Jamaica."

"Yes, I know."

"I hate when you do that."

"Yes, but I do know my actresses."

All of Andre's wives were actors. My quitting acting was not on the radar at the time of our Jamaican tryst. Would we have married if it was?

Andre dismissed the news when I first quit. "We all love to hate the business," he said, assuming my negative mood would pass. "It is a cliché, Ardennes." I was relieved not to have to explain or defend myself. I wasn't sure I could. I only knew I was serious.

If I was in crisis mode, I kept it under wraps. For all I know I'm still in crisis mode now. But the time slipped by pretty fast from that week in paradise to now, when I first began to suspect there were other ways to make one's way through the world than the one I was following. True, that week involved money and property and to some extent colonization, at least in that we were the foreign visitors with money to burn while the native population cooked and cleaned and waited on us. Andre's friend, the villa's owner, seemed well regarded by his staff; if there was any underlying misery or complaint, they hid it well. I guess I found things easier there. If poverty was the way of life, its relief may have been a general lack of complexity, and that appealed.

One morning, early—I was up with the sun, the coolest part of each new day—I heard bleating at the heavy wire fence along the property line that ran steeply uphill. I followed the cries toward the avocado and lime trees, halfway up, and found a pair of goats, a mother and child, and the mother's head was stuck in the fence. I tried twisting and pushing her out by the horns, but the wire was too thick. If she hadn't been stuck, I wouldn't have gotten so near and that gave me a thrill, the intimacy of touching the horny appendages that only her imprisonment allowed. I talked to her quietly, her rectangular black pupils not panicked but surprisingly calm—or fatalistic. I told her not to worry, we would free her.

I found Andre on the terrace with a carafe of coffee. He too liked the early morning and was chatting with the gardener, Gladfellow. I interrupted, telling Gladfellow about the goat.

"Thah goat a'wa in thah fence, ma'am."

"Whose goats are they, Gladfellow?" Andre asked.

"Mon up the village, he no take care at all." (He said ah-*tall*—as if it was a one word melody.)

Gladfellow wasn't usually that way. He'd taken me on a tour of the property, naming all the trees and plants. He'd shown me the low-growing ground cover called shy lady; when you bent down to touch the tiny leaves, they folded in on themselves like shy ladies. He'd taught me the time of day to best spot the male long-tailed Jamaican hummingbirds—the doctor bird—that came to suck the nectar of a certain row of bushes with honeysuckle-type flowers. He spoke softly and gently. But the goats would eat everything, even the shy ladies if they got through to the land. They were a nuisance, and stupid, he said, and that one in particular had a stubborn head.

"Then you won't help me free the mother goat, Gladfellow?"

"Not me, Ma'am," he said with his sweet, low laugh. He knew the goats better than I did, but I couldn't just leave the mother to die in the fence. It was her kid doing most of the bleating. Gladfellow headed down to the pool to fish out the leaves and debris fallen in overnight. There was always a skim of little night bugs on the surface in the morning.

"Andre?" I said.

He put his coffee down, placed a straw hat on his head and stood up. "Where is this baleful goat?" he said, touching my neck with the warm hand that had in the night felt the length and breadth of my flesh. Together we freed the goat. She skittered off with her kid without a backward glance.

"No manners in nature," Andre said.

"None needed," I answered.

On Sunday afternoon we heard gospel singing from the village church a ways up the hill; sorrow redeemed in song, or just letting it all out in clear, strong voices. That night the village rolled with reggae: church in the morning, partying all night, music and tree frogs keeping time. I was tempted to go up the hill to join in but it wasn't my party; it wasn't my life to celebrate. The Jamaicans went at it until the night was replaced by a golden dawn and tranquil morning breezes.

I took myself by surprise with tears when we finally said our good-byes to the island. It hadn't hit me yet that I was a wife again. I was just sad to leave. Within two months I was on location again, leaving Andre behind in New York City.

I never made it back to Jamaica, though I surely thought I would. I suppose I could fly there tomorrow if I wanted. I waited until Detective Collins's voice mail came on after about six rings, and I left a message. He called back two minutes later. He'd screened the call? He sounded coolly surprised to hear from me, saying there'd been no further developments in the Machin case. In fact, there was no case at this point. I said I wasn't surprised, but that was not why I called.

When I said I thought I was maybe being stalked, the Detective's first question was if I knew the individual. He slipped pronto into cop jargon. I wondered if people were always stalked by people they knew, or could it be a person in passing? He seemed to consider the question. Maybe I didn't sound sufficiently concerned because after a pause he asked why I'd called him.

"You're not located in my department. I'll get you the number for the East Hollywood precinct; it's over on North Wilcox."

"No, that's all right. I'm probably making something out of nothing and I can find the local police if I need to. Thanks, Detective Collins; I'm sorry I bothered you. It's just your card was in my pocket."

"You didn't bother me, Ms. Thrush." He seemed to be making up his mind, and if things can be sensed over the phone, I sensed *he* sensed he was going to regret what came next. "Is the person there now?"

"No, I'm at the hotel. There's security. It's not impossible, but I don't think he'd try to break in."

"What makes you say that? Then you do know the man?"

"He works in a shoe store. He showed up at the lobby last night and twice today while I was out running errands. He just appeared. . . ."

"I'll be there in an hour."

"You can do that? You won't get into trouble?"

Detective Collins laughed, unkindly but he also sounded amused. "I don't *get* into trouble, Ms. Thrush; I *make* trouble for those who do." It sounded like a movie line, if he'd meant it to or not, and I laughed. I gave him the hotel address and pass code to the security gate and hung up.

I looked around to neaten up, but nothing was out of place, so I paced back and forth in front of the big sitting room window. I took the new scarf and sweaters out of their bags and placed them on the bed. I realized I hadn't eaten and pulled what was left of a rotisserie chicken out of the fridge and made myself a hasty sandwich. The day had turned pleasantly warm and clear; I opened the balcony door and stood looking out over the hills as I ate. The mountains in the distance dissolved into a faded blue blur with a roll of clean white clouds balanced above.

An hour came and went. No Detective Collins. I felt pretty silly. Eddie Tompkins hadn't done anything to me. Why did I assume he meant me harm? He only wanted a job. He'd seemed nice enough, if too all over me in the shoe store. He saw me as an opportunity and I'd dismissed him. I hadn't even bothered to mention him to Andre. There was a time when I was hungry for work, times I asked my mother for help with the rent. Things eased up some when Joe and I pooled our resources, and then I started auditioning for commercials and that stabilized us for a while. At least I'd never had to work in a shoe store. I must have looked like a sign from the gods to Eddie Tompkins. I remember telling Joe I had no choice: "You have to be aggressive. You can't just stand there bundled up with talent and hope somebody notices. There's tons of talent rolling around out there."

Joe said an artist had to work her craft and that excellence came with time and concentration. Sure, he was right, but he wasn't an actor. He didn't have to trade on youth or sex or some physical quirk. He knew I was torn on that point. He knew I despised the sex-as-sales-pitch part of the business, but was I going to change that? I wasn't even standard beautiful. I was always going to have to crash through the gates. I'd crashed through all right and landed pretty high up on the heap. I never got to tell Joe just how much of what I found there I loathed.

I was about to call Detective Collins, tell him to forget it; I'd overreacted. I'd call Eddie Tompkins and tell him, very nicely, I couldn't help. I would suggest he call what was left of Harry's business, assuming Machin Talent would continue without him. I could name one or two other agencies; he could use my name to secure an interview. I might not mean much these days, but Andre sure did. After that I would insist he not contact me again—

My cell phone went off in my pocket. It was Detective Collins. He'd parked, but I hadn't told him my room number. I looked over the balcony wall and waved, indicating the staircase past the laundry, and held up a V for two, second floor. In a minute he was standing inside the suite, wearing a suit and overcoat, I think the same tie as the other week. He seemed taller, or the rooms smaller. He was so much more a guy than I what was used to; I couldn't help it, he was physically more masculine than all the other men I'd been with—put together. Acute manliness might be good in a cop.

"Detective Collins, please come in." He walked past me, with authority. "I'm afraid I've wasted your time, Detective."

He was busy taking in the sitting room, and then a glance into the bedroom. "Big windows," he said. The plate and glass from my lunch were still out on the balcony table. "There's a guy out there, across the hill. That your stalker?"

I looked out. I'd been here days before I noticed White Shirt; the Detective cased him in ten seconds. "That's White Shirt; he lives there."

"White Shirt, huh? Well, he's looking over here. Is that usual?"

"It's his garden. And he's not the man I called about. Would you like to sit down?"

"No."

For a good-looking man he had a pretty lousy bedside manner. That movie line came back to me, the one that always got a laugh. I tried a variation: "How do I call off the cavalry, Detective?" The line fell flat. Maybe I couldn't act even if I wanted to; there was a thought.

"Why the change of heart? You were threatened?"

"No. The shoe store's just a job; the guy is an actor looking for a break. He asked me to give his card to my husband, Andre Lucerne—he's a director. I might have done the same thing once upon a time."

"Followed someone?"

"Hey, I know a pair of actors who dressed up as heavies and went to Al Pacino's New York apartment with toy guns, demanding a job on his movie."

"It work?"

"It did, but they were only on screen for ten seconds."

"Does your man have a gun?"

"He didn't pull one." I sounded annoyed.

"Does he have a name?"

"Actors tend to be bleeding liberals, Detective, and show-offs with insides like scared little rabbits."

"That include you?"

"I quit the business, remember?"

"So we drop it?"

"I won't press charges."

"If he's carrying a weapon, you won't have to."

I handed over Eddie's card. Detective Collins studied both sides. "Where's the shoe store?"

"Down on Sunset, the Shoe Horn or something like that."

He looked up. "That discount dump near the In-N-Out?" I nodded. He looked at my shoes, then flipped the card over again. "This address is there." He lifted his chin toward the hills. "Maybe he knows your White Shirt pal? Maybe they're in it together . . . extortion, possible kidnap. Maybe *you're* in on some kind of setup."

I shook my head. "Back up. White Shirt has a Mercedes sports car in his garage; Eddie's in the shoe store—"

"Could be lovers."

"I'd have seen them."

"They don't want to be seen. But they've seen you." He lifted a shoulder. "You have binoculars here?"

"*No!* What do you think I am?"

"You tell me."

I sat down on the couch. This was turning out badly. What did I expect?

"What did your husband say about giving Eddie a job?"

My voice came out muffled. "I didn't give him the card."

"No?"

"Andre's on a movie; he's all over the place all times of day and night."

"He's busy?"

"Movie people make lousy spouses. You don't need a gossip columnist to tell you that."

"Would that include ex–movie people?" I shrugged, looking down at a small brown stain I hadn't noticed on the carpet before. He said, "I guess they don't call it Hollyweird for nothing." Was he making a joke? I looked up and laughed. I couldn't help it; the line didn't fit the character saying it. "You have a nice laugh," he said.

My cell phone rang. I let it ring.

"Answer it." He nodded once toward the phone in my hand.

I picked up the call. "Andre?" I listened, then said okay and we hung up. "My husband is stopping by for some new sides—script pages—he forgot. With his assistant director," I said, facing the officer of the law whose presence in my hotel room was beginning to unnerve me.

Detective Collins stuffed Eddie's card into his pocket. "Mind if I keep this?" He didn't wait for an answer. "I'll go up the hill, check out this address and get back to you," he said, moving toward the door.

"You don't want to meet Andre?"

"What for?"

Detective Collins wasn't gone six minutes before Andre and Carola came in. They'd probably passed each other in their cars.

I guess I took my cue from the Detective and didn't bring him up to Andre, or Eddie Tompkins either. I kept up a busy chatter, giving Andre the scarf, showing him the new sweaters. "A good color," he said. "And cashmere. Perfect." He gamely tossed the scarf over his shoulder. He glanced in the mirror, made an adjustment, and thanked me with a kiss to my cheek. Turning to Carola—who I only then noticed looked pale with worry—he said he'd look over the new pages now. He found them on the table, where until a few minutes ago Eddie Tompkins's card had sat. "We will see if they are an improvement for her." The word *her* was loaded, a freight train of contempt. I understood Andre had been calmly indulgent about the scarf, that his mood underneath was murderous. He put his glasses on, moved toward the bedroom, and read the pages.

Carola confided to me in a low voice the lead actress was proving a disappointment.

"Can't learn her lines?"

Andre looked up from reading. "She is a whore." His tone was glacial.

Carola shook her blond head, chewed a fingernail. "She knows the lines but brings nothing to them."

I knew the actress's work. Luce Bouclé was all right, if too reliant on her physicality over a character's interior, not gorgeous but compelling to watch, French. I'd joked when Andre cast her, "Have you fallen for another actress?" And he'd joked back that I was jealous at last. I wasn't.

"She is impossible, devoid of spirit, a *corpse*!" Andre almost shouted. Poor Carola visibly shrank. Andre was not a man to raise his voice, so when he did, it was that much worse. His burst of anger would have to do with the fact that he alone had cast Luce Bouclé, had auditioned no one else. I was tempted to ask if she'd auditioned well, but this was not the moment to suggest that a mistake had been made even if I meant it humorously.

Andre tossed the pages onto the bed. He'd read them standing in the double doorway to the bedroom. He'd had the writer come up with changes that would nurse the actress along, give her less to say but more reaction. "This is all explanation," he said of the fix. He picked the three pages up off the bed and swatted the paper with the back of his hand. "Utter junk." He handed the pages to me. "Ardennes, will you read this?" I scanned the first page. "No, no, out loud, please."

He was asking me to read cold? I glanced at Carola. She was a wreck, biting whatever was left of her fingernails. I breathed. I took a minute to read the first page to myself, breathed again, exhaled, and read as convincingly as I could.

"No," Andre said. "Stop. Don't go on, please. This is terrible. *Terrible.* Carola, have you the original with you?"

Carola nodded, dug into her bag and pulled out a script. She looked up at Andre, a question on her face. Andre looked at me. "The pages?"

Carola hurried through the script, found the needed pages and handed me her battered copy.

"Andre, I'm not a circus dog to bark on cue."

"Ardennes, just, please, read for me." He spoke in his director's voice. I felt a chilly spasm down my neck, and my buttocks clenched. What I wanted was to carefully put the script down, to say firmly, no, I would not just please read for him or for anyone else. But

Andre had on that demanding yet wide-open listening face I knew so well. It was a face I'd not been able to challenge as an actress. I wet my lips, suddenly deathly thirsty. "Ardennes? Will you refuse to help us for one moment of your day?"

I looked at the page. At a glance I could see the writing here was real, lines an actress could chew and digest. The character, Anne, is talking to the police. I let out a hard breath and began: "Mr. Lawson is no longer at this address, Officer. He's gone, you see, and now there is laughter again. There's a trail of lies and slime behind Mr. Lawson, and no one cares where he's gone. . . . Do you know how to kill a garden slug, Officer? You lay traps with stale beer; they die and the flowers live. I wonder who sat down and made that discovery about the beer. Have you ever heard of that trick, Officer?" I continued with the scene, already feeling Anne's ache and her crazy hope. The directions called for her to execute a little dance, suddenly to dance, her body knowing she is free ahead of her mind. The dance is not described. Andre and his actress would have to work it out. I thought of Beckett's *Godot*, Lucky's dance. But no, this would be faster, lighter, stiff—because Anne is lame—but graceful.

Carola and Andre were silent when I finished; they looked rapt. I broke the silence, handing the script back to Carola. "I have such a headache all of a sudden." Andre looked steadily at me for what seemed like a very long pause, even for him.

"Come, we'll go," he told Carola.

"The sides?" she asked him.

Andre shook his head. "Leave them; they are worthless. We know now how the lines are meant to be spoken." He went for the door. "Oh, before I forget, Ardennes, here is the extra key to Grant's room—302—on the other end." He gestured toward the room to the right of the landing. "I have lent him the printer you were using.

If you need to, just go take it." He tossed the plastic pass onto the table and went for the door again. I hadn't realized the printer was gone and wondered when it had been taken off my desk, and by whom.

Carola reminded me that Grant Stuart was the second AD. I glanced at the white-and-gold passkey on the table and nodded. She said she hoped my headache would soon pass. She followed Andre out, closing the door. I felt sick on top of a splitting headache, so when Zaneda knocked on the door soon after they left, it wasn't my make-believe ankle injury that was killing me. I'd forgotten I was supposed to be hurt.

Hotel maids know everything. The shoes you wear, the undergarments. They witness the bed stains; the time of the month and the signs of sexual activity. A good maid has seen it all. Disheveled bath towels thrown on the floor, the makeup and the creams, the brush full of hidden gray hairs, and the paperwork left lying around—they see that too, if they bother to look. My sense of the staff at the Hotel Muse is that they are involved, they cooperate, and they report back. The Muse is friendly, the snooping not malignant. The Hollywood location suggests a certain sort of guest, film people, journalists, and plenty of foreigners; not your typical Hollywood tourist hole. All the more reason to keep a lookout.

Zaneda was friendly and bright. Alma, her alternate, was also amiable, with better English and shrewder, more on the lookout for tips. Our extra coffees and teas and bath products, the bits of attention here and there, reflected that and also the awareness that Andre was an important figure. Plus we are long term, which called for greater investment on the maids' part. I had cachet too, whether they knew it or not, though the mystique was faded. Not that the tingle of elusive fame once achieved is ever entirely extinguished.

With so much of Andre's crew occupying so many rooms we were bound to make waves. Sometimes there was partying late, loud with the pungent smell of weed carried on the nighttime air. Once or twice management made a call, which I fielded on the house phone. Those calls should have gone to the line producer, but Andre had negotiated the rooms and was staying here and was in charge, so complaints—though they were never quite that—went to the head of the movie family, and since I was here so much of the time that, by proxy, became me. Management was always apologetic.

The maids asked me questions too. So I shouldn't have been surprised when Zaneda asked if everything was all right. Detective Collins had arrived in an unmarked car and left minutes before Andre and Carola replaced him in the suite. The Detective had stayed perhaps twenty minutes, long enough for Zaneda to observe him come and go; long enough for a possibly illegal immigrant to sniff out the law. Zaneda could have been anywhere: changing another room's sheets, carrying out a big bundle of wash to be picked up in the hotel van, or bagloads of trash, or fluffing pillows and scouring sinks and toilets—unseen eyes seeing everything.

But what did she mean by all right? If she said she'd seen a man come and go, she'd be stepping on my privacy. The man that had come and gone could have been anyone, a lawyer, a producer . . . but there was that cop stink to him, and gentle Zaneda would have the wariness natural to a third world transplant. Anyone who says hotels are anonymous has their head up in the dark; hotel walls have eyes and ears and mouths that talk.

She rang the bell. She hadn't cleaned the rooms, she said; was running late with more guests than usual for early spring. We were standing in the doorway, and I let her know I'd made the bed already. She looked at my ankle.

Sharif's unopened box of Epsom salts was on the kitchen counter, right behind me. Assuming she'd seen me, Zaneda had surely noted I was not limping when I went out in the car and again when I came back. I wasn't favoring the foot now. Good thing I'm not with the CIA; I couldn't even remember my own cover story. Word was out I'd hurt myself on hotel property. Was that what Zaneda meant by asking if I was all right?

I stepped aside from the doorway. A drafty current was wheezing down the open-ended corridor. "See what you think, if the room needs cleaning."

She didn't come in. "Is up to you. But fresh towels, soaps? Whatever you need."

"I'm okay, Zaneda, thanks; *está bien, todo bien*. Will you come back, clean tomorrow? *Mañana?*"

"Tomorrow is Alma."

"Ah, you're off? Wait one minute." I went for my purse, not limping—the hell with it—and found a twenty. Usually we tip a ten to the maids every week or so. I gave her the twenty. Her eyes lit up at the amount. She made the usual polite protest. "For *los niños*," I said. She said okay and took the money with thanks and a quick glance at my ankle, then tried for my eyes. I'm guessing she was guessing the big tip was for the man who'd come to my rooms, *la policía*, and for her ignorance of that fact. I reached down to rub my ankle, making it seem unconscious. I might make a lousy intelligence agent, but I could still perform. I smiled and closed the door.

Alone, I was left to try and untangle a day that was beginning to feel like a trashy airport novel. Should I dive into a bottle of scotch or scrounge around for an aspirin? I didn't do either; the aspirin would sit badly in my stomach and the scotch would change nothing. I was rattled, but not by Eddie or the sudden involvement of Detective Collins in my life; those things were trouble enough. What Andre had just made me do was worse.

The hardest thing about ending a part on stage is coming down from the high, shutting that down. This happens in film too if the part has any meat on its bones. Even if the acting is a struggle from word one to word last, the body systems quicken. You might feel like you're about to have a stroke standing up before an audience or in front of the camera's cold eye as you utter your first line. Maybe there isn't a molecule of saliva in your mouth and an ocean is pounding inside your skull and you are sure you are trembling so if you have to pick up a prop—a glass, say—that could slip and crash and shatter into a thousand pieces, there is still the rush. Get past the first sentence and hear your voice take control, your body snap inside the character, and *feel* being heard, listened to, watched, *seen*, clung to . . . not ego but power, the power you own over the words. With a good part the writer's voice comes alive through you, the emotions rising naturally out of the words, no gimmicks to rouse a tear, a laugh, a shout. Maybe I got that from Joe, about the writer's voice, or maybe from reading so much, I don't know. But even the crap parts, done truthfully, carry a rush. Never mind that it's not you; never mind that it's all an act. . . .

Okay, let's lay it bare: It's a sham, entertainment, a passing waste of time, a *numbing* of time; a make-believe magic show of inconsequential emotions and tired stories told over and over again; a three-ring circus of prancing ponies, seminude girls and pretend tough guys, manufactured machismo, guns shooting blanks, and simulated sex. For all that, some of us believed it was real. Some of us remembered what Aristotle talked about. Some of us understood somewhere deep down that our job was to say things that couldn't be said, emote to catharsis, pass through taboos and yearning and fear and hope and all the other murky misunderstandings we call communication and mostly fail at miserably in real life. Good theater embraces that, attempts that level of communication.

Andre's script—*The Dance*—is about Anne Dernier, a ballerina, and her agent, Mr. Lawson. She's an Isadora Duncan type, an original. Mr. Lawson—always Mr. Lawson even after they become lovers—wants control, to take her to the top. He gives up all his other clients for her. She's spry and joyous—the actress would want to tap a bit of Gelsomina from Fellini's *La Strada* (well, I would). Mr. Lawson ridicules her childlike sense of play. There is a scene at an amusement park, Anne and a boy spinning, the Ferris wheel lighting up the night sky. "It's like dancing!" Anne says, throwing her head back. But there is an accident; she's thrown from a ride, the Mouse—not even a dangerous ride, but her belt was not secure. The carnival turns to sideshow horror; her legs are broken. Mr. Lawson has followed her—he thinks she's fallen for the boy, but the boy is only a friend, a fellow dancer. Lawson sees the accident and abandons Anne. Years later he finds her tending bar at the same amusement park; her friends are carnie types—clowns, snake charmers, magicians, dwarfs; outsiders.

"Serving drinks to nobodies. Always drawn to nobodies," Lawson tells her.

"I like freaks," she responds. "They're more real."

There is a clown, Mr. Chuckles, whose unrequited love for Anne has evolved into devoted protection. She could choreograph, Mr. Lawson tells Anne; she was a genius, being lame shouldn't stop her, why did she give up? Chuckles tries to warn her against Lawson, but she falls under his spell a second time and makes a comeback.

Lawson finds her an apprentice, a young dancer who looks a little like her younger self. Anne's dances become darkly comic, modern Grimm's tales: strange, filmy figures swirling across the stage—a Powell/Pressburger tone, the critics' note. She attains an audience once again and begins to slip out of Mr. Lawson's grip. She attempts to make him laugh, the one thing he cannot control; if he laughs, she wins. She tells him there are rhythms beyond the ego and that he misses everything essential, is only half human. He seduces the young apprentice, letting Anne know *he* is in control, that he will humiliate and torment her if need be. Mr. Lawson is killed and suspicion falls first on Mr. Chuckles, then on Anne. The audience won't know if she's killed him or not; there is a trial, but nothing can be proved, and of course the audience wants him gone. Anne forms a dance troupe with the young apprentice as her lead. Her tragicomic ballets are beautiful: sensuous and grotesque, haunting and mesmerizing.

I started going over the lines I'd read to Andre and Carola. That opening line about Mr. Lawson had to be read with a kind of mad euphoria but at the same time innocence. I'd lifted my hand at one point, the free hand not holding the script. I remembered every modulation and tone change. I didn't remember every word, but close. If I kept churning the lines, all the words would come back to me of a piece. I picked up the new pages Andre had thrown down. He was right; they were terrible, the life sucked out of them.

I'd been critical of the script when I first read it in New York. Andre deflected my angry words, saying the script could be changed as needed.

"Don't lie!" I said, theatrically loud. "This isn't a draft."

"I thought you would like it."

"My liking it or not has nothing to do with anything."

"And why not?"

"I don't act anymore!" I gestured dramatically toward the script lying on the coffee table between us, a silly flourish. We were in New York, Andre's loft, where I'd moved after our island wedding. I still kept my apartment uptown. I'd sublet it to actor friends I'd known since the starving theater days, way back. They were my only link to Joe because they'd remained friends; he'd inherited them from me. I charged only maintenance and taxes, utilities. They would never get past struggling in the theater world, but at least their quest was uncorrupted, which translated into their being broke. Anyhow, I got to keep my apartment, my just-in-case escape hatch. I'd learned to keep escape hatches at the ready.

"Tell me what is so terrible in this script?" Andre asked, watching me, scrutinizing me with those director eyes. I kept silent. "So," he shrugged, "you don't *act* anymore. You still *think*; you still understand how to read a script, no? It is paper, it won't bite you. Amuse me." He smiled.

"Humor me; you mean *humor*," I said, instantly regretting my nastiness.

"Go on."

"Okay. For one thing, how is an actress supposed to play this?"

"This what?"

"This, this running joke idea—"

"What running joke?"

"That she is joyous and funny—goofy—this laughter she wants to elicit from that horror Lawson. How do you direct that? How would I—how would the actress play such a vague concept?"

"This is not difficult to solve. . . ."

"And why would she fall for Lawson in the first place?" I was growing heated. "Plus, this business of not using Lawson's first name; it's contrived. Even in bed, Andre?"

"He was her guide; she is a performer, *aspiring*, young but an original, a force . . . yet with all the sensitivity and doubts of a great talent . . . she needs him."

"*Great talent*; that's not specific!" He'd said the word *aspiring* with that European emphasis that sometimes made me hate him because he sounded so *certain*. I've never trusted immaculate certainty. Not since Joe.

"Okay. Why would she fall for him a second time? She's not *aspiring* anymore, not after the broken legs. And he abandoned her. She would hate him."

"Ah, the actor here is critical. He is older—remember that—twisted, yes, but a magnet nonetheless, very attractive, worn, a bit worn, but . . . the lines can be changed to satisfy, to convince the actress."

He meant "magnetic," but I'd run out of steam to mock him. I didn't want to mock Andre, play the bitch. I stood up, trying to gather my thoughts. Something about the script was bothering me and I wasn't getting at it. I walked over to the wall of windows. It was raining outside, hard, like a Kurosawa film.

Andre had lived at the loft with his second wife—bought it with her. I was a case of marital musical chairs, I'd joked. I'd added a few touches, taken a back room for a small studio, my inner sanctum, my private corner of earth. I'd thought briefly of renovating the state-of-the-art kitchen, but that was ridiculous, only something to bury myself in. I'd let Andre believe I was taking notes in my studio for a possible book. I was in fact keeping a notebook. Not a diary. Writing and reading diaries is deathly boring; the last one I'd kept was as a tiresomely sincere eleven-year-old. Mostly I lay about and read books in my inner sanctum.

After quitting, I walked. Everywhere. I went to museums, sometimes to the country, to an inn I liked upstate or to visit friends with country houses. I did not go to plays, but I went to many movies. I usually kept Andre in the dark about my days and whereabouts. We knew not to question each other, to give each other space. His casual beddings were apparent from our beginnings, but he was discreet, never in the gossip columns. I could have had affairs too, if I'd wanted, but I lacked Andre's distance, his director's way of seeing people as objects outside himself. Anyhow, New York is generous in its anonymity; it was easy enough to disappear. Once in a while I'd be approached, spoken to in that way the public has of assuming an actor is their personal property, part of the price of a movie ticket. But I was free for the most part to simply be a woman in a city. Garbo came to mind more than once.

I refined my cooking—with little excuse not to make dinner at home, though Andre liked to dine out several times a week. I even learned how to put together small dinner parties. For a while that was interesting, but I always imagined Joe watching me as I attempted to justify to myself the bourgeois ritual of witty conversation, good wine and clever desserts. Andre didn't care about the dinner parties one way or the other, and they soon petered out. This would be when he was in town, but he was often not, chasing down his next film: research, financing, securing his actors and the all-important script—he was always in on the script. Where Andre was consumed, I was adrift, and I could feel his disapproval grow as time passed and he understood I really meant it when I quit acting. The ruse that I was planning a book was a way to try to keep his disapproval at bay. That pretense followed me to Los Angeles, along with the workbook, which is at my little desk in the bedroom, in the drawer below the computer. It is a grade school, black-and-white, lined notebook.

Anyhow, rain was slithering down the windows that New York evening in metallic sheets, making it impossible to see outside. The daylight was gone, replaced by orange crime lights and a murky blue gray. Once all the paperwork was in place Andre would leave for L.A. He had finalized his cast and crew, his director of photography, designer, locations—the whole company. He would begin the yearlong journey of making a film. So why was he asking me about a script already in place? I turned away from the windows. "Would you like a drink?"

"I would like to hear your objections to the script. If, for example, you imagined yourself playing the part."

"On a rainy day in hell, Andre."

He tilted his head. "That is cute, that saying. Maybe today is such a day." He affirmed his thought with a double nod of his head and a solid smile. I laughed. Andre had a thing for rain in film; it was almost a trademark, the number of rainy scenes in his movies. His actors and hairdressers could plan on difficult hair days. We looked at each other, hearing the rain pour down from the heavens, tapping on the glass. He laughed too.

I couldn't stop myself going over and over the tape in my head. Had I gotten the lines right, delivered the goods, *owned* the words? Why care how I read to Andre and Carola? I'd done him a favor; it would not happen again; I would make sure, beg as he might—like the *penitentes* I'd seen in Mexico, walking on their knees over Coke-bottle caps, sharp side up, begging Dios to forgive. Really, how dare he do that to me? I felt cold and hot at the same time. I recognized the feeling, the doubts mixed with desire; hanging on for the director's approval like an orphaned child. Suddenly the rotisserie chicken from earlier wasn't sitting so well. I ran to the toilet, making it just in time to vomit.

"*Oh,* Joe," I said out loud, wiping my mouth with the back of my hand, a line of thick spit trailing along my chin. I used to vomit like that over a part; my doubts, my terror of not getting the character right mangling my gut. I couldn't see any way around it.

"Is it worth it?" Joe once asked, standing over me, my head halfway into the toilet bowl. I remember draping my arm over the cold porcelain and looking up at him and saying I didn't know. He reached down to gently pull the damp hair off my cold, sweaty brow.

"I've seen you look pretty drawn over your work. So I guess none of this comes cheap." He sat down next to me on the bathroom floor.

"No. I guess not."

He pulled me to him. "Come here; you're done puking for now."

"I stink. . . ." I said, leaning into him, my breath like a city dump.

"You know you're good. You don't need to beat yourself up. Just be confident; the goods are in place for you to use: Go ahead and use."

There was no one to pull my head up out of the toilet bowl when I was throwing up my brains over a role while living alone in L.A. No one but Harry to tell me I had the goods. Ah, Harry, whaddaya have to go and die like that for?

After I finished flushing the chicken out of my gut, I lay down on the bed, the curtains drawn and lights off. My phone rang next to me. Before I committed to coming out west, when I was still in New York, torturing us both with indecision, Andre insisted that I have the phone on me at all times. We'd joked about our coast-to-coast leashes. I still kept the phone nearby. I picked it up and glanced at the number: ID BLOCKED.

My vomit-sore belly tightened. It was him again. Or was it? Whoever it was. The phone was still playing its jingle. Do I pick up, only to be hung up on? Where was Detective Collins?

I pushed talk but didn't say anything. Once again whoever was there hung up without a word, not even heavy breathing. I hit end, laid the phone back down on the bed beside me and closed my eyes. "Is that you, Eddie? You're making a big mistake. The sheriff's in town."

I was asleep and it was dark outside when the phone rang a second time, and this time it was the Detective. I must have sounded like I was answering from the crypt. He asked if everything was all right. The answer was everything was all wrong, but most of that had nothing to do with him, so I said I was fine.

"I ran Eddie Tompkins's tags; there's nothing out on him. His address is the bottom of Hillcrest Way. So he's not watching you from there."

I didn't know what to make of that, so I said, "Oh."

"Maybe he is just after a job, like you said. You didn't report him—officially—so I couldn't do much more. I asked him if he was a friend of yours."

I sat up on the pillow. "What did he say?"

Detective Collins sounded irritated. "He said no."

"Why was he following me?"

"He said he wasn't."

"He came to the hotel—"

"You want to file a report yet?" I shook my head. "Ms. Thrush?"

"No."

"Didn't think so. The next time you see him hanging around, call the East Hollywood police. Okay?"

"No."

"Why not?"

"Someone called my cell again, number undisclosed. They clicked off when I answered. That's three times it happened." There was silence on the other end. "Detective Collins? Thank you for what you've done—"

"I don't see Eddie Tompkins for this. I'm still not sure there is a 'this.' What we have is an out-of-work actor, a couple of coincidences near where you and he live. And the phone calls . . . could be the press, could be the same jerk can't dial his phone right."

"You think I pushed the panic button?"

"Could be . . . If you see Eddie again, call me. Or anything else gets the hairs up, call."

"I can call you?"

"If it's important." I was tempted to ask how he defined important but thanked him again and hung up.

I supposed the Detective knew his stuff and I should stop worrying about Eddie Tompkins. That left the phone calls. I couldn't explain anyone wanting to harass me. What for? Still, three coincidences? I doubted Detective Collins really believed that.

I stood up too fast and felt woozy from all the throwing up. I was thirsty like dry dirt. I waited a minute until my head cleared and went to the bathroom to run a hot tub. I had no idea where Andre was or when he'd be in. With the water running, I didn't hear the phone when he called to let me know he'd be very late. After a half-hour soak I felt better. Maybe I could eat something, if there was something there to eat. Oatmeal appealed. I wrapped myself in the hotel waffle robe we were not supposed to be privileged to up here in the poor cousins' quarters, but Alma had brought a pair up for us and now we were spoiled and there were always two clean white robes at the ready.

I picked up my blinking phone on the way to the kitchen. Andre's message said he'd be at an important meeting: "Things going on." Problems in movieland, I guessed. I decided I shouldn't return the call, that I'd be an interruption. I stopped, hearing noises outside on the driveway and the parking areas, cars pulling up and people calling out. I recognized Andre's crowd. I slipped out onto the balcony, hugging the wall so as not to be seen. The crew was coming home, and by the sound of it in jolly spirits. Someone yelled that he'd get the beer and be right back. I recognized Renny and a few others. Then I heard Carola's distinctive voice and Portuguese accent.

If Andre was still working, how could everyone be here? Meetings? Okay. But without Carola, his right arm? She was in on everything. Now I would definitely not call Andre back. I slipped inside and closed the balcony door. Was Andre coaching Luce Bouclé, one-on-one? Desperate to make it work, using flattery, seduction? Or insults, proffered in private? Andre was known to try anything to get the performance he wanted. I stirred oatmeal into soy milk and water, the flame under the pot on high, picturing the actress's responsive face.

I ate at the computer while trolling for news on Lucille Trevor. Information was slim. I was just about to call it quits when her name popped up under an old movie-star fan magazine. Someone had sat around and archived old fan rags, going all the way back to the silents. There used to be dozens: *Star Album*, *Movie Fan*, *Movie* magazine . . . gossip and scandal—Clark Gable, Liz Taylor, Robert Mitchum, endless Garbo, Brando, Monty Cliff, Kim Novak . . . the list went on and on. Movie stars! When I was a kid my dad sometimes called me his little actress. If I was being particularly emphatic I'd be labeled his own little Sarah Bernhardt. Until I understood who he was talking about I thought he was saying *Sahara burn hard*, like I was giving him indigestion. My grandmother, also misunderstanding the reference, would buy me movie magazines, which I devoured huddled in an armchair at her house. Finding me with my nose in one when she came to pick me up from Grandma's one Saturday afternoon, my mother asked why her daughter was reading garbage.

"I thought the child wanted to be a movie star," my grandma said.

"I do!" I shouted, poking my ponytailed head out from behind the magazine, though it was the first I'd heard of the idea. My mother asked what happened to nurse or doctor. "You don't get to wear evening gowns," I said. My grandmother nodded approval. To her a girl was meant to dress up, to be as beautiful as she could be and put it to good use.

My mother promptly put a stop to the magazines. "My daughter is a more perfect version of me; her motivation must find its way beyond costumes and airs," she told me—more than once.

It turned out Lucille was from Delaware and grew up in Wilmington. I'd pictured her as a Midwesterner. Instead she was from the first state to ratify the U.S. Constitution, thereby becoming the first state in the union (that bit of trivia was in the issue: padding for Lucille's lightweight resume). The fan mag linked me to the *Wilmington News Journal*—called the *Journal Every Evening* at the time—and here was where I sat up straight in my uncomfortable hotel desk chair: A clipping from the local news: "First State's Youngest Ballet Dancer Takes First Prize."

So then, Lucille was a dancer. A dancer? Not an actress?

The clip said at eight years old she was the youngest ballerina from Delaware to audition and win summer placement to study with the prestigious New York Ballet Corps. There was nothing more until an accident report in the same paper nine years later:

> Lucille Trevor, fifteen, of 55 Maple Avenue, was hurt when the car her father was driving was struck by a delivery van on the morning of April 10th. David Trevor, a decorated war hero, was listed in critical condition after the crash. The driver of the truck, Reginald Barr, insisted Mr. Trevor's car ran a red light. There were no witnesses. Lucille Trevor sustained severely broken legs, thus ending, her mother said, her daughter's dreams of becoming a professional ballerina.

I stared at the blank wall above the small desk. I'd moved the desk to the other side of the bedroom, away from the window and glass balcony door, so I was in a kind of cave. I'd bought a used desk lamp at a thrift store, and a cushion for the hard chair. This was my tiny haven, equal to the surface of the desk, where Andre believed I was at work on a book. The wall was a calming off-white and empty. The Muse was free of the usual banal hotel art, matching the couch or bedspread fabric. There was a modest flower print in a simple frame over the bed and two forgettable but not irritating prints in the sitting room. I'd tried to move them, but they were stuck in place. Staring up at the wall with only the soft glow of my shaded thrift-store lamp creating an arc of yellow light, I felt sick. Not throw-up sick. The oatmeal had done the trick settling me there. No, this was a more profound sickness, a dull sensation that gravity might fail, the earth slip off its axis and the sky turn permanently black. I felt the noose of something tightening and I did not know what that something was. Coincidence, a little voice let me know, the eerie kind that wants to upset all previous knowledge, coming out of nowhere and making a scary kind of pattern where none should reasonably be: Lucille Trevor's legs were broken in an accident. An aspiring ballerina . . . hopes dashed . . . sound familiar, Ardennes?

I scanned but found no further news about the accident. I mean, did her dad subsequently die of his wounds? Did Lucille graduate on time after months of surgeries and traction? Nothing. Two back-arrow clicks brought me to the movie magazine link again and a tiny notice I'd missed: the Lucille Trevor Fan Club. How sweet; a B-movie actress with a homegirl fan club. I never had a fan club, not that I knew of—do they exist anymore? The link led to Jody Pechard, Lucille Trevor Fan Club president. There was a studio head shot of Lucille and a listing of five movies, walk-ons or minor characters. The text said, "Nearly every member went Friday night to the Arcade Theater to see Lucille's latest Hollywood venture." No mention of a limp, a wrecked dancing career, twisted legs, or a handicap. Lucille had healed. Ballet was over, but Hollywood beckoned. Was that what happened?

What did it mean that Andre was directing a script about a ballerina whose legs are mangled in a freak accident? Nothing. The earth was safely on its axis, the sky was only nighttime black and objects were not floating free in the hotel room. And Andre's Anne didn't go to Hollywood; his Anne quit. . . .

Just a small world of zany coincidence, I told myself, about as convinced as that Santa and the Tooth Fairy had the same mother; something didn't fit. I had only one lead left to locate: Lucille Trevor's obituary—

"*Ah!*" I gasped, feeling a hand on my shoulder.

"At work on your book?"

"You scared hell out of me, sneaking up like that, Andre!" I glanced at the computer clock: one A.M.

"Did I sneak?" In fact he had a glass of brandy in his hand.

I quickly bookmarked the site and clicked back to the main screen. Andre walked to the sitting room, I followed. One look at his face told me his mood was even darker than earlier. "Any more of that brandy?" I asked.

Andre poured me a small glass, and I sat down on the couch. He stood over me and placed a hand on top of my head and left it there for a minute while he looked down at my face. "What is it?" I asked.

He shook his head and removed his hand. I bit my lip, thinking about telling him about Eddie Tompkins and having called Detective Collins; maybe he could use a diversion, and maybe I should tell him I'd been riding a roller coaster ever since Harry died, that I was noticing strange coincidences. But that would be a big load on him when he was clearly already overloaded. Trouble is, I was no good at it anyway; true confessions of my private fears hadn't worked with Joe the few times I'd tried, and I'd given up on that route of personal revelation. Anyhow, except for Harry, what was there to really tell? One of the reasons Andre had gone through two actress wives was that they didn't know how to shut up. Somehow he hadn't taken that into account before he married them. I was the exception. So talking now probably wouldn't help either of us. I decided to let things lie quietly—if unsettled—where they were.

"I hope this works out for you, Andre."

"Ah, yes. You did a wonderful reading this afternoon." I stiffened. "Carola thought me remiss not to say so. Now I have. Thank you."

"Was she with you tonight?"

"Carola?" I nodded. He hesitated. "No, she was not." He gave me that look again, like he was drilling past my head into some other part of me, searching for something that was lost. "It's late," he finally said. We turned out the lights and headed for the bedroom, leaving the brandy glasses where they were.

As we brushed our teeth at our separate sinks, I thought of Harry again, and I remembered what I'd wanted to ask him. "Andre, why were you so glad that day I was going to lunch with Harry?"

"Was I?" he asked, neatly spitting toothpaste suds into his sink.

"Yes. C'mon, you were gleeful."

"Harry was good for you."

"*For* me or *to* me?"

"Both."

"Harry Machin, deal-maker of the earth?"

"Perhaps you underestimated him."

"You didn't think I was going back, to sign—"

He touched my neck, stopping on his way to the bedroom. "I was glad for an old comrade, *if* I was glad."

I finished my nightly face routine and went to bed. Andre was already asleep. I lay in the dark thinking about Lucille, then about Eddie Tompkins, and then Detective Collins's image stood in front of me. They drifted in and out as I slipped off to sleep. One thought stuck: It was only by accident—or coincidence—that I overheard Sharif in the lobby, when my passkey died, and learned of the fire and Lucille Trevor's fate. On that unresolved note, I fell asleep.

I lingered in bed next morning. Andre was up; I barely heard him make a pot of coffee, and then he was gone for the day. The sun sneaked past the curtains in a single blinding beam trained right on my eyes. I sank deeper under the down quilt. As usual all was quiet around me. I could stay in bed all day if I wanted, nestled in warm nothingness. Eventually I jumped up to open the curtains and skittered back into bed. I could see a bit of the hills past the coral tree, nearly denuded now of red flowers. Birds were busy chirping and doing whatever they did all day. I felt safe in bed, on a fluffy island that would dissolve once my toes hit the carpet. I finally got up for good to put on a pot of tea. It was ten o'clock.

I turned the computer on and washed up. My plan was to find Lucille's obit and any other scraps I could on the ill-fated actress. The miserable house phone rang as I was dressing. The call was from the front desk, not Sharif—Phil, I think it was—letting me know I had a package and did I want it sent up to the room. I said yes and quickly finished dressing. Arturo knocked on my door a few minutes later with a box, the long kind you'd expect to see flowers come in, only this was a brown box that had gone through the mail. Inside that box was a long white flower box, and inside that were two dozen roses, but the roses were burned dead and three Mexican Day of the Dead dolls lay next to the long, thorny stems. One doll was in a tux, another in a white gown, à la Carol Channing in *Hello, Dolly!* with a wide-brimmed satin hat and feathers, and the third was a sexy Barbie-doll type with a pile of big brown hair.

That trip to Mexico with Fits was the first time I'd seen Day of the Dead dolls. I fell in love with the idea of celebrating the dead: Mexicans partying on graves. lighting candles, eating cake and candy shaped like skulls, playing music and singing and dancing the whole night, a fiesta for the buried. I bought my first doll on that trip. Every time I've been down since I've picked up a few more. There's a small collection in the New York loft. Who here besides Andre and Fits knew that? I looked for a card. There was none.

Was Fits playing a joke? Or was Eddie taking revenge on me for calling the cops? Why the seared rose petals? They broke apart when I touched them. It looked as if they'd once been red and yellow passion roses before someone took a blow torch to them. Ow! I pricked my finger on a thorn. I watched a globule of deep red blood form and widen, and sucked it out.

I walked out onto the balcony, then walked quickly back inside again. The day was warming nicely, a lovely spring morning. I wanted to let the fresh air in but closed and locked the balcony door. As I was drawing the glass curtains closed—which I never did during the day—I noticed White Shirt hanging two sets of sheets out on his line. I watched until he was done. He leaned over the railing, over his garage, before turning and moving out of sight. I'd been neglecting White Shirt. When Andre was on nights I sometimes sat outside with a candle lit on the balcony table, bundled in my coat to enjoy the night. It would be colder in New York, I'd tell myself, so I might not feel as chilled sitting there. Most nights one or two of the searchlights were busy sweeping the Hollywood sky, suggesting red carpets and glitz. I'm sure White Shirt could see me those nights, or at least my little candle flickering in the dark.

Could White Shirt have sent the roses?

I decided the strange delivery qualified as "getting the hairs up" and dialed the Detective. He was quiet a minute on his end. "No idea who sent the flowers?"

"Look, they were burned on purpose; this isn't a friendly *Thinking of you* delivery. . . . And it's not my anniversary." I heard a hint of something like alarm in my voice, but I didn't feel alarmed. If I felt anything it was way underneath, and it ran along the lines of wanting something to go away or not be true, like information I didn't want but that wanted me.

"Yeah. All right, I can get there around noon, maybe sooner."
Was he coming on his lunch hour? "Meantime, sit tight. Don't go
out or let anyone in. And don't touch the roses. Got it?"

I said yes, and we hung up.

I went to the kitchen to put on a second pot of tea, mostly for
something to do so I wouldn't have to stare at the dead roses. As I
stood, breaking the rule about watching the pot boil, I replayed the
tape of Eddie Tompkins calling out to me: *"Miss Thrush! Ardennes!*
Please, a minute . . . I only want to talk. . . . I'm a good actor. . . ."

The first time that happened, someone calling out to me so fa-
miliarly in public, I jerked my head around to see who it could be,
what unexpected friend had shown up and was calling me. It was at
an affair in New York, the Museum of Modern Art's Film Department. I was becoming a known entity and, as a New York actor, had
been invited as a VIP guest. All the New York actors were out that
night for whatever the gala or charity was all about. It was autumn,
a crisp evening with golden hues. I was in three-inch heels beneath
a new at-the-knee-length dress and light cashmere coat. Harry had
been after me to advance my wardrobe for just such evenings and to
quit saying no to every invitation I received. I'd spent some money
on my hair too. The do at the MoMA that night must have been
pretty special because Joe was with me. He turned his head too
when my name was called. I was holding on to him for dear life, not
to break my legs in the shoes (he'd mocked them the whole way
across town in the cab I'd insisted on taking—he would have put us
on a crosstown bus with a free transfer to the downtown bus). The
voice sounded familiar, but it turned out to be a press person, a
paparazzo calling from the middle of the street, from behind the
flimsy police barricade at the museum entrance. He wanted me
to turn around for a photo. I stopped. I was terribly polite then,

inexperienced. He yelled, asking what my plans were: "Any big movies coming up, Ardennes?" I shook my head, and Joe pulled me inside. The guy was instantly on to the next personality. I think I remember it was Susan Sarandon coming in after me.

"What bullshit!" Joe let out once we were inside. "There's a bar here, right?"

I was startled. I'd bet my jaw was hanging open in the photo. "I thought he must know me, calling like that. That's really very rude."

"Rude, yeah. You're a public commodity now. This is what you wanted, right?" Of course he disapproved and it was my fault and I wasn't able to get him to go to another event like that again, except Cannes. I never got used to that unwelcome familiarity. So when Eddie called me by my first name I had the same sensation of invasion, of ownership just because I worked in the movies, only Eddie was more persistent.

I turned the tea water off and phoned Fits.

"Hey, darlin'," he said in a too-loud voice.

I pulled the phone away from my ear and examined it for a second as if it might bite. "Fits? It's Ardennes. . . ."

"The lady from the forest; how do, sugar poo?" I didn't say anything. "Funny, I was thinking about you this very morning, lying in bed. You know those are the best moments of the day; you leave the dream world and see yourself for a clear few seconds sans the accumulated lifetime of bullshit on top. Best time to figure things out. So there I was with you on my mind—"

"Fits, listen—"

"Not like that, baby. I was thinking, maybe Ardennes got it right walking away. This business is full of shit."

"Well, there's plenty of that going around. Politicians, religious leaders . . ."

"But in Hollywood it's systemic. 'What do you do? Me, I enter-
tain.' It's a lousy charade, and you figured it out."

"Not exactly," I said. "It's not like I became a brain surgeon in
Rwanda, saving people. What's with the cowboy act, Fits? Have you
been drinking?"

"Certainly not! I'm gearing for a part. You couldn't tell? That's
not good," he added, sotto voce.

Oh, the hoops a good actor leaps through to get at a part. Even
Fits, who rarely had the lead, prepared hard no matter how small the
role. Too many actors were bums that way, doing the obvious, rely-
ing on eye-candy looks, playing at it; a charade, like Fits said. To
prepare for *Separation and Rain* I stood outside in a rainstorm for
twenty minutes in just my panties. My nipples hurt for a week after
that, a wonder I didn't catch my death. It rains in nearly every scene
in the film, and every character got to make a comment on the
weather: classic Lucerne.

"Interesting part?" I asked.

"Not bad; an indie about a director who fakes his own death—
comedy. Pay stinks, of course."

Fits had seen my enchanted response in Mexico when I'd bought
my first Day of the Dead Doll. I'd said to him, "This is the kind of
ritual I could sink my teeth into: drama, emotion, fun, and death.
How can you improve on that?" And Fits had shot back: "The gay
Halloween parade in the Village?"

"So, thanks for the bouquet."

"What bouquet?"

"C'mon, Fits, very funny."

"Ard, baby, you lost me."

"You didn't send me a bouquet of dead roses?"

"Someone did?"

"Hang on, Fits." I heard tapping on my door, brittle, like long fingernails. "Someone's at the door, I gotta go." The Detective, I guessed.

"I didn't send any dead flowers," Fits said. He sounded like himself again, not the character he'd be playing. I said okay and hung up.

I called out softly, "Detective?"

The tapping came again, and I got up sneaky-like and tiptoed to the door. I looked out the peephole, and there stood Sylvia Vernon, Mucho tucked under her arm, his eyes staring like big black marbles.

"Oh, Sylvia, give me a second," I said through the door. I had to hide the box of dead flowers the Detective told me not to touch. Never mind his telling me not to let anyone in. I moved the box very carefully over to the bed, shut the louvered blinds on either glass door and closed them tight. I trotted back to the front door, pulling my cotton sweater off partway, seemingly pulling it over my head as I opened the door. "Sorry, Sylvia, I overslept—you caught me off to a late start. Come in."

She clacked her low-heeled slingbacks across the kitchen tiles and into the sitting room, where she planted herself on the couch, placing Mucho on the floor. The dog made a beeline for the bedroom doors. Watching Mucho, Sylvia said, "What? Ya have a man in there?"

I laughed. "Two." I laughed again, forced this time. "The bed's not made."

Sylvia smoothed her white capris, crossing her legs, and drew a cigarette pack out of a sweater pocket. From another pocket she located a black holder with a ring of rhinestones where the cigarette fit in. "I thought I heard Arturo," she said, fitting a cigarette into the holder. "I'm getting a late start myself this morning or I would have nabbed him. Something's going on with my fridge." She had a sultry kind of drawl I hadn't noticed in her speech before. I was thinking how to tell her it would be better if she didn't smoke, but she didn't light up. "I quit," she explained, "but only after the doctor held a gun to my head." She held the cigarette and holder in her left hand as if she were between puffs.

The full-time residences aren't entitled to maid service, though the owners are obliged to keep up maintenance. I'd heard a rumor the family who owned the property was looking to sell the thirteen-acre Muse parcel. Quarrels among the heirs, Sharif had let it be known. I brought that up, asking Sylvia if she knew the place might be sold, and would that be a problem for her.

"Renter laws are pretty protective in Los Angeles. They'd have trouble kicking us all out. They're not letting anyone else in, I can tell you that. Next to and above me are locked up empty, downstairs too. Only you and me on this floor, and that film fellow at the other end of the landing. Plans are to renovate, but why bother if you're selling?"

"Don't they lose money having them sit empty?"

"They're losing anyhow. The restaurant's in trouble, hardly any patrons some nights."

I was stalling before pouncing on what I wanted to know: Lucille and the fire and what Sylvia knew. "I was just putting up a pot of tea. Care for some?"

"Never touch the stuff. If you have coffee I'd be tempted."

"I have," I said. I went around the corner to make some, figuring I'd join Sylvia in a cup. I thought I heard her moving. She said something, and I turned the water off. "Did you say something, Sylvia?"

"I was just telling Mucho to leave off the bedroom."

"Oh." I glanced around the corner just in time to see Sylvia sit back down.

I brought out the coffees, skim milk, sugar and a couple of croissants from the lobby breakfast I'd stuck in the freezer, they microwaved soft in a hurry. I had packets of the hotel cherry jam too, napkins; a nice little setup.

"These from below? They don't let us in on those goodies either," Sylvia said, eyeing the croissants. She helped herself, smearing each bite with jam.

"Sylvia, did you know . . . I heard there'd been a fire next door—years ago—and I think an actress died."

"What of it?"

"Just curious." I went for nonchalance.

"I watched a couple of your films the other day," she said, changing the subject. "You weren't bad." She didn't look at me while paying the compliment.

"So they say."

"Mucho, come here!" The dog was not letting go of the bedroom doors, sniffing at the carpeted threshold like he was on to a bag of bones. He did not obey his mistress but began to dig at the carpet. Sylvia took a hard pull on her unlit cigarette. "There was a fire all right," she said, as if she hadn't just shifted topics. "I stayed with Lucille sometimes when I came in from Vegas. That was the actress who died, Lucille Trevor. We first hooked up when she came out to the casino for a film, a revue number. I coached the gals how to dance in pasties and boas. She was the lead dancer but only a bit part in the movie."

"So she could still dance?"

Sylvia's eyes met mine, hers silvery blue and cold as ice. I lowered mine to the floor. I was caught red-handed, and stupid to boot.

"Then you already knew about Lucille? Why ask me?"

Let's see if I could act my way out of this one. Play it cool, hold her gaze, steady, calm. I forced my eyes to stay on hers. They burned, and I fought not to blink. "I'm working on a book, well, researching one, about Hollywood actresses." I glanced at the dog still sniffing the bedroom doors. "Not the famous ones . . . more, what about all those girls who come out here with a dream only to end badly?"

"Plenty of dreams don't make it, probably most. What happened to yours?"

I was beginning to see the brassy side of Sylvia Vernon. I glanced up at the clock on top of the TV cabinet. The Detective would be here soon. I had to get rid of her. "Mustn't have been all that interesting," I said, going for I-couldn't-care-less.

"And Lucille's was?" She tossed me that icy stare again.

I stood up. "Sylvia, I have an appointment. . . . I'm sorry to cut this short. . . ." (What a rotten exit line: an appointment?)

Sylvia stood too and Mucho came running. She bent down to pick him up. "No worries. You should stop by, visit the scene of the—accident. If you stand in the closet with the door closed tight, you can faintly smell smoke still stuck in the walls." She angled her head back, looking up at me, watching my face. I turned and walked to the door.

"She was a beauty," Sylvia said, stopping in the doorway. "Thanks for the hospitality," she added, her tone more snarl than farewell.

I closed the door quietly behind her. Oh, boy, did I blow it. "Dammit, Ardennes!" I quickly gathered the coffee cups and plates and loaded them into the sink. I ran to the bedroom to carry the box of dead roses back into the sitting room. My cell phone rang and I left the white box on the bed to find the phone on the dining table. I dropped the brown mailing carton on a chair as I said hello.

Detective Collins was on the other end. "I'll be there in ten minutes," he said.

"You remember the gate combination?"

"Of course."

I put the phone down on the side table and saw Sylvia's rhinestone cigarette holder, almost hidden behind the vase of lilies. One of the long white petals had fallen off. The cigarette was gone. I remembered her placing it on the saucer, wasting a perfectly good smoke. I ran to the bedroom and dropped the holder into the desk drawer. Then I ran to the kitchen to wash the dishes to be rid of any trace of Sylvia's visit. I'd disobeyed the Detective by letting her in. Curiosity—Lucille—had killed that cat. The last of the crumbs was wiped away when the Detective tapped lightly on the door.

The same thing happened when I opened the door to Detective Collins as the last time: the size and presence of the man caught me. He wasn't *that* big; there was just that . . . je ne sais quoi. I smiled and waved him in, thanking him again for coming.

He looked around. I guess cops do that automatically, like thieves who can't help casing any room they enter. "You have company?"

"What?"

"That stink's not your perfume."

"Oh. The maid must have sprayed something." Now I was lying to him. That would be the maid he'd told me not to have in. "Yesterday, I mean."

"Uh-huh. So, where's this package got you all hopped up?"

It was on the rumpled bed I'd lingered in, exposed now like an invitation to random lust. "I'll bring it here," I said, moving quickly to the bedroom.

"No, you will not," he said, following me just as fast. He lightly pushed me aside and leaned over the box and the tangled bed. The lid was only resting, not all the way closed. He slipped on a pair of latex gloves picked out of his pocket and gingerly lifted the lid, which he placed next to the box. He fished around carefully inside. Dried petals fell at the slightest touch. He felt beneath the green florist's paper. "No note?"

I shook my head. "Watch the thorns." A couple more petals fell away as he lifted one of the Day of the Dead dolls. "I sort of collect those," I volunteered.

He gave me a hard look and replaced the doll. "No name on the box. This how it was delivered?"

"No, it was mailed. That box is on the chair." I indicated the dining chair by the balcony door.

The Detective nodded. He walked over to the mailing carton with me following like a nervous cat. "Any return address?"

I was close enough to him to feel his body heat. "Nothing familiar." There was a Los Angeles postmark, but the last digit was blurry. The return address was from down toward San Diego, Corona Del Mar.

"Probably fake," the Detective said of the address. "Unless you know anyone from there?" I did not. He took out a pad and pen and copied the post office numbers and return address.

"What about fingerprints?" I asked.

The Detective removed the latex gloves and put them back into his pocket. "Too many people touched things to bother. And, look, anonymously sent dead flowers don't constitute a crime." He paused as if to punctuate what came next. "Okay, here's the deal: I talked to my boss—" My brows went together; I made a gesture, a pushing-something-away motion with my hands. "Just hear me for a second." There was a slight eagerness in his tone, just a fragment. "He caught on before I did: Sure, it was Harry Machin's death brought you to Beverly Hills precinct, but you're—were—an actor and felt safer talking to a cop you'd already had dealings with—"

"I thought you said there was no crime. Eddie was nothing, the phone calls are nothing, and maybe my husband sent the flowers!" I was speaking way too loud.

"Could he have?"

"*No!*"

"What you need is discretion and to feel safe, and I've got the okay to do that."

"You've got the okay from your captain to make me feel safe? What does that mean?"

"You're afraid."

"I am *not* afraid." But that wasn't true. I was, right down to my knees, into my skin, my DNA, and he knew it before I did. I felt a case of the hiccups coming on. I suddenly wanted to talk to Joe. I wanted his suspicions of the system, wanted him to tell me what did I expect from the vicious world I'd chosen; why was I even talking to the cops? Fits had just said it: a business full of phonies, and now someone was sending me dead flowers and hanging up on me and who knew what with Eddie . . . Harry dead like that! It wasn't until the Detective was standing next to me holding up a paper napkin from the table that I realized tears were streaming down my face. This must be what they call weeping. I hiccupped. "I'm sorry," I whispered. I took the napkin and blew my nose and shook my head. "I'm sorry," I said again. Apparently that was all I could think of to say.

"What do you have to be so sorry about?"

Was that the cop talking? I looked up, I couldn't be sure if he was seriously concerned or being on-duty polite. Sincere won,

I guess, because he took my chin in his hand. He did it with such authority. Hold me, I thought. I did not say those words out loud, but he folded me into his arms and did just that. I pretty much did the rest, responding to him with everything I had.

He placed his hands on my hips and ran them up, then down my torso, slowly, like a blind man reading Braille, his fingertips taking in my length, my curves, my folds. His hands were warm over my sweater. He moved lower onto my loose linen pants and the sides of my thighs. I pulled away. He pulled me back, firmly, and I got a good whiff of whatever he put on in the morning: shaving cream, deodorant, and maybe cologne. I was glad I'd closed the curtains. His back faced the balcony door; one of the dining chairs was pushing into my back, or I was being pushed into it. That was when I saw Grant Stuart's passkey lying innocently on the table.

"Not in here," I said, my voice low. The Detective put his mouth over mine, and I ate into his greedily. "Hang on, Billy," I said when we were done with the kiss.

"Billy?"

"No one ever told you you look like William Holden?"

"No."

I held Grant's passkey up for him to see. I grabbed my passkey and said, "Come with me." The Detective hesitated. I stood by the door, opened it and checked both directions. To get into Grant's room we would be briefly exposed at the landing; it couldn't be helped. For all I knew Alma was in the room right now cleaning. There was the chance Grant was not on set and was in there himself. I'd say I was coming for the printer if he was. For someone who'd been reasonably faithful, I was suddenly scheming like a pro. The Detective came to the doorway. I held up my palm, then fast-walked to Grant's door and inserted the key. The green light came on, and I pushed the door open.

His room was a large single, a small sitting area with two stuffed armchairs, a couple of low tables, and a TV cabinet like mine. The wall to the left was full-length mirrored closet doors ending in a tiny kitchen alcove with a sink, countertop two-burner stove, coffee maker, and below-the-counter refrigerator. The bathroom came next, and the king-sized bed opposite, behind the sitting area. The balcony drapes were closed. A small desk on that side of the room held papers and the printer. Grant was a very neat guy, not a single personal item lying around. I turned and waved the Detective in. I watched him slink down the corridor like a big tomcat on the hunt. He hooked the do-not-disturb sign on the door, closed and locked it. The bed was made, but the Detective chose the floor.

My heart raced as he removed my top and next the linen pants. I stood still while he got out of the overcoat and jacket. I hadn't seen the gun before this. He yanked off the holster and laid the piece carefully over his jacket. I loosened his tie while he unbuttoned his shirt.

We made good use of the carpeted floor. When he entered me, easy at first, I was a tingle of open nerves, a mix of excitement and feel-bad all over because this was a strange body inside my body. Why the hell I thought of Joe at that particular moment when it was Andre I was betraying is anybody's guess, but none of that lasted too long because I wanted what the strange body was doing like a desert wants rain. I could feel as lousy as I wished to later on.

I didn't count on him being so tender when it was over, but he was. He got up and found a towel in the bathroom for me to use. He sat back down on the floor next to me and watched my face like a man, not a cop. I was afraid he'd say something, but he didn't. He touched my hair and finally did say, "You have a lot of it, a brown halo."

I lay with my head on my arm, looking up at him. "What *is* your name?"

"Devin—Irish, of course, a cop. The Gaelic is fawn, stag, or ox."

"Which are you?"

"Take your pick, depending on the time of day."

"My first husband was Irish. . . . I don't know why I said that."

"No crime in it."

I laughed.

He reached for his shorts and white undershirt and stood up. He looked even more Billy Holden in his underwear. I was partially covered with the bath towel, but he studied what he could see of me as he dressed. He'd lifted the tie over his head, so he only had to loop it back on and tighten it. I watched him replace the holster and the gun and then the jacket. He was back on the job.

He helped me to my feet and I looked around for my panties, but froze hearing a voice outside. Someone had stopped just outside the door. I felt my heart fall about a mile and thump as it landed. I pictured Grant walking in on the director's wife, naked as sin next to a man wearing a gun. Then I heard Sylvia say, "Mucho, quiet," real low. She seemed to linger at the door. The Detective moved next to the wall, so if the door opened he would be ready. I heard the low clack of Sylvia's heels on the landing, then die down on the carpeted corridor to her apartment, past my suite, and then her door bang shut.

"Just my neighbor and her dog," I whispered. Now all the Detective and I had to do was sneak back to my rooms. Well, I did anyhow.

Once I was dressed he signaled me to be quiet. He opened the door a crack, then wider, and gave me the okay, wordlessly telling me to go first and open my door. I ran back for the sex-soiled towel and took it with me. He waited until my door was unlocked and I was inside. There was no noise from Sylvia, so I waved him in, but he waited a minute before coming down the corridor. I was thinking, now what? I'd just done a cop on my husband's second assistant director's floor. I had to hand it to myself for knowing how to complicate my life. I watched the complication walk toward me; at least I'd picked a hot one.

The Detective walked inside and I shut us in, quiet as I could. He went out on the balcony and looked over the railing wall in both directions. He came back in and asked if I wanted to get some coffee. I asked about the box of dead flowers. We put them back in the mailing box and tucked the lot up on a high back shelf in the walk-in closet, all the while not saying a word to each other. I grabbed a hat, scarf, key, wallet and my phone, and we walked outside. I was on automatic pilot. I'd wanted to replace Grant's towel with a clean one of mine, but the Detective said to do it later. We walked to his car in the visitor's slot, and he opened the passenger-side door for me to get in. Just then Alma came out of one of the rooms opposite, where there was a landing and a short flight of stairs to the driveway. She was holding a bundle of dirty white sheets. Our eyes met; she smiled. I waved. She took in the Detective as she closed the door behind her. Great.

We drove past Highland and left onto Ivar, then up to Yucca, where the Detective parked illegally, placing an LAPD card in the window. We walked to an old-time coffee shop just off the corner, a place only an insider would know about. A line of booths, long lunch counter, and wide blinds along the windows to keep the sun out. The decor was Formica and plastic, and either lunch was over or business was slow. We took a booth, and a puffy blond waitress came over with two menus. "Haven't seen the likes of you around here lately, Dev." She smiled as she spoke, not wide so much as knowing.

He nodded. "I don't get over here much anymore."

The waitress passed me a hard-to-read but not unfriendly glance as she handed me a menu. "You want to know what's good today?"

"Nah. Cheeseburger, fries, coffee. A couple'a extra pickles," the Detective said, handing back the menu.

She turned her waiting eyes on me. I don't eat much red meat. Andre eats none, but I was suddenly hungry as a wild beast for hard-core protein. "I'll have the same, only no coffee. Do you make shakes?" She nodded. "Vanilla, please."

"How do you like that burger done?" She meant me; apparently she didn't need to ask Devin Collins how he liked his.

"Medium," I said.

Now what? Were we supposed to make small talk, like what just happened on the hotel floor hadn't happened? Were we supposed to explore its meaning, linger in its glow? Or should we discuss what was going on with me and how I was going to be made to feel safe? It was pretty clear discreet was out.

"I lived over here," the Detective said. I felt he was letting me know he hadn't slept with the waitress. *If* he hadn't. I didn't say anything to the news. "I was downtown—homicide—and it wasn't a bad commute."

"What happened before . . ." I started to say, but I didn't know what to call him: Devin, Detective, Billy?

He cut in, not done yet with what he had to say: "I shot a guy, a known killer wanted for a list as long as my arm. Trouble is, he was unarmed, his gun just out of reach. I didn't aim to kill, only to take his shooting arm out. Police commissioner thought my actions a little too Harry Callahan and moved me over to Beverly Hills burglary. No one was sorry to see the bad guy go down, only nobody else wanted to do the job."

I didn't know anyone who shot at people. At least not for real, I only knew movie bullets. For a second I thought he was making it up; that would be the tone deafness actors can get for real events. "Did he die?"

He glanced over the mug of coffee the waitress had set down in front of him, steam rising. "I got what I aimed for, so no. He went to jail, where he resides to this day."

"I should be impressed—"

"My wife was killed on the 10 just prior to the shooting. A pileup on a foggy afternoon."

"That's too bad." I looked over the menu again like I'd forgotten something, and then up at Billy (Billy's what I'd settled on). "You don't have to tell me any of this."

"Just saying why I left the neighborhood, how being transferred out of downtown to Beverly Thrills was a result of my being too mad at the bad guy, or at something."

"About your wife?"

"The marriage stunk; at least for her it did. Pretty much we were spared divorce proceedings." He pulled a toothpick out of a pocket and carefully unwrapped the paper covering, just to be doing something with his hands, it seemed. "She was on her way to her boyfriend's in Santa Monica when the tractor-trailer took her and five others. No winners."

"Oh."

"So, sure: No explanations required, I'm just telling you how I stand." He gave me a that-means-you look. Only it seemed to me he had just explained a lot.

The waitress came with our order. There was a big pile of fries next to an old-style flat burger patty. I pulled the bit of paper off the straw end and took a long suck on thick, cold vanilla shake. I looked up to find the Detective watching me. It was the first time I'd seen him smile.

I took a big bite of burger after loading up on ketchup. "Mm, this is so good." Billy nodded, chewing. "So," I said, my mouth full of meat, "this guy's dad is about to turn ninety and he wants to give him a really special birthday gift. So he hires a call girl—good looking, classy—and takes his dad to the hotel. Only Dad's just feeling old. His show is on TV, he tells his son, kind of cranky. 'C'mon, Dad,' the son says. 'You don't turn ninety every day.' So they shuffle down the hotel hallway, and the son, turning to leave, tells his dad, 'Go ahead and knock on the door.' The call girl was told to say, 'I'm the special on your special day!' She does, and the old guy stands in the doorway. 'The special?' he says. 'I'll just have the soup.'"

"That was a joke?" the Detective said, perfectly deadpan.

4

Andre's Troubles

A tree stands outside Andre's New York loft. Soho doesn't have a whole lot of trees, and this one—I have no idea what it's called—took off so that by the time I came along as Andre's third attempt at until-death-do-us-part, it had already grown up as high as the fourth floor. In summer the crime lights backlit the leaves orange-gold at night. Mornings I looked out at leafy branches sunlit a pale green, with sparrows chirping and twittering on and off all day long, sounding like things were all right with them. That tree made me feel okay living in the loft, and I started worrying that it would somehow die. Cities are hard on trees, and lately there was the long-horned Asian beetle killing certain types, maples mostly. The Parks Department started cutting them down to prevent the beetle spreading. Even big old trees in Central Park were axed as a precaution. That seemed like a pretty failed remedy to me, but maybe amputation was better than a chemical attack, some sort of tree chemo that would take out even more greenery and do who knew what to the birds and maybe to people too.

I'd been talking about buying a small house upstate, maybe in the Catskills. I've got plenty of money lying around, and I spend very little of it. Andre didn't want me to kick in on the loft payments. He had no mortgage and maintenance was low for New York. He'd bought the place from an artist at a time when it was still possible to get a good deal downtown, before Soho turned into one giant designer mall. Andre wasn't interested in a country place. He wasn't against the idea either. We'd had good visits to friends' places up north, taking walks, spending casual afternoons on long days that didn't translate into his wanting a commitment. "Were you thinking of working on your book? Because you could rent a house for that," he said the last time the topic came up, before he left to start his movie. Renting would be a sensible way to see what I liked. But what did sensible mean to me? What about my existence pointed with any certainty to making straight-ahead, logical sense?

As for my imaginary book, to Andre's expectant look I said, "I suppose the country would be a good place to write." I was fibbing, though not entirely; I hadn't said a country house for *me* to write in. He nodded and busied himself with something else. Discussion closed.

My dad caught me smoking once. The other kids at school were experimenting and I went along. I'd gone into the vacant maid's room, beyond the kitchen, not counting on the smoke being noticeable through the closed door. I was apparently too dumb to open a window. It was a Saturday, about a year or so before my dad died. He showed up after I'd already nearly choked to death inhaling and flushed the butt down the toilet. He came into my room and asked me if I'd been smoking. I said no. It must have been so obvious. He said okay, that I shouldn't take up the habit, but to tell him if I was considering the idea. A little while later I confessed. He'd been so damn nice about it; I'd almost wished he'd accused me so I could have acted out, belligerent and tough. But that wasn't his style, and I couldn't let the lie stand between us. It wasn't Andre's style to accuse either, but with him I didn't have so much trouble letting a lie stand.

I can't say why I thought I wanted a house in the country. I can't even arrange flowers in a vase, so the idea of gardening meant hiring someone, not me getting out a hoe, goatskin gloves and knee pads. I wasn't about to take up a hobby, and I certainly wasn't going to write a damn book. I'd just see that tree outside the loft window and wonder if life wouldn't be better surrounded by green. Even in winter it seemed special to have a tree alive and breathing tree breath, connected with deep roots meandering under cement and macadam, poking and pushing through whatever stood in its way, branches reaching up to a cluttered sky, eating the light and drinking the rain. It made me happy knowing the tree stuck with it. Did that translate into a bucolic life in the country? If I had a house in the mountains, I might be there now instead of showering in the middle of a Los Angeles afternoon after having randomly slept with one of L.A.'s finest.

I'd run for the shower as soon as the Detective dropped me off. Tossed my clothes onto the floor and headed for the hot water. I couldn't get out of the car fast enough. He took my arm and said he'd be in touch. I said, "Okay, Billy," and he let go. As I scrubbed I tried not to picture us together, though I could not deny the pleasure, the hunger I'd—or we'd—sated on Grant's floor. I wasn't trying to wash him away so much as do the polite thing by Andre and at least rinse away the odor of sex. There wasn't going to be a second time, of that I'd make certain. I was conveniently forgetting that the Detective was in my life now, on the case for what was beginning to look to me like not much more than creepiness. He'd said himself no laws had been broken so far, and no one had threatened me in any direct way. Creeping a person out with dead flowers is, by itself, not a crime. All I could conclude was that somebody wanted to get my attention.

Wrapped in a towel, I sat down at the computer to look into flights back to New York. Running away would solve plenty. Assuming my creep was L.A. based, I'd be free of him, and that would take me away from the Detective too, of us entangling ourselves further. And I wouldn't have to face Andre knowing what I knew about what I'd done—which wasn't much. I could also go to Jamaica; that was something to consider.

I never deceived Joe. We didn't need anyone else to satisfy us. We were chaste that way, wanting only each other. We crashed in flames and burned our love to death. You don't get that kind of purity twice.

My hands dropped into my lap. "Joe," I whispered. I still had the occasional sex dream starring Joe.

I sat like that for several minutes. I wondered if he'd seen Harry's obit in the papers, if he knew he was dead. If somehow my name had come up in anything he'd read or heard. If he cared anymore one way or the other what befell me, who I slept with or where I went.

"Why not?" I'd said to his long-ago objection to my signing with Harry. "Do you know how big Machin Talent is? Huge, that's how big. Harry takes on very few clients. He *invests* in his actors. I'll get work, Joe, real work."

"Sure, you will," Joe said. "But what does that mean?"

"What do you mean, what does it mean? I'm going to have a

crack at some plum parts. I'll make us some decent money for a change—well, there's no guarantee of that, but it's certain I've reached as far as I can on the route I'm on now. Oh, Joe, if I can bring in better money, you won't have to do electric work ever again! You'll be free to write full-time."

"I don't mind doing electrical when I have to, and I can write like I do now."

I didn't understand. It was a conversation we'd had a hundred different ways a thousand different times and were not able to cross a bridge to understand what to do. Joe didn't say what he really wanted me to do, and I only saw what I thought was the road to where I was supposed to go, where I *wanted* to go. If he'd said to me, don't do this, don't sign with Harry, don't be an actress in movies, what would I have done? But he couldn't because he didn't believe in telling me what to do—not directly. I was free to make mistakes, which he must have thought I was doing most of the time. I didn't want him to say it outright either because then I'd have to choose—which I did anyway, didn't I? So we danced around the question until events took over and the question no longer mattered and the dance stopped. So why do I feel like I'm still stuck on the same dance floor? And what in hell did I just do with Detective Collins?

I dipped my forehead into my left hand. Oh, what have I done?

I glanced to the right and saw Grant's dirtied towel lying discarded on the floor just inside the bathroom. "Christ!"

I looked back at the computer screen: Find a flight to New York tonight or sooner, I told myself. I could be packed in five minutes. But that wasn't what I did because when I hit my bookmarks I saw Lucille's name in capital letters and hit that instead. Presto, I was back at the newspaper piece about the car wreck and Lucille's blown ballet dreams. That toggled in my mind with Sylvia saying, *I coached the gals how to dance in pasties and boas. She was the lead dancer but only a bit part in the movie.*

What? That couldn't be right; no one would cast a girl who'd had two broken legs *as a dancer*, certainly not half naked in a Vegas lineup. Sylvia made that up. She lied. Why? What was Sylvia up to when I went into the kitchen? What was Mucho so interested in at the bedroom door? He practically scratched his way under the carpet. Could he smell the dead flowers? I had that sinking-universe feeling again. . . .

My cell phone pealed out. I found it on the third round of its jingle, fallen off Andre's side of the bed.

I flung myself over and across, commando style, nearly landing head first on the floor. The screen read, ID BLOCKED.

"Hello?"

CLICK.

I felt cold.

I hung over the side of the bed for a minute, naked, feeling the blood rush to my brain. What was that, hang-up number four?

I sat up. The towel I'd wrapped around me was on the floor by the desk. I hung it up in the bathroom, got some underwear and jeans on and a lightweight cashmere sweater. It was three o'clock. I took Grant's towel and balled it up in a corner on the floor by the tub so Zaneda or Alma would take it in the morning. I took an unused towel from my rack and folded it under my arm. I found Grant's passkey next to mine on the table and walked out to the hall and over to his room. I knocked and called out, "Grant?" and waited, called again and unlocked the door. I quickly hung the clean towel in his bathroom and came back out, careful not to look at the place on the floor where I'd lain with the Detective, lain as Bathsheba had with David while Uriah the Hittite was out fighting the war.

I opened the door and Mucho burst into the room. "Mucho! No!"

"Mucho! Come!" Sylvia said almost in unison.

The little rat ran right over and sniffed the place on the floor, then ran back out to Sylvia, who scooped him up just outside Grant's door. The dog looked pleased.

"Frisky little bastard, isn't he?" I said, instantly regretting my anger. "I'm sorry, Sylvia; he frightened me."

Sylvia eyed me, her head back, a wise-to-me look on her pointed face. "I wouldn't wonder," she said. I reached out to pet the dog's head, but he growled, pulling his lips back wide, showing razor-sharp little teeth. I yanked my hand back. "Muchie, don't be a little terror," Sylvia said, offering me a faint smile that looked more like an accusation. I tried to smile back. "That was some fella with you earlier," she added, stroking Mucho's miniature head.

Earlier where? The first problem was what to do with my face. The second was the platoon of lies that were lining up in my head like soldiers on a parade field, arms tight at their sides, prepared to salute the general making his rounds. Maybe that's all an actor ever does: lies. First it's memorizing someone else's words, then it's becoming the character—physically and emotionally: total immersion, consumption, transformation; speaking, moving, inhaling and exhaling that character. And what happens to the real-life actor, the person inside? Swallowed up, dissolved; sits in a corner on hold, an abandoned self watching from the sidelines as the fictional character takes over. An actor can personally be as stupid as a doornail, impossible to converse with, yet speak Shakespeare with eloquence and truth. Good, bad, evil, comic . . . no matter the part as long as the actor is a true vessel bringing the character to life. Is that not the profoundest form of lying, right up there with the sociopaths?

If I were Andre, I'd condescend to Sylvia with Eurosophisticated bemusement. I'd even manage to turn the tables on her. But my lies were stepping up on the field: Lie number one, sir! (A starched salute.) Go on, soldier. He was my cousin, sir! Soldier number two? Sir, my lawyer. Number three? My long-lost brother, sir. Number four? What man, sir? Five? Number six, seven, eight, and nine, et cetera: the plumber; special delivery; the phone guy; my personal trainer; accountant; sir, my physician; sir, a case of mistaken identity . . . you nosy old cow, sir!

The general frowned: At ease, men; company dismissed! Tenhut, two, three, four . . . The general had not lied his way to the top, and he had yet to find anything that frightened him into silence, so he whispered bravely in my ear, and I repeated to Sylvia: "You never met Lucille Trevor in any dance review."

Mucho growled at me. "Shut up!" I said, firm, not loud. I surprised myself giving the miserable runt what for. The beast seemed to settle down in his mistress's arms, as if that was all he needed to hear. Sylvia, on the other hand, did not settle down. She looked to be thinking things over, and the things she was thinking looked to be dark clouds forming across the leathery horizon of her brow.

That was when my phone rang, for once a blessing. I yanked it out of my pants pocket, answered without checking the caller ID, the most innocent of smiles passing over my countenance for Sylvia Vernon's benefit, even a wash of goodwill for petite Mucho. I was off the hook—for now. Clicking Grant's door shut behind me, shrugging as I brushed past her—what could I do, my shrug suggested, I had to take the call—I headed for my room, tossing the casualest of waves over my shoulder toward Sylvia. Ta ta.

The Detective was the second-to-the-last person in the world I wanted to speak to at that moment, Andre being the first. There was a pause between us on the line when I didn't respond to his identifying himself.

He broke it: "There a problem?"

"No." I closed my door.

"Okay . . . a couple of items: That Corona Del Mar address checks out fake, as expected. We got a little lucky on the PO, though. The Hollywood Postal Store is underutilized; in fact they might close the place, so—"

"I've been there. I had to ask three people on the street how to find it, down that underground parking below the Kodak Mall—"

"Right. The clerk remembered the long box because of its odd shape; people don't usually mail flowers USPS. The guy hasn't got much to do—probably bored stiff—and he thought it could be a rifle—maybe a little excitement to his day—but the box didn't have the heft—"

"Did he see who sent it?"

The Detective took a beat. "Gee, I didn't think to ask."

"Sorry."

"It was a kid, maybe twelve years old."

"A *kid?*"

"Probably someone passed him a couple of bucks to drop it off, waited outside and took the receipt. We won't find the kid, but it would be someone seemed trustworthy, not to set off stranger-danger alarms, maybe even someone the kid knew. So it's likely somebody nearby. Could be Eddie."

"Is that what you think?"

"No."

"I don't know anybody nearby."

"Sure, you do; you're just not putting two and two together."

"Thank you."

"For what? It's my job." He was quiet again for a couple of seconds. "That doesn't include what went on earlier. . . ."

"Detective? No explanations required, remember?"

"Sure."

If he had more to say, he wasn't going to get the chance because Andre walked into the suite just then, trailed by Carola, looking more worried than ever. I said into the phone (my liar soldiers back on the job), "Oh, Dottie, Andre just walked in. I'll call you back?" I didn't wait for a reply. I hadn't bought my plane ticket. I hadn't prepared anything for Andre—whatever throes of remorse might hit me—having wanted to take the coward's way out. But never mind all that, what was he doing here at this hour? And he hadn't called first. Shave a couple of hours off and I could have been getting out of Billy's car, or Grant's room. At least I'd showered. I was glad Carola was with Andre so we didn't have to be alone, though they both looked pretty dog-drag miserable. "Andre, is something the matter?" (How could he possibly suspect anything; it *just* happened. . . .)

Andre addressed Carola: "Drink?" She nodded. He pointed to the scotch bottle on the liquor shelf, and she nodded again. "Ardennes?" he asked me.

"No, I don't think so." Andre was quiet as he got ice for two drinks, pouring a hefty amount of scotch into each glass. His face was set hard as he passed Carola hers. Would he confront me with her here? "Andre?"

"Ardennes?"

I felt the pit of my stomach tighten. The way he glanced at me, quick but loaded. How could he know? Did I have guilt smeared all over my face? Could Alma have told? So soon? Not Sylvia? Someone from the production was here; saw me leaving Grant's room with the Detective? Oh, I'd have to come up with something huge. This was awful. . . . I don't think the best actor in the world could lie their way out of this one. Was I going to have to confess? Jump off the balcony? It wasn't as if Andre would start a big wronged-husband row, though he'd probably rather I'd gone to a different location. I just didn't *want* him to *know*.

"I've stopped production," Andre said. He downed his drink, poured another. "Carola, out of the kitchen. Come sit." He was standing at the table. She'd lagged behind near the door, as if she might make a fast dash for it. "Why is it so dark in here?" He pulled back the glass curtains; L.A.'s afternoon brightness spilled over the sitting room.

"You shut down your movie?" That's what this was all about? I almost laughed with relief—but of course it wasn't funny.

Carola sat on the couch, literally on the edge of her seat. I looked from Andre to her and back to Andre. He shrugged. Carola said, her voice barely above a whisper, "Andre—we—fired the actress."

"No!" Fired Luce Bouclé? Oh, boy. This was the stuff tabloids dined on: "Production Halted: Actress Booted out on Her Fanny!" It was something every actor lived in dread of happening to them. I don't think Andre had ever taken such an extreme measure before. I felt almost as if it were me he'd sacked, but maybe that was the other issue, which for the moment, happily, was fully eclipsed.

"Carola, not so gloomy. We are well rid of her; we will shoot around her scenes until she is replaced."

Carola didn't look convinced. They'd probably been shooting around the lead for days. There was the bond company to consider, and how would the producers take the news? The film would begin hemorrhaging money, if it wasn't already. Not to leave out the actress herself: contract broken, her people in a fury. *Variety* and all the other rags would milk the story dry; focus especially, cruelly, on how the actress would try to save face.

"Andre? What will you do?"

"It must be contagious. You are gloomy too, Ardennes? I will find a way." He passed a hand along my guilty back, the same back Detective Collins had recently made his own.

I moved away. "I'll see if there's anything to eat."

"We are not at a funeral, no need for a spread," Andre said, looking into his second drink.

Not quite a funeral, but any way you looked at it the situation was bad. I pictured Jonas Campion taking the news. Producers have heart attacks over less. Campion wasn't the type, but someone under him was going to choke on this one. Andre—if Campion could make it stick.

"You're not concerned?"

"Concerned, not hysterical," Andre replied nasally.

"I'll get some cheese and crackers to go with the drinks," I said, heading into the kitchen.

The Christmas after Daddy died I sat in a chair for hours. I'd refused to go with my mother to my grandmother's, where aunts, uncles and cousins gathered as they always did for a gigantic meal and piles of gifts underneath an enormous, bright-as-day tree. How was I supposed to celebrate? How could my mother? I had no way to know it would be Grandma's last Christmas, and except for some childhood cats I'd had no experience of death.

I was the only one I knew at school who wasn't freaked by the idea of my parents *doing* it. I mean, they didn't paw each other in front of me or act like sloppy teenagers, but they were organic, natural, so I wasn't grossed out by the idea of sex between "old" people. That Christmas my mother was alone for the first time since I'd known her. She must have been dead inside, but it wasn't her way to draw attention to herself. He'd been sick with leukemia, caught too late. After about a year of wasting away the disease suddenly accelerated, and the shock of seeing him gnawed alive from the inside was numbing. I was away at boarding school for most of the ordeal, so I only got to see him that way at Thanksgiving. He was gone the day after I returned to school and I had to turn right around and go back home.

I'd been sent out of the city for the last three years of high school because my mother didn't like the tone of things for city kids those days. I don't think she thought I'd join a gang or anything moronic like that, but to me it felt like I was being hauled off to a Connecticut prison. It was actually all right at the all-girl revue, as we called it; I made more mischief there than I probably would have back in New York. I think Dad didn't like me being sent off either. I was only a two-hour train ride away and I came home any weekend I wanted. Still, I was the only one of my friends to be shipped out.

Woulda, coulda, shoulda had no place in our little household. We were forward-thinkers who treated trouble as a nuisance to be weathered. The line we used when something really bad came along was *At least it's not the Ardennes.* Even when he realized he needed help, way past the subtle, then stronger signs of something wrong, my father said the six months they maybe could have salvaged for him with earlier rounds of chemo was not something to cry over. If he had one regret, it was his first wife. He wished he'd seen more clearly before they married that she was a depressive. Her mental states hurt him and eventually their kids and, of course, her too. He didn't understand depression. Who does? he asked. He regretted too that he probably hadn't cared enough, possessed sufficient compassion to stick by her. She became a cloud over the household. She got custody when they split up because at the time two things were true that aren't any longer: Depression was a matter of bucking up, and children belonged with their mother, almost no matter what.

We had a conversation about all this one time because I told Dad my stepbrother was wacko and had threatened me. "He hates me, Daddy," I said. "Does he have to come here?" I was six, and my stepbrother, Alec, was about to graduate from high school.

"Alec doesn't hate you. He's mixed up," Dad said. "Can you try to be nice to him anyhow?"

"He's mentally ill!" I said. That was what we all said about anybody we didn't like in the first grade. That it might be true was meaningless because I didn't know what the words meant in the first place, but hearing that must have hurt Daddy. Alec was a troubled teen, but he straightened out in the army. He didn't see action like his father, but time stationed in Germany gave him a different perspective, I guess, because he took the GI Bill and became a legal advocate for soldiers. He behaved gently at Dad's funeral. He'd started to look like my father, which was very weird for me at the time. I guess Dad knew his son turned out okay. I don't know.

I didn't mind my half-sister, Arlene, so much. She was older than Alec, so she'd basically always been an adult. I just assumed she'd started out that way and I had trouble with the idea that she was my sister. She always acted surprised when she and Alec came to see Dad—which by the time I was six was nearly never—that there was this little kid running around and that I was *her* half-sister. She painted my finger- and toenails pink once, wedged cotton wads between the toes and told me I had to blow on my hands and feet until the polish dried and to quit squirming. That's pretty much my whole childhood memory of her.

Anyhow, I sat in a chair in my room for hours on end, not turning on a light as Christmas day waned into Christmas night, taking only bathroom breaks and trips down to the kitchen for milk and cookies. I wasn't thinking so much about my father being dead. I was thinking about myself and the promise I'd made him to go college. My mother had gotten me hooked on books early and I figured I could give myself as good a liberal arts education as any school could, and one that would mean something to me, so why should I waste time at a university? Dad wasn't against acting or the arts; he just knew what a tough life it could be. My parents didn't baby-talk me, and they didn't hide trouble when it came, like the insecure times when my father wanted to quit one job for another, or when he struck out on his own with insufficient financial backing. Our family didn't believe finances ruled. There was always enough to live on and sometimes—more often than not—plenty of money for the three of us to live well. If he could take chances, why couldn't I?

So his dying sort of set me free. When my mother came home that night, laden with the gifts I hadn't been there to open, I let her know I'd be saving her a bundle because I wasn't going to school after I graduated. I would have dropped out anyway, I told her, so I was not blaming breaking my promise on Daddy's dying. She looked tired as I made my case, seated in her armchair on the other side of the round lamp table from Dad's armchair, in a corner of the living room with windows that overlooked the Hudson River. The armchairs were raised up on a little triangular platform—like a small stage—with a couple of Persian rugs instead of the wall-to-wall carpeting in the rest of the living room. I think the stage had been there when they'd bought the place, so I was used to it, but none of my friends' apartments had a stage. I stood where I always did, in the middle distance between the king's and queen's armchairs, just at the edge of the platform. It was where I'd stood for years, giving little declarative performances. My parents were my first audience, more so than the typical only child's attention seeking—which I effectively was, growing up. I hadn't sought their approval so much as I secretly watched to see how well I performed vis-à-vis their response. I even think they were complicit, or at least he was, calling me his little thespian when I came to them about a science project or a hated homework assignment, and maybe I hammed it up a little extra to please him. My mother would caution against showing off. Her sense of decorum was her own—not something lifted from a code of etiquette. Julia Thrush's carriage was impeccable right to the end, and, luckily, I inherited that from her, and her long legs. Her modulated voice was clear into her seventies, and she had a melodic laugh. When it came around to teenaged rebellion my problem was more about there being nothing to rebel against than anything they did that I found offensive. I'd slouch on purpose to annoy her; answer Dad in irritated monosyllables, but that didn't last long.

She didn't argue that Christmas night, didn't try to convince me to go to college, waving her hand impatiently when I told her I despised the whole concept of school, gearing up to pitch my case. "Don't use a word like *despise* as if it was chewing gum, Ardennes. And try not to exaggerate; words are powerful tools as they are. What will you do if you don't go to school?"

I glanced at Dad's chair to see how I was going over with him. Naturally part of me was bluffing. I meant what I said, but the prospect still scared me and I was game to being talked out of my decision until maybe summer—I needed a bit of wise resistance to test my resolve, but that was Daddy's job. It's so inconvenient when people die. You can go ahead and imagine what the deceased would say in a given situation, but you're only filling in blanks. Dead means dead. I think it came home to me in that moment, when I needed him to say it was okay for me to break my promise. He probably would have talked me into trying one semester, but he was silenced for keeps. I was on my own.

As I looked at his empty chair my lips began to quiver and my eyes filled with tears and my face got hot and I fell on the floor and threw myself over my mother's lap—drama queen in pain—and cried until I was weak. She kept her hand on my back until the flood subsided, her dress drenched with my hot tears and snot. "Get us each a glass of red wine," she told me when I was played out.

"For real?" I said. We were going to share a glass of wine? *Quelle* sophistication. I was suddenly grown up! That meant being fatherless hardly mattered in that heady moment; it would be Mom and me from now on. And so the two of us made a plan: I'd stay in the Riverdale apartment with her, and I'd audition at the Actors Studio or maybe sign up at HB Studio. If no one would take me I'd find a theater group, some acting venue: hit the sidewalk auditioning for plays all over New York. There were theater groups like weeds back then, from Brooklyn to the Bronx; artists could still live and work on the cheap—the city had not yet been made over in the image of big-box developers artificially ratcheting up rents and profit margins in real estate heaven. We'd give it a year, we agreed, and see where I stood. Then, like an utter child, I sat at my mother's feet and opened my Christmas gifts. My mother gave me Uta Hagen's *Respect for Acting*.

"Mom! You knew all along." I threw my arms around her, ready for another spasm of overwrought emotion.

She gently pushed me off so I was seated on the little stage; a tableau of mother and daughter, father gone missing.

"Ardennes, listen to me. . . ."

I turned my face up in rapt attention; I would obey my queen's every command. "Ardennes, you have a kind of drifting mind . . ." I was no longer rapt. "I can't think of another way to put it. Acting—listen, now—" I was ready to bolt, off the stage, out of the room, race down the hall to my room and slam the door shut behind me. "Steady," my mother said, using the one voice I had yet to disobey, which she used only rarely and which on that day had an added note of fatigue. I heard the note and stopped.

"I'm listening, Mother."

"You have talent to spare; I have no question of that. But you will make things harder for yourself than they have to be."

I had no idea what she meant.

I still don't. My head in the refrigerator, I was wondering, as I often have since she made her inscrutable pronouncement, exactly what my mother meant by a drifting mind. Way in back I found some cheese to put with crackers to feed to Carola and Andre, who were downing scotches like lemonade on a hot day. If my father could weather setbacks, so could Andre, once he stopped bottle diving. It wouldn't help at all for him to learn of his wife's recent indiscretion with a cop, so I could in reasonably good conscience bury that for the—

Who was that knocking at the door? My face must have blanched at the sight of Grant Stuart standing on the other side when I opened up, smiling under a young head of beach-blond hair. Had I left something on his floor: panties, perhaps, a bullet fallen from the Detective's holster? Was he here to warn me, unaware his boss was at home?

"Ms. Thrush . . . it's an honor—I mean, we met before." He held out his hand.

I barely brushed it with mine, thinking what the honor could be, this time or any other. I waved him in. "It's Grant, right?" He nodded solemnly, not quite taking his eyes off me, just shy of staring. It seemed as if humor had deserted Andre's production company altogether. "Andre and Carola are inside," I said. "Can I get you a drink for the funeral party?" I indicated the living room area.

"What? Oh, no, thank you." He walked toward the others in the sitting room. Grant looked Midwest trusting to me—Iowa, perhaps—too trusting to suspect his floor had been the recent scene of illicit activities. What was Grant Stuart doing in a dirty business like film production anyhow?

Andre and Carola were on their separate phones. I followed Grant. He sat down heavily next to Carola, on the couch. I stood leaning along the dividing wall to the kitchen.

Andre ended his call. "Grant?"

"Sir." He stood up. Such Midwestern manners, probably votes conservative, queasy in his sexual orientation—deep down—and that neatness to his room; nothing against neatness, just a little out of touch with himself, I'd say.

"We have a situation—care for a drink?" Grant declined again. "I have no idea how long production will be halted, Grant, but it will be."

"I know. I was thinking, Carola is doing great and Timmy O'Malley is ready to step into second AD. I'd like to be excused—

no contractual difficulties or anything—I just want to head back out to Iowa."

Huh, got it on the first try.

"You have not been happy?" Andre queried.

Grant sat back down. "Oh, no. It's just I may not be right for this sort of thing; I've enjoyed immensely—working with you has been an education, an honor—"

Double bingo; I must be psychic today: He doesn't belong in this dirty business, and he knows it, sensible boy. None of this was funny. . . . I was just the odd wheel in the room, and a broken one at that—

"I think you said you wanted to write screenplays, no?" Andre said. Grant nodded, looking humbled and slightly noble. "You are dismissed with all my good wishes. And you will receive credit on the film." Carola was now off her call and listening. "Carola will handle your room bill with the hotel, and any monies due, of course."

That would certainly take care of any future hookups in room 302. Any taint of sin would shortly be scrubbed away by Alma and Zaneda.

Carola nodded. "I'm sorry you're going," she told Grant without waiting for his response. She turned to Andre. "That was Quinn just now, and the others, they wanted to know—"

"Does he want to jump ship too?"

Grant stood up. "I should go. . . ."

"No, he only wanted to know the latest," Carola answered Andre.

No one noticed Grant leave. Well, I did. I walked behind him to the door and smiled at him as he left. I thanked him. "Thank *you*, Ms. Thrush," he said. As a writer he'd need work on his rejoinders, poor kid.

"No news to anyone for now, Carola; they must sit tight," Andre was saying as I turned from seeing Grant out. "We'll see what the money hounds have to say. . . ." His phone rang again. He let it ring. "Ardennes!"

I came around the corner, cheese plate in hand, my expression quizzical at hearing my name called with such vigorous determination. I wanted to say, *Yes, dear*, but knew I was in no righteous position at the moment to use an endearment. I placed the plate on the coffee table.

"Ah, there you are. We are going to Century City." His phone rang again. He looked annoyed as he glanced at the caller ID. "Come, Carola—" He seemed to think better of it, excused himself, and went to use the toilet.

"We have to see the producers," Carola said weakly. She looked as if she'd rather be going to an abortion clinic for a D and C.

I glanced at the empty glasses on the coffee table. The cheese and crackers sat, unwanted. "What do you think they'll do?"

Carola shook her head. "I've never been in the situation before." Her Portuguese accent was thickening; the stress, no doubt, or the scotch.

I carried the glasses to the sink and started to wash them. Andre came out of the bathroom, all manliness in charge, on the phone again. He was confirming whatever was being asked of him on the other end. His voice sounded off. He stood in the kitchen looking at me. I turned off the tap, a wet glass in my hand. His call ended.

"Andre? Get a PA to drive." I rinsed the glass and followed him into the sitting room, drying my hands on my pants. My doing so usually annoyed Andre, but not today.

"Sorry? Ah, Carola can drive. I want to keep the crew out of things for now. Come, Carola."

"She's had as much to drink as you."

"I'm fine, Ardennes, really." She remained seated.

"You don't look fine, Carola. You don't either, Andre. Is it imperative that you go to Century City today, this afternoon? It can't wait until morning?" My God, I sounded just like my mother.

"Absolutely not," Andre said.

At the same time Carola said, "No, we must be at that meeting!"

And that was how I ended up driving to Century City, where Andre would face the producers to answer for firing his lead. My preference was to be on a plane out of California bound for almost anywhere else in the world, but my preferences were about to be thrown off a cliff.

Century City was home to Campion Productions, a Hollywood powerhouse. It was a city within a city, an island of tall, gleaming buildings west of downtown, out toward the Pacific. Not a short ride from the Hollywood Hills without traffic. Carola sat in back, her phone silent, her eyes shut. I wondered the landscape didn't spin on her with all that scotch; that the boat didn't rock. Andre was on the phone more or less steadily, and I did my best not to listen while fielding early rush-hour traffic. Off Hollywood, I headed for Fairfax to Santa Monica Boulevard for the haul to Avenue of the Stars, on to Constellation Boulevard and finally Garden Lane. A long drive along dreamy-sounding streets that were anything but, the GPS girl smoothly telling me when to turn, rewarding me with bells.

"Andre?" He was off the phone for once. "What time is the appointment?"

"Hmm? Ah, no concern, when we get there. They are waiting."

None too happily, I'd guess. Traffic was gummy but moving

steadily. With luck we might make it in under an hour. The GPS cooed with updates. Andre closed his eyes and briefly the mood in the car was pleasantly quiet, as if a storm that could break into deadly chaos over our heads had been averted. Andre didn't look like a man in trouble, but he wouldn't. The quiet was giving me a chance to think, and I did not want that chance, so I was glad when my cell phone pealed off a ring.

I reached for it, out of the top of my purse. "Hello?" It was Detective Collins. "I'm driving," I said, "one hand on the wheel, one with you." (That was suggestive; why'd I say that?)

"A brief update." He sounded official. "There's a warrant out for Eddie Tompkins's arrest."

"What for?" I sounded excited—or scared.

"I don't know yet. I was informed because I made those recent inquiries. . . ."

"I thought you said you didn't do that?"

"Well, I did. I'll fill you in when I learn more. Meantime, both hands on the wheel." He paused. I was about to say good-bye. "Are you alone?"

"No."

"But okay?"

"Yes." He hung up.

I hung up.

"Good news?" Andre asked. I looked over at him. He had a silly grin on his face. Booze-induced, I supposed—or hoped.

"I'm not sure."

He reached over to pat my head. "What a good wife you are, transporting me safely." His hand glanced down and lightly touched my right breast.

I nearly flinched. Good wife!

Carola came to life in the backseat. I wondered if she was going to roll down the window and throw up; she looked white as death. "I had such a nice little nap," she said.

Andre turned to face her. "Good, that is the spirit. Take things in step."

He meant stride. I glanced at Carola in the rearview mirror, but she didn't smile.

My cell went off again, in my lap. Andre picked it up. I nearly hit the brakes. He glanced at the caller ID. "Andre?" I fought not to shout: "Give me my phone, please."

"It reads, ID BLOCKED," he said. "Secret lover?"

I grabbed the phone and threw it still ringing into my purse. I glanced at Carola again. Her eyes had gone big. I smiled, shrugged as if to say, what a silly man. "Actually, someone has been making anonymous calls lately," I said to the car, not addressing Andre. And this latest would be number five.

"That's scary," Carola said.

"Who might it be?" Andre asked. He sounded off to me again.

"I have no idea. It's probably nothing." I tried for a light tone. The GPS informed us we had arrived, destination on the left.

"You go left here, Ardennes," Carola said, pointing.

"Yes, up to that steel-and-glass abomination. Head straight for the valet," Andre said. He glanced at his watch. Suddenly he seemed all business and churchman-sober.

I wanted to stay with the car or go for a walk, steer clear of the meeting. Andre could call me when it was over. I'd taken Fits's Salinger with me, so I was all set to find a hideout and wait. What I needed was a hole to crawl into, call Billy to find out what was going on with Eddie Tompkins. Was it safe to conclude that this latest news took him off the list of possible mystery callers? But Andre was telling me to head for the building valet. I suggested he drop me off. I'd find a dark bar or café where a person's features were hard to distinguish, the sort of place Fits would know of, no matter where in L.A. Andre wasn't having any of it.

"No. There is no place for you here, Ardennes. Among corporate towers you are a lost bird; your little wings will fail. Come with us," he insisted.

He was right about me and office towers, but wouldn't it be worse for me *inside* the bowels of the steel-and-glass abomination? Still, I'm not helpless. "There is nothing diminutive about my wings, Andre."

He glanced up from his phone and gave me one of those intense looks with his deep gray eyes, a look that used to unnerve or arouse me and always put me at attention. He held his gaze, then let go, smiled ever so slightly, and said, "Here we are."

A smartly uniformed young Latino stepped out of the valet station, leaned into the window I'd opened, all crisp and ready to serve. "Good afternoon, ma'am."

Andre leaned into me. "We are expected at Campion Productions; Paul Thames."

"That would be elevator J," Sharp Latino said, pointing the way. "If you'll head there I'll follow and park your car. When you are ready to leave, they will call down for us."

"Right," Andre answered, and I drove to the elevators.

We passed through reception after some awkwardness with my name not being on the appointment roster. The lobby receptionist was an unattractive woman with rigid determination, in the German shepherd vein. She was sorry, I would have to wait downstairs, but the others could go right up. "That won't be necessary," Andre said with that distinct brand of Eurodisdain. "Jonas Campion knows my wife; there has been a lapse, easily corrected."

"Sir, procedure," the receptionist declared. A uniformed security guard stepped up, either to defend the canine miss or put me under lock and key. Andre was already on his phone. Twenty seconds later the receptionist was defanged by a ten-second phone call from above, and we were ushered to the inner sanctum of one of Hollywood's invincible string pullers.

This had been Harry's quarry. He knew the money men and the money knew him. And they all intimately knew each other's lawyers. Some of the personnel in this building had once had a great deal to say about my own financial health, from a distance mostly except when our paths crossed at certain parties, do-or-die award nights, or happenstance meetings at an in restaurant. This was anonymous corporate America, the ticking heartbeat of an economy, impersonal and all powerful. The twenty-first floor was not for the Harvey Weinstein types who wanted hands-on involvement and name credit on their films. This crowd usually did not do indies. Andre was one of a few exceptions and was duly distrusted. Gatekeepers, flunkies like Paul Thames, whose name *would* appear on films, fronted for the real investors, and his head would roll all by its lonesome if a movie failed to fill seats. Complicated and boring stuff—at least to me—and I was scanning my interior for a place to install my mind while the others negotiated the current cloudy weather in search of a bright ending to the problem of Andre's production sans a star.

Paul Thames was a paunchy Brit with a perspiration mustache even in the frosty corporate air and soft, limp hands, one of which I had to shake. He more or less ignored Carola (I assumed by his terse tone they'd met before) to focus on me as Andre made the introductions, cutting him off: "Quite! Pleased as hell to meet you after enjoying your fantastic work, and looking forward—"

Now it was Andre's turn to cut in: "We should get down to business. Where are the others?"

"Right. We'll meet upstairs in conference," Thames said. He moved aside, held out his left arm, indicating I should please go ahead. I stepped aside and indicated that Carola should please go ahead. I followed her, and Andre took his place in the queue, leaving Thames to bring up the rear as we filed back to the elevator bank.

The twenty-third-floor conference room held smashing views of Santa Monica and the shimmering Pacific beyond, a power view that left me cold. Andre cast an ironic eye toward such tired symbols of worldly success too and was, I knew, ready to turn mocking if need be. He didn't like being at Campion Productions any more than I did. At least he had motive. I felt like a trapped skunk.

So it was all in place, the view, the big-boy players, and the administrative assistant (a.k.a. hot secretary) to match: three-inch heels, cool demeanor, even cooler hair, and just this side of pricey slut in her stuck-to-the-skin dress. Sleek efficiency with a cute behind that didn't quite go with the rest of her statement.

Jonas Campion—the man in charge—extended a warm greeting, mostly to me, indicating to Cheryl (Cheryl Li, of the cute behind/cool demeanor) to bring whatever was required by way of refreshment. The sense of expectation in the conspicuously appointed conference room—no detail left to the imagination—was palpable. I was an actress, ergo expected to exhibit a certain air, a breathy flourish, big gestures, commanding presence. Alas and ah me, I am not typical in this regard. I did not expect all company present to cleave to me. I know actors often feel compelled to perform, to own the stage even if it consists of a table for two and the interlocutor is a friend. This must be tiring for them and is often tiresome for others. I don't borrow ideas either, to seconds later make them my own, and I don't deflate postsocial situations. I deflate *in* social situations and perk up when left to my own devices. So any ideas of being entertained, that a prima donna had entered the room, were destined to be disappointed.

Andre's agent, Kurt Tayker, was present, looking ready to pounce as needed. Andre had only contempt for him, calling Kurt a viciously unenlightened man who had one purpose in life: making money through the talent of others without being burdened by a particle of comprehension of that talent. He could have been a fishmonger, Andre said, or a suit salesman; a good fish, a well-cut suit, or a Hollywood star, the particulars meant nothing. He made Harry Machin look like Marcus Aurelius. If you talked to Kurt Tayker—a man destiny had given the perfect name, a little joke by a playful God with an Olympian idea of the inanity of human intercourse—you were always divided between his phone and himself. "I have to stay connected," I once heard him tell Andre in his whiny, perennially complacent voice. It was a cocktail party at the Soho loft, a time to relax, but the glow of Kurt's phone was always on, a bluish fairy in his hand, linking him nonstop to the West Coast. He glanced at it every other minute. When I suggested he turn it off and enjoy himself, he grew churlish. I'd just quit the business, word was out, so Kurt had little to lose in not being phony polite to me. He was no good at it anyway. What he was good at was making deals, taking the toughest line possible, and winning, his way. Andre said he was a necessary evil, a pit bull to keep the producers off his own face. He'd say, "Go see Tayker," and that usually kept a money worry from blossoming into gangrene. No one wanted to tussle with Kurt if they could avoid it. So how would that work out now with this enormous problem of Andre having just tossed his lead?

There came a long pause as everyone settled into their chairs, during which time I stood awkwardly by the door, still entertaining faint hope of escape until the man in charge seized the reins at the long oval table. Campion pulled out a chair for me, at his side, facing the view, and I obliged, all hope withered. "On to the business at hand," he said.

Jonas Campion had come up fast. I remember Harry mentioning him as a jackal with surprisingly original tastes. He was one to watch and watch out for I think was how Harry had put it. I felt I ought to warn Andre, but how could I? Toward me Mr. Campion was all pleasant skies and balmy afternoons: "Ms. Thrush, in this room we are all fans. It is an honor." More honors; I'd be wearing medals on my breast before the day was out. Why all the fuss over a dropout anyway?

Big deal, I'd been nominated for an Oscar. I didn't win. I hadn't owned the town. I barely knew the names, Harry needling me all the time to show my face. This was well after Joe. Did I care about not getting the golden statue to place on a mantel I didn't even own? Sure, it ached like pins in my heart not to win. I bought a new dress for the stupid ceremony. I waited in line for the toilet along with all the other overdressed actresses with high hopes that night. I took Fits as my date—strictly friends at that point. He whispered in my ear, "Fuck 'em," when I didn't get the prize, and that made me smile—for real—which saved me from that cruel moment when the camera pans the loser's face for national television consumption.

The Mancini brothers hustled me at one of the afterparties. Fits insisted I go to a couple: Never let them see you sweat a loss. They had a part for me, the brothers said, and could they messenger the script first thing in the morning? Sure. One of them said I should have won; I was never able to keep clear who was which. Maybe they were twins. I read the script and turned it down. It was not a vehicle for Ardennes Thrush the actor but for what they saw of me as a person: an exaggeration of me as a shy, secretive type working as a spy for the other side (of something). "Their characters lack sympathy," I told Harry. "I suppose that's the point, but must they *insult* their characters too?" That may have been the precise moment I knew I was going to quit, when I threw the script across the floor and called Harry to tell them I declined.

"Not going to call yourself? The Mancini brothers are big, and they approached you personally, Ardennes."

"So?" I said, and Harry did the dirty work for me.

Anyhow, the flattery trifling gotten over with serious talk could begin, and I could cringe inside myself. I was the only one free to enjoy the view. Poor Carola, already petite, seemed to have shrunk to the size of a seven-year-old. I wanted to grab her hand and run with her, out of school, into the fresh air, to frolic in the beckoning sea out beyond the windows. She sat next to Andre, hands clasped tightly in front of her.

Campion cleared his throat. "Andre, problems with Luce Bouclé? I'm very surprised. I've seen her work. She's highly considered—"

Here Paul Thames made the mistake of interrupting: "I . . ." he hesitated for a flicker of a second as Campion turned his head in his direction. "I was not certain from the outset she was ideal for the part."

"How nice to be right," Andre said.

Campion smiled. Sort of. "The money for this—" he paused to

glance at some papers before him. Cheryl straightened her spine, alert to any need the papers might give rise to, ready on short notice to shuffle others into place. "The money for the project is coming out of—" he lifted his hand off the table and flipped it palm side up.

"Australia," Cheryl prompted.

"Right. Ouch. That would be Amos Matterly." Cheryl nodded. "Those Aussies can be a particularly nasty lot when things go south. Was there much arm twisting to get him on board, Paul?"

"Yeah, you know, the usual—and I can't say I blame him—his people wanted a stronger—I should say *bigger* name, male name, opposite Bouclé—"

"Nothing new there," Campion said. He sighed, seemingly at the tediousness of it all. Or was I reading that into it?

Kurt Tayker, who had so far maintained submarine silence, not even greeting the others, barely a nod to Andre, inserted, "Matterly can be handled."

Jonas Campion studied him for a brief, who-let-the-pestilence-in minute. "And just how difficult will the dismissed actress be for us?"

Here a legal eagle who'd been quietly nursing the sidelines stepped in: "Her people are demanding full compensation for the original contract—they won't get that, of course—*and* they want damage control from the director; a generous statement from Mr. Lucerne on the order of saving her image and future worth, et cetera. We are working up a statement now and a walk-away offer—"

"She was fired for *incompetence*," Andre said, the last C like a snake's hiss. Kurt Tayker held up his hand, palm facing Andre.

Paul Thames threw in a shrill, "We can't possibly say *that*!"

Kurt Tayker again, eyes on Andre: "I don't see why not. She did not live up to expectation or reputation." His strategy seemed to be to give no quarter; get the smear machine going at once, discredit the bitch.

Legal Eagle put in, "We don't want to be libelous . . . Mr. Tayker."

"No point in that," Jonas Campion added calmly. "I'll need a figure, and soon, what she'll agree to, and of course with our regrets things did not work out. Could we say she's preggers, or whatever sends her quietly off into the night? Let's find *something* to use. . . . We have a situation, money flowing into the abyss, and that has to be staunched either by canceling the project or getting back on track as close to immediately as possible."

Kurt leaned back, satisfied, apparently, that no one was suggesting raking his client over the coals, firing him too. It looked as if, so far, daggers would remain sheathed.

Campion continued, "Any chance of Matterly threatening to pull out?"

"Not yet," Paul Thames said, "but I wouldn't be—"

"Fine," Campion said, cutting the lackey to the quick. He then turned to me with his deep, almost black, blue eyes revealing not an iota of emotional susceptibility. I tried to hold his gaze, suddenly wishing I had Harry at my side, his girth to hide behind, or that I could just dive under the table. "Ms. Thrush, you are prepared to step into the role?"

Ms. Thrush, you are prepared to WHAT?

Who shot that rifle into the room, sent the bullet ricocheting past my head, shattering the glass and the view with it? Who turned out the lights and sucked the air out of the vents so that it was suddenly impossible to breathe, like a window popping out of a plane at thirty thousand feet, the pressure dropping fast? Who was playing such a sick joke? Was that my name uttered as the shot rang out?

Instead of looking at Andre, I looked to Carola, perhaps because she seemed incapable of subterfuge. She appeared genuinely surprised. I knew then that the designing Judas among us at the conference table was Andre. Slight chance I was wrong and it was that limp rag, Thames. He looked badly uncomfortable. Andre? Cool as Cheryl Li, not a ruffle to his countenance. Our eyes met for a fraction of a second. After that I was pretty much a numb blur. The gunshot I'd imagined hearing made my ears ring.

I insisted on driving back. The reverse route was more or less as crowded with evening traffic. The occupants of Andre's car rode in stiff silence; I might as well have been driving a hearse. I must have been the only one who'd failed to see the proposal squatting like a rhinoceros in the middle of the conference table. It must have been there all along, but I hadn't been let into the loop, wink, wink. I was the only one blind to an idea as big and obvious as Mount Everest; the last one in is the loser. Of course it made perfect sense, and so convenient: Ardennes Thrush steps into the role of Anne Dernier. Even better, her coming out of retirement takes the focus off dear old dumped Luce Bouclé. The press runs in the other direction: "Actress Ardennes Thrush teams up once again with husband-director Andre Lucerne." Who cares anymore about Luce? Some might suggest that was the plan all along: to stage a dramatic comeback in what is reported to be Lucerne's greatest work.

If there ever was a time when I did want to throw a first-class, foot-stomping, actressy hissy fit, this was the day and Jonas Campion's conference room the place. But I couldn't; doing that would sabotage Andre. If he'd acted out of desperation . . . if he'd had no choice . . . even if he never really believed I quit, I still couldn't shut the door in his face in front of everyone. I will shut it—slam it—but not until he has found another actress. What if the Australian, what's his name, said to sign me or he pulls his money? Then Andre had to try the gambit. Or did Paul Thames or Jonas Campion make ugly threats to sue? No; why would the Aussie insist on me, or Campion or Thames? Reasonably good actors are a dime a dozen in this town. Something else was up.

I was glad for the traffic moving at a quicker pace, which meant I had to pay closer attention. Good, pay attention to the road, not the screaming voices inside my head. How could Andre *do* that? How could he not approach me first? Because he knows . . . he knows I don't want this . . . knows, but he has a need . . .

He *betrayed* my trust! Andre traded on my goodwill, or counted on it. And he got it; I didn't say no. Did I? I felt like yelling into the car, in front of Carola: I slept with a cop today! The Detective, Billy, Devin, a very desirable man. What a thirst he brought up in me. . . . what about Eddie Tompkins? . . . I wish I was on a plane right now, sailing through the air toward New York City, nestled in deep and innocent night. . . . I should move back uptown, leave the Soho loft. . . . Why isn't Andre's phone ringing off the hook? . . . The silence of a dead project . . . the phone stopped ringing: Sorry, buddy, "The End"? But how *did* the meeting end? I didn't say anything. Never leave the stage silent for more than a minute. *Hamlet*, Act V: the silence of bodies strewn all over the boards; the silence of dead characters. Was it over? How did we get out of the conference room, the building? Did Sharp Latino bring the car around? I only remember saying, "I'll drive," and nobody objecting. I did not say, "No, I will not do the part." I couldn't think for that rifle shot reverberating in my head. What a lousy mess . . .

I looked over at Andre. His eyes were closed, but he wasn't

asleep. Carola sat shoved all the way into the corner in back, staring out the window; a caged animal searching for a way out. Andre's phone was not even in sight. He looked severe, the lines of his face, his cheeks, cragged, beaten up around the chin. No question, he was a good-looking man, like granite today. When was the last time we—no, no, don't go there.

It was solidly night by the time I parked at the hotel. Andre kissed both of Carola's cheeks, bade her good-night. "No thinking," he said. The morning would suffice for that; rest was what was called for. Carola returned a halfhearted smile and saluted the director. Would there be a movie to report to in the morning?

"There isn't much here if you're hungry," I said to Andre once we were inside. "I can make popcorn."

"Okay." He was already at the scotch bottle. It was getting low; I'd have to replace it in the morning.

We acted as if nothing had gone wrong. As if he were off for the weekend and we were just ad-libbing, suddenly finding ourselves alone together without a plan.

I popped the corn in the microwave. The cheddar and crackers were still out on the plate where I'd left them earlier. We sat outside on the dark balcony. I wrapped the cashmere shawl over my shoulders and lit the single candle on the table. Andre was on his who-knew-what drink. I sipped a glass of red wine. We didn't talk but sat for a long time. A silver-white moon crept up into the eastern sky. The usual spotlights were waving intermittently from some Hollywood locale, meaning nothing, a symbol of a gone era, now just a tepid gesture of pre-fabricated glitter. Everything seemed cheapened to me. Even the Frenchie hills opposite. White Shirt's car was in the garage, the same dim light on. A few people were on the patio of the Spanish house; a dinner in progress?

"'The night is fine,' the Walrus said,'" Andre said. "A pleasant view," he added as if seeing it for the first time. What would he do if he lost his film?

"I'm tired," I said, gathering the popcorn bowl and empty cheese plate, my glass.

"I will sit a while longer."

I nodded in the dark and went inside to wash the few dishes. When that was done I turned out most of the lights. I closed the curtains, up to the balcony door, and glanced over at White Shirt's; one lonely light was on upstairs and the flicker of a screen. The dinner party at the Spanish house had moved inside. I'd sat for hours on the balcony where Andre now sat and never once had a mosquito shown up. I couldn't remember if I'd ever experienced a mosquito when I lived here in a house with a garden. I guess the trade-off was snakes and coyotes. What a crazy city. I felt a sudden fondness for old L.A., for the hotel I was living in and had been wandering and—now—sinning in, for the city that had once been my home away from Joe that I'd associated with all that went wrong with us, with Joe's everlasting disapproval and my guilty misery, except when I was working. Except when I was working L.A. was an empty pit to me, a loathed, sprawling place without content . . . why did I now feel affection?

I washed up, and when I came out of the bathroom Andre was standing in the bedroom. I might have imagined it, but he looked forlorn, like a boy who has lost a favorite toy, a baseball mitt or postcard, a kid's precious object, leaving him perplexed that a dear thing could suddenly go missing. A probably unhealthy mixture of desire and shame—or did I mean pity?—took hold of me and I moved toward him. I approached and he reacted coolly, nothing boyish or vulnerable in his emotional shift. I embraced him anyway. He put his arms above my shoulders: not a return embrace. How furious he must be with me. . . .

I pushed into him, my legs on his, wrapping a hand around his neck, bringing my face in close until I could smell his familiar odors. My right hand pressed the small of his back into me, and I could feel his penis lying in his trousers. He lightly pushed me away. Not harsh, just turning me down, firm but gentle. But I wanted him; or did I want Billy, or to make up for Billy? Apparently either one would do. Or was I trying to prove something? Like what?

"Andre . . ."

"There is no need for words. This was just something thrown on the table, you stepping in." I wanted to protest. "Shhhh," he said softly.

I stepped back. "No need for words?" I tried not to shout. "What are you going to do?" I meant about his movie.

"Are you asking the right person?"

"Am I asking the right person *what*?" Frustration was rising, ready to explode. I wanted Andre to be angry, to tell me I was self-ish, that I was ruining his film and for what reason? *He* should raise *his* voice and let me have it from the gut, smash in my teeth, some-thing, anything but that cool, collected calm.

"We won't get anywhere shouting."

"I wasn't shouting," I hissed. "Do you have to act like my father?"

"I am not quite old enough," he said, heading for the bathroom. I followed.

I lowered my voice, remembering how sounds travel via the bathroom vent. "I meant so, so *rational* when you know perfectly well you're bitterly unhappy with me."

He unbuttoned and took off his shirt to wash up. I looked in the mirror at his taut, wiry frame, abdomen every bit as tight as Detective Collins's. What kind of animal was I to desire my husband only hours after consuming another man? And Andre had just rejected me, wouldn't even argue. His cold response was more punishing to me than shouts or threats.

Joe and I never had that problem. No makeup sex with us; we went at it even in the middle of whopper fights, no matter if we were talking or not. Sometimes it was better when we weren't talking, exciting, as if we were perfect strangers on a train. . . .

Andre went into the small toilet chamber. I followed. "Are you coming in here too? Fine, come in." He lifted the toilet seat, and I turned and left. I tore the covers open and fell into bed. Andre flushed, came in, turned out the lights and climbed in next to me.

"Andre, listen, please—"

"It has been a long day. If you don't mind I'd like to sleep now."

"*I do mind!*" There, I shouted. Now what? Not a word of protest from Andre. "I *won't* do it. Do you understand? I won't." There, I said it.

He sat up, tossed the quilt back and got up out of bed. He reached for his pants and pulled a clean shirt out of the bureau. The bedroom doors were open, I watched him take his wallet off the dining table, his watch and phone, stuff them into a pants pocket. He started to go, turned and unplugged his phone charger and put it into his pocket. I sat staring from the bed. I wanted to scream, to beg him not to go, but I was numb again and too afraid to say a word.

"I am going to a hotel to get some rest. Good night."

"You're in a hotel," I said, but not loudly. He nodded once and left. "He's in a hotel," I told myself, finding that enormously funny. "He's already in a hotel!" I started to laugh, but not for long.

Now what? The vacuum left in Andre's wake pressed in on the pit of my stomach, and cold radiated out of me like I was sinking into a swamp and couldn't possibly survive the night, the hour, even the next five minutes. It was a familiar miasma: the mire of other people and my utter inability to swim successfully among them. Darkness spread in me, a heavy black blanket. I did not want that blanket on top of me. I did not want that blanket smothering me ever again. I lay on the bed in an agony of flailing emotions: doubt, fear, and failure, a loathsome stew of chaotic yearning with no end in sight.

What did I dread so in Andre's leaving? What could I do to not smother in my sudden solitude? And these people are telling me to go back to work! Look at me! How could I ever think I could be an actor? That arrogant Campion and all the others this afternoon . . . Jonas Campion . . . I felt filthy just thinking his name, yet what is he? A harmless businessman, he's successful, so what? No, wrong, he is *not* harmless; none of them are. I wish I could tell Fits. I *should* tell Fits. He would know Jonas Campion's tone; he'd know the presumption of the producer class, "gilded pigs," he called them. And he knew Kurt Tayker. He had a special loathing for "that pus-brain prick," he called him. Fits told me he'd once asked Kurt if he had a wife, and if his wife could stand him. Kurt's response? A shrug. Fits was an insect to Kurt; the only difference between him and all the other insects was that Fits wouldn't stay in line. Maybe Fits could walk me out of this quicksand.

Or should I call Billy? And say what? Rescue me; I've been abandoned? I looked at the clock by the bed; it wasn't that late, just midnight. Maybe I should call Joe. Oh, that had to be the bottom line of desperation.

I grabbed the phone and dialed Fits. I got my voice under control, "I'm a mess," I said.

"Move over," Fits answered.

"Where are you; is there a free stool at that bar?"

"I don't know. I can't see that far."

"Fits . . ."

"Darlin', I'm sitting here smoking a little weed, petting my fa-vorite cat, with a six A.M. call staring me in the eye."

"Oh. You should be getting your beauty rest."

"But I ain't. So what's the hurt?"

I let out a hiccup. I told him about Andre walking out, the meeting, and the proposal I replace Luce Bouclé, adding, who Andre'd fired today, and that he had probably done the whole thing on purpose to trick me into taking the part.

Fits was characteristically unmoved. "I don't get it," he said. "What's so bad about jumping into the role? You took a vow or something, like a fast not to act? What is it, *religious*? I got an actor friend with bone cancer, sometimes the morphine doesn't do the trick, and she's on the way out and would give a hipbone to act one more time. Why? Who knows? Never quite showed them what she had, and now she finally *gets* acting and it's too late? Or am I bring-ing you down?"

"That's terrible, Fits." I hiccupped loudly.

"Is it? As bad as figuring out the business you gave your heart and soul to is filthy rotten stinking and you're good but not up to incorporating the stench into your immaculate worldview? We get used to it, darlin', we get used to it, and once we do it gets better; you only have to relearn how to breathe."

"Fits . . ." I stopped myself from mentioning the Detective. I saw the whole thing through his eyes, and even I would have to laugh given Fits's probable take: *You slept with the law? Was his gun on and everything; he hot or what? Then—bang—you try and jump your*

old man? C'mon over and do me. Jesus, Ardennes, you're on a freakin' roll.
I'm hip. Not to the cop, maybe, but a good lay is a good lay. I guess.

To my silence Fits said, "Okay, Andre walked out. Ya want me
to come over and tuck you in, sing 'Kumbaya'? Ride, the storm,
baby, ride the storm."

"How long does it last, Fits?"

"As long as it has to." He yawned loudly into the phone, and
I saw his face as clearly as if he were seated next to me on the bed.
"You figure out the dead roses?"

"No . . . an admirer, I guess." He laughed, and we said good-
night. Before hanging up he said he'd give me a call after work tomorrow. There *would* be a tomorrow. . . .

I came across some papers while clearing out the old Riverdale
apartment. My mother was gone and I was left to sort through her
and my father's effects. Her dying had been so sudden—a massive
stroke—that there was a teacup and plate still on the kitchen table.
She was a tea drinker like me—or me like her. My half-brother had
been Dad's executor, which years ago had taken care of what he'd
meant Alec and Arlene to have. I called them both to see if they
wanted anything else, like Daddy's military dress uniform and two
pistols from the war. Both said they didn't think so, but then Alec
called back to say he would stop by if that was all right. Considering
he lived in Maryland he would hardly be stopping by, but I said
sure, okay. Arlene chatted for a few minutes but had no interest
whatsoever in revisiting Daddy's past. She did say she'd seen my
movies and that her husband thought me "top drawer." Arlene was
leading what my mother would call a purposeless life of expensive
distractions.

The apartment walls echoed with the silence of my missing family. The little stage by the windows would hold no more performances, at least not by me. My audience was gone. Mom and I went to see every one of my movies; I'd fly back to New York for one day sometimes just so we could go together. Sometimes I had to warn her that she might not like what she saw. Joe joined us once or twice. Anyhow, I sat on the floor by the stage leafing through Dad's army papers, thinking I'd make a bundle for Alec of his war history, when I came across a disturbing couple of documents. There had been a complaint, all the way up to the Pentagon, against Dad regarding what had gone on in the Ardennes Forest. A wounded soldier, it seemed, had been left behind to die, to bleed to death, I imagined, on the pine needles amid spotty snow and the roar of German guns, the day my father led the others out. I looked up at the empty stage. "Dad?"

My mother died nine months earlier, and I'd been paying the maintenance fees on the apartment. My accountant was after me to sell or rent, so I was there to clear the place out, a chore I would gladly have put off another six months and equally gladly gone on paying. Joe and I were on the rocks we'd be shipwrecked on until we finally ended the misery, so I planned to stay in my old bedroom rather than in the West Side apartment among our anger and lusty hope, at least for a day or two. I had a fire going in the fireplace, though it was spring. I wish I'd left the old army papers alone. When I read the complaint I felt as if I'd sailed out of my body. Dad had always been modest and pooh-poohing of the whole Ardennes affair, never talked directly about his feelings about the war, and that incident in particular. "Soldiers don't discuss what they've seen," my mother cautioned—more than once to my prying questions. She let me know not to expect too much from Daddy in that way. He did tell me of the first time he'd seen a dead German soldier. The corpse had been abused by passing GIs: propped against a tree, a rigor mortis hand held up by a branch, pointing the way for the Allied troops coming up behind. What sickened my dad was seeing that they'd placed the dead soldier's family photos in his other hand. He said you had to respect your enemy, and the dead. Now here I was reading a complaint that said he'd abandoned one of his own.

I right away called Joe. He took the subway up, and we sat in the apartment after I showed him the report, then had sex in my childhood bedroom and slept cramped together in the twin bed. We went to a diner for breakfast the next day, the same one where I used to hang out with my friends. We talked sweetly, steered clear of any *topics of disruption*, and he told me to come home that night and to quit talking to the dead. "Most people don't have heroes for daddies anyhow, Ardennes," he said. I felt the space where he left out the words that I should grow up.

We kissed on the corner near the subway entrance and I went back to the apartment that had been my home. But what was home now? Riverdale? L.A., where most of my work was centered? Or the small West Side flat with Joe? By then we could have afforded a bigger place, maybe even a three-bedroom. But it would be on my dime and that apparently did not sit well with Joe. My grandmother once told me a man does not want a woman supporting him. That sounded like prehistoric news to me, and still does, but I suppose there's something to it in a never-make-it-to-the-top-of-the-brain sort of way. Did Joe think I was trying to emasculate him? Why would I do that? I adored his penis—in a non-Freudian sense. He didn't act insecure; why would a smart, talented guy care where the rent money came from? Dottie once said, "The caveman is there underneath every one of them, Ard, honey, they just put loincloths and leather over that detail. Keep the info tucked in your mind so you don't accidentally get clubbed." We'd both laughed.

I returned to the pile of papers on the floor and found I hadn't read the whole story. The case against my dad had been dismissed after all. No verification, no corroboration to the complaint, the army report went, concluding no wrong done. My dad always said the army never admits a mistake, and it had decorated him, so, while it looked as if the situation ended there, I had a lingering sense that my dad might have done something less than on the up-and-up: like left a wounded soldier on the forest floor. He didn't desert because he went on to other battles. But you're not supposed to walk away from a fight. But are you required to commit suicide?

I started imagining the scene—colored by too many war movies watched growing up with Dad narrating, telling me what was fake, what rang true in a battle scene, or with the guys sitting around waiting for orders, which, he let me know, was mostly what soldiers did when they weren't being shot at or bombed. So I pictured him with the dying man. Half his men thinking: The guy's a goner, no saving him, load him up on morphine and get the hell outta here before it's all of us lying with holes in our guts. And the others, the altruistic half, saying, Captain, we can't leave him like that. Make a stretcher out of a blanket and carry him out—under heavy assault.

And Dad standing there, figuring what to do with the soldier— just a kid, who'd blacked out again anyway, so at least he couldn't hear his fate being decided by a twenty soldier-year-old newly minted U.S. Army captain. The greatest moral dilemma of Dad's young life, maybe of his whole life, and what was right and what was wrong and couldn't someone else make the decision for him? If it was a horse, he could shoot it. He could pull out his gun to force any soldiers who objected to leaving the good-looking kid behind (he would be good-looking in the movie version, to wring out one more tear). So, did Captain Thrush give the order to retreat? Who would have ratted out whatever happened that day? Who talked out of school? Which soldier under Dad's command was bitten by remorse or doubts or post-traumatic stress or plain old fear? Who had a conscience that wouldn't leave him alone? The documents in my hand didn't say.

Did my father kneel down briefly by the unconscious maybe already dead kid and say, *Sorry. Soldier, be at peace*, and then give the order to move out? Is that what happened? Or did he pass sentence and live with that the rest of his life so that the decision made him a better man when it could easily have gone the other way and turned him into a mean and haunted cynic, even a criminal? Had Daddy lived his whole life with an awful secret buried in his heart?

I was left with a tugging undercurrent, a nagging doubt that he might have been a quitter—at least in that one instance—in the midst of a battle no one had excused him from fighting. And if he was, wasn't I one too—just a plain old common ordinary quitter?

It turned out Alec didn't come up after all, and I was relieved. The thought of spending a night in the apartment with him had made me uneasy. I ended up sending him the uniform. I carried the pistols down to the West Side on the subway and stuck them in a shoe box, with the plan to sell them to a World War II gun buff. I didn't, and for all I know Joe still has them somewhere in his life.

I don't know what made me think of that episode in the Ardennes, though it has long been there at my emotional fingertips, rearing up at the worst possible moments—like now—to remind me that I can never be certain. But through the fog of all the doubting and smothering I was able to see that Fits, for all his nonchalance, had caught me and was there for me. Fits would be there for anyone in trouble. He'd have come over if I'd asked, or I could have gone to him. Not a thing was solved, but there *was* Fits, and that was a candle glow in the dark. And this brought up the Detective, my supposed protector in what was or was not a real situation of someone stalking me. It was close on one A.M. Where was Andre now? Probably sound asleep wherever he'd checked in for the night. Was Andre a glow in the dark? I'd been careful never to test him. Of course he was, at least as a director. . . .

I was tired, and I knew things would look just as black and unresolved in the morning, so I told myself to go to bed: Sleep, Ardennes, sleep. I laughed dully. Not like Grandma used to say: "It'll all be brighter in the morning, Ardie, sweetie, you'll see."

Instead of turning out the lights, I dialed the Detective's cell and got his message voice. What did I expect? Cops sleep; they're not required to keep their phones on, the way off-duty police must carry their sidearms and ID. Are they? I left a brief message: "It's Ardennes, Detective. Sorry to call so late. I hope you're sleeping well." I paused enormously, stupidly, and then added, "Good night." The call made no sense. But neither did anything else, not after a day like this.

5

Indio

After calling Billy I actually slept. Time just moved along and plowed everything in its path and in the morning I awoke refreshed. For a full minute I forgot Andre was not beside me, somewhere on the island of our giant California king. That's right, I reminded myself, he's in another hotel. Okay, no matter, I felt very clear for the first time in a long time, and I was pretty sure I knew what I had to do.

First things first: shower, tea, breakfast—I was ravenous after another day of near zero nutrition. Opening the curtains revealed exquisite skies: pellucid, pale blue, no clouds other than the usual puffers over the San Gabriels, and the mountains were shining to bursting, snow visible like veiled virgin brides. No sign of the pollution ring hovering over downtown and the hills. The air had been wiped clean, scrubbed, the temperature crisp, though it would likely heat up. Gone were the ghosts of last night.

I sat at the table with my tea and a big bowl of cereal and

banana. I found one last croissant in the freezer and heated that. I could have wolfed down a he-man breakfast of pancakes, eggs, home fries and toast. I thought about jumping into the car and driving over to the Detective's diner. My mother made fun of my diner taste. I'd tell her it was my personal bit of white trash coming out and she'd say, "I don't know from whom." Not from her French-Scottish people, only a generation down from Canada.

Not Daddy. The Thrushes were English from way back, though things got muddied a drop when his grandfather married an Italian—northern, Dad always added—the one lapse into snobbery from a staunch egalitarian. I thought about that, and in this wide-open day I couldn't see Simon Thrush as a man who'd left a soldier to die alone in the field. I decided the soldier had already died, and I was willing to let it go at that, not pick it apart and insist on leaving a hang-nail of doubt. I had a lifetime of picked-over doubts that I would not let go of, a whole filing cabinet marked: UNDECIDED DOOM.

But Grandma must have been right: Things did seem brighter this morning, only I had a giddy feeling I'd forgotten something important and couldn't think what. I turned the cereal box upside down for a second bowlful, but only a couple of flakes fell out. Put it on the list, I told myself. Today I was going shopping. Head out to Trader Joe's on La Brea, fill the larder. I was going to cook a proper dinner, and we were going to sort everything out. I was practically whistling. The song "What a Difference a Day Makes" and the rejoinder *twenty-four little hours* circled inside my head like a plane waiting to land.

My first mistake was turning on my cell phone. I'd recharged before going to sleep, the charger plugged in by the bed. No message from Andre. He would still be asleep was my guess; I wouldn't call and chance waking him up. Unless he was already awake, and doing damage control. Billy had returned my call, telling me to return his when I got the message. I couldn't tell much from his neutral tone. I lay back on the bed and played the message again. It didn't sound so neutral the second time. I played it again. Longing struck. I felt his weight on me, I felt him . . . it's funny how the exact memory of sex slips away, like they say about pain: You can't recall the exact sensation. You can recall the longing. . . .

It was just after nine o'clock; probably Billy called from work, but why not from home as soon as he got my message? I hit call history; he'd phoned about eight minutes ago. Probably didn't want to wake *me* up in case my phone was on, but now, like it or not, we had to get down to business. I decided not to return his call. Not just yet. That was the second mistake.

I brushed my teeth and applied the usual minute amount of makeup, mostly under my eyes, where my mother said the Italian grandmother showed up and left her mark. No else in the family had the dark circles. They're not that bad, but the makeup people treated them like leprosy, constantly reworking my eyes for every scene. Caking was an issue in a close-up. Joe said it was a sign of character—he meant real, not as in playing one. I did what I could with the circles, tossed my hair around, and went to clear the breakfast things.

As I dried my hands on the dish towel, wisps of thoughts crept out of that yet-to-be destroyed UNDECIDED DOOM file cabinet. A whole new document, the subject: *What are you so chipper about, Ardennes?* Slam the door! I told myself—don't listen—but the fact was there, as real as the gorgeous L.A. day beyond my balcony—into which I planned to go in a few minutes, this being no day to be stuck inside—that nothing had in fact been resolved. "It will be," I whispered aloud. "It will be."

My third mistake was answering the doorbell. The do-not-disturb sign was not out. The maids always rang the bell before unlocking the door. But would Alma or Zaneda come this early? The desk people called before sending up maintenance or a package. Carola or any of Andre's people would call. I half decided, for whatever reason, it must be Grant Stuart. My inclination was to ignore the bell, retreat to the bedroom until whoever it was went away. But the maids would come in if I didn't answer. I moved into the bathroom; I could say I hadn't heard the bell. It rang again. I should listen to the little inner voice . . . but then I thought it might be Andre and that he was being formal, making a kind of separation between us, putting me on notice that things had grown seriously strained, hence he was announcing his arrival rather than entering intimately as a husband. But I knew it was not him—the little voice did. I think I *wanted* it to be him. Wanting it to be him was revealing. If I hadn't wanted it to be him, it would have been revealing in the other direction. I walked to the door. I didn't look through the peephole. The fourth mistake.

I opened up with the determination of a fresh ocean breeze and who should I see standing there, throwing a curve to my wind, but Sylvia Vernon, diminutive, unsmiling, her face all business, and not good business either by the look of her. She pushed in. Why didn't I push back? My fifth mistake.

"Where's Mucho? And what's that in your hand, Sylvia?"

By way of reply she waved the gun, indicating I back up, which I did. The piece was small, a .22 if I knew my movie guns, and it looked old. Sylvia had her heels on and leggings and a long linen tunic top. No hat this time, just her bright Carol Channing hair. I could have kicked her, she was that close and so much smaller, but I reminded myself this was not a movie take, no one would call *Cut, try it again*, if I missed, no director was in charge, and the moment for me to try any stunts quickly passed. Besides that, part of me wouldn't go around kicking old ladies. The result was Sylvia in charge.

"You're coming with me," she said.

The clarity I'd felt since waking up vanished into something like a heavy sadness for the whole world, a weary sadness that it was all so unknowable. All our little and big struggles, hurting each other along the way, the importance we place on every little gesture as one day turns into the next until we think we have it figured out, or stop short of that and settle on some approximation of what we think we were meant to be. I felt like lying down. But Sylvia was aiming that pistol at me and I had no idea why. Hers was the second gun in my life in as many days, if you count the Detective's piece. And that made me think of my father and the pistols I'd lost track of, and it came to me all at once, a minirevelation: My father was a kind man, as a father but also to others, and he was not a man to run from a fight. And that thought, in the current moment of an ex-stripper pointing a revolver at me, made me feel the most outrageously glad I'd ever felt. That would explain the giddy feeling from before. I slammed the drawer shut on that DOOM file with all my mental might: I was certain my father never left any soldier to die alone while he ran out of the Ardennes Forest to save his own skin. I wanted to tell Sylvia: He would never have named me after the scene of his own disgrace! The sin of the father did not visit the daughter. There was no sin. Ha!

"What's this all about, Sylvia?" I asked almost gaily, as if the two of us had arranged a lunch and she'd made the reservations; dressy or casual? My energy returned. I was curiously unconcerned, though Sylvia had to be insane to be pointing that gun at me.

"Never mind. You pack up a weekend bag: panties, tops; what you'd need for a few days."

"All right. Can I ask where we're going?"

"No, you cannot. Hand me that cell phone."

She'd caught me looking at it on the table. Dumb, Ardennes, dumb. I stepped cautiously over to the table and picked up the phone to hand to her. She shook her head, the gun steady. "First change your answer message; say, 'I've gone away for a few days. I'll return your call soon. Thanks.' Make it convincing."

"Hi all," I said into the phone's voice-mail recorder, keeping my eyes on Sylvia, my voice steady. "I've gone to Indio for a couple of days. I need to think. Back to you soon. Thanks."

"Why'd you say Indio? That some kind of trick?"

I shook my head. "You said make it convincing. I went there once to rest after a long job. It's in the desert, nothing there—"

"I've danced Palm Springs. I know Indio; it's a dump."

I kept surprisingly cool. "They have a polo club. . . ."

"Get packing."

As I walked toward the bedroom, I said over my shoulder, "You sent the dead roses, didn't you, Sylvia?"

"You're a pretty smart cookie."

"Why?"

"What did you do with them?" I told Sylvia I'd hidden them in the closet so my husband wouldn't find them and become alarmed. If she'd seen me with Billy, that didn't mean she knew he was a cop. I steered clear of mentioning him. "Get them," she barked.

I retrieved the flowers. Next I grabbed what clothes I thought I'd need for a couple of days and tossed them with my toothbrush into a weekend bag. I asked if I could take my vitamins. That was all right with Sylvia, and any medicines, she added, "Take those."

That was hopeful; she wouldn't be killing me if I was allowed to take my vitamins. Right? Fits's J. D. Salinger was still in my purse, so I'd have something to read if ransom was her game and there would be downtime. I started thinking of all the standard movie lines when a character is facing a loaded gun: *Why are you doing this? What do you want? You don't have to do this. You won't get away with it.* . . .

"Let's go," Sylvia said, pointing the way with the short muzzle. We stopped in the kitchen to put the dead flowers into a white trash bag. Now I was holding that, my purse and the weekend bag, and a brown barn jacket.

I stopped again at the door. "I forgot my hairbrush. I'd never leave without it; my husband will notice." I was stalling, trying not to leave the suite; in the suite there was the chance of Sylvia's plan being disrupted; after that . . .

"Fine. Go get it."

"What about the hang-up phone calls, Sylvia?"

"What about them? Get the brush."

I did, and I added a jar of face cream, and we were at the door again. She already had my passkey. Out in the corridor I started to turn right, toward the landing. "No, go to my door. Push it open." I obeyed, expecting Mucho to fly at me the minute Sylvia's door opened, but no Mucho. Did she kill the miserable runt?

Sylvia shut the door behind us and locked it twice. Her place was the same size as mine but completely different. Most of the walls had been knocked out to make a kind of loft. Painted white ceiling beams were exposed in a beach-bungalow effect with all-white walls, floors, beams, shag rug, and furniture. The only splash of color was a pair of bright magenta throw pillows on the white couch. Even the balcony chairs were white. As with my suite, we entered via the kitchen. Hers was smaller. I didn't have more time to look around. Mucho started barking from what I guessed was the bathroom, located inartistically smack next to the couch, lined up with the kitchen plumbing. Sylvia ignored Mucho's frantic yaps.

"Drop the garbage bag." That was the last I'd see of the roses; too bad about the Day of the Dead dolls. "That way," she said, pointing to the opposite end of the room, toward a small bedroom. "Keep going." We entered the bedroom, also all white, airy with a big window looking out on her balcony. The room was pin neat. A low bureau held all sorts of cosmetics and perfumes. Above it hung a large, framed color photo of a woman in showgirl gear: boas, sequins, pasties, G-string, satin dancing shoes, garter and white fishnets, topped by a feathered headpiece. The woman, who was not smiling, had to be Sylvia in her prime, looking not so much hard as tigerish and sensual: bright red mouth, full and slightly pouting. Her body was full too, and curvy. An all-around sexy dame, she looked like a handful. It made me think of the old rat-pack days, Sinatra and his crowd, Dean Martin and the others; boozy, womanizing old Hollywood.

Sylvia let me take a good long look at her stripper portrait before pointing to a walk-in closet. I saw the light switch was on the outside. I followed where the gun pointed and went in. The light was on. The closet was stuffy with Sylvia's clothes and stale with sweat and old perfume. It was carpeted in the same white shag. The walls seemed thick, where I could see the walls for all the old gowns and shoes and the rest of Sylvia's wardrobe, looking like it went back fifty years. The floor was mostly clear of stuff, and there was a pillow and a small pink flannel blanket meant for a child's bed and, just by the door, an old-fashioned porcelain chamber pot with a lid.

Sylvia started to close the door. "Wait! This is it?" I asked, something close to terror inching into my voice. "Sylvia!" I said to the closed door. "I'm claustrophobic, Sylvia; even a blanket over my head terrifies me—" I started to cough. Panic was folding over me, white and hot at my throat. I banged on the door. The light went out. I yelled as loud as I could and banged with both fists.

"There's a flashlight and a bottle of water on the floor. Now, shut up."

"Sylvia? Wait! Please open the door." I tried to calm myself, or my voice anyway. *"Sylvia?"* Nothing. Then I heard scratching and hard breathing by the door. Mucho. "Mucho!" I called, like the little beast was Lassie and could go get help, save me from having fallen into the well. "Mucho!"

"Mucho, come here." That was Sylvia. I started screaming and kicking the door.

"No one can hear you; you might as well save your breath," Sylvia said.

She'd already let me know no one lived next door to her or below her and, like my suite, no one above either. She must have made a point of telling me that. But the closet wall would be an exterior—also like mine—connected to the hallway where the maids came and went, and maintenance guys; activity. Only nobody cleaned her rooms, and I was the only guest on the floor except Grant, on the other side of the landing. The filled-to-bursting shelves lining both walls would serve as insulation. I was pretty well isolated.

Think of something, Ardennes. "Sylvia! What about my car, Sylvia? *What about my car, you maniac?"* If I'd gone to Indio, how could my car still be parked outside?

I didn't notice a chain on the outside of the closet door when I walked in. She opened the door a few inches, and I hurt my shoulder shoving as hard as I could until the short length of chain stopped me. Who installed the chain for her; hadn't they wondered at it on the outside of a closet and realized she was planning something diabolical, like a kidnapping?

"My car, Sylvia," I said through the gap, my lips touching the door frame. "Andre will see it and . . ."

"You're not too observant, are you? It's been gone since yesterday. I returned it to Enterprise. Paid up with your American Express card; contract canceled."

"You're lying. They'd recognize me, a nice-looking guy—Dave—they'll figure out—"

"Not at LAX, where I dropped it off. Busy airport, they don't notice much. By the way, you owe me for the cab fare back."

"I owe *you*, you sick old witch?"

"Keep a civil tongue, Miss."

She shut the door tight. I heard her tell Mucho to come along, and then I think the bedroom door closed. I was breathing hard. How much air could the closet contain, and for how long? The old clothes held whiffs of deodorant, cologne, and camphor—mothballs maybe—and what was that? Smoke! The fire lingering in the walls? Didn't she say something about that? I was sweating all over and scared, my gut wobbly as a bowl of Jell-O, hands icy cold. I'd be happy to face the gun again, anything but this wardrobe tomb. I slumped down on the floor and pressed my face to the door. My eyes grew used to the dark and I saw the thinnest strip of light under the door, piercing through in spite of the thick carpeting. I put my hand along the strip and felt a draft of cooler air. It was hot in the closet. "Please," I said into the dark. "Please . . ."

After a while, maybe ten minutes during which I tried with all my might to follow the breathing exercises I'd half paid attention to in a long-ago yoga class, I calmed down some. Joe had a good laugh over that: "Yoga, so perfectly L.A," he'd said. "It's better than sleeping around," I'd joked back. Kidding like that didn't go over well on the phone. I knew the calm was temporary and I'd better take advantage of it, so I crawled on all fours until I found the water bottle; there were two next to the flashlight. I turned the light on and shone it around my prison walls. Surveillance took all of two minutes.

I drank some water and leaned the flashlight against the pillow. She'll have to feed me at some point; she'll have to open the door to pass in some food, and that's when I'll kill her. Unless she plans to starve me to death? She's small, she's old . . . she has a gun. I don't care; I'll overpower her, let her shoot me . . . if she fires the gun someone will hear it.

I didn't have my watch, so no way to tell the time. I guessed going on eleven. Wouldn't Andre have come back to the hotel by now? And the Detective? He'd be calling my cell again. Fits would call too, later on, he said, after work. I'd be missed. *The phone charger is still in the wall! That* will be noticed; I would never leave without the cell phone charger. Ha. No, Andre won't notice. He'll be scrambling for a new lead; he's fighting off the wolves . . . he must hate me so much by now. He'll call when he realizes my car is gone . . . he'll get the message. Will he believe I've gone to Indio? Without leaving a note? Will he get the Indio clue?

A bird attacked us there, a screech owl.

Indio was a bit of fast thinking. My friend—a set designer, another abandoned victim of my quitting—drove us to an estate there after a long, complicated shoot. We were both exhausted. Andre was in New York. We sat all afternoon in the hot tub. It was winter in the desert, so not roasting hot; the Santa Rosa Mountains were pinkish-violet hazy beauties surrounding us. The house was huge, with a caretaker who made himself scarce so we were alone, tooling around the hacienda with its artificially watered gardens and lawns, waterfall and infinity pool. We saw a roadrunner shoot across the lawn and laughed our heads off because he zoomed just like in the cartoon.

Beverly mixed pitchers of margaritas as the sun set. I made guacamole, and we grilled some dinner and were outside afterward, lounging, feeling no pain having downed serial margaritas. Later we stood by the pool on one of the big marble terraces, looking up at stars that looked close enough to pluck, when something dive-bombed out of the dark, screeching like a bat out of hell. We screamed, clutching each other while he turned and came back at us. I was taller and felt the breath of a wing on my hair and pictured razor-sharp talons slicing into my scalp. We ducked and ran, clinging to each other, into the house, laughing in our terror. No one heard our screams. We found out later it was a screech owl and that he'd once attacked the owner. Next day we packed up and left.

I called Andre to tell him about the attack. He didn't react much, maybe because I woke him up in New York. Will he remember the owl attack? Will he put two and two together and realize I'm saying I've been attacked? Will he? Oh, Andre . . .

What about Billy when I don't return his call . . . except he'll think I'm running away from him, from yesterday. He's a cop; if I was being stalked—I *was* being stalked—he wouldn't focus on any postsex regrets. Unless he's insulted; he is a man. No, he's a cop; he'll smell trouble. Billy, I *am* in trouble. . . .

I decided to dump everything out of both bags, starting with the clothes bag. I changed from the jersey I was wearing into a white t-shirt, and I took off my jeans and put on a little white summer skirt I'd tossed into the bag. I placed my Mason Pearson brush near the door; maybe I could smack Sylvia in the face with it, poke her eyes out. My purse might hold a file or something sharp, like the keys to the Soho loft, and could be used as a weapon. I found an opened bottle of water, who knew how old, a tampon, lip gloss, sunglasses, eye drops, an umbrella—too small to hit a person with—really old gum stuck to its wrapper, oh, a couple of hard candies, boarding-pass stub, loose receipts. No nail file. I emptied out my wallet next. . . . How did Sylvia get my AmEx card and the car keys? I flashed on her moving around when I went to make us coffee—that was only yesterday—how long has she been planning this? Everything was lying right out on that end table . . . where Andre's lilies were, probably running low on water by now.

What day is it? That table I bought should be delivered today or tomorrow; they said within two weeks. Haven't two weeks gone by? The desk will call. Sharif will wonder why he hasn't seen me. The maids will wonder. Or am I supposed to disappear, fall away into nothingness, into whatever happened to that guest who walked the gardens and spied on her neighbors?

"Sylvia!"

She must have been right outside the door because she answered immediately: "What?"

"What do you want from me?"

"What do *you* want?"

"What?" No answer. "Sylvia, open the door, please. I won't try anything. I can't hear you. . . ." She opened the door as far as the chain. "Thank you." No reply. "I'll need toilet paper, Sylvia. . . ."

"You think I killed Lucille Trevor."

"Why would I think that?"

"They all did."

"Do you want me to ask you if you did?"

She laughed a little hyena's laugh. Mucho's head pushed into the door and growled. He was small enough to fit through the crack, but he stayed outside. "What were you doing snooping into all that?"

"Nothing. Sharif—at the desk—told me about the fire. I was curious, that's all."

"You have nothing better to do?"

"Apparently not." She turned and left the room. I could hear her heels clacking lightly. The carpeting swallowed most of the sound. "Sylvia?" I said softly. I grabbed the little compact mirror out of my kit and held it outside the door. The bedroom door was open. I moved the mirror around. The bedroom curtains were shut; the room was fairly dark. I heard her heels again and pulled my hand back inside.

The closet light went on. "Back into the corner, all the way into the back," Sylvia commanded. She held a lit flashlight on me through the opening. She tapped the revolver on the door frame. "Stay there. Don't move a whisker."

"Okay. I'm back as far as I can go." She unchained the door and threw in a roll of toilet paper and two granola bars, then slammed it; I heard the chain go back on. At least she left the light on.

The silence that followed was more determined. I drank some more water. I opened the Salinger, forced myself to read. Zooey was going on about something in the bathroom, his mother seated on the closed toilet seat, chain-smoking. He's in the tub and wants to get out, but Mom wants to talk about his sister Franny and her troubles, and she's not going anywhere until they do. Zooey is an actor in a family of geniuses. Why would Salinger write about actors in a genius family? Since when are actors geniuses? It was no use trying to read. I tossed the book. It was so hot in the closet. I drank more water. I felt like crying but couldn't. It practically goes with the territory that actors can pull out the tears on cue, but I couldn't have cried right then if I was being paid a million dollars. I drank some more water.

The closet had two rods full of hanging clothes on both sides and shelves above the rods, and below for shoes. On the back wall were two sets of high shelves but no rod, just a pile of clothes on the floor. The shoe racks were filled to capacity. More shoes spilled loose out onto the floor to the left of the door. There were boxes and clothes folded on the shelves, except for the top shelf along the back wall. That one held white Styrofoam heads, some with wigs on them—strawberry blond, fiery red, brunette and black—some bald. Lipstick had been painted on the faces where lips would be if the heads had lips. I didn't like the heads. They were harmless but had the feel of a Halloween scream movie. I drank more water. It was so hot.

I tried the door, pushed it with both hands as hard as I could. Then I realized it wasn't locked, so I shoved as far as the chain would allow. All was quiet outside my prison. I had the sense Sylvia had gone out. I couldn't hear a bird chirp or a car, not a human voice anywhere. I sat on the floor feeling drowsy. . . . I shook my head, drank some more water. . . . I could hardly keep my eyes open—

I didn't need my little mirror to tell me it was evening when I woke up. My head felt mushy. No one had broken down the door to liberate me, and now my hands were tied and attached to my waist by lengths of—oh, very funny, Sylvia—black fishnet stockings, the old kind that you'd need a garter belt to hold up. She'd tied me up and doped me first to do it. I thought as I tugged my hands apart, how could diminutive Sylvia have lassoed me all by herself? Doped or not, she'd have had a struggle. Did she have help? My mouth was dry as sand. I shook my head like a wet dog, trying to clear it. My body felt stiff. My hands were tied about ten inches apart so I could use them, but clumsily. I couldn't lift them much higher than my chin.

I had to pee. This was going to be tricky. I lifted the skirt and lowered my drawers and with no way to balance myself I squatted over the pot. I forgot the toilet paper. It was over by the water, only I couldn't reach it tied up. I fell on my knees and then down on my stomach and moved the toilet-paper roll with my chin until I got it near my hands. Getting back up and over the bowl was a workout. What would happen when I had to move my bowels? Had Sylvia thought of that? Christ! I twisted around and shut the lid over the pot so I wouldn't smell my own urine. Then I grabbed the water bottle and dumped what was left into the bowl, tossed Sylvia's Mickey. Trouble is, I was thirstier than ever. "Shit," I said out loud. I reached for the other bottle and examined the seal. It wasn't broken, so I opened it and took a long drink.

That was when I smelled smoke. "Sylvia! What's going on?" If she was there, she didn't make a sound. I pushed my face up against the door. What if she set the room on fire and left me there? Is this what she did to poor Lucille Trevor? *"Sylvia!"* Nothing. "Answer me, you bitch, *Sylvia!*" Not a word. "Are you going to set me on fire too? Are you smoking in bed? Everyone knows I don't smoke! It won't work this time!"

"So you *do* think I killed her?" She opened the door to the chain and moved back.

She was smoking. No lights were on in the bedroom. I took a breath, coughed. "Well, how does it look to you, Sylvia? You take me at gunpoint, lock me in the closet, dope me, and tie me up. Did I leave anything out?"

"You found the sandwich?"

I hadn't seen a sandwich, but there it was on the pillow, a small tray with a paper napkin and a glass of milk, nice and neat; white bread, no mayo or mustard or Swiss, just a wilted piece of iceberg lettuce, the crusts cut off. I was hungry. "How do I know it's not laced?"

"Smoking is such a lovely habit," Sylvia said thoughtfully. "Your generation ruined it for all of us."

I looked out through the door opening again. I could see half of Sylvia, and that half was stubbing out the cigarette. I thought she said she didn't smoke anymore? I picked up the sandwich, sniffed it, and looked at the meat. I shrugged and took a bite. I waited a few minutes and took another. It would be in the milk, I figured: no milk. I wolfed the sandwich down.

I heard Sylvia moving. She turned on a lamp by the bed. "I saw the young woman, Krolla? The one always with your husband—"

"Carola? You spoke to her?"

"We've spoken several times. She knows I was in show business."

Show business? That's a laugh! "She's first assistant director on my husband's film."

"Yes."

Why *not* talk to Carola? Sylvia lives here, she walks her dog . . . why would I be the only one she chatted up? She could have chatted with all of Andre's people.

"They are considering Nicole Kidman."

"*What?*"

"To replace the French actress."

"Carola told you that? Nicole Kidman? She's all wrong; she's brittle."

"So? Why do you care?"

The Australians; they must have said to forget Ardennes Thrush, go for Kidman. Andre would never do it. I think he'd abort the film first. Sylvia had to be mistaken.

"Lucille was bitter," Sylvia said in a thoughtful tone I hadn't heard before. "But not brittle. She was a good actress and might have been great. They were noticing her up top. I pulled all the strings I could with the actors that liked to see me strip—and there were plenty of those, and they had *real* strings to pull, I could name names—but she wanted to dance, wouldn't let it go."

I peeked out through the opening again. Sylvia was fitting another cigarette into a zebra–patterned holder. She did not light the cigarette. Mucho was asleep on a cushion next to her, on the floor: the Peaceable Kingdom. They made a team, all right. I almost laughed. At least the drug was wearing off, my brain clearing.

"Her skin was flawless, like pearls. Her mother kept her from the sun, the little ballerina. That was me in her Vegas dance number, my body—in the movie. They said I had million-dollar legs. Some said million-dollar everything else, and they all had good looks at most of it."

"Why are you telling me this, Sylvia?"

"She believed she was more disfigured than she was. The limp wasn't so noticeable as she thought; the scars were bad, but makeup could hide them easy enough. As long as she didn't dance." She laughed a kind of sneer. "Hollywood! Lucy flung herself at the men, and the animals flung back. She only toyed with me. Here in this apartment." She grew thoughtful again. "I massaged her aching legs. I used oils and creams, touching her . . . when she let me. . . ."

She trailed off into her sordid memories. I pictured Lucille and Sylvia on the bed, Sylvia inching slowly closer. Did she kill Lucille because she rejected her? Why drag me into it? Andre cast Kidman? Never!

"Did Carola really say that, Sylvia?"

"I was out with Mucho. We say hello."

"How did she seem?"

"Serious."

"Did you see Andre—my husband—demand ransom or something like that?"

"You should rest."

"I'm plenty rested. You knocked me out, remember?"

"I used your own Valium and a sleeping pill. No harm."

Ah! Then she'd gone back to the suite, rifled through my bedside drawer, maybe all the drawers. Did she take my computer, my address book, the cell charger? I only kept the Valium around for emergencies, like flying. I wasn't used to full doses, never mind a sleeping pill on top. "I'm wide awake! And I won't drink the milk."

"Drink it. I only needed to be able to tie you up."

"I'm pretty sure you're out of your mind, Sylvia."

"I could very well be."

"Can't you tell me what you want?"

"I want to rest." And with that she kicked the door closed, almost on my eye, locked it, and shut off the light.

No, no, no! Blackness again. I fished around for the flashlight. I was afraid of the batteries not lasting the night. I wanted so badly to cry. I thought of my father in the Ardennes Forest. Was he this afraid under the winter trees, the Nazis ceaselessly firing their big guns? I was sorry now I'd tossed the Valium water into the chamber pot. There wasn't a sound from the bedroom outside the closet. I might as well be dead. I drank the milk.

I am dead.

I've been dead since Joe.

Is that true?

Why did I marry Andre?

At twenty I played Blanche DuBois. A hole-in-the-wall theater downtown, the play staged by a moody Yale Drama dropout. He was a rich kid; his parents paid for the production, gave sonny a chance to sow his oats, and then they'd rein him in. He hated his mother, and from the little I saw of her I understood why: a clenched, dried-out woman, meanness itself to the imaginative soul. He cast me the day I auditioned; we slept together almost immediately. I was too young for Blanche, but he got me there. He rehearsed us hard. I stayed in character even in bed with him, right down to the Southern accent. The production received no press, not one review, but we got audiences, full houses every night and standing ovations. I hired a guy to video the production and that was how I got my Actors Studio audition.

I met Joe at a reading there, a play by a friend of his. I was reading, but not the lead. Joe came up to me afterward. He had this smile—sweet, like a child's, only he smiled so rarely. We went out with the others after the reading and then the two of us alone. He had this intelligence, any topic I brought up. Not cheap opinions, but knowledge. I told him it wasn't the applause in acting but *getting* the character, and then the audience to go along, seducing them into believing what I did with her; a creative act to take a character and make her breathe and bleed and feel; a magical illusion.

I couldn't take my eyes off Joe. I stopped seeing the *Streetcar* director, Dennis, cut him off just like that. I don't know what became of Dennis. He didn't show up again in the theater, not that I knew of, so Mommy must have worn sonny down. It wasn't like we would've lasted; Joe just sped things up. Dennis knew Blanche, though; boy, did he ever know Blanche DuBois. Tennessee Williams would have leaped for joy at that little nowhere production. I think I maybe gave my best performance under Dennis, a close second under Andre—no pun intended.

And now I'm dead.

Part Two

Then, sharply, as a headache can suddenly
stop, something yielded, long griefs eased.

—E. Annie Proulx,
The Shipping News

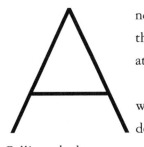

1

Sylvia's Closet

Andre told the Detective he had doubts. He thought his wife would have left him a note at the very least.

"You don't believe the message that your wife went off to Indio to think? She's never done this sort of thing before?" Detective Collins asked.

"Not like this." Yes, Andre admitted, he'd been upset and was wrong to have taken off, gone to another hotel for the night. Yes, it was an unusually bad moment between them, but she still would have written a note. He was sure of it. He remembered that his wife had gone to Indio with a friend once, but the name of the friend—a costume designer or set dresser or whatever from a film she'd worked on four or so years ago, or maybe earlier—escaped him. He was sorry; he just wasn't good with names—or dates. To Detective Collins's suggestion that perhaps he hadn't listened, Andre suggested perhaps not always.

He'd been in New York, he explained, and she'd awakened him

to tell him about an incident, forgetting the time difference. "With the bird," he replied when asked what incident. "The bird at night was all I ever knew of Indio."

"What happened?"

"They were attacked by some sort of owl. Ardennes called around midnight, West Coast time; I was asleep."

"You weren't concerned, two women alone in the desert?"

"We spoke the next day. Brenda! That could be the friend's name."

"No last name?"

"I'm afraid not. We laughed about the bird attack the next day. She went back to L.A., packed up, and returned to New York soon after."

Detective Collins was quiet, thinking things through. Andre was seated at the dining table; the Detective stood leaning on the wall separating the kitchen. "Do you think your wife *could* be in Indio, left the phone message instead of a note?"

"I don't think so, but I can't defend that idea—I mean why I think not. Why would she go there?"

"Why mention Indio if she didn't go there?" Detective Collins was thinking out loud. "To say she's been attacked?" That got Andre's attention. That was when the Detective let him know about Eddie Tompkins and the series of hang-up phone calls.

"Why didn't I know anything about this man?"

"You tell me why your wife never mentioned she was being stalked."

Andre moved—abruptly, for him. The Detective took a step closer. Andre was slim and compact at just under six feet; the Detective was broad, imposing, muscular and solidly six feet tall, a little over. Andre turned to the open balcony door. "This man—Eddie?— you say was arrested?" He stepped out onto the balcony. White Shirt was outside, on the edge of his lawn above the garage, leaning out over the railing. "I've seen that man before, Detective, looking over here like that."

Detective Collins walked out onto the balcony. "Can you tell from here where he's looking? With any degree of certainty?"

"No, of course I cannot, but he has been there before. I've remarked on it to Ardennes."

"What did she say?" Andre shrugged. "Is it possible Ms. Thrush went to New York?"

"Again, without saying a word?" He brushed past the Detective, who followed him inside.

"You said she was upset after the meeting; we know she felt threatened."

"Isn't that something the police can check, if she took a flight out?"

"You haven't filed a missing-persons report. No crime has been committed that we know of. So far we have an upset wife who possibly took herself off."

"Is that what you think?"

"What I think doesn't matter without some clear sign of foul play."

"Wouldn't stalking satisfy?" The two men were quiet. "Detective, Ardennes—my wife—is an actress. Her emotions are raw, impulsive . . . Yesterday she seemed . . . confused. I would say almost panicked—last night."

Detective Collins shifted his weight. "And yet you left her alone?" Andre had already said it had been a mistake. "I'm trying to follow, Mr. Lucerne; are you suggesting she left on her own or not?" Andre shook his head; he didn't know. "Say she is in harm's way. You argued; convince me you're not involved; you lost your temper, things got out of hand. . . ." He tapped the table once with his left hand.

"I will not address that absurdity."

The Detective pocketed his growing disdain for the movie director, tried not to sound dismissive of the forsaken spouse. "You mind if I have a look around?"

"Of course, please look. Perhaps she is under the bed."

There was a knock on the door. The Detective put a hand up, went and stood behind it; he nodded to Andre, who said, "Yes?" The Detective opened the door and Carola walked into the kitchen. Detective Collins stepped out. "Carola, this is Detective—I'm sorry—"

"Collins."

"Of course. This is my assistant director, Carola Santosa."

Carola looked up at the Detective. "Hello. Any news of Ardennes?" she asked.

"When did you see her last?"

"Last evening when she drove us home from a producer's meeting."

"How did she seem to you?"

"Not too happy. None of us were. . . ."

"Have a seat, Ms. Santosa." Carola walked past him and sat down at the table. The Detective opened the refrigerator door. "Not much food in the house." He opened and closed the kitchen cabinets. He looked at Andre. "Who drinks tea?"

"My wife."

"It doesn't look as if she took any with her. Tea drinkers tend to be particular. Would she have left without it?"

"Probably not. Where does the tea take us?" Andre added, lifting his hands impatiently.

The Detective leaned on the short refrigerator. "You and Ms. Santosa are close?"

"We work together, closely."

The Detective moved along to the living room, on the prowl. He opened the TV cabinet, examined the couch, slid a hand under the cushions. In the bedroom he asked if there were any medicines Ms. Thrush took and if they were missing. Andre said she took vitamins. He looked into the kitchen cabinet. "They seem to be gone," he called to the Detective.

Detective Collins nodded. "You said you don't think she took many clothes?" he called to Andre. He noted a plugged-in cell phone charger at the bedside table. He'd seen another one at the dining table. A quick perusal of the drawer told him this was where Ardennes slept. He made a note: She left without her phone charger. Not likely. He opened the bureau drawers, scanning the contents.

"She couldn't have; she didn't have that many things here to start," Andre said, walking into the bedroom.

The Detective moved to the bathroom. "Her face creams missing?"

"I guess so." Andre now stood in the bathroom doorway, watching. Both men briefly appeared in the wide mirror over the two sinks.

"You guess so what?"

"There seem to be fewer."

"You don't know your wife very well, do you?"

"I know my wife."

The Detective was in the closet now. He saw that the box of dead flowers was gone.

"Her computer is not here," Andre said. He glanced around the bedroom as if it were someone else's. "Maybe she *did* go away for a few days and we're making something out of nothing."

Detective Collins returned to the bedroom. "Uh-huh. Where does that leave she wouldn't have left without a note?"

Andre ran a finger over his lip. "Perhaps I was wrong and I've wasted everyone's time, Detective—"

"I was on my way over here when you phoned, remember that?"

"Ah, yes, your card on the table . . . I only meant to find out if she had spoken again to you . . . and now the stalker . . . I am not sure what to think."

"Don't leave out the phone calls." The Detective did not mention the delivery of dead roses and Day of the Dead dolls. He passed his hand through the shallow desk drawer and picked up Sylvia's rhinestone-encrusted cigarette holder. "Your wife doesn't smoke, correct?" Andre confirmed that. "She did the wash?"

"*What?*"

"There's a lot of quarters in the drawer."

"Oh, yes. She likes doing laundry. There is one here, just below. You find me somewhat distracted, I'm afraid, Detective . . . Collins. But isn't the computer a hopeful sign? I believe she was writing some sort of book; she may have wanted only to do that. You know, get away to work?" The Detective would have said, why not say so, why all the mystery, but Andre's cell phone rang for perhaps the tenth time. He looked at the screen. "I have to . . . Carola, will you take this for me? Dammit. It's Jonas Campion. . . ."

Carola ran up to Andre. She took the ringing phone from his hand. "Should I say Ardennes is missing?"

"*Merde.* No. Tell him, tell him—stall, say there is a problem; no, don't say that. Say I am on another call; say things are moving along, I will get back to him." Carola nodded and walked to the sitting room with Andre's phone. "You see, if the press gets hold of all this . . . that was the production company head, Jonas Campion."

He pointed toward Carola on his phone. "The point is, we do not *know* she's gone . . . missing."

"This Campion wants Ms. Thrush to replace the lead, that's what you said earlier; do I understand correctly?"

"*I* want her in the role."

"She told me she no longer acts."

Andre eyed the Detective as if seeing him for the first time: the essence of manly handsome. "Ardennes Thrush is at her best potential right now. The part is a silk glove tailor-sewn for her."

"I see."

"Do you?"

The Detective, unseen, slipped Sylvia's cigarette holder into his pocket and closed the desk drawer. "Inconvenient as the news might be, Mr. Lucerne, I think your wife may be in real trouble."

The first look of genuine concern crossed Andre's face, as if the situation had slipped out of his control. That was the way Detective Collins would describe his expression. "I'll file a missing-persons report if you think that will help," Andre said. The Detective nodded.

Back in the sitting room, Detective Collins asked Andre to retrieve his laptop out of his car. They would look up Ardennes Thrush's filmography, find out who'd worked on her last films, and try to locate the name of the production person who'd taken her to Indio. Andre wanted to send Carola, but the Detective said he wanted a word with her. He didn't want a word—more to take a reading. They waited while Andre went out to his car, the silence between them as thick as wet felt. Detective Collins did not have the sense Carola was up to anything, at least not regarding Ardennes directly.

"You're friendly with Ms. Thrush?" he asked.

Carola smiled. "I admire her! She's a great actress—"

Andre burst into the room, the computer held under his

arm. He'd hurried up the steps from the parking lot and was breathing hard. "Look, Detective Collins, I checked; her car *is* gone. I don't see where we are going at this point. If she *did* go to Indio, or somewhere to be alone, to think, as her phone message—why not let it go at that?"

"That would satisfy you?" Andre was quiet. "What company did she rent her car with?"

Carola had taken Andre's computer and set it on the table, and was waiting for it to boot up. She looked up at the two men. "I can answer that. We all use Enterprise."

"Did the film rent her car?"

"No," Carola said, "but Enterprise may have given her our group discount. The lot is over on Ivar Avenue."

The Detective nodded. The lot was near the diner where he and Ardennes had had lunch. "I'll have to go back to my precinct to clear this case with my captain. Get some blue on board."

"You are going to bring in more police? Aren't we getting a bit carried away?"

"What would you suggest, Mr. Lucerne; we pour ourselves a smoky single malt, sit back and wait for your wife to walk in the door?" He looked at his watch, then at Andre, his eyes revealing nothing.

At that awkward moment Fits showed up. He knocked twice and rang the bell. Carola looked at the Detective, who nodded and slipped out of sight behind the bedroom door.

"Hello there, cutie," Fits said, eyeing Carola when she opened up. He saw Andre and walked past her. "Mr. Lucerne, I'm a friend of Ardennes's, an actor who has enjoyed your work."

Fits had come from the set. He wore his usual loose clothes, a kind of urban-cowboy-biker look, his graying hair long and chaotic. He still had face makeup on. To Andre's amused stare, he added, "I came from work. My character's a ruffian—with a good heart."

"Matthew Fitzgerald, if I am not mistaken," Andre said, smiling broadly. He was looking Fits over. "I wonder we haven't worked together."

"I wonder the same."

The Detective stepped out from behind the door. Both men turned to face him.

Andre took over. "Mr. Fitzgerald, this is Detective Collins—"

"Everyone knows me as Fits," Fits said, nodding to the cop. "Quite a little fete going on here. Is something the matter, Detective?"

Detective Collins lowered his eyelids halfway. "What brings you to the party?"

"I came to see Ardennes. I didn't expect a crowd."

"Fits, this is my AD, Carola," said Andre; he seemed to want to control the conversation.

"Pretty," Fits said. "So, ah, what's with the convention?"

"Will you step into the bedroom, Mr., ah, Fits?"

"We've hardly met, Detective . . . and it's just Fits." He followed Detective Collins into the bedroom. The Detective closed the double glass doors.

The king-sized bed didn't leave much room for two big men, one round, the other tall. "Have a seat," Detective Collins told Fits.

Fits sat on the bed. The Detective pulled out the small rattan desk chair, seating himself on it backward.

"Did Ms. Thrush expect you today?"

"No. I said I'd call, but they wrapped my character early. We're shooting at Universal Shitty, traffic was weird, like there were no cars; I took it as sign and came over."

"You've been here before? You know the gate combination?"

Fits made a laughing grunt. "No, I popped in behind a garbage truck."

"That can be verified."

"He's still out there. Verify."

"How'd you get the room number?"

"I saw Lucerne trot up the steps, first door I knocked was wrong, guy inside set me straight. Can I ask a question now?"

"Why'd you decide to pay a visit?"

"Besides that we go way back and way deep and she sounded pretty unhappy?"

"For starters."

"She called late last night. She had a fight with Herr Director." He pointed with his thumb toward Andre in the sitting room. "Apparently he walked out."

"Why would she call you?"

"Like I said, we have a history."

"An intimate one?"

Fits leaned back, amused. "Is this off the record? 'Cause I'm not a kiss-and-tell sort of guy."

The Detective paused. "Did you call her today?"

"No, I came over, like I also said."

"Would you call her now, on your cell phone?"

"What's this all about?" Fits asked, punching Ardennes's speed-dial number. He listened to the message. "It's Fits, baby. Call me," he said into the phone. He hung up, put his phone back into a breast pocket. "Indio?" he asked the Detective.

"Mean anything to you?"

"Polo? I mean, who goes to Indio?"

"So you have no idea where Ardennes Thrush is?"

Andre knocked on the bedroom door. "We think we have a name, Detective."

Fits stood up. "What's going on?"

"Fits, I can count on your discretion? You won't repeat what you learned here?" It was Andre talking.

"I haven't learned anything."

"Ms. Thrush said absolutely nothing to you last night about going away?" It was the Detective talking.

"You spoke to Ardennes?"

"Sure. She called me after you pulled your little disappearing act to another hotel. Nice move."

The Detective walked purposefully to the sitting room and stood over Carola at the computer. "We think it has to be Beverly Henry, production designer on Ardennes's last feature," Carola said.

"Hey, I know Beverly Henry—well, I worked on a film she was on, good lady, talented," Fits said as he walked past Andre.

"Have you got her information?"

Fits was already punching into his iPhone. "I never toss a connection. Here it is, Detective." He showed him the number.

"Would you mind calling? Keep it friendly . . . just how are you . . . Ardennes said something about going to Indio—"

"Got it." He pushed talk and walked out onto the balcony. "Hey, is this Beverly, yeah, Fits here . . . you remember . . ." He moved out of earshot.

Andre said, "I could use some coffee. I think there's some hotel brand. Detective? Carola?" They both nodded, and Andre went to the kitchen to put together a pot. Carola followed to help.

Fits came back into the living room. He shook his head. "Beverly hasn't heard from Ardennes in a couple of years. When she dropped out—of acting—she kind of dropped out on her people out here too."

"But she spoke to you?"

"Yeah, I looked her up after her agent, Harry Machin, died. We had a drink at Musso and Frank's the other day."

"How was she then?"

"Pretty lost." The Detective nodded. "So, ah, what's the Beverly Henry connection, if I can ask?"

"She went to Indio with her after her last film, to a friend of Beverly's ranch out there."

"So she's supposed to be in Indio now, but you don't think she is?"

"She could be."

"It's kind of nowhere down there, except for the Salton Sea, which most people think is a chemical dump. Not that many hotels to choose from. Not the best place to get lost in. Or maybe it is."

"And conveniently close to the Mexican border."

"You think maybe Mexicans have her?"

The Detective shook his head. "I don't think anything and I think everything at this point."

Carola put out four cups and a container of milk. Andre poured the coffee. "Detective?" he said, then paused. "I was thinking, there has been no request for ransom. There has been nothing."

That remark brought forth no comment from the Detective. There was a brief silence while they drank their coffee. Detective Collins set his empty cup down on the side table. "Okay. You have my numbers. Mr. Lucerne, you hear the slightest peep, a hint of a peep, find me. You too, Ms. Santosa." He handed Fits a card after writing his cell and home phone numbers on it. "I'll report back after I check up a few things. All right?" He glanced all around. There were bashful nods. "Mr. Lucerne, you will go to the Hollywood precinct to file a missing-persons report, agreed?" Andre said he would go right away.

"Mind if I walk out with you, Detective?" Fits asked.

The Detective nodded and they left together. On the steps Fits said, "What about a trace on her cell?"

"Right. Outside of the movies, that doesn't happen like magic."

"Ya know, some actors take off *after* they achieve big fame. Ardennes didn't—she wasn't super huge yet, but on her way, I'd say, and she just walked away."

"And that bothered you?"

"Huh? Well, yeah, it wasn't very polite to her friends. And I don't know why she did it."

"Quit?"

Fits put a hand up; a braided black leather band adorned a thick wrist. "Hold on, I just thought of something. Somebody sent Ardennes a bunch of dead flowers."

"Oh?"

"Yeah. She thought I did."

"You didn't?"

"My sense of humor's not that profound."

"When was this?"

"Two days ago . . . three. Wait a minute, my cell history. Yeah, here it is." He showed the Detective the time on his phone. "It was yesterday." The Detective glanced at Fits. "What? I have a recovering pothead's sense of time, okay?"

Detective Collins suppressed a smile. "Okay. She say anything else?"

"I wasn't paying real close attention until she mentioned the dead flowers. Then she had to go; someone was at the door."

"What time was that again?"

To the Detective, Fits's information meant someone had definitely been to see Ardennes *before* he arrived, and that someone had been female—he'd gotten that much from the lousy perfume Ardennes tried to pass off as the maid's cleaning products—and the dead roses had already been delivered.

"You've been helpful. If you think of anything else . . ."

"Yup."

The detective and the actor got into their cars and drove off. Fits turned left, the Detective right, toward Beverly Hills. A block later he turned around and headed for the Enterprise Rent-a-Car on Ivar Avenue. It took over twenty minutes to find out that Ardennes's contract had been canceled, but not at that location. Another few minutes turned up LAX as the drop-off point, and she'd paid a fee for a different drop-off location. Ardennes's American Express card had been used, and the gas tank had not been full, another penalty. No one remembered seeing who'd dropped off the gray four-door Nissan Sentra. They'd gotten what they were owed; what did they care if the customer or her great-aunt Tillie paid up? The Enterprise employee name on the receipt was Dave, but that was from the Ivar location, where the car had been picked up. He came to the desk and said he remembered Ardennes. "She's some kind of actress, right? I thought I recognized her," he said.

The Detective wondered that no one had recognized the actress at the airport location, but LAX was nonstop, and actors did come in. . . . Even for basic cars like the one in question? Sure. And they sometimes covered up with wigs and things. The key was that Ardennes Thrush had been with Andre and Carola, on their way back from Century City, around the time the car was being dropped off at LAX. The Detective thanked the clerk, gave him a fax number, and asked that a copy of the receipt be sent over to the Beverly Hills precinct. He asked one more question: Any damage to the vehicle, anything unusual inside? Negative on both counts.

Unless Ardennes had wanted to take herself off, had gotten someone else to drop off the Nissan for her, then gone to another car-rental company or bought a plane ticket to Disappearsville, Detective Devin Collins had a missing person on his hands. He thanked the Enterprise people and entered his own vehicle for the trip back to Beverly Hills. How long would he be able to keep the case out of Hollywood's hands? More to the point, how much trouble was Ardennes facing? Attacked by a bird had to be a clue tied to Indio, he told himself, reasonably certain that was not where his victim was located. That was all he had to go on.

I did finally let it out that first night in the closet, cried myself to sleep, and I had no Kleenex but a few ragged bits from the bottom of my purse. I took an iota of revenge by blowing my nose on one of Sylvia's fuchsia-colored blouses, which I then tossed near the chamber pot. I cried like badly needed rain. It didn't change much, or maybe it did. I fell asleep trying to remember the last time I'd cried with such abandon, freely, fully, emptying the heart of poison and hurt. Maybe when Daddy died. After his death I put the brakes on that much raw emotion, as if feeling too much could kill me. There was Joe, the hell of that ending, but it was only when I acted that I let it out, where I was safe to let go what I refused to otherwise touch. And now? Now that I'm no longer an actor?

A thin strip of gray light shone under the door when I woke up. Either it was raining or just dawn. The closet had turned cold in the night. The plaid pink flannel blanket was placed over my shoulders. Sylvia must have covered me, and I must have slept through it. The flashlight was off. I didn't remember clicking it off, so Sylvia must have done that too. Did she lie about the milk, or did I really sleep that soundly? Babies cry themselves to sleep why not grown-ups? Yeah. I'd bet the milk was spiked.

I turned the flashlight on and stood up. I stretched as much as I could with my hands tied. I peed and drank what was left of the water. I did some squats and tried some crunches, turning my back and my neck this way and that. Take control, I told myself. I struggled with the little flannel blanket, to get it around my shoulders again when I was done stretching. Then I set to work with my loft keys to try to pick through the little diamonds of the fishnet stockings, one diamond at a time. They weren't silk or nylon but acrylic or some such sturdy stuff and tougher than I thought the material would be. I wasn't making much progress.

When I heard Mucho sniffing at the door I hid the keys inside the pillowcase and sat very still. Sylvia turned on the closet light and opened the door up to the chain. Again she ordered me to the back, showing the gun.

"The piss pot stinks, Sylvia."

"Good morning," was her reply. She wore a long, gown-like robe with satin edging and feathers at the collar. I recognized it as the one she had on when I ran into her in the laundry. Her slippers were gold lamé ballet flats. She looked so small. I thought of rushing her as she pulled out the food tray from last night. "Don't move!" she barked, pointing the gun like she'd read my mind. She shoved a new tray in with her left hand. It held a raspberry cheese Danish, a pot of tea, a cup and a small pitcher of milk, a fresh bottle of water. Two teabags, so she knew I liked it strong even if she didn't have the real deal loose tea. In some ways Sylvia was a very considerate jailer. She removed the chamber pot last.

I watched these maneuvers from the back of the closet like a well-trained pet that wants to bite its mistress, to chew her arm off, but knows better than to try.

"What if I refuse to eat?"

"You won't," she said as she rechained the door, leaving it open and the light on.

Day two of captivity.

Fits called the Detective's landline early, from his car on his way to the studio. "What's the time?" the Detective asked, sounding groggy. His nightstand clock read five twenty-eight A.M. He sat up, threw off the bedding so the cold, not-yet-light morning air would wake him all the way. A window was open. A car suddenly honked outside.

"I thought of something in the night, waited till I was on my way to work—you never know when you'll get a break on set—you awake?"

"Go ahead."

"I remembered a phone conversation with Ardennes a couple of days ago. She told me there'd been a fire at the Hotel Muse, but it was like fifty *years* ago. She thought maybe some burlesque queen murdered an actress in the fire, something like that."

"What was the actress's name?"

"She didn't say. Maybe she was losing it, huh? Maybe she's slipped off the deep end of the planet. . . ."

"What's the connection?"

"The stripper lives in the hotel. I think she called her Sally or Salome, something with an S."

"All right. Thanks."

"You find anything out yesterday?" The Detective was quiet. "I want to help if I can."

"She turned in her rental car. Or somebody did."

"Huh. Hard to get to Indio without wheels."

"Think of anything else, call." The Detective clicked off. He sat up, covering his groin with the sheet, though he was alone in the room. Why would Ardennes care about a fifty-year-old crime? He glanced at the clock.

After breakfast I got busy going over all sorts of things in my mind; plenty of time to ruminate in my cell. Sylvia had closed the door but left the light on. The closet didn't warm up like yesterday and I wasn't as panicked, for the moment. You have to learn to take the calms between storms, is how I see it. There could be little doubt Sylvia was mad as a hatter but not pathological—at least I didn't think she was. Of course, I could be dead wrong, and, mad or not, she seemed capable of anything.

So I sat there trying to remember a conversation with Joe. It involved one of those phrases he'd repeat that I never believed he meant, one that sticks and works its way back into the brain like a virus. The phrase was *Do whatever you like*. The first problem was the word *like*, which I always mentally wanted to correct to *want*. There is a critical difference: Doing what you like is flimsy, indulgent, whereas doing what you want is firmer, more of a stand. *I'd like to play the piano* spoken on a summer porch over mint juleps with Chopin playing in the background: a whim. *I want to play the piano*: formidable, a statement of purpose.

Meanwhile, I shifted my interpretation: *Do whatever you like = I'll have nothing to do with your folly*. Subtext: *and suffer the consequences*.

"Ardennes, if you want to go from stage to screen, if you want to star in a TV series, go ahead, sign with this Harry Machin you think is the center of the universe; by all means do whatever you like."

Further interpretation, arrived at in the acquired wisdom of my solitary prison musings: *Don't seek my approval.* As in, go on up that trapeze; don't mind me while I pull away the net. Did that mean I'd expected Joe to catch me if I fell? Was that what I wanted, or what he'd thought I wanted, for Joe to provide me with a safety net? I wouldn't *want* a safety net pulled. But what net? Since when has there ever been anything in place to catch me if I fall?

My parents had this perfect marriage, this ideal love for each other. Only my perfect mother had an affair with an imperfect married man before she met my dad.

She told me about it when I was a dewy-eyed teen. I'd developed a killer crush on my English-lit teacher, who was married. I became pretty silly about the whole thing, imagining all sorts of signs that he returned my adoration but was trapped—unhappily, of course—in a marriage to a stringy, ungenerous older woman—or so I imagined. One day, unable to stand it any longer, I left him a note asking if he would see me after school, away from campus. The teacher, Mr. Russell, called my mother. She in turn called me home that weekend and sat me down: Why did I want to see Mr. Russell outside school?

I bellowed, bursting into tears, "He *told* you?" I was ready to die, to sink right into the kitchen linoleum. My mother waited patiently until I ran out of heart-wrenching ammunition and protest. She made us chamomile tea with honey and asked me what attracted me to the teacher.

"How can I say? Just *him*! I can't help it! This is *love*, Mother. For God's sake."

"A crush, Ardennes," she corrected, her tone controlled. "You're so young. You think you want to die, but you are lucky Mr. Russell is a good man."

"Lucky? I wanted to run away with him and he called my mother! I'm such a jerk."

"No, you're wonderful. Your mother, though, *was* a very foolish girl once upon a time." And she told me the story. The guy sounded like a real bum. He'd visit her one weekend a month where she was teaching, at a private school in Pennsylvania. He'd been her college professor. She told me she finally found the courage to tell him it was over. Of course it wasn't, and she was in agony for a long time. "If ever I was going to become a tragic poet, that was the time and he was the material. Happily, I did not write one single line of poetry."

It was winter; outside, the day was gunmetal-gray and heavy, as if weighted with snow. The light in the kitchen was disappearing around us. "Do I have to go back to school, Mom?" She nodded. "I have to *face* him?"

"It will be all right."

I shivered. "I'm going to my room for a while." I planned to lie down and die of grief. I was halfway down the hallway, past the master suite, my parents' big bedroom that had always been special, both welcoming and a room I felt not quite privy to, when I ran back to the kitchen. My mother was still seated at the table, very straight in her chair, hands wrapped around her mug, already cold. "Did Daddy rescue you?"

She laughed lightly. "No. He came along a little later."

"Do you love him more than the other guy?"

"Improper question," she said. I understood she'd shared something big with me and that I would have to live with the blanks in the story because suddenly I wanted all sorts of dirty details: what the guy looked like, the sex . . . had she ever seen his wife? She told me to go do my homework. I froze at the kitchen door, turned around. "Does Dad know?"

"Homework, now."

By the time I made it back to school on the train that Sunday night I had transferred her experience to me and made it mine. I saw plainly the next day that Mr. Russell was too slight, with arms like sticks. Did I want to be held by a pair of sticks? What he had was a voice; he could read Shakespeare, short stories, even poetry and stop a class of fidgeting girls. Other than that he was just a nice guy, and a good teacher. Perfect love? Romeo and Juliet? All the mortifying embarrassments we live through before we even turn sixteen . . .

Anyhow, Joe said Harry Machin ruined me. Because of Harry I took parts Joe thought beneath me. He wasn't entirely wrong. But he had a punishing contempt for missteps in those he admired. The trouble is, Joe was on a constant lookout for missteps. *Do whatever you like, but I disown your mistakes.* . . . What happened to humans err, forgiveness is divine? Only the divine can say forget it, not a big deal, try it again?

Okay, now change the argument: *Ardennes, do whatever you want.* But I didn't need him to tell me that. I *did* what I wanted. I ran for it, and then I slowed down . . . and then I quit. Joe won.

Joe won?

And Andre? Andre married three actresses—

Sylvia was back! She unlocked the door. I looked up. I had taken to lying in the back corner of my cell. I'd made a nice little nest for myself out of a pile of dresses and things bundled on the floor. "Are you hungry?" Sylvia asked. If she minded my making a bed of her clothing, she didn't say.

Was it lunchtime already? Hadn't I just eaten breakfast? Funny how fast the sense of time dissolves when you're locked away from clocks and cell phones and media of all sorts. "Not very. I could use more water, preferably not spiked."

She told me to push the breakfast tray to the door and go back to my corner. I felt like saying, "Yes, Mistress," but didn't. She took the tray out, chained the door, and came back a few minutes later with a bottle of water, leaving it just inside the door. Mucho stuck his nose in and barked once. I'd started to hate that dog.

"There is activity in the vicinity of your room," Sylvia announced. I stood up in my cell, walked over to my prison door. Sylvia sounded oddly satisfied, if not outright pleased.

"What sort of activity?" I asked, but she was suddenly gone and I was locked in again. I heard the TV or radio go on, loud.

I t was the doorbell, and Detective Collins was ringing it. He held his badge up in front of Sylvia's peephole. She opened the door, her right hand held modestly at her throat. "Sylvia Vernon?" Sylvia smiled vacantly. "I'm Detective Collins. I've been ringing your bell several minutes." Sylvia studied the badge. "Can you hear me, Ms. Vernon?"

"I was resting, with the TV on. Nothing to watch; junk as usual. Those soaps are the bottom of the pit. How on earth do women watch such trash?"

"Is that your dog barking?"

"Mucho!" Sylvia ran to the bedroom, opened the door, and scooped up Mucho. She closed the door. The Detective stepped into the kitchen and then a little farther in. The TV was still blaring in the bedroom. Sylvia returned to the Detective, Mucho in her arms. "You're the gentleman from the other day. I saw you with my neighbor, Ardennes Thrush."

The Detective didn't skip a beat. "You two are friendly?"

"Mucho! Stop that growling or I'll shut you back in the bedroom." She tapped the dog's nose. "No, you wouldn't like that, would you?" Mucho quieted down. "That's better. What did you say?"

"You and your neighbor are friendly?"

"We've had tea."

"When did you last see Ms. Thrush, do you recall?"

Sylvia pulled her body back at the waist, looked up at the big Detective from her just-over-five-foot-two frame. She smiled. "That would be with you."

"Funny, I don't remember seeing you."

"I had the idea you didn't want to be seen."

"And what were you doing while I wasn't being seen?"

Sylvia laughed. "I have a large balcony, a lookout on all the comings and goings from my own little tower. People are interesting to watch, don't you think? Especially in a hotel, where all sorts of behavior goes on." She lifted her brows suggestively.

"Seen anything interesting lately?"

"Lieutenant, can a lady ask why she's getting the third degree?"

"It's Detective. When was the last time you spoke to Ms. Thrush?"

"Back to Ardennes; am I sensing something amiss?"

"You don't have to answer, Ms. Vernon. For the moment."

"Threats, is it? Well, let me see. Mucho, when did we last see Ms. Thrush? Two days ago, I think. Wouldn't that be the very day I saw you? Yes, she invited me for coffee. She was expecting someone, so our visit was brief. Maybe it was you she expected?"

"Did she seem concerned about anything?"

"No . . . I don't think so. Is something wrong with Ardennes? She doesn't see her husband much; she's so alone. . . ." Mucho started to whine. "You think so too, Muchie?" She smiled at the Detective while petting Mucho's head. "Hollywood can be such a lonely town, don't you think?"

"The name Lucille Trevor mean anything to you?"

It was Sylvia's turn to not skip a beat. "I knew Lucille. She died in a fire in this very apartment, a very long time ago. Why?"

"Thanks for your time."

"Don't you want to read me my rights?"

"Have you done something naughty?" Sylvia smiled a flirty little smile. Detective Collins turned to go.

Sylvia stepped into the hallway after him. "You know, there was one thing, not much to it, but a man did come by the other day. Heavyset, wore one of those leather biker vests." Sylvia shuddered, perhaps with some bad biker memory. "He and Ardennes seemed to have words. I think he may have shoved her."

"Where was this?"

"The parking below my balcony. They weren't shouting, more like hissing cats, so I couldn't catch what it was about."

"Would you know the man if you saw him again?"

"Of course. He was here yesterday afternoon." The Detective gave Sylvia Vernon a hard, scrutinizing look. "But you still haven't said what this is all about, have you?"

"Thanks again for you time, Ms. Vernon."

"Call again, Detective. Anytime . . ."

All the while Sylvia was toying with Billy I lay in my dungeon, hands over my ears against soap operas blaring on Sylvia's TV with even louder commercials in between: ads for everything from hemorrhoid ointments to remedies for erectile dysfunction. I had no way to know he was at the door, how close we'd been for those few minutes. It was well over thirty hours since I'd seen daylight, heard a bird, seen the wind in the trees, or had a bath. Now I was being driven mad by daytime TV.

Hours passed with nothing from Sylvia. The evening news was on. Maybe I would be reported missing on the broadcast. I didn't care. I'd crawled as far back as I could and hidden under some of Sylvia's gowns, the pillow over my head. I hadn't eaten since morning. I was out of water. I'd sucked on the stale candies from my purse and was out of supplies. I felt exhausted even though I'd hardly moved in two days. I yanked at the fishnet rope. Did she drug me again? Or was it just the dark and the not knowing that made me so sleepy? A kind of escape? I shook my head and tapped it. I needed to wake up and start thinking. And where the hell was Andre? How much time was he going to let go by before calling the cops . . . And Billy? What kind of cop was he? Shouldn't a SWAT team have stormed the place by now? What would Joe say to my present predicament. . . . You know, Ardennes, you need to stop referencing Joe. Really? Says who? Says I. And who are you? You. Me. Us. Joe didn't want to be anybody's daddy. *Nobody's daddy. Nobody's mommy* . . . I was singing. Who said anything about a daddy? I was so in love with Joe, but was there a whiff of that idea in him? I mean, the man never had a doubt in his life that I knew of. So? What would Simon Thrush say? He'd say: What page are you on, Ardennes? Yeah, what page am I on?

I was seven before I realized my handsome daddy was old. It was Father's Visiting Day at school, some of the girls acting like real twits, excited brides awaiting their grooms (Freud wasn't entirely off). I saw the day as an opportunity. I already hated math, and the dads were due just as we were set to open our dreaded red-and-blue workbooks. I was watching the clock. "Arithmetic is canceled today, students," Miss McCarthy announced as the fathers filed in. Most of the fathers filed in; what about kids without—dead, divorced, unwilling or unable to get time off work? What about daddies who hit their kids or preyed on them sexually? Whose idea was it to pretend we all lived in a happily-ever-after world? I had it pretty good, but then I saw how old my dad was compared to the others. He had all those *gray hairs* mixed in with the brown! How come he was so old? My half-siblings were old too. This was not normal. He smiled at me and winked. I waved back, involuntarily, but I wanted to climb inside my desk. The fathers lined up in the back of the classroom and our teacher welcomed them. I didn't hear the rest of the presentation. I would rather have done numbers. There was a chink now in my total adoration, like I'd caught Daddy with his pants down and seen something scary. That never happened; years went by in blissful ignorance before I saw anything scary between a boy's legs. Big deal; I had an older dad. I just didn't want the other kids to see. I didn't go over to him, kept my eyes on my sneakers when he came to claim me. I'm sorry, Daddy . . .

I WANT TO GET OUT OF HERE!

I banged as hard as I could on the carpeted floor with my tied-up fists until I was short of breath and worn out, all to no avail.

When Sylvia finally turned up again and unlocked the door, I didn't move a muscle. Come get me, you old witch. Come get me.

At least the TV was off. She shone a flashlight on me, and I blinked, a deer caught in the headlights. I kept still. She left the light off and unbolted the chain. This was my chance, but Mucho burst in and tore at me, all ten inches of him at face level where I lay on the pile of Sylvia's clothes. I sat up. He growled and paced in front of me as Sylvia put down a tray of covered food. She held the gun in her hand the whole time, using her right hand to slide the items into my prison.

"Mucho! Come!" The dog ran to her, and she slammed the door, rechained it, turned on the light and opened the door to the chain. "Bon appetit," she said.

"Is it nighttime?" No answer.

I was disheveled, hungry and glum. I tried to resist, but the food smelled good. I dove in.

The Muse doesn't have much of a kitchen, no complicated cuisine; the breakfasts, sandwiches, and snacks but no dining room, only limited room service down below. Up top we didn't even have minibars. Sylvia had helped herself to a stainless-steel dish cover, a tray with the hotel logo on it, and likewise the table linen. There was a white carnation on the hotel tray, set in a tiny glass vase, and a meal of capon, carrots, red potatoes and avocado. The food was precisely prepared and delicious, only there wasn't enough of it. Minute bones were all that remained on the plate when I was done. I licked it clean. Dessert was sliced papaya. I was still hungry.

I crawled to the back of my cave to digest. The day must have remained cool because the closet wasn't hot at all. That was yesterday that it was hot, right? Or was it the day before? What difference did it make? You're supposed to keep track of time, I told myself. How? I asked back. Make marks on the wall, like prisoners in movies do? I wonder if Sylvia locked Lucille in this very closet. I had my pillow and my little flannel blanket, the flashlight. The light was still on and the door was open to the chain. I should be trying to escape. Isn't that what they tell prisoners of war? What about *The Great Escape* with Steve McQueen; wasn't that a true story? He was supposed to be a messed up guy, or did Hollywood success mess him up? Probably Hollywood did. All the lackeys, even the lowly PAs on a set have attitude, as if being in the vicinity of a star gives them an edge. For *what*? Stars are objects in the night sky, diamonds the atmosphere wears of an evening. Luminaries! Crap! It's all filling and no cake. Is that why you quit, Ms. Thrush?

I was beginning to see certain advantages to captivity: a chance to think, guilt-free, to clarify everything that needed examining. Clear out the mental dust, wipe away the cobwebs, rearrange the files—a life's work, in other words. Here I lay committing the sin of idleness; an empty chair, enforced downtime, and oodles of it. If only I wasn't so sleepy. Maybe that's what I really want to be when I grow up, a prisoner. Silly, silly me. Old Sylvia's a pretty good cook. Where is old Sylvia? Out reconnoitering? It must be late, moving toward the end of day two? And I'm still supposed to be in Indio, thinking? Where's the cavalry? I didn't go to the moon, Billy, I'm right here. What about all those horror movies where the girl is abducted? There's always a cabin in the woods, miles from the nearest gas station, only bears to hear her cry out. What's that supposed to be about? Primal insecurity? At least Sylvia won't rape me before slitting my throat. And there's that hideous movie where the madman throws the drugged woman alive into a coffin and buries her. Who thinks this stuff up? Why? What's the thrill for the sicko? Fear of annihilating solitude, death of human contact? He imagines himself buried, reaches sexual climax while she slowly expires, but not before waking up in a narrow box six feet under? I shivered, stood up, did some clumsy, hand-tied jumping jacks, stretches, squats. I was not sorting anything out. . . . I lay down again. I'll make lists, that'll pass the time. Start with my directors and work my way through all the other actors . . . every part I ever played . . . no matter how small . . . get a handle on all of it . . . Maybe I should do charity work when I get out of here. . . .

Eventually, clean out of profound thoughts, with a little help from whatever Sylvia was slipping me, I fell asleep again. It was downright cold when I woke up. The closet was black. I felt chilled, but no way to put a sweater on while tied up. I wrapped the blanket tighter and crawled to the door; it opened to the chain. There was a low light from somewhere. I got my compact and stuck the mirror out as far as my hands could go. I saw a little half-moon nightlight plugged into the wall near the bedroom door. How quaint, in case Sylvia had to go wee in the dark, not to break her old kidnapper's dancing legs. Mucho lay at the foot of her bed in a regal, downy little bed of his own, and he was snoring pretty loud for such a runt. I could just see the rise and fall of Sylvia's body under the covers. It was the middle of the night. I flashed my light along the closet walls, careful to avoid the wig heads. My dinner things were gone! The chamber pot was empty and clean, and there were new water bottles. I'd slept through Sylvia clearing the dinner things? The potty removal too? Dammit, she drugged me again! I couldn't have slept through all that activity. Was she still using my Valium, or what? Well, I was wide awake now. I should start yelling, wake her up; why should Sylvia rest peacefully? Maybe someone would hear me yelling in the quiet of night. Andre must be asleep next door. Right next door, for shit's sake! Only he was way on the other side from my closet domain.

I didn't yell. I sat there, my mind running like a high fever. Nothing to conclude, I told myself. Hours went by. I think. Maybe not, maybe only ten minutes. One Mississippi, two Mississippi . . . I imagined myself in one of those vegetative comas, fed by a tube, sponge-bathed, my body creamed against bedsores, fingernails cut so they didn't grow into claws, hair combed each day, trimmed when required, teeth brushed, shades opened and closed accordingly morning or night, cheerful chatter from the day nurse filling the waking grave of my room. Not that I would know, being a turnip.

What a great part that would be to play, just lying there acting in voice-over . . . lying there thinking all kinds of things with my vague coma-way of knowing. Fed and brushed and bathed; no worries. But what if I could hear and feel and had not even an eyelash motion to communicate with, just an endless tooling around in my brain over absolutely nothing? I'd want to yell, kick, scream; I'd go mad and no one would ever know. . . . The equivalent of being mentally buried alive. There I am, buried alive again. This is not good. Quick, change the topic. But if I am buried alive, did I do the burying?

Okay, Ardennes, think of something else. . . . One Mississippi . . . breathe . . . two Mississippi . . .

Then it was morning again, and Sylvia was waking me up. There was a new tray. It was oatmeal this morning, with milk and butter, toast and jam, and tea. She looked at me as I lay in my corner. I like oatmeal, and I suppose I was hungry, but I didn't budge a muscle.

"Sick?" Sylvia asked. She was seated on a vanity chair in the open doorway, wide open, revolver in hand. The balcony curtain was open partway, I could tell by the extra light outside my jail. It must be a sunny morning out in the world.

"Not sick, Sylvia, hungover from all your doping." She didn't react. "I've been wondering what I did to make you hate me so much." I didn't sit up. I watched her sideways, my head on my pillow, cheek in both tied-together hands. I imagine my not eating her food irked.

"I don't hate you."

"What, then? I'm locked up three days. Why?"

"Your oatmeal is getting cold."

"If you let me eat with the door open, I might jump you." She waved the gun by way of reply. "Sure," I said to the gun. "But would you really shoot me, Sylvia? I don't think you killed Lucille. You loved Lucille. And I don't think you'd shoot me any more than Mucho."

"Try me."

I shrugged and slowly rose. She sat straighter. I crawled over to my bowl and picked up my spoon. I ate, and I drank my tea. There was a banana on the tray too. Mucho wandered into the closet. Sylvia called him back. I finished my breakfast while she watched, feeling like a death-row prisoner eating her last meal, the warden looking on.

"Do you look at pornography, Ardennes?"

"Oh, are we having a conversation? How pleasant. Yeah, I've glanced online, occasionally, casually. Why?"

"Even at my age I love a woman's body. I made my living showing mine. No touching, though. The men did not touch Sylvia Vernon, even when I was getting almost too old and the dance numbers too raunchy and I needed the money. I've displayed enough of myself to make a clock blush, but I kept the men off. These girls today have it bad with lap dances and back rooms. That's not dancing."

I'd heard this from her already, the tragedy of stripping today. Was this feminism on Sylvia's part? It's not as if anyone was going to pay her anymore to spread her inner sanctum open to the klieg lights. "Is it money you're after, Sylvia? You don't have to go to Andre. I made a ton on films. I'm not greedy, and I'm happy to share." I meant it too; I had enough money to live comfortably for two lifetimes.

"I've wondered what you do now you no longer act. Actors don't seem to know what to do with themselves when no one's looking."

"You're not in love with me or anything sad like that, Sylvia?"

"I could be. I've watched all your films. That first day in the laundry, when you waltzed in out of nowhere, I thought I must be dreaming. What was Ardennes Thrush doing in the Muse laundry room? And you were as down-to-earth as a mouse."

"A mouse?"

"Beautiful, and not always a mouse. Who frightened you? Who took your nerve away?"

"What makes you think I'm frightened, other than of the muzzle of your gun, Sylvia?"

"What do you want?"

"I've been asking you the same thing for three days, Sylvia. One of us must know."

"It doesn't matter what I want."

"It matters to me; I'm living in your closet."

Detective Collins informed Andre that his wife's cell phone was off or out of commission; for the moment untraceable. It was noon of the third day. He'd been all over the place looking for leads. He'd sat on the phone at the precinct to check flights to New York, with no luck. He didn't request manifests for all the flights out of Los Angeles, which would get to be Homeland Security-complicated so he went with his gut feeling that Ardennes would fly to New York, *if* she took a flight out. He'd gone to Enterprise Rent-a-Car at LAX to show Ardennes Thrush's picture around, then to the other car rentals, but came up empty. All a waste of time, but the gumshoe work couldn't be avoided. His boss would need to know every avenue had been walked. He was losing time when every minute might matter.

Andre Lucerne and Detective Devin Collins were seated at the cluttered table, an unlikely pair. The balcony door was closed against a cool day, the seesawing of spring making up its mind. "The last activity was the morning she went missing." He didn't mention any calls made to or from him. He let Andre know Ardennes's car had been returned to Enterprise at LAX and that, as far as he could tell, she hadn't replaced it with another car.

Andre nodded. "Why LAX, I wonder, if she didn't take a flight out?" He stood up to open the balcony door, to let a little air in, the two men at the table making a heavy presence. He did not sit down again. The Detective watched him. "I wanted to say—I thought about it in the night—she would not have left without her blue and white teapot. She drags that black tea everywhere. The pot is here, on the shelf. I feel surer now my wife is missing."

"Good for you, Mr. Lucerne. Ready to face facts, are we? Have you recast your film?"

"No, I have not. Your position is important, Officer, but the significance of the situation may escape you, used as you must be to this sort of thing."

"Still worried about the press, huh?"

At this point Andre made a visible effort to control himself. "If my wife has been taken against her will, what do they want with her if not money?"

"Any number of things: sex, torture, murder, thrills . . . use your imagination." Andre was paying close attention. The Detective softened his tone. "It's also possible none of the above and she just wanted out."

"You mean flew off somewhere?"

"Not on an airplane. We checked as far as we could, unless she went someplace exotic and unexpected." No need to go into details—or the lack.

"What do we do now?" Andre asked. He looked to be struggling, as if he were not certain how to react. That was how Detective Collins saw it.

"We see what Matthew Fitzgerald has to say. I've had him picked up. He won't like it."

"You suspect him?"

"Currently I suspect everyone." He looked at Andre to be certain he understood that by everyone he meant *everyone*. His cell phone rang. "Yeah? Okay, bring him up. Fits is here, and not too happy."

There was a commotion at the door. Two uniformed officers brought a raucous Fits into the suite. Detective Collins nodded to the officers and told them to wait outside.

"What's the idea, Detective? You want to get me fired or what?"

"Sit down, Fits. Quietly, please."

"Yeah, well, screw you. This better be good." He slumped down onto the couch and shoved his hair off his face with both hands.

"The lady next door says you had an argument with Ms. Thrush. She heard you below her balcony."

"Oh, yeah, and when was that?"

"You tell me."

"You send cops over to my set; they don't arrest me but drag me over here. You could have asked me this on the phone."

"The waiter at Musso and Frank's also said you had an argument with Ms. Thrush, that you left in a huff without finishing your drink."

"I'm not that much of a drinker." The Detective was quiet. "We met at Musso's, yeah. I was angry with Ardennes, sure, for quitting, for throwing her talent away. But I don't qualify that as a fight. Not even close. And I tipped that old goat of a waiter well."

Andre was seated at the table, listening. "Where is my wife, Fits?"

"In my hip pocket. I could ask you the same; she's *your* wife."

The Detective stepped in: "You're saying you did not argue with Ms. Thrush here at the hotel, a few days ago?"

"Yesterday was the first time I was ever at this hotel—or whatever day that was. You got the wrong guy, copper."

"It's been three days, Detective. Do you think this man is lying and that he is involved in Ardennes's disappearance?"

"Oh, not so fast, director-face. Besides, why would I take her; she's missing, that's certain? 'Cause where I left off, that was just speculation."

"Someone is lying, Fits. Either you or the lady next door."

"Try the lady next door," Fits told the Detective. He rubbed his hands over his chaotic head of hair. "This is fucking bullshit. . . . I'll go talk to the cunt myself." He stood up.

"*Sit* down, Fits." It was as close as the Detective came to raising his voice.

To me Sylvia was the eccentric at the other end of Mucho's leash. I didn't picture her on the telephone or shopping or bathing or doing much of anything other than dressing large and walking her dog. So when her phone rang and she slammed the door and locked it, I had to adjust my image of her.

She must have walked out of the bedroom with the phone. I heard her smoky laugh and something like "You do know how to get a gal interested. . . ." But that was all. A short time later she was back, unlocking the closet door, opening it to the chain. She sat on the little cushioned vanity chair, crossing her legs. I could just see her left profile from my bed of rags, where I'd retreated when she'd gone for the phone.

"Yup, looks like your crew is going back to work; that fellow Olive let me know just now. You'll be glad to know the long faces are gone."

"*Who?* Do you mean Olav, the Norwegian, the sound guy? And they're not my crew, Sylvia; it's my husband's movie. I have nothing to do with it. Sorry to disappoint."

"Sound? I thought he was props?" I lifted my hands, palms open, and shrugged. "He *said* his name was Olive. That's what I've been calling him. . . . Anyway, he asked me for a drink."

"Olav did?"

She primped her never-out-of-place, plastic-looking hair, reached for the leopard-patterned cigarette holder, installed a fresh smoke but thankfully did not light up. "You think I'm too old? It so happens Olive and I went to the Hollywood Bowl just the other week."

My eyes were bugging. How did I miss Olav and Sylvia? I also wondered about her hearing, or maybe she just didn't listen too well.

"Of course he's gay as the day is long, but I take it unkindly you think my pubic hairs are too gray to entice."

"I don't think anything of the sort. And Olav is not gay. His girlfriend came out for a long weekend just before shooting began. So better watch your panties." Apparently old Sylvia still enjoyed the idea of turning men on.

"Not gay? Could've fooled me. Bi, then. Well, they *are* going back to work."

My guess was Sylvia was only guessing, or outright lying, trying to rattle me. But she must have talked to Olav, and maybe they had gone to a concert. Still, all Andre could do was work scenes that didn't involve the lead; even if he had replaced Luce Bouclé, the new actress couldn't possibly be ready. Sylvia's point, of course, was Andre going back to work with me still missing, her little game of torturing the prisoner. Or did he believe my message about Indio, and did Billy buy that too, and absolutely no one was looking for me? I felt fury rising up into my throat. Shouldn't Sylvia have made some sort of ransom demand by now? "What do you want with me, Sylvia? If you plan on killing me I ask that you get it over with; otherwise, tell me what it is you fucking want!"

"Such melodrama. Who said anything about killing anybody?" She harrumphed. "You actresses are all alike. You know, it was a wartime buddy of Lucille's father who brought her out to Holly-wood, took pity—according to Lucy. He stepped into her daddy's shoes after the car crash. Helped himself is what I saw. He was a start-up director; she was all of eighteen. He paid her train ticket, gave her a screen test, and found her a bit part. After that she signed a slave-wage contract with MGM, and he moved her in here."

"So this *was* her flat? And her father died in the accident. And you *did* meet in Las Vegas?"

Sylvia wasn't angry this time that I knew so much. She warmed up. "Lucy watched my revue and asked me to teach her for a B part she wanted badly—only because of the dancing. I took one look at her legs and told her she was nuts. She cussed me good: 'Just teach me to sex dance, you whore.' They let me be her body double— which didn't leave her much to do. 'Course, I didn't take any pay. I did it as a favor, and after that she thought she owed me. Lucille didn't owe me a thing, I'd have body-doubled her whole life if I could have." Sylvia stopped talking. She held the unlit cigarette to her lips. Mucho watched her, his small body trembling the way those tiny dogs do.

My own body ached all over from inactivity, sleeping on the

floor and being tied up. I was beginning to disappear. I would soon be forgotten, a cold case. I didn't know why Sylvia was taking me down memory lane with Lucille Trevor's story—a need to confess, maybe—but I decided keeping on her friendly side was in my best interests.

"You think she was abused by her daddy's pal?"

"I *know* she was." She pressed her lips shut tight, and we were quiet a couple of minutes.

I figured she was in a softened frame of mind and took a chance. "Listen, Sylvia, any chance of a shower?"

She thought about my request. "I'll bring you a bowl of hot water and a soap sponge."

"I can't exactly change my shirt all tied up like this, can I?"

"I'm not running a hotel!" she snapped.

"I didn't ask to check in!" I snapped back. If she was going to relent and untie me, it would be a mistake. "How about it, Sylvia? I'm becoming a health hazard."

Instead of answering, she bolted up and slammed the closet door shut, locked it and turned out the light.

"Sylvia?" I called out. "I only wanted to wash up." I heard the bedroom door slam. A minute or two later there was frantic barking from Mucho, apparently stuck in the bedroom.

Detective Collins rang her bell a second time. The chain was on; Sylvia opened the door and peered out. Mucho continued to bark in the bedroom.

"Back for more, Detective?" She closed the door, undid the chain and opened the door, pulling off a bright magenta dish glove that she'd grabbed from the sink before opening the door. "Forgot something?"

"Mind if I come in?"

Sylvia pulled the door open all the way. "As you wish."

The curtains were open on the balcony, flooding the place with light. Skies were intermittent sun and clouds, but Sylvia's white shag rug and white decor caused a glare. The Detective needed a second to adjust his eyes. There was slow jazz playing from a radio in the living room. Detective Collins glanced around. Stew was simmering on the stove in a large red Le Creuset pot.

He lifted the lid. "Company coming?"

"You're welcome to join me."

"Smells good. Nice little home you have here."

"What can I do for you—again, Officer?"

He pulled the black rhinestone cigarette holder out of his pocket. "This belong to you?" Sylvia considered the question before answering. "A simple yes or no, Ms. Vernon."

"I was thinking, where did I lose that darn thing? Where'd you find it?"

"In Ardennes Thrush's desk drawer; any idea how it got there?"

"She must have found it. I stopped smoking, you know. I only hold the cigarette, unlit. I miss it awfully, but the doctor—well, you don't want to hear about all that. Can I have it back?"

"Not yet. The actor Matthew Fitzgerald, that's the man you say you saw with Ms. Thrush, says you're fictionalizing about them having an argument. Two days ago was the first time he was ever here."

"And which of us do you believe, Detective?"

"I hear management wants to convert all the units up top to hotel rooms, eliminate the apartments. That could be problematic for you, living on a retired stripper's pension. Or don't strippers get pensions? I forget."

"Renters are protected in Los Angeles, Detective. The law is on my side."

"That's a good place to keep it, Ms. Vernon." He tossed the cigarette holder into the air and caught it. "I'll get this back to you once the case is closed. Thanks again for your time. Oh, enjoy the dinner party."

Sylvia followed Detective Collins to the door. "I still don't know what this is. . . . Oh, my, things do look serious," she said, eyeing the two uniformed cops who'd brought Fits to the hotel, lingering in the hallway. "Hello, boys. Care for a cup of coffee?" The cops looked to Detective Collins, who made a "no" tick with his right forefinger. They said no, thanks. "Knock twice if you change your mind," Sylvia said before closing and chaining the door.

I couldn't hear a thing, but I could tell something was up. Was attention finally being focused on Sylvia? I heard her tell Mucho to shut up. She opened the closet door and told me some new actors had arrived. She said one had rung her doorbell by mistake. She'd gone out on the balcony to see the fresh young faces. "Lookers too," she said. "Think what you're missing all locked up."

"What do I have to do to get un–locked up?"

"Don't you know?"

"Give me a hint."

"What do you want?"

"Keep asking me that!" Dammit, she was annoying. She turned to leave. "Wait! I *want* to go outside, into the sunlight. That's what I want." I sounded pathetic.

"I have to check my stove," she said, dismissing me. Sylvia stirred her stew, then filled an oversized bowl with hot water. With a bar of soap and a washcloth in her apron pocket and a fresh towel over her arm she walked slowly, carrying the bowl on a tray, into the bedroom and then to the closet. The usual instructions followed, and I hovered in the back while she pushed the tray in, water sloshing as she did.

The water wasn't very hot by the time the chain was back on. She gave me my privacy to bathe. I crawled to the bowl. I wasn't standing up much anymore, moving on the ground instead, like a caged animal on all fours. I rinsed my face and under my arms and ran the cloth between my legs after removing my panties. I patted myself dry as best I could with tied hands. My T-shirt was damp, and so was my fishnet binding. Nothing I could do about it. I had two clean pairs of underwear, I put one pair on and tucked the dirty pair into my bag—why the modesty; who cared? I took a bottle of water—she'd left three this time—and brushed my teeth for the first time since my captivity. I wondered about lunch. Something smelled good when she opened the door. What a civilizing effect even a miserable facsimile of a bath and a change of panties can bring. I sat back in my lair. I picked up the Salinger and managed to read a few pages before dozing off. Zooey and his mom were still in the bathroom.

Detective Collins spent the afternoon of day three poking around the hotel. The staff was already abuzz that something was up. He'd fill out the picture, though he didn't count on learning much. Something was eating at him from his last visit to Sylvia Vernon's apartment. He was pretty sure he'd caught a whiff of the same cheap perfume he'd smelled in Ardennes's suite. Was the former Vegas stripper up to no good, beyond being a hard-boiled old broad? It looked as if she might have made up that yarn about Fits and Ardennes arguing. Why?

First he had a chat with the hotel manager, Doug Warren, who was newly placed. This was unfortunate for the Detective because Warren didn't yet have his hands on things in a way that would have been helpful, the nuances and details of the hotel that can reveal so much. Tall and pimply, as if his sebaceous glands hadn't quite made it out of high school, he wore glasses that slipped down an oily nose at regular intervals. Fortunately he'd inherited a loyal staff, and a hardworking assistant manager in Mary Kay Alton, a natural blond who knew how to handle her staff and any tricky guests.

Doug Warren said he'd only met Ms. Thrush once, when she'd first arrived. He rarely went to the upper-level rooms himself.

"I hear you're planning on turning the apartments up top into rentals. Business is good, then?"

The manager shook his head. "They're a complete loss. Rent control is killing us."

"Yeah, those pesky protections. You buying out leases?"

"We don't quite have the budget in place for that at the moment. But as people look to leave—"

"Sure, apply a little pressure—"

"No, nothing like harassment. Not at all. Ours is a reputable establishment, Detective Collins."

The Detective placed the manager as Canadian or Minnesotan. "There are some vacant apartments; Ms. Vernon in 304 seems to be one of a couple of holdouts in that wing. Why not begin renovating around them?"

Mr. Warren lowered his voice, though they were alone in his office with the door securely closed. "Detective Collins, the family that owns the Hotel Muse property is looking to sell. Those units are currently worth more sitting idle."

"I see; so it's lucky you have Andre Lucerne's crew taking up so many rooms and suites."

The manager shook his head, adjusted his tortoiseshell glasses. "Frankly, my predecessor gave them rather too sweetheart a deal." He shifted in his swivel chair. "Water?" He reached into a small refrigerator behind his desk and pulled out two bottles of spring water.

The Detective nodded. "Thanks." He reached across the desk for one of the bottles.

"I have to say, Detective, I'm not quite certain what the problem here is. You say Ms. Thrush has gone missing?"

"It's not certain." He looked significantly across the water bottle, still at his lips.

"Then in what way can I help? Negative publicity if a guest *were* to go missing from the property—well, you see where this could lead, I'm sure."

"Right. This town is all about image. But you will arrange for me to talk—*quietly*—to some of your staff. The maids who work up top, the desk people . . ."

"Of course, of course." He hit a number on his phone. "Mary Kay? Can you come into my office? Yes, now." The assistant manager materialized in a matter of seconds. The manager made the introductions. She was pretty enough, if just the wrong side of missing her gym days, and looked like she could use a couple of days off or what the locker-room gents might call in need of a good plugging by her boyfriend; bring some color to her cheeks. The Detective stood up. "There's a little problem—"

"I'll take it from here, Mr. Warren," the Detective said without looking at the manager. "Ms. Alton, have you seen Ardennes Thrush in the past, say, three days?"

"I heard something was wrong . . . but no, I haven't. She doesn't come down much anymore now they have Internet up top. Is she in any danger?"

"How did you find her when you last saw her?"

"Oh, lovely; she's a lovely person, not a stuck–up, actressy bone to her." She leaned in as if confiding. "And, you know, she was nominated for an Oscar? I'd say there's an inwardness or solitariness— yes, that's the word I'd use; she's a solitary person." She nodded her head as if to indicate she was done making her point.

"Not upset or distracted?"

The assistant manager considered the question, wrinkling her nose, scrunching together a constellation of pale freckles. The Detective saw Mary Kay Alton as one who'd had other plans—perhaps to be an actress herself. Probably something creative that would fade as she did. "No, I don't think so," she said.

Doug Warren guarded no hidden ambition; he was content managing a boutique hotel and all its personnel; the job gave him just the amount of authority necessary to face the bathroom mirror each day. The Detective knew the type. At the same time as he sized up the inconsequential manager, he decided Fits was squeaky clean, at least with regard to Ardennes's current circumstance. And that made Sylvia look bad again. The cop in him didn't care as long as his case was solved and Ardennes Thrush was safe. But Devin Collins—private citizen—preferred Fits to be clean and—for reasons he couldn't satisfactorily explain—did not want Sylvia to be as dirty as she was beginning to look. Was it the old cliché of the stripper and the law? The soft spot for a girl who'd turned hard by years of exposure to johnny-boys who only saw her as a ticket to self-pleasure?

He didn't know and was not about to spend time guessing. He just didn't see Sylvia Vernon as a determined criminal.

"Okay, Ms. Alton, thanks. I'll talk to the desk personnel now."

"Oh, I just remembered, Ms. Thrush was going to join the gym, L.A. Fitness. We have an arrangement with our guests to use the facility. She seemed excited about that."

"Did she join?"

"I can check for reimbursement receipts, but I don't think there would have been time, I only passed her the information the other day, a note in her mailbox. She called me back to inquire."

"Will you check on that for me? Now, the desk people . . ."

"Sharif is on today," Mary Kay Alton explained in a brisk, businesslike tone. "And Christine, but Christie's in back. We have two clerks on at each shift, though usually only one is actually present at the desk." She moved toward the door.

The Detective thanked the manager, who'd stood up. Mr. Warren let him know he hoped nothing was seriously the matter. Security was good at the Hotel Muse; he wanted Detective Collins to be assured of that.

The Detective nodded. "Sure, adverse publicity. I got it."

Sharif snapped to attention, ready for the grand jury. Whatever the Detective might ask he'd have details to spare, taking matters very much to heart. "She's a beautiful woman. I confess I have a small crush. Last time I saw her . . . let's see . . . a few days ago. I miss her so at breakfast, we had such nice little chats." He smiled conspiratorially. He told the Detective about Eddie Tompkins's curious visit, not adding much to what Detective Collins already knew. "Ms. Thrush didn't seem to know who he was. An aggressive fan, I supposed. These actresses can't be too careful, and Ardennes—er, Ms. Thrush—wasn't very."

"Careful?"

"*I* don't think so. . . . So, the last time I saw her? Yes, I remember. She was locked out—*again*. Wait a minute; she hurt her ankle—was that before or after?"

The Detective leaned an elbow on the reception desk. "To the best of your recollection."

"After, I think. Yes, she was on her way out and twisted her ankle—Ms. Thrush likes to walk, a real New Yorker. Anyhow, she limped back into the lobby. She seemed very bothered by it. I asked if she needed a doctor. She didn't, but she wanted a ride back up to her suite. I had Manuel—no, Arturo drove her, and later I sent a box of Epsom salts up for her to soak her foot. Epsom salt is the elixir for *so* many woes, Detective. Hermie took it up—that's Hermie Martinez, our head of housekeeping. She left it at the door because Ms. Thrush had gone out in her car, which surprised me. In fact, I was worried; using the ankle seemed like a bad idea. She has fantastic legs!" He paused to breathe.

"That was the last contact?"

"She had a delivery . . . flowers, it looked like—a long box."

"Who delivered?"

"The post office. Now I think of it, she had another delivery yesterday. Mr. Lucerne asked me to hold on to it."

"What was it?"

"A large box from Bed Bath and Beyond."

"Who delivered that?"

"UPS."

"Okay. I'll need to take a look at that box, and I'd like to speak with Ms. Martinez."

Sharif pressed a button under the desk, and the other clerk, Christine, materialized. Sharif asked her to locate Hermie, and he and the Detective waited, the silence between them burdensome. Sharif started to say something, but the Detective got there first. "How did you find Ms. Thrush that last time you saw her, aside from the ankle?"

"She was, she seemed—not unhappy, too much *to* her for that— but a little sad. Maybe that day with the ankle, a little anxious. To me she was never less than gorgeous."

The Detective thrummed the desk, studying poor, pudgy Sharif, guessing at sweaty palms and a fumbling love life. But what was up with the ankle? Detective Collins put two and two together, and it added up to the second sighting of Eddie Tompkins. Ardennes had told him about it but must have skipped some details, like a feigned injury. He remembered seeing a blue and white box of Epsom salts on the kitchen counter. That was when he placed the cheap perfume on Sylvia Vernon for sure. It had to be.

Ms. Martinez couldn't add much to the others' accounts. A squat woman in a navy-blue skirt and white hotel blouse, with too much plum lipstick coloring an ample mouth, she too found Ardennes sweet, *dulce*, she said. Yes, she had driven up the box of salts and left them on the door handle.

"How did Ms. Thrush seem when you last saw her?" the Detective asked.

"I would say she was a woman, how can I say it? Contained to herself."

The Detective nodded and thanked her. Christine had nothing to add. She hadn't even met Ardennes. The box from Bed Bath and Beyond held a small, glass-topped garden table. Detective Collins found nothing in the packing or contents relevant to the case; another waste of time that couldn't be helped. He thanked Sharif again.

He hadn't parked his car before the maids up top knew a policeman was coming to question them about a guest. Alma and Zaneda also sang Ardennes's praises. "Kind, *y muy guapa, la señora!*" Zaneda said. No, she hadn't cleaned the rooms in a day or two, and then it was her days off. "She do not all the time want me to clean. Her rooms almost did not need me. She like me to make the bed, and the bath."

They were standing in an unoccupied room in the wing opposite the one containing the Thrush-Lucerne suite. Detective Collins faced the open door. The women sat down together on the bed.

Alma was the blunter of the two. "I seen her with you, Señor. She get into your car."

"Did you see me before that?"

"I see you," Zaneda said. She looked down at her hands, nervously. "The day I come late to her rooms because she took the do-not-disturb off." She thought a minute. "She give nice tips, for my kids."

"Where did you see me, Zaneda?"

"I see you came that day and go to her rooms." She looked Detective Collins sharply in the eye, just once.

"And you, Alma? You haven't cleaned the rooms lately either, correct?"

"A German film team came to take up four good rooms, so they need us down below. They are good business below. Better tips. But I cleaned yesterday, late. Mr. Lucerne ask me to."

"Mr. Lucerne asked you to clean?" Alma nodded. "Okay, when did you last see Ms. Thrush?"

"I saw Mrs. Thrush go out with Mr. Lucerne and the Portuguese girl, Santosa—last time I saw her. Mrs. Thrush was driving."

"Did either of you see her limping?"

"*Quale?*" asked Zaneda. Alma translated. Neither woman had seen Ardennes with a limp. Then Zaneda remembered: Arturo had driven her up, and he'd told her about the ankle. "*Sí*, when she falled on her foot?" She pointed to her ankle. The Detective indicated yes. "No, not limp."

He pulled out a picture of Fits and showed it to the women. Alma had nothing to say, but Zaneda recognized him. "I see him in movies." She smiled.

"You like the movies?" He watched a dimple come to life on the left side of her small mouth.

Zaneda nodded, smiled shyly. "*Sí*, movies make me dream."

"Sure, dreaming's open to everybody, and it's free. How about here, at the hotel?"

"*Como?*" Alma translated. Zaneda giggled, covering her mouth. Alma looked at her. "*Sí Sí, aquí,* here today—yes. He comes with two policemens, just like in the movies." She laughed again. Alma's eyes went big.

"But not before that?" Fits might have been missed, slipping in behind the garbage truck.

"You have not been to her rooms since your day off?" Zaneda shook her head. She looked at Alma, who shrugged. "Alma, this is important: Did you see Ms. Thrush drive her car away three or four days ago?"

"No."

"Did you see anyone else drive her car away?"

"No." She thought a minute but said no again.

"Okay. Last question: Do either of you clean Ms. Vernon's room, 304? It's okay, I won't tell anyone, but maybe she pays you cash once in a while?"

"That crazy old lady with the dog—she too cheap!"

"Why do you call her crazy, Alma?"

"Look how she dresses, like a old *putana*. People like that, they pretend they don't see us."

Zaneda asked her something in Spanish; Alma answered in Spanish. Zaneda said, "She not so bad. She talk sometimes to Señora Thrush. I don't know the *mujer* is loco, only old. I see Señora Thrush all the time walking, in the little gardens and down in the road. Always walking, always she is alone. Is good she have a friend, no?"

Detective Collins glanced out through the open door just in time to see Sylvia Vernon withdraw her head from over her balcony wall. Friend or foe? he asked himself. He looked each woman in the eye. "Neither of you knows where Ms. Thrush is?" Neither did. Alma was likely the less trustworthy of the two, but Detective Collins didn't see either of them involved in Ardennes's disappearance. He thanked them and let them go.

He'd already told Fits he was free to go. Fits had told him to shove it when he'd offered to have the uniformed officers, Mike Berry and Paul Bedford, drive him back to Universal City. He said he'd pay for his own cab. What he wanted Detective Collins to do was call the studio and say there had been a mix-up, that he—Fits—was not involved in any criminal activity. "I don't need those stiffs with anything to hang over my head. See?"

"Fine," Detective Collins said.

"And where are you, anyway, as in: Where's Ardennes? You're an amateur, Detective Collins, as in: You don't know what you're doing. I could *act* a better cop," he said before taking off.

While Detective Collins was harvesting clues, Andre made a quick trip to Century City, with Carola behind the wheel this time. He let Jonas Campion know his wife was missing and suggested they keep a low profile on the news since the circumstances were anything but clear. She may have, as Andre put it, "been encouraged to leave with someone not of her own choosing." His tone was impatient.

"Missing? Good God. Since when?" Jonas Campion asked. He glanced at the ever-poised and ready Cheryl Li.

"A day or so."

"Or *so*?" He composed himself, leaned back in his desk chair. "Listen here, Andre, first there was the Bouclé incident. A perfectly good actress. Now this. We have a bottom line to consider; there is an end to our patience."

"The police feel they are getting close," Andre lied. Carola studied the floor.

Jonas Campion stood up. "The police . . . wonderful. Cheryl! Get that idiot Thames on the phone—not up here; I do not want him in here—and tell him to get a piece in *Variety* ASAP: Andre Lucerne will begin shooting . . ." he fished the air for the title . . . "*The Dance* next week. Keep it under wraps who will replace Luce Bouclé. He's to drop a few actresses' names, get a little intrigue going. And, Cheryl, not a word leaves this office about Ardennes Thrush gone missing. Not a word." Cheryl nodded firmly: her high heels clacked efficiently past the carpeted portion of Jonas Campion's office onto the terrazzo flooring and out to her desk. To Andre Campion said, "You begin shooting first thing next week. I will assign a lead and work out the details if you haven't found one by then. Ardennes Thrush might be the best actress for the part, but we can't wait—of course we hope for her safe recovery. Find someone, Andre. Don't jeopardize that Aussie money. You see my point, I'm sure." He eyed Andre significantly.

Andre was quiet a moment. "Producers do not cast my films,

Jonas. *I* cast my films." His voice was as icy as his native Alps. "Your concern for Ms. Thrush's well-being is touching. Good day, sir." And with that he took Carola's arm and led her out of the office, barely fifteen minutes after they'd arrived.

Jonas Campion sat down at his desk, the brown calf-leather seat emitting a deflating sigh. "Shit," he announced to the air around his desk. He reached for his phone but recradled it a few seconds later. "Shit," he said again, more emphatically. He sat a minute. "Cheryl!" he called out.

We're running out of time, Miss," Sylvia said when she finally returned. I was back on my pile of old clothes. I'd put on a pair of sweatpants after my sponge bath and was reasonably comfortable. I did not reply. What difference did the time make to me? "Ardennes?" The light was on, but Sylvia pointed a flashlight into my face.

"I heard you. Turn that thing off!" I blinked. "Running out for what? Should I make out a will: 'All my worldly wealth goes to my good friend and jailer, Sylvia Vernon, in memory of our intimate time together'?"

"You have to decide; it's now or never: *What* do you want?"

I yawned. "I'm missing your point, Sylvia."

"What's wrong with you?"

"I must be getting Stockholm syndrome. I'm starting to like my little lair. Of course, my muscles are atrophying, my hair's a nest, I can't change my shirt, but all in all it's not too bad. The food is excellent. And something smells yummy."

"Why'd you shack up with that detective?"

"You weren't in my life yet."

"What are you doing married to the Swiss?"

"They make very precise timepieces, didn't you know?"

"Do all you actresses need to ruin yourselves?"

I leaned on my elbow, one hand hugging the other in my binding. I'd become a regular lazy little odalisque. I'm sure it was Sylvia's doping potion or I'd have been on the floor in a thousand crumpled nervous pieces by now. I snapped my fingers. "Why don't *you* audition for Andre's film, Sylvia? It's about a dancer whose legs get mangled in a carnival accident. Sound familiar? You could try for the body double if acting's not in your line. What a plot coincidence, huh: The character was a ballerina before her mishap. That'd be a lot safer than kidnapping. Isn't kidnapping a capital offense? Better make ransom contact with my husband soon, before the FBI comes on board, eh, Sylvia? He's worth plenty." Maybe the cobwebs were clearing and I was actually on to something. I sat up. "I'm thinking you couldn't have pulled this little caper off all on your own. . . ."

"Shut up."

She looked agitated. I must have hit a nerve. "No need to get testy. I'm only trying to help."

"You *sound* like her. . . ."

"But I am *not* Lucy. Do you understand that, Sylvia?" I think I finally had her off balance.

She softened her tone. "You're lonely. I can help."

I laughed without mirth. "Is that what you told Lucy when you locked her up and set the closet on fire?"

"She was found in bed."

"So? You dragged her there after the smoke knocked her out. You took a chance; you could have been killed too, but it worked out, right, Sylvia?" She shook her head. "No? Okay, just a thought; can't hang a girl for thinking."

"They're looking for you. You haven't much time left to decide."

This was a bit of good news. But why tell me? "Oh, for God's sake, decide *what*, Sylvia?" We had begun to snarl. It seemed to me that neither of us meant to; well, I had the right, but why was Sylvia all worked up? I suppose she was on edge, an old lady holding a woman hostage. I looked at her. Nah, she was a pretty tough bird. Besides, she was keeping me docile on sedatives. "Whose idea was drugging me, Sylvia?"

She ignored the question. "What do you care about?"

"Me? I care about plenty."

"Name three things."

I thought about that. "No."

"You didn't care about acting."

She knew how to cut the fat off the meat, get right to the gut of the matter, didn't old Sylvia? Maybe this was what I would have tried to tell Harry if his heart hadn't given out, but Sylvia was doing the asking now: "I probably cared too much."

She was quiet. Mucho was looking at me, his head cocked. It seemed like he was smiling. I coughed and looked up at Sylvia. She looked stricken. "Sylvia? What makes you so certain I'm not in love with my husband?"

She waved a hand impatiently.

"Bluffing? Well, you could be right. We married in a mood: a snowy night . . ."

"I *am* right."

I leaned back on my chaise of old clothes, the stale smell of them no longer bothersome. I was hungry; we'd skipped lunch.

"Maybe I just wanted to be in love. . . ." I heard myself and wanted to laugh, I sounded that drifty—that was my mom's word, *drifting*. Well, well, revelation upon revelation. She was always saying, "Be clear, Ardennes; be clear." When I was small I thought of windows and Windex. Or like when Grandma would say, "What a perfectly clear day we've been given today; we should learn from it." Which also confused me because I didn't know who gave us the clear day—nor did I have a clue what we were supposed to learn from it. Later I figured my mother meant clear à la the March Hare: *Then you should say what you mean.* But I don't think that was it either, but more like some tall-order wisdom that I would have to catch on to when I got a little wisdom of my own. In other words, I forgot about it.

Sylvia put Mucho down. "Is it girl talk now?"

"Your turn at sarcasm, Sylvia?" I shot back.

"Ah, whaddaya mean by *love* anyhow?"

"I don't know." I looked up at the closet ceiling, the bare light fixture that had been my sun for the past couple of days. "Shooting stars? The kind in the sky, I mean."

"Fireworks, huh?"

"Sure, except fireworks don't last; then I think moving on to something deeper is the trick." I thought about Billy. He was good on the floor but maybe not so stellar on the job; why hadn't he found me yet? On top of everything else, had I slept with a second-rate cop?

"How's the deep part going so far?"

I shrugged. "I'm better at theory. What about you, Sylvia?"

"What *about* me?"

"Didn't you ever fall hard?"

"Lucille . . ."

I sat up again. "You had it bad for lame little Lucy, huh?" She nodded. "So you were a lesbian stripper?"

"I had men. One I liked, only he was my uncle and that was a no-no. Didn't stop us, but it couldn't go anywhere, and I was in far more over my head than he ever was. He liked consuming my flesh all right. Not to mention he had a wife."

"Why your uncle, if you don't mind my asking?"

"Who knows? My mother's brother; maybe it was father desire—mine took off before we were introduced. I was barely fifteen when I seduced Uncle Jack."

"Oh." Right about the time in my life when I was innocently pining for literary Mr. Russell. *My* daydreams hadn't gotten past kissing; I didn't know enough to go any further.

"He was a stinker to let me, not a man of principle, but that type never worked out for me as it turned out. I started dancing and found I enjoyed the girls in the dressing room—ladies' bodies more. Being on stage with nearly naked women was a real turn-on. Imagine my little secret—not that I was the only gal to ever try and climb the harem walls." She massaged her neck. On her right middle finger was a chunky garnet ring. She had a habit of twisting it while holding on to the gun. I wondered if it was glass or the real thing. If real, who gave it to her?

"Maybe the men I wanted to love were just too clumsy with me. Or we're all just too clumsy with each other . . . who knows?" I said, unintentionally mimicking her.

Sylvia's head shot forward. She looked at me with total concentration, her expression stern—or maybe alert, animal-alert. It lasted a matter of seconds. "All this reminiscing isn't getting us anywhere." Her tone turned hard as rocks.

I looked at her, not the way she looked at me but seeing her clearly the way it sometimes happens when you think you're seeing but then, when you do look—really look—you see you haven't seen at all and are only just in that moment seeing what is before you. It was her looking at me the way she did that made me look back at her the way I did. "Where are we trying get to, Sylvia?" I asked softly.

She pushed herself off the doorway. "Too much chatter! We leave here tomorrow morning."

I felt a shiver of panic, a snake of fear slithering down from my heart to my gut. The announcement seemed sudden. Where would she take me, to another hideout? Or was she going to dump me somewhere? Were they getting close to finding me?

I made my voice sound unconcerned. I'd cooked up a plan and decided now was the time to play it. "Ah, gee, I was just settling in. Must we leave?" She didn't react, seated now in her chair with the gun at her side, in her right hand. "Sylvia, listen." I made myself sound embarrassed. "I had my little bath earlier, and there was spotting." No response. "Did you hear? I'm about to get my period. Could you go to the pharmacy and get me tampons? I'll pay you back. Sylvia."

She just stared at me. For a minute I thought she was going to ask for proof. I was lying. In fact, I was a day or two late and trying not to panic, though I didn't see how it could be possible. I'd thought of that too, to ask for a pregnancy test, but decided not to jinx myself. My plan, once she was gone, was to bang on the walls with her shoes. It wasn't much, but it was all I had. The subterfuge was the only way I could be certain she'd be out of the way. But she just kept on staring. My little trick, this entirely unanticipated piece of information, had her stumped. She looked seriously flummoxed. "Sylvia?"

She finally snapped out of it, seemed to decide what to do. Of course I was gambling she didn't have any monthly gear lying around anymore, also that she wouldn't just let me bleed all over the closet. "Sylvia, if you don't get me some sort of sanitary aid I'll have to use your clothing. I think the white blouses and gowns would go first, and of course there's the nice white carpeting. C'mon, Sylvia!"

She agreed. She'd be gone twenty minutes, she said. She closed me in and turned the TV on, blaring again. I waited what I thought was ten minutes, then started banging and yelling with all I had. I stopped to listen. No Sylvia running back in to stop me. And nobody else either. The only gambit I had failed. Nobody heard me pounding for my life.

Detective Collins finished with Zaneda and Alma and headed back to see Andre. He nodded to Officers Berry and Bedford, waiting in their squad car, on his way up to the suite. A few minutes later he was talking on his cell phone out on the balcony when he saw Sylvia Vernon walk out to her car. She waved girlishly to the uniform cops. The Detective went inside and asked Carola—who had just returned with Andre from Century City—to follow her. "Just follow, Carola. Call me immediately as soon as she stops anywhere. Don't go after her. No heroics, got it?" Carola nodded. She looked nervous but game. "Good."

He walked Carola to the stairs, then called Berry and Bedford to tell them to follow her, telling them Sylvia Vernon was their objective. "The subject's car is a light blue, two-door Toyota. Follow at a distance." He read out the license number. "Go easy, like you're on a break, not looking for anything particular."

Carola called fifteen minutes later. Sylvia had parked in the garage, taken a ticket and gone up in the elevator to Long's Pharmacy, on Hollywood. "You were supposed to call me, not stop." the Detective said.

"I know, but I didn't want to lose her. I'm going into the store. I'll say hello if she sees me, and I'll see what she is doing." She hung up.

Detective Collins stepped into the hallway and called Officer Berry to tell him to stay close to the parking garage exit. "Watch for the subject. When she exits follow her, again at a distance. Got it?" He called Carola to tell her to come back to the hotel immediately.

"I don't like this," Andre said when the Detective came back into the suite. "Carola should not be doing this."

"Doing what?"

"Police work!"

The Detective didn't like it any more than Andre. He knew his captain would hang him out to dry if he found out he'd used Carola. "I don't like it either."

"I assume you know what you are doing?"

"Don't you have some paperwork, an actress to hire?"

Ten minutes later Carola burst into the suite, out of breath and excited. "I sped like wild! She didn't see me. Can you believe she was buying *tampons*? Isn't she a little old?"

The Detective smiled and told her she'd disobeyed orders.

Andre put his arm around her shoulder. "That was foolish," he said, but lightly.

"I know. I was so scared!"

Detective Collins didn't let her know he'd told Officers Berry and Bedford to stay with Sylvia once Carola was out of the way. He did his best to confuse everyone. Officer Bedford called to say Sylvia was on her way up to the hotel. "Good," the Detective said into his phone. "Were you seen?" Officer Bedford said he didn't think so, and they'd continued straight on the avenue when she turned up to the hotel. The Detective told him they could head back to the precinct, where he would have been already if Sylvia hadn't sidetracked him. He hung up, looked at his watch and swore. "I have to go back to Beverly Hills. Don't talk to Ms. Vernon, either of you," he told Andre and Carola. "That's an order, Ms. Santosa. I have a hunch she may have seen something and is afraid; that's why I wanted to know where she went. It looks like that turned out to be nothing, but we don't want to spook her and lose a possible lead." He was manufacturing and thought it had to be obvious.

Andre looked skeptical. He said he was confused. "What would the lady next door have to do with Ardennes?"

"Quite probably nothing," Detective Collins said. "So everybody sit tight."

Andre and Carola promised not to do anything. "We have no wish to do your police work for you, Detective." Andre said, sounding irritated.

The Detective looked at his watch again. Rush hour had begun. He made a showy exit, hoping Sylvia Vernon would see him leave the hotel. He felt certain now she was up to no good, had maybe been paid to make Ardennes available to someone with foul intent. Even he did not think to conclude—yet—that Ardennes was being held by a seventy-year-old former stripper.

Municipal offices were closed by the time the Detective made it back to the precinct to ask his boss to clear a search warrant affidavit. He knew the request would not go over well.

"*On what grounds?*" Captain Cortez bellowed. "I gave you the actress when the talent agent's housekeeper yelled foul, a simple open and shut; *you* turned it complicated. I let you go ahead with this, Collins, to my eternal regret. We don't even know the woman is missing." He tugged at his sort-of-off-white, too-tight collar.

"The husband filed a missing-persons; there's been no contact for three days. The car's been turned in—not by the actress. I could go on, sir." The *sir* sounded as sincere as a mattress salesman.

Captain Cortez bristled. "Yeah, the man filed in Hollywood. Go ask *them* for a warrant. You got yourself bumped outta homicide, Collins, all by yourself. Even I thought you can't louse up the usual Beverly Hills break-ins, but look what you've gone and done. You want to be a hero, join the armed forces. Beverly Hills is one of the safest cities in the U.S.; we don't do violence here, see?" He looked at his watch. "It's late already; you wouldn't get a warrant until for tomorrow morning anyway. You're lucky *I'm* still here. I am not bothering any judge after hours on what you're giving me. Where you wanna look, anyhow?"

"Lady next door."

"You astonish me. Since you came over from downtown you been more or less a bum around here, filling your shift like I fill my shoes. Now you're all jacked up some used-ta be actress wanders off and you think the dame next door secretly has her under lock and key?"

"Something like that."

The captain reached for a pack of cigarettes on his desk, shook one loose, looked at the cigarette, and dropped it into the wastebasket. "I hear your uniform cop brother Roy over in Reno got himself into some hot water. Dumb must run in the family." He paused to see how the L.A. Detective Collins would respond. He didn't. "I probably shouldn't discourage you, finally doing something besides clocking in until early retirement. But this is bullshit; you're up to something more than a missing person. I can smell it."

Detective Collins scratched the back of his neck, sniffled once, and looked at the door then at the captain.

"I'm gonna regret this. Go the fuck ahead and search next

door. I'll set up the warrant for first thing tomorrow." The Detective turned to go. "Make it neat; I don't want to hear from the hotel or Hollywood about knifed mattresses: Look under the bed and close the door carefully behind you when you find nothing. Got that?" Detective Collins was already out the door. Captain Cortez called after him, "You get two uniforms; take Berry and Bedford. I'm gonna regret this," he added to himself. "I can feel it." He fished the cigarette out of the trash basket and put it back in the pack.

Detective Collins ran into Officer Berry in the parking lot. Berry was in his civvies, headed for home. The Detective let him know he and Bedford would be needed early next morning.

"Back to Hollywood?" Officer Berry asked.

"Yup." He wished the officer good-night, then stopped, called to him from his car, "What other use you think a tampon could be put to, Mike?"

Berry grinned. "Besides the usual?"

Officer Bedford, coming down toward his car, heard this. "My aunt used to use them to stop up mouse holes. Dipped the suckers in poison and shoved them in."

Officer Berry asked, "It work?"

"I don't know. My moms made her stop in case one of us kids visiting got snoopy and pulled one out, got at the poison."

"I've pulled a couple out," Officer Berry said.

"But did you do it with your teeth?" Officer Bedford asked.

All three policemen laughed.

"Bright and early tomorrow, boys," Detective Collins said, getting into his car. He'd laughed with the others but felt anything but merry. In the morning it would be four days since Ardennes Thrush had gone missing.

2

Release

Sylvia returned with the tampons. She was quick about it and I'd had to shove the heavy pump I was using to bang on the walls under my clothing-heap bed. If she heard me making a racket she didn't let on, and I'm guessing she didn't. She tossed the box toward me and stayed where she was. I made a big show of opening the package. "You're not going to stand there and watch, are you?"

"I'll get dinner, and then you better sleep for a while." When she left I tossed the box into the corner.

She returned with a big bowl of stew. I didn't mention I don't eat red meat if I can help it, I was too hungry to care about the cows. I devoured the meal in big sloppy mouthfuls, including a home-made biscuit. She ate from a tray balanced on her lap, watching me eat like a greedy child. I think she enjoyed that.

She told me to eat up and pack my stuff nice and tidy. "All of it. Any traces will be burned, so no tricks."

"You still haven't told me where we're going, Sylvia." I was hoping she'd change her mind.

"You'll find out soon enough."

After I finished, I asked for more. She brought me another bowlful, a second biscuit, and a sliced, perfectly ripe juicy pear for dessert. I thought of that scene in *The Godfather* where De Niro, as Corleone, brings his wife a pear after he's been fired from his job, how she appreciates the fruit as if it were a piece of gold jewelry. I told Sylvia she was a first-class cook, and only one thing was missing: How about a glass of wine? She accommodated, bringing me a glass of red and one for herself. We sat like pair of doves, her on the other side of the doorway, gun in hand, me in the closet, seated cross-legged. The door was wide open. She didn't have a tight grip on the weapon, and she was drinking. It almost seemed as if she was tempting me; that we were just enjoying a glass together and maybe she was flirting. I more or less immediately nixed the idea of going for her as likely to get me shot in a tussle.

"You're not deciding," she said as she tossed off her wine.

"If you mean what I think you mean, I may have and I may not have already decided. I may even have decided days ago. But so what; if you're going to kill me, why bother?"

"If you are going to die, all the more reason to know; no point to your last minutes on earth if you don't tell yourself the truth."

"So philosophical, Sylvia; I didn't know you had it in you. I wonder, did Lucy tell the truth—in the end?" I didn't say this with any particular venom.

"I wouldn't know," Sylvia answered.

I wanted to keep her talking, maybe convince her to stay where we were. "Did you cook for her?"

Sylvia was quiet a minute. "She had the tiniest waist. She *looked* like a ballerina. I had a jewelry box once; that stinker Uncle Jack gave me. It had a little ballerina inside, wearing a pink tutu."

"Did it have a music box; did little ballerina spin? What happened to it?"

"What?"

"To the jewelry box?"

She shook her head. "Gone, like everything else." She twisted the ring on her finger. "Lucille had long, thick shiny brown hair. I brushed it. . . . But then, see, this guy wanted to be with her. He was a rotter; anybody could see that. I tried to explain to her. She didn't want to hear it. I said he was a pimp—"

"Was he?"

"I just said it!" she almost shouted. She was waving the gun around, from side to side.

I edged toward the back of the closet. "Sylvia? It's okay . . . Sylvia?"

Her voice came out raspy, "She told me to get out, to take my sick jealousy and get out. She was drinking. . . ."

"Are you saying—"

"I'm not saying anything, hear!"

At least the gun was down at her side. We sat a minute, me bound up, Sylvia on the other side of the closet door. "Sylvia?" I said almost in a whisper.

"Push the tray to the door."

She sounded so tired.

She cleared away the dishes and shut me in again, slamming the door.

When she left with the dishes I thought of hiding a credit card or some ID under the pile of clothes or in a shoe box, somewhere it could be found as proof I was kept here. I didn't do that, though, and I can't say why. I could see myself I wasn't making much sense. Maybe it was the steady dosing of Valium—or whatever it was. I could see Sylvia lived in her own solitary weather patterns, was unpredictable, but did that mean she was deadly dangerous? Just before she came back I hid the box of tampons under some clothes on a high shelf.

She told me to pack while she watched. I pushed the packed bag and my purse to the doorway, and she dragged them out, closing the closet again. Only the chamber pot, the flashlight and half a roll of toilet paper were left. She hadn't said a word as I packed. I didn't like the grim set of her mouth.

"Can you at least leave the door open, Sylvia?" I called into the dark. She'd turned the light off when she locked the door. I was panicked again because I was going to be taken from the hotel, and that meant I might never be found; the darkness only accelerated my fears. I thought, if I do die, at least I held Detective Devin Collins inside me. The act may have been meaningless, but I'd rather die as a woman who'd known a man before her end, as if that carnal fact would make me less dead. *"Sylvia!"* I yelled. I pictured her driving me into the mountains or out to the desert, being left to die, vultures circling like in an old Western. I pounded on the door.

"Knock it off!"

I continued to pound until she relented. That was better, and with the light on I saw she'd missed Fits's copy of *Franny and Zooey*. I'd missed it too, half hidden under the pile of clothes. Should I leave it or take it to my next prison? If there was going to be a next prison. Fits's daughter had penned her name inside the jacket in girlish pink ink: "This book belongs to MISSY FITZGERALD." Fits once told me her real name was Littlemiss Fitzgerald, and it was legal. She'd been a C-section preemie, and her mom was out of it when he had the birth certificate filled in. She was too tiny for a name, he said. I decided I'd better keep the book with me.

"Sylvia? What's going on?" I heard light scraping sounds on the closet door. "Mucho?" No, the sound was too high up. Then I heard something metallic drop to the carpeted floor. Only later, when she let me out, did I see that Sylvia had unscrewed the chain from the door. She'd applied quick-drying filler and a layer of white paint, an attempt to hide the evidence.

I lay pressed up against the door, Missy's book next to me. I'd fall into an uneasy sleep, start awake, and drift back again. As usual it was impossible to tell the time. There was no noise outside the closet door. Sylvia must be asleep. I looked around my cell. I'd be leaving . . . so what? Let's not go dripping sentimental. For the moment I wasn't afraid, but something was chewing at me and finally made it to the top of my head: How come Sylvia never came in here to get her clothing or shoes?

In the bedroom was the bureau with Sylvia's blown up photo in pasties and G-string, I think a night table, and some sort of armoire, white and cheap like an IKEA low-end item. What else? Wait a minute! That IKEA piece must be for *her* clothes. I jumped up. The shoe I'd used to bang on the wall was an old-fashioned pump. I opened several shoe boxes: all old-fashioned. I sucked in my breath when I found a pair of small ballet slippers, scuffed white satin with long ribbons and hard toes, a girl's size; Lucy's? I studied the dresses more closely: all old. A wool coat with a fur collar in a style Judy Garland might have worn in one of her ingenue roles. There were waist shirts and filmy, flared dresses and cocktail gowns in '50s glamour style. They had to be Lucille's. Saved since she died? Jeepers creepers, I'm stuck in a clothing tomb. The things on the floor were newer and smaller. I think *they* were Sylvia's. Here I was, an actress stuffed into a dead B actress's closet. There must be some symbolism there.

Poor, doomed Lucy. Was I next? I flopped down again by the door, staring at nothing. I wondered if Lucy's dresses would fit me, but I think I'm a little taller than she was. I decided I'd better snap out of it. I'd better jump Sylvia when she came to get me. This time I meant it. She deserved to die for shoving me into her private mausoleum. She'd slip up and I'd overpower her. Okay, she didn't deserve to die, but she was going to get a fight. I tried to stay alert, to be ready, but it wasn't much use. How could I stay awake shut in a closet sedated with who knew what? Reading would only put me to sleep faster; thinking was no help. I decided to spend the night leaning up against the door, to be ready when she came to get me.

When the door pulled open I fell backward, popping awake. I thought fast and went for Sylvia's ankles with my tied-up hands. But Mucho leaped on my arm and took a bite just above the binding on my right wrist. I howled and pulled back. "Damn rabid beast!"

"Serves you right," Sylvia said. "Back into your corner. Now!" Pointing the gun at me, she pulled the chamber pot out and slammed the door, turning the key to lock it. When she came back she had no hair. I stared at her. Her head looked like a chick's back: sparse tufts of red and gray. She was a redhead?

"Put this on." She was holding her Carol Channing hair, a wig.

I stayed put, turned my back on her, sullenly nursing my wound. "No."

She stuck the cold muzzle into my neck. Mucho growled next to me, his breath coming in hot little puffs on my leg. I grabbed the wig and put it over my big hair. She told me to move to a chair in the bedroom and sit. She adjusted the wig from behind while her other hand held the gun pressed into my back. Mucho watched every move. He looked happy as a clam, ready to strike my jugular at Sylvia's command. The puncture wound looked blue; I pictured lockjaw setting in. Sylvia walked me back into the closet, locked me in again, returning a minute later with peroxide and a cotton ball. First she's all set to shoot me; next she's cleaning my hurt. After that I was back in the chair, where she wrapped my brown barn jacket over my shoulders and, reaching over me, buttoned me up with one hand.

"Get up." I stood, nearly losing my balance. I was pretty tightly wound in the jacket, an ambulatory mummy. She stuck my weekend bag into my two hands, then placed my purse over my right shoulder, crosswise over my chest so it hung along my left arm. She took one quick look in the closet, turning over my nest of clothes. She found the book near the door. "Nice try," she said, shoving it into my bag. She shut off the light and locked the door, putting the key into her pocket. No point mentioning I hadn't meant to leave the book.

I stood waiting, feeling as foolish as a department store dummy.

"Muchie, in!" The dog jumped into an oversized purse Sylvia held open. She tucked the gun into her coat pocket, aiming it at me, and said, "Let's go. Try anything cute and one of us gets hurt, and it won't be me." She had the noir dialogue down.

I walked clumsily to the door. We took the back way from Sylvia's apartment, where the reported coyote sighting had taken place. I saw the clock on her stove as we left: almost four A.M. I was hoping the security guard would drive by, but Sylvia would have thought of that and timed his passes. Her car was parked next to the back stairs, already unlocked. "Drop the bag," she whispered. I did as I was told. "Get in." She guided my head the way cops in movies do, closing the door soundlessly. There was nothing I could do, bound as I was, other than scream, and I didn't.

She tossed the bag into the trunk and slipped into the driver's seat, where there was a cushion all set up so she could see over the dash. She let Mucho out of her purse. "Stay," she told him, and he sat between us, letting me know where I stood with a warning growl. I was pinned by ten inches of dog flesh and a stripper. This would be amusing, seen from the outside or via a camera lens, a real slapstick comedy.

We drove out through the gate and past the lobby area, took a right, and then the next right higher up into the hills. That was bad. We drove winding, dark streets past big houses like sleeping fortresses, up and up, heading for Mulholland Drive and Runyon Canyon. Perfect. Was the plan to take me out there and shoot me? It was a cold predawn; I was close to shivering in a dirty t-shirt and lightweight jacket. She could leave me to die of exposure. Or a rattlesnake or coyotes—maybe a mountain lion would chew me to shreds. My stomach sank. I thought of Joe. Hey, Joe, how about this: a dead serious wilderness right in the heart of Hollywood, and they call it a park. See what you missed? Shame on you. He came out exactly once and didn't even walk Runyon Canyon with me.

Sylvia slowed down at the upper parking area but then kept going. She threaded through the hills until she came down onto Sunset and from there dropped onto Santa Monica Boulevard.

"Are we going to the beach? Why not take the 10?" I said, both to break the silence and to express relief that I hadn't been dumped in the canyon. Bodies of water have always reassured me. Any horizon will do. Unless she planned to toss me off the pier, things were looking up. There were nearly no cars on the road. Sylvia's wheels barely touched macadam; she missed every stoplight for several miles.

Mucho began to growl. Sylvia said, "I don't drive and talk too well, so just pipe down." But I hadn't said anything for ten minutes. I looked out the window at the waning darkness, black fading to gray. My wrists ached from the fishnets and my legs felt jumpy. I closed my eyes to try to rest. No luck. I noted Sylvia wore leather driving gloves and a beret. With her trench coat and tufts of hair poking out, she made quite a statement, like an out of commission spy who'd forgotten to make the wardrobe change. *Mind if I call you Marlowe?* Fits had said what seemed like eons ago. Is Fits aware I'm missing? Of course he is. Not Joe, though. Joe's not aware of anything about me. There's an uneasy border between people, and I wonder if we ever really cross it, ever really reach each other for more than day trips or skirmishes.

Joe was wrong about me. He couldn't see past the few crappy jobs I took, or Harry guiding my career. I took the shit work because I wanted to practice my instrument. It's that simple. Joe was such a purist. It's not like I made the Hollywood drug scene, only briefly hit the party circuit, dipped a toe into the serial sex; was I supposed to sit in bed each night reading the autobiography of John Stuart Mill? Joe missed my struggle and condemned me like I was enemy territory. I think that was what made me ache so badly, that and no longer folding his t-shirts as a wife—when I was at home to fold them.

"Good-bye, Joe," I said aloud.

Mucho growled. "What's that?" Sylvia said, briefly turning her eyes on me.

"I'm done with my first husband."

"That's progress."

"It took too long and hurt like hell reinvented."

She shot another quick look over my way. "One down, one to go."

That was almost funny, and funny was far preferable to sitting next to her with a case of the scared, sorry ass blues. "What do you have against this husband?"

"I think he's a snake."

"Why would you think that?" She didn't say anything further. "My arms are killing me, Sylvia," I complained, mostly by way of something to say and to keep things neutral.

"Nothing I can do about that now," she said, keeping her eyes on the road. Her grip on the steering wheel was tense, her head bent forward as if she was driving through fog, though we were still moving bullet fast.

"Okay, so what do you think matters more, Sylvia: love or work?"

"What's this, sticky question hour? Who says you have to choose?"

I didn't say because I think that's the setup. It certainly is the setup in the arts. Anyone who tries to live normally and answer to the muse is either lousy at normal or cheating the muse. "How do you know so much about me, Sylvia?" I asked instead.

"What? Oh, besides that you're a public icon? That little notebook you keep."

"Really? There's nothing in that notebook; jottings, gibberish to make Andre think I'm writing a book." She glanced at me. I couldn't read the look. Old Sylvia knew how to hold a poker face. I doubt she'd read a single word of the notebook. "So what'd you think of what you read?"

"When did I agree to a Q and A?" she snarled.

We were almost at the beach. Light tinged the sky, blue gray filling in with faint backlighting. "Almost home," she said not looking at me.

What did she mean by that? My grandmother used to refer to death as going home; home sweet home, she'd say. "Why home?"

I asked. Mucho suddenly barked with that extra piercing small dog sound that cuts right through the eardrum. Sylvia was as startled as I was. We both said, "Shut up, Mucho!" He lay down, and we were quiet again. My brain was racing. The endgame was near; what should I do?

There was the pier and the Ferris wheel, still lit up. And there was the sea, the Pacific, nearly colorless, rippling to shore just as gently as a lake. Sylvia turned right onto the Pacific Coast Highway, heading north. We drove until she suddenly pulled over on the ocean side, against traffic. We were at one of the empty stretches between Malibu and Santa Monica. The car lurched to a stop on the pebbled shoulder. Sylvia told Mucho to stay. She left the keys in the ignition. "Let's go," she told me.

I didn't move. "The Muse is your purgatory isn't it, Sylvia: living in the very rooms where your lover died. Right, Sylvia? You have me all mixed up with Lucy. Am I getting warm? Lucy had to decide too: Let go of the ballet dream, take the second chance she'd been thrown, right? Did you lock her in to try and force her to decide? Did Lucy kill herself in the hotel fire? Or did you accidentally kill her? It was so long ago; let it go, Sylvia. Don't make things worse. . . . Listen, I can offer you a pile of cash. Let's turn around and go back, Sylvia, before it's too late. What do you say?"

"Why do you actors have to talk so much?"

She got out of the car, took the bag out of the trunk and yanked open the passenger door. "C'mon." A car was coming down the road, headlights bright in the early light. She lowered the gun. "Move it!" She walked me to the cliff, over the narrow beach, boulders and rocks down a steep decline. She held the weekend bag; the purse was still around my neck. I stumbled all over the place and fell. My chin hit a rock. I swore loudly. Sylvia helped me to my feet. She was pretty spry for an old girl, all those years of dancing, I supposed, and why was I thinking that . . . and why was she carrying the bag? To throw into the sea? Was that the plan?

"Sylvia?"

"Okay, stop." I tried to turn to face her. Now what? "Face the water!"

"Can I sit?"

"Yes."

I sat hard on a boulder, hurting my rear. She tossed the bag past me; it tumbled down to the beach. We were almost at the bottom. The sound of the surf was loud, though the waves were fairly easy. There was a breeze. Sylvia suddenly yanked the wig off my head and when I turned she was already scrambling up the hill. Halfway to the top, she turned. I looked up at her. She had the blond wig in place. "You're free," she called down. "I hope you decided."

I stood up, facing her. "That's it? That's all you have?" I called to her. "*That* was the plan?" I looked at her face, anger boiling inside me coupled with one word: *stupid*. Stupid, stupid, stupid—I yelled up at her: "*That was the plan, Sylvia? Why?*"

That was when she pulled the trigger.

She shot me—*she shot me* . . . sheshotmesheshotmeshotmeshot-meshot echoed; the shot was stunningly loud, but I didn't feel a thing. I dove down, the sand cushioning my fall. It was not like in the movies at all except for the cop dialogue suddenly playing in my head: *Shots fired, officer down; repeat, officer down.* Stillness followed, as if the universe, offended, held its breath; the stillness of a Sergio Leone Western, only instead of the blades of a windmill squeaking the waves resumed licking the shore in lacy folds, bringing back the sound and rhythm of life. The universe exhaled. *Move!* I yelled to myself. I rolled under a rocky overhang; if she planned to fire again, she'd have to come back down. I expected the beach to be running red, but there was no blood. I reached under the jacket—my fingertips came back tinged red. I wiped them hard on my jeans as if the blood were someone else's and had AIDS or cooties or even a common cold. I'm alive, I told myself, not hemorrhaging. Okay. Stay calm. I am calm, I told myself back. Did she mean to kill me but missed? My heart was beating too fast.

Less than a minute had passed.

I waited. The thing about quitting is how good it feels. At first. So what now, Ardennes? Lie here and see the naked truth before the lights go out? Or just think stupid thoughts until Sylvia fires again? I looked up to see a sharp ledge of rock above me; I lay back and started rubbing the fishnets along the edge. It took forever to wiggle my hands to the point where they were loose. I was close to bursting with frustration. "Oh, please, let me get untied! Please . . ." I grit my teeth till they felt like breaking in half.

No sign of Sylvia. I stood up very slowly to a crouch, ready to dive for cover again if I had to, but still no sign of her. I grabbed a stone and tossed it up, hitting a boulder higher up. I waited. Nothing. I went to work unknotting the fishnets at my waist and let the stockings go to the waves. The sea could eat them. They were evidence, but I didn't care. I'd ripped all the buttons but one off my jacket, freeing myself. My t-shirt was bloody from my chin cut. The jacket sleeve had a hole in it, scorched and dark. I touched my chin and shivered. I stood a minute to look at the sea, now almost blue. Behind me the sky over the Santa Monica Mountains was lavender. Two dolphins suddenly leaped out of the water, two black forms jumping for joy. "Hello, fishies," I said, my heart warm and deep; I knew then that Sylvia was gone and I was truly free of her.

I waited, but the dolphins didn't show again. I walked to the water's edge and cupped my hands, tossed foam and water onto my chin; the salt stung. I held my breath and cupped water onto my upper left arm, just below the muscle. *Ah!* I bit my lip hard; the salt was like acid on my flesh. I lowered the jacket and chanced a look. The bullet wound looked like a zigzag of raw meat. No hole. I'd only been grazed. Sylvia, what did you do? Did you wait to see that I wasn't dead? More freezing saltwater stopped the bleeding, which was more welling than flowing. I took the smaller of two scarves from my bag and dunked it into the ocean, then wrapped the wound tightly, sucking in my breath as I did. I carefully placed my arm back into the jacket and tossed more water onto the left sleeve as a kind of ice pack. In the bag I found a sweater, a burgundy cashmere Andre had bought me, and wrapped it around my neck. I was very cold but did not want wool near my open flesh.

Maybe five minutes had passed.

I tried to scramble back up the cliff the way Sylvia had, but three days' immobility had left my muscles floppy. And the drugs were slowing me down too. Maybe that was why my arm didn't hurt. Or was that something the body does, endorphins kicking in, acting like morphine to ease the shock? I picked my way, holding the bags in my right hand. Halfway up I saw a blue-black metal object stuck between two rocks. The gun! Sylvia dropped it? Or tossed it? The handle was wedged. A couple of hard tugs and I had it in the palm of my hand. I turned the chamber, the way Dad had shown me, making sure the safety was on first. It wasn't. He'd wanted me to know how to handle a gun, just as a precaution, that a girl should never feel helpless. He made my mom learn too. The old army pistols from our house, last seen in a shoe box at Joe's . . .

The chamber was empty. Either she had only one bullet or took only one with her. The gun looked old. Where'd she get it? Was she supposed to shoot me, or had Sylvia gone renegade on the plan? I couldn't see her premeditating to kill me; maybe her aim was no good or she didn't mean the gun to go off. I left the bags and climbed back down the rocks and threw the gun with all my might into the Pacific, far enough out, I think, that it would be a couple of days before it washed up, hopefully down toward Mexico.

I climbed back up the rocks to the road, my purse over my right shoulder, the weekender in my right hand. I had to decide which way to go. Walk north to one of the Malibu houses to ask for help, where intruders were as welcome as mudslides and typhoons, or go back to Santa Monica to find an open coffee shop? The few cars on the highway were speeding in the just beginning to glow morning light. I headed for the houses. Even if I was seen as a threat and the police were called, I'd be better off than in a more public setting like a café. I walked for twenty minutes, growing warmer as I did. I kept my left hand in my jacket pocket to keep the arm still. A jogger came by from the opposite direction, meter thingy on his arm, form-fitting spandex, and headband: the jogger statement. "Hello! Listen, please stop; can I use your phone?"

"Don't have one on me!" he yelled as he ran by, giving me a wide berth.

"Like hell," I yelled back at him. "Thanks!" He must have though I was a vagrant. Sure, a lady bum with cashmere around my throat. It was true I hadn't brushed my hair lately, or washed my face. I sat down on the rocks to rest a minute. I opened my purse and found Sylvia had put in a new bottle of water. She was full of contradictions. The seal was good. I snapped it open and took a long pull. A female jogger came toward me. She didn't see me until the last minute, running into the road when she did. I could have been a killer lying in wait. "You should be more careful, all alone like that," I called out.

She swung her shoulder and gave me the finger. "Crazy person," she called back in a high-pitched, teenaged voice. What a nice bunch of caring people lived in Malibu. Once upon a lifetime ago I rented here.

Cars were steadier now, a growing stream. Morning had stamped out the dark. I pushed myself up and started walking again. The houses were getting closer, and I was getting nervous. I wasn't sure what day it was, let alone how to approach a strange house, ring the doorbell and ask for help. Is this how I would be if I hadn't been Ardennes Thrush, successful actress? How, homeless? A nobody was the reply, and that idea did not sit happily. But I'd been chasing an-onymity for two years, and I was not now walking with great pur-pose, not racing to the first house for help. This must be how guys were who rode the rails, moving across the country from job to job or bar to bar, seeing the world from the ground up as they roamed the landscape. There were the dry hills to my right: cactus, scruff plants and brown grass, the breath of wilderness under the city sur-face. And there was the sea to my left: rocks and surf, seagulls and dolphins, all under a cloudless sky. I walked, strolled really—almost enjoying an aimless freedom I knew had just about spun itself out— when a cruiser pulled up next to me.

"Lost?" a nice looking cop asked. Nice until I looked deeper into a pair of cold eyes. He was there to protect the money and the movie stars who made Malibu home, a place where nobody walked. Period. A little brain birdie let me know not to say what I was thinking but to let the cop do the talking until I figured out when to mention I'd been missing for the past few days.

A second officer stepped out of the passenger side. "Okay, hold it right where you are." No *Ma'am, or are you all right?* or *Looks like you took a spill*. Did I appear dangerous? He came around the car, right hand at the butt of his gun, close enough for me to read his name tag: Officer Brown, like his eyes. Only he wasn't; both cops were white, and that didn't seem like a coincidence considering the neighborhood. "Nice and easy," he said as if he was talking to a spooked horse. I hadn't moved other than to turn my head in his direction. The sun chose that moment to pop over the hills, shining right into my eyes. I squinted. It must have been later than I thought, after six, maybe even going on seven. "Step back and put the bags down, nice and slow." He was overusing the word *nice*; better get the writers out here for a dialogue fix. I tried to tell myself this was real, but it wasn't working because at the moment nothing seemed real and hadn't for the longest time, and now things felt downright absurd. Plus, I'd taken a bullet—not quite, but Fits was going to howl over that one.

I placed the weekender on the ground and awkwardly lifted the purse off my shoulder and over my head. My arm started to pulse. I moved unsteadily. I probably looked drunk. Good thing there's no walking while intoxicated to go with the DWI or I'd be up on that suspicion too. I bet that rat runner who said he had no phone called the cops on me. The other officer, who'd watched the proceedings with a mixture of bored fatigue and slight interest (I was clearly not the usual pickup), unfolded himself out of the driver's seat. He was very tall. His name tag read, Roger.

Officer Brown was saying something, but I was noticing early rush hour cars slowing down to rubberneck our little side of the highway performance. Cop Roger hadn't bothered to pull all the way onto the shoulder. They never do. Cars had to maneuver around the cruiser's tail end, creating another potential hazard. That used to drive Joe mad, how the police stopped on a city street, sometimes more than one car, sometimes blocking an entire intersection, snarling traffic. But Joe and I were done. . . .

"Wake up, lady; I said to place your hands on the hood, legs apart."

"What for?"

Officers Brown and Roger exchanged bemused glances. "I'm going to have you dust the hood. Or maybe I'm going to search you. So spread 'em." It seemed to me the policeman lingered an extra couple of seconds at my crotch. When he tapped my left arm and I jumped in pain, all interest in my personal assets vanished. Hands were on guns. (More guns; what a world!) All of a sudden I felt so tired.

"What the hell!" Brown said, grabbing me by my right arm while reaching for his cuffs.

"Oh, no, please don't. I just got untied." I turned to face him.

"You better quiet down, lady." He pulled my arms behind me and was about to apply the cuffs when Officer Roger told him to hang on.

He was looking at my beat up, black-and-blue wrists. "What did she say just now about being tied up?"

"What?"

Officer Roger didn't look happy. "Cuffs in front, and keep 'em loose," he told his partner. He picked up my purse and began searching through the contents.

Officer Brown yanked my arms forward, and I was once again in bondage. "You gonna sit quiet if I put you in back?" I nodded. My arm was throbbing. He opened the door, and for the second time that morning my head was held as I was guided into a car.

"Can you tell me what time it is?" I asked. Neither cop replied. They were too busy with my purse.

"This yours, or did you steal it?" a surly Brown asked. He was out for blood.

"There should be a photo ID, New York state driver's license in the wallet. It will look like me," I said. I suddenly missed the calm of Sylvia's closet.

They found my license, held it up, conferred, and Officer Brown kept it. Next they rifled through the weekend bag. I knew there was nothing fishy in there, and I was growing impatient for my one phone call. Finally they put my bags in the trunk and got into the car. "What are you doing in Malibu, Ms. Thrush?"

I wondered if there was an APB out on me. I decided then and there not to cooperate.

"Officer Roger, will you please call Detective Devin Collins of the Beverly Hills precinct?"

Officer Brown snapped his head around. He was reading my license number, about to call in on me, see if I had any outstanding anythings attached that would give him an excuse to lock me up. "You were asked a question, Miss."

"What was it again?"

"Why are you walking the Pacific Highway at dawn with bruises on your face and arms? You into some kind of S/M shit or what?"

"I'd like a phone call."

"Don't get smart; you're in a world of trouble—"

I cut in on Officer Brown. "Officer Roger, will you please call Detective Collins of the Beverly Hills precinct?" Working actress that I'd been, I already had his cell phone number memorized. I recited it to Officer Roger.

"What's with Beverly Hills; we have a nice precinct right here near the shore," he said.

"He was working on my case." That came out wrong. Both cops

turned to face me. "I thought I was being stalked, and he was handling the situation."

"Where you staying in Los Angeles, Ms. Thrush?"

"The Hotel Muse, in Hollywood. Please, make the call." I
recited the number again.

They did, eventually, call Detective Collins, but not until taking forever to clear my name in their computer files of crooks, rap-
ists, murderers and terrorists. I was hungry, and my arm was waking
up to a world of pain, but I kept resolutely quiet, figuring anything
I said would be held against me.

The search warrant was executed for seven A.M. By seven fifteen
Detective Collins and Officers Berry and Bedford were inside Syl-
via's apartment. Sylvia must have taken a jet back from the beach.
She was in her peignoir, the bed mussed with sleep, shades down.
If they thought to look at her car, they'd have found the engine was
red hot.

"A little early for coffee, boys," she said at the door. "But
come on in." Her wig was off, and all three men registered the
chicken fluff.

Detective Collins presented the search warrant. "Ms. Vernon,
I'm going to ask you to sit in that chair and not move while we
search your apartment. Do you comprehend?"

"No coffee, I take it." She sat down, crossing her legs demurely.
Mucho had let up a steady stream of barking protest. The Detective
looked at him, and Sylvia called the dog and got him quiet on her
lap. "Am I allowed to ask why I'm so honored, Lieutenant?"

She was ignored. "Easy, boys, no damage," Detective Collins
cautioned. Officer Berry was in the bathroom, the hamper turned

upside down. Officer Bedford was turning over the couch cushions. The Detective walked to the bedroom, straight to the closet. He ran a finger along the fresh paint, over the holes where the chain and latch had recently been unscrewed. The paint was still tacky. He pulled out a doctored double-blade knife—one blade filed to an ice pick that could puncture a liver, an eye or a cheap old lock—and had Sylvia's closet picked open in three seconds. There wasn't so much as a crumb to indicate meals had been served and a prisoner held. Sylvia had sprayed the room with air freshener, and the window by the bed was open just enough.

The Detective's cell phone rang.

I heard the following from the backseat of the squad car: "Detective Collins, this is Officer Roy Roger of Malibu/Lost Hills. . . . Yeah, that's right, Roger . . . Agoura Road Precinct. Ah, we picked up an Ardennes Thrush walking along the Pacific Coast Highway. She says you been handling some stalking case. . . . No, a couple bruises, a little unsteady, but . . . yeah, she should be looked at. So, ah, what do you want us to do? . . . You mean here? In the car? No, it's not hot, but we gotta call it in. . . . Yeah, okay."

Officer Roger grunted. "He says to wait here. Seems she's been missing a few days. I don't like it. We should bring her in."

Officer Brown was waiting for a report. He was on his laptop playing a game while he waited.

"What the hell, Ralph. Take the cuffs off her."

"Why?"

"Quit pissing around."

The computer boinged. Officer Brown read a short report. He shook his head, frowned. "I got nothing. Wait, looks like a missing-persons from Hollywood . . . Hang on; she's some kind of big deal actress. I never heard of her. You?"

She was me, sitting in the back. "Is he coming?" I asked.

Officer Roger's phone rang. "Yes, Detective . . . no . . . yeah." He got out of the car and opened the back door. "Detective Collins wants to talk to you." He handed me his phone.

I smiled as I took the phone with both hands, the cuffs clanking as I did. "Hi . . . no, I'm okay." Detective Collins said he was in his car, on his way. He wanted to know if I was hurt; he was going to get me to the hospital. "I'm a little wobbly. . . . I'll explain everything. I just need to catch my breath. Did you tell Andre?" He said not yet. He was driving hard to Malibu, the siren on, cars moving out of his way.

"Get here fast, okay? Both hands on the wheel."

Billy was all business. He outranked them, but that didn't mean Officers Roger and Brown had to like their—what was I, not a suspect—pulled out of their hands. Billy wore a taupe suit and white button-down shirt open at the collar. Was he studying me the way I was him? Everything else moved to fade. It was just the two of us on the highway, a gorgeous day in Malibu. Sounds of the surf fade up to music . . . Are you sure you don't want to be a movie star, Billy? The burning in my arm, growing intense in waves, broke up my impossible fantasy—

No, Billy was not studying me, and Officer Roger was saying something. Billy didn't look too receptive. Officer Brown said they'd need to file a report; was he going to take responsibility? Detective Collins responded that he'd sign any damn report they filed, only now he needed to get me to the hospital. "And get those cuffs off her!"

He tossed my bags into his car; we were set to speed off. "Thank you, Officers," I said to Brown and Roger. "You've been very kind."

Officer Brown said, "You're removing evidence, Detective—just so you know."

"Evidence of what, Officer?" Billy said in a flat voice that said everything and nothing while opening the passenger door for me. He gently closed the door behind me. He was done talking to the uniforms.

We didn't say much in the car. I drank what was left of Sylvia's water. "They were only doing their jobs," I said, embarrassed.

"Right. Those cops are dicks."

"Billy, couldn't we just go to a diner for breakfast?" I leaned into him, dirty underwear, bloody bruises and all.

He shook his head. "We need to make certain you're okay. Then you take your time and we'll sort this out. I know where she kept you, the closet, right—"

I sat back, faced front. "I won't press charges."

"No, of course not." He looked me over. I was afraid he'd touch me and afraid he wouldn't. I'd be a puddle if he did.

"Listen, Billy, I'm trying . . . I need to keep clear what matters—what I need to do. It's been a bizarre couple of days, but I'm all right."

The Detective, in full cop mode, glanced at the blood on my t-shirt, the not-quite-coagulated chin gash, the bruised cheek and wrists, the ruined left sleeve of my jacket. "Uh-huh."

It was a longish drive to Santa Monica–UCLA Medical Center. He'd already called in we were on our way and hit the lights and siren at the hospital's emergency entrance. We were met by a nurse and a young doctor who looked like he couldn't have been much older than twelve. They made me ride a gurney in, though I was perfectly capable of walking. We made quite a dramatic entrance.

The doctor seemed shy about feeling me all over. I told him things looked worse than they were, that I'd always bruised easily. He had no comment. A nurse drew blood while he asked a slew of questions. The doc was first interested in Mucho's bite, giving me a tetanus shot when I couldn't remember the last time I'd had one. He cleaned the chin cut and put one of those butterfly stitches on to hold it closed. When he got to the arm he changed course. He removed my makeshift bandage and didn't like what he saw, cleaning the wound extra carefully with warm water and saline. I told him I'd put cold seawater on it. "Bet that hurt," he said briefly meeting my eyes. "It was a smart move," he added. I looked at the wound; it was mean, like a thick worm had gouged a bloody red canal into my flesh. He gave me another injection, antibiotic this time. As he was pushing the needle in my ears went funny. I shook my head and reached up to tap it.

"Ms. Thrush?" I couldn't hear him clearly. "Ms. Thrush?" Billy materialized, looking at me with gigantic concern on his handsome face. Odd, he doesn't know how good looking he is; very un-Hollywood. I could wrap my legs around that . . . can't imagine what his wife saw in the other guy—I tried to tap my head with the heel of my hand, but those bees needed to quit pulling cotton through my ears—

Ms. Thrush?" The doctor was shining a piercing light into my eyes. I shut them. "Can you hear me?"

I could! "I died for a minute," I said. I was flat on my back.

"Your blood pressure dropped. Nurse, start a fluids drip." He told me he'd be back in a minute. Where'd Billy go? How long was I out? I closed my eyes, I must have slept. I don't remember the nurse sticking an IV needle in. Maybe fifteen minutes passed, maybe two hours. The hospital was Sylvia's closet all over again but with a doctor treating me who looked like his mom still packed his lunch. I had only one thought: I have to get out of here.

A thin curtain separated me from the ER hyperactivity surrounding my bed. I felt the chaotic energy of the place like a current and wanted to yell, *Stop*. I called, "Detective?" The nurse showed up, telling me Detective Collins was making some calls. "Listen, I need to go home."

"That wouldn't be wise."

"Okay, how about if I have to go to the bathroom?" She helped me up. I was suddenly unsteady. She came with me, pulling the IV pole alongside us like a mechanical pet. The bathroom smelled of recent vomit and didn't look too clean. This time the spotting on my underwear was real. I told the nurse, and she gave me a couple of pads; the hospital didn't do tampons, she explained; toxic shock and all that. At least I didn't have that worry, about a pregnancy. Billy was standing guard when we returned to my cubicle. I smiled at him, but I'm not sure it came out that way. I felt as if I must look very pale. He was quiet.

Finally Boy-Doc returned. He and Billy stood at the foot of the bed. The doc said nothing terrible had shown up in my blood, no toxins or illicit narcotics, but there was diazepam and zolpidem.

"What-pidem?" I asked.

"Like Ambien," he said. "A sleeping dose." He didn't ask how it had gotten there. "If there's been sexual abuse," he suggested, avoiding my eyes, "the nurse will bring in a rape kit."

"No sex," I said, careful not to meet Billy's eyes.

The doc signaled to Billy and they moved beyond the curtain for a huddle, only not far enough that I couldn't hear. Young Doctor said the arm wound was not consistent with the others. "That tissue damage is no scrape, more like a bullet grazing."

"You're certain?"

"Certain enough."

"Can you prove it?"

"I looked at her jacket; the fabric appears to be burned, but the seawater she applied compromised any residue." He shook his head. "I'm not a forensics doctor. I do see it all, working the ER, but I can't prove that's a gunshot. I'll write it up as suspicious; best I can do."

They came back to me, sitting up on the bed, my feet hanging over the side. I was ready to go. Billy looked grim.

"I'd keep her overnight for observation, Detective," Boy-Doc said.

"Hello?" I said.

Apparently I wasn't to be addressed directly. I was a specimen, an oddity, a victim, and that seemed to imply an object to be handled at a remove, in the third person, as if victimhood created a discomfiting setback from the norm, like maybe it was contagious or self-inflicted, and generally unhealthy. "I'm right here," I said. Boy-Doc's hands fell to his sides. Billy looked mostly at the curtain behind me. "I haven't been raped or beaten or starved or even verbally abused. I *am* hungry, however, so if you gentlemen will give me a moment's privacy I'll get dressed and, if the Detective is willing, some cafeteria food. My treat. You're welcome to join us, Doctor. After that I'm going home. Please take this needle out of my arm." It was a convincing act, if I do say so, because I felt like a piece of rotten meat.

The Doc didn't like it but looked ready to move on. "I'll write a prescription for antibiotics and ointment. Keep the face cut clean and the arm *very* clean and lubricated; watch for infection. Have someone look at it in a day or two." He reconsidered, asked if I wanted a painkiller. I said no, thanks. He reached up and pulled the curtain closed around my bed; the beads made that metallic sound of mini–ball bearings as they scraped along the metal rod. He nodded and turned to go. He seemed to have aged since I came in.

"Thank you, Doctor," I called after him, but he was gone, on to the next casualty of violence or pain or unforgiving illness.

The nurse came in with my clothes and release papers for me to sign, in triplicate. She removed the IV needle and stuck gauze and a Band-Aid over the hole. I was a patchwork now of assorted boo-boos and applications, like a cartoon figure who'd fallen out of the sky. Nurse held on to the plastic bag of clothes a minute and asked if she hadn't seen me in a movie. Her eyes were fastened on the bruise on my face. I was a walking *Enquirer* piece, straight off the supermarket tabloid shelf. I smiled and thanked her for my clothes, and she drifted away.

Billy went to the hospital pharmacy while I dressed. His badge got him quick service. He'd brought my bag in so I'd have clean clothes to put on. My arm ached badly now, but I was otherwise returning to the everyday, my ordeal in Sylvia's closet already retreating to some other realm of consciousness. The present asserts itself very efficiently that way, or the brain dismisses fast what it doesn't like, starts a glaze over events as quick as it can. I'd find a time to examine all that had gone on in the past few days, but not now; now I wanted to eat and not think. I didn't want to discuss my time with Sylvia with the Detective, in either a law and order context or a personal one. Open and shut . . .

I heard his cell phone chime as I was hooking my bra closed. I'd found the last clean pair of panties but no clean bra; the one I put back on was grimy with sweat. What I needed was a bath. I hurried through the deodorant, hiked my jeans back on, pulled a white cotton V-neck gingerly over the bad arm, tossed a scarf around my neck, ran a brush through my unclean hair and found a barrette to hold it back and I was ready to face breakfast.

Billy was talking to Andre when I pulled back the curtain. I signaled no, I did not want to talk to him. "They're still having a look," he said into the phone. "It seems your wife may have been shot. . . . That's right. No, grazed it looks like . . . Yeah, I'll bring her back ASAP." I looked daggers at him for telling Andre I'd been shot.

"He wanted to drive over to the hospital. I discouraged that, but I had to let him know you'd be returning to the hotel."

"I know. It's okay. Come on, Billy, I need food." I said.

We took a long, winding set of corridors to the cafeteria. I wanted to loop my right arm through Billy's as we walked, but that probably wouldn't have been sensible. We weren't on a date. I was glad when he took hold of my arm. I was still a little weak-kneed. After several minutes' walk through the hospital's shoe-squeaky hush we came to a brightly lit cafeteria with windows facing a small courtyard garden. I picked up a tray and insisted the Detective take one too. He said okay to coffee, but I stuck a plate of peach pie on his tray as well.

I like cafeterias; they're so reassuringly direct. I like the little windows with sandwiches and diced fruit bowls, puddings and Jell-Os lined in neat, colorful rows, and the hot tables with people in hairnets ready to heap servings of turkey or chicken, meatloaf or fish, with dead-looking sides of once green now gray vegetables and gravy with a thick, greasy skim on top. Only it was still breakfast, so I got a bowl of oatmeal, French toast, fresh fruit, tea, and a banana. I dumped a pile of little rectangular napkins on my tray. You needed ten to do the job of one, which made no sense if saving money or trees was the point. Despite my arm hurting like razor blades, I was in a good mood.

Billy carried my tray, and we took a table by the window in the nearly empty cafeteria. I dove into my oatmeal as he went back for his tray. The oatmeal was pretty bad—the spoon stood up in it—but milk and two packets of fructose, meant to pass for maple syrup, helped. Billy sat down opposite me.

"Do you know there's no such thing as French toast in France?" I asked him. "It's called *pain perdu*—or lost bread—stale bread that would be thrown out, but waste not want not, the peasants dipped it in milk and egg, *et voilà*, a new dish was born."

Billy nodded. "Interesting."

"No, it's not. But this is our second meal together." I smiled. He didn't.

He sipped his coffee, shoved pie around with a fork. "You didn't eat in four days?"

"I ate, and I ate well. There just wasn't time for breakfast today."

"What did she want?"

I thought about that. "She didn't really say. Or she did, but it wouldn't make sense."

"Tell me anyway."

I waggled my finger.

"Your line is you went off of your own free will?"

"I didn't say that."

"No one shot at you? No one was hurt?" He pointed to the jacket I'd put back on. One button left and an irreparable tear in the sleeve: burned black from the bullet, edged in white from the salty sea.

"Maybe she's some sort of wacky prophet."

"Sylvia Vernon? More like criminally insane. She took a shot at you; what was that? Sport?"

"You shot at someone." His reaction was slight, a barely noticeable flicker in his eyes. "Cops aren't licensed to kill," I said. This time he didn't react at all. Detective Collins disarmed an unarmed bad guy, and he paid a big price for it. With him it had to be black and white: Sylvia crossed the line, had committed some very serious crimes, and should pay. If Billy wasn't a cop I'd break down and tell him everything, but I didn't have that luxury. And I had no desire to punish Sylvia Vernon.

"Some people went to some trouble for you," he said. I was quiet. "Not that anybody minded, but you act like you think this is some sort of game."

"Billy, listen, please, I had a chance to think. I had all the chances in the world to think before—before the last few days—but I didn't. You could say my hand was forced; you could say my hand *needed* to be forced, and scaring me was the method. You could say a thousand things, but you can't say I was really harmed; shaken, scared, and, yes, hurt a little, but . . ." I waited, but he didn't respond. "Couldn't we stop the world, just for a few minutes, you and me?" What did I want, a motel room off the highway for a quickie? To rest a minute in Billy's arms? It would be so simple. And so temporary.

We looked at each other until I picked up my fork and took a bite of *pain perdu*. Billy pushed his phone toward me across the table. "You better call your husband." I pushed the phone back. I wasn't ready to call my husband. He put his phone away. "You think there's any chance he was involved?"

"Andre?" I blinked. "The Swiss are very law-abiding," I said. I reached over to my big wound; the arm was screaming pain at me.

Maybe I should have taken the painkillers the doctor offered. But I'd had enough doping for a while.

Billy watched my face. "If there were others, they're still out there," he said. "You can live with that?"

I think he said that to see how I'd react. I didn't. I finished my breakfast, and there was no getting around that it was time to head back to the Muse.

A security guard hurriedly approached Billy as we walked back toward the emergency room exit. The guard said they'd shooed off a couple of reporters, but they were still hovering outside.

"Sorry," Billy said to me. "The squad car call must have been intercepted."

I made a face, shrugged. "Even parasites have rent to pay."

He smiled briefly, barely cracking his lips. "Listen, it'll hit the Hollywood blog universe within five minutes that you've been hurt or arrested—"

"Maybe that's the idea: Get me some fast ink."

"Whose idea?" I shook my head. He looked at me, but I didn't have any more to say. "Okay. You have a hat or scarf or anything in that bag?" I did. He told me to drape the scarf over my head of notoriously unruly hair—only he didn't say the unruly part. "And take that beat up jacket off." Done for the moment with me, he asked the guard, "Any chance of an orderly and a wheelchair?"

I wrapped the scarf as stylishly as I could. "Let's not fuss, Billy. I've been through the press before. I can just race past."

Billy said no dice. He smiled. "Wouldn't do your image any good."

"Thanks."

The guard came back with another security guard and a wheel-chair and the nurse from before, holding a pillow wrapped in a baby blanket. "Here you go, Ms. Thrush," she said, handing me my new-born pillow. I smiled and cradled the little darling in my arms. I sat in the chair and laid the folded jacket on my lap.

"Good," Detective Collins said. "Here's the plan: I drive out. Give me, say, ten, fifteen minutes, then wheel Ms. Thrush out the main entrance." He turned to the first guard and told him to keep a lookout, not to exit until the car was under the entrance portico. "Got it?" The nurse was to handle the wheelchair.

In the parking lot the Detective fielded questions from two bloggers and maybe one legitimate reporter: What was my condition? they wanted to know. Was it true Ardennes Thrush had been arrested? Billy asked how they were so sure I was at the hospital. A scruffy guy in cargo shorts shoved an oversized Nikon at him and asked for a quote.

"Here's a quote," Billy said. "Beat it."

The escape plan worked, and we were soon safely on our way back to Hollywood—no lights and sirens this time. Billy told me about the jerk entertainment reporters lying in wait and asked how I put up with that kind of crap. "You get paid way too much money for the inconvenience of giving up your privacy," I said. I looked out the window onto Santa Monica Boulevard. This time I could see the mini-malls, low-rise buildings, occasional sidewalk palms tucked under the L.A. morning light. Away from the water, the haze was building. It was going to be hot.

We drove the slow route across the city while Billy filled me in on what had gone on since Sylvia had taken me (his words). All about Andre and Fits—how he'd had to test Fits, and Fits having been none too happy at being pulled out of the studio by a pair of cops—about Carola's bravery. I asked a million questions, interrupting often. Billy was clear and patient, as if he were giving testimony, recalling details and impressions. I laughed when he told me about Fits.

"Fits is solid gold," I said. "He's made some real dog movies, but he's had a bunch of fun bucking producers and taking home big chunks of movie pay. Good old Fits."

"The hotel staff thinks you're an angel."

"Sure, I tip well. What about Eddie Tompkins; why was he arrested?"

"Unrelated. His boss said he had his hand in the shoe store till. Tompkins says otherwise: It was the boss with sticky fingers."

"He didn't seem like a thief. Poor guy, he really needed work." Billy shot me a that's-no-excuse look. His recounting ended with the aborted early morning search through Sylvia's apartment.

"You knew. You figured out the Indio clue?"

Sitting next to the detective in the big, unmarked car, I felt like I was in high school and Billy had his driver's license and maybe we'd cut school, were going for Cokes—or malteds, like the other day. We'd drive to some secluded spot seniors knew about where we'd make out until our lips ached and he'd work out my bra clasp and maybe get a hand in my pants. Forbidden fruit of the teenage variety; my breath caught and I felt the reckless thrill of being with a boy nobody approved of and, too bad, I was free to make out if I wanted. Only I wasn't. And Billy wasn't older than me; I was older than him. I didn't care; I just wanted to drive up into the hills, climb into the backseat, and fuck the living daylights out of both of us.

Billy was calmly answering my question—which I nearly forgotten I asked. He was, I noted, very literal: "I *didn't* know you were there. I just figured you had a reason for mentioning Indio. Lucerne supplied the story of the bird attack."

"You're a good cop. You would have had me today."

"Today could easily have been too late."

Billy pulled into the upper Hotel Muse visitor's parking space, and who should come strolling toward us, just as cool as the morning dew, Mucho in tow, but Sylvia Vernon. She wore a wide-brimmed lavender hat atop her wig, a purple and white striped smock over yellow capris, and the usual slingbacks. She's going to break her neck one of these days in those shoes, was what I first thought. Seeing her had no other effect on me, not so much as a dart of hatred for my recent warden and possibly failed assassin. She scooped up Mucho and sidled next to the Detective's open window. Red lipstick filled the tributaries along her scored lips. Up in the hills it was hot and bright, Sylvia had to be warm in her getup.

She leaned in. "Find what you were looking for, Lieutenant?" The Detective kept silent, only turned to face her, eyes obscured behind polarized sunglasses. She addressed me next, her own eyes invisible behind oversized, white-framed sunglasses. She didn't look at me as if she were seeing a ghost. "People were worried," she said. I didn't react either. Besides that Billy would be watching for the smallest sign to pounce on her, what was there for me to say to Sylvia Vernon? Thanks for the memories? Boy, it hurts to be shot? A breeze fluttered Sylvia's hat brim and Mucho's big ears. I'll say this for old Sylvia; she might be crazy as corn, but she's the most unflappable lady I've ever met: Tallulah Bankhead and Mae West bundled into a reduced package.

Detective Collins said, facing front, "If it was up to me you'd be in lockup right now, Ms. Vernon, and that piece of fluff that passes for a dog yapping himself silly in the pound."

"Well, I'm glad it isn't up to you," Sylvia said, looking briefly over her glasses—mostly at me. The wall she'd built around herself over years of exposing her body to countless men, which had only gotten bigger after Lucille Trevor died, was up now like a fortress. As if on cue, Mucho barked. Sylvia pushed herself off the car and, hugging her dog close, turned toward the stairs. I watched her walk away. That little mutt in her arms was about the sum total of Sylvia's world, that and a pain in her being that was never going to let go. I'm going with the idea that she was trying to do something for me, whatever else she got herself caught up in, however confused her mission. The way I saw it, old Sylvia wasn't one of the bad guys, and I'll take confused eccentric almost every time over tight and sure. That's just how I called it.

"You know what you're doing?" Billy asked me. I nodded. "You'll have to file a report *and* sign it."

"I know." My good mood was souring.

"They'll ask questions; better have a story ready, and it better be convincing."

I looked at him but didn't say what had to be obvious: I was considered a pretty good actress; being convincing was my job. I tried for a smile, but none would come. I wanted sterling, not an actor's pose. I do know the difference between a real smile and a fake. "Listen, Billy, the weapon will never be found—assuming I'm saying there was a weapon. And I'll deny everything. I'm sorry I got you dragged into my mess." And I meant that, truly.

He looked at me. He'd already told me, others didn't get him into messes. We sat, by unspoken agreement reluctant to give up the moment between us.

I took a deep breath and we both got out of the car. The Detective opened the back door and reached for my bags. I stuck both hands into my ruined jacket pockets, possibly to hide my bruised wrists, or maybe as a way to calm myself. The next step was not going to be easy. I found a folded up scrap of paper in my right pocket. I took it out, unfolded it, and read a typed message: *Computer, notebook, and cell phone bottom bureau drawer*. Hardly the note of a murderer. I looked up at Sylvia's balcony and smiled, just in time to see her pull her Carol Channing head back. I shoved the paper scrap back into my pocket. I didn't think Billy saw, but he did. He didn't say anything, but I knew he was on to my every move. "It's nothing, Billy."

"Uh-huh."

"Try not to be angry with me, okay?"

If he was going to answer, he didn't have the chance. Carola came down the steps just then, bounding two at a time when she saw me. "Ardennes!" For once she didn't look worried. Her eyes were round, her smile beatific. She saw the bruise on my face and pulled back from embracing me. She scanned my jacket and went for my hands, taking the right one carefully in hers, lightly resting a finger on the discolored wrist. "I am so happy to see you!" Unqualified, genuine happiness. I thought Andre was lucky to have her.

I reached over to take her head of long, streaked blond hair into my hands and kissed the top. She stood just about to my chin, which I carefully kept from touching her hair. "I hear you showed bravery under fire?" She blushed deep red. "I'm very glad to see you too, Carola."

She looked at Detective Collins. "Thank you for finding Ardennes." He had no response to that other than a slight nod of his head, which meant pretty much nothing. And, anyway, technically, *I* found *him*. "Andre is upstairs," Carola told me, unnecessarily.

"Yes," I said, and she stepped aside to let us pass. In that moment I saw, from the way she stepped aside, the quiver of modesty in her expression, that she was so in love with Andre. I wish I could have laughed and hugged her.

I slowed to a crawl once we were in the darkened corridor leading to my and Sylvia's doors. Did Detective Collins have to be with me when I entered the suite? Did I have a choice? Was I still official police business?

Sylvia must have slipped the passkey into my bag. I'd seen it there earlier, at the hospital. Billy grunted when he saw it. "We could get prints off that," he said, making the correct assumption it had been stolen and returned.

I held the card in my hand for a few seconds before inserting it into the lock. I shook my head. "Gloves," I said. The Detective wanted Sylvia badly, but as long as I had anything to say about the matter he wouldn't get her. I hadn't cooked up a story for the police yet, wasn't sure what I planned to tell them regarding my sudden disappearance. I was thinking along the lines of a row with my husband: I'd gone to stay with a friend, I could say. Dottie came to mind. She'd stick by me if asked, but I'd hate to have to do that to her. The bruises were going to be tougher to explain. The way I saw it, I hadn't done anything wrong. My Indio message would corroborate that I'd gone away to think things through. Nobody had gone to Indio to look for me, so far as I knew; I'd lost my way and ended up north. If pressed, I'd say I didn't care to mention where I'd gone to privately conclude my marriage was over. Whatever I said wasn't going to add up, but that line should raise eyebrows sufficiently to knock the police off the scent. If I wasn't complaining, where was the crime? I could add that I needed to think about accepting the offer to replace Luce Bouclé. There was truth to the last two parts, but none of that would satisfy the press hounds; they'd stick around, smelling lies to pick over and embellish, drag through the mud. As Harry Machin would say, "They're inevitable so put them to good use. No one believes half of what the Hollywood press says anyway."

"Detective Collins, could I ask you to give me a few minutes alone with Andre?"

"I can leave now if that's what you want." I shook my head.

The lock blinked green; I turned the knob and handed the pass-key to Billy. "Just a couple of minutes, okay?"

Andre was on the phone, facing the balcony. He turned and saw me and said into his phone he'd call whoever it was back.

We stood a minute looking at each other, a sea of tension flowing between us. I smiled as if remembering something pleasant. He came toward me; I met him halfway.

"Ah, Ardennes! My God, Detective Collins said you were shot—"

"That wasn't part of the plan?"

He looked at me for a long moment before giving in and answering. "Ardennes . . . you were not supposed to be taken from the hotel, not hurt in any way." I shook my head. He came up to me, carefully—as if I might break—taking my right arm, guiding me into the sitting room and over to the couch. I didn't sit down.

"What you did to that poor woman, Andre, to use her grief like that—don't tell me you paid her; I don't care. What you did to her was cruel, just unforgivably cruel." I took a breath, waved my arm, the good one; almost a swipe, but at nothing. "I'll do the part," I said.

There were two quick knocks on the door. Devin Collins opened it and came in.

Andre turned to face him. "Detective Collins, I am grateful, and I—"

"The deal isn't quite sealed, Mr. Lucerne. Ms. Thrush will have to make a statement. She doesn't seem to want to indict her captor, who may also be her shooter."

Unseen by Billy, I shook my head slowly at Andre. "*Was* there a captor?" he asked the detective.

Billy was among the artists now, on a different stage, where information traveled by less direct paths. His cop's intuition would take him only so far into the realm of facts being, in and of themselves, not all that interesting. He wouldn't understand how we made our worlds up. . . . Billy's universe of cops and robbers and killers isn't as real. We *played* cops, and wrote cops, could create a libretto for a policeman's opera, get into the cop soul, but we couldn't any of us *stay* in character as a real cop. The next few minutes were going to bewilder and anger Detective Collins. It couldn't be helped.

Billy turned to me. I gave him nothing, only shifted my gaze back to Andre. "The money is still in place?" I said.

"Of course, with you in."

I nodded. "When do we start?"

Andre shrugged, expanded his arms. "Now?" He bit his lip. "If you are able."

"I'll need a bath. . . ."

"No, yes, yes, of course. We can rehearse as soon as you've reread the script." He glanced at my torn jacket sleeve. Some fancy camera work would be required to hide my run-in with Sylvia and her gun. Kind of like Lucille Trevor and her disfigured legs—or Anne Dernier and hers.

"Five minutes to learn my lines!" I turned to Billy. "Okay if I come in tomorrow to make a statement?"

"Sure. Or the next day, or after that." Something like loathing passed over his face. He probably felt used. "You'll be careful of her, Lucerne?"

I answered before Andre could: "Mr. Lucerne will be moving out, to another room or, if he likes, another hotel."

"Does that concern me?"

"It might if my safety is in question."

"According to you it never was."

Now it was Andre's turn to be left out in the cold. But he'd need no translation for what just passed between me and Billy.

Andre sat on an armchair and crossed a leg over his knee. Mimicking him, I suppose, I sat on the couch, directly opposite. Billy stood, a fulcrum between us.

"So I gain the actor but lose the wife," Andre said. It was not a question.

I thought of Sylvia: One down, one to go. I said, "It's what you wanted. Or maybe what you need, like the song says."

Billy pulled one of the two dining chairs out and sat down. He didn't cross his legs.

"Still here, Detective?"

"Until Ms. Thrush assures me she'll be all right."

The balcony door was open on the warm day. I could see the hills up to the observatory. The San Gabriels were shy behind a thickening haze. The air looked to be turning ugly; by evening a familiar gritty feeling would descend on the City of Angels. I didn't care a hang about White Shirt at the moment, though I could see his house and two sets of sheets on the line, one off-white, one lavender. Very soon I wouldn't care about much beyond my character. I would become Anne Dernier and all else would be peripheral, distraction and confusion. Andre would direct, and he would have me—or Anne—

totally. I would be under his and her thrall all the way to my bones. I both dreaded and longed for that immersion. We would rob each other, me and the character; get at a truth rarely known in real life. I thought of Harry. I'm back, dear old Harry; rest in peace.

I turned to Andre. "Harry's gone. I don't have an agent."

"Kurt can make up a contract."

"Yeah, no, thanks, not Kurt. Fits will have someone."

He twirled the fingers of his left hand. "Luce Bouclé's terms, to the fullest."

"You cast her on purpose." Andre bowed his head. "You really do stink," I said, but not with malice.

Detective Collins stood up. Andre and I turned to face him. He looked at me, haunted suspicion in his eyes. "Taxpayers' money was used here, if that matters to you."

"Meaning?" Andre asked.

"Meaning I hope this episode wasn't some lousy Hollywood publicity stunt."

"Ah. Sincerity is overrated, though, don't you think, Detective? No one was seriously hurt, hmm?" Andre's tone could freeze ice.

I winced for Billy's sake. "No," I said quietly, not looking at him. "We're just talented imposters."

I looked at Andre—the easier male, the one of waning potential.

"We're a long way from the moon over Montego Bay," he said to me.

Andre and I had been married five days. The other guests left that morning. The staff was gone for the day, or in their quarters, so we were alone. The Caribbean spread before us; lights on the hills along the bay twinkled and swayed but felt temporary in the night, as if they knew they had no business on an island where wild jungle grew over neglected civilization in a matter of days. On the lip of the horizon a tour boat made slow passage on its way to Mexico, the size of a tiny bathtub toy with strings of white lights, a floating fiesta. Tree frogs were already long at their surround-sound calls, like thousands of tiny glass bottles rubbing their legs together in the dark. The moon pushed up orange behind the lush mountains until a black shred of cloud caught on it; moonlight seeping out beneath the veil as in a dark Ryder painting. We soaked in the hot tub, leaped steamy, naked bodies into the cold pool. The shroud tore away and crystal moonlight lit the landscape black and white. Venus, balanced to the moon's right, beckoned, forever unable to embrace her sister. It was a night for poetry or sex. We chose the latter. Andre spread blue and white striped towels on the ground beside the pool and we fell on each other. His passion was never white hot; he made few sounds, enjoying an unorthodox placement of a hand or finger. He was a considerate lover without letting go of the balance of power. That night he was an athlete, a yogi of endurance; entering me and withdrawing, whispering into my ear, back in, a fit of movement and out again until I pulled him into me, insistent and yearning. Fits once asked me if Andre was a director in bed. He may have been that night. Too bad for him he took possession just as the idea of quitting began to germinate in my deepest folds.

Oh, I suppose he cast a spell that night, but now we were here in the Hotel Muse, and the spell was broken. This was not going to be a baby-torn-from-the-womb ending. Not Joe and me ripping everything to miserable shreds before letting go of the tatters. "It was a lifetime ago, Andre, and so much has changed."

I took my jacket off, even though I felt cold. Andre glanced at my bandaged arm. I wanted him to see it. I reached for my cashmere shawl, from the back of the couch where I'd left it how many days ago.

"Yes, you've returned to your senses," he said. "This madness of not acting is over."

I'd just spent three days in a dead woman's closet. I'd calmed myself in that claustrophobic hole, my smelly lair on an old stripper's gowns. I'd been shot at, for Christ's sake. How could Andre be so certain I wouldn't press charges and the whole abduction come out? Because he knows me that well, that's how. Even with bullets flying. Even if I wanted to, turning him in meant turning Sylvia in, and that was not going to happen.

"Dear Andre," I said, "how you've manipulated everything."

He laughed, but not smugly. "You are going to be magnificent, Ardennes. Acting is where with all my being I believe you belong."

Andre was not complacent. It was just that his unfortunate European intonation and his enormous, driven confidence made him sound it. He was acutely present and boyish again, watching me. He'd risked a great deal to get me back in front of his camera, blind to the selfishness of it. If Andre Lucerne was a businessman, he'd be a billionaire. He goes after, and gets, what he wants. Sylvia was only a pawn; I bet he paid her well.

After that moonlit night came a dangerous storm. We woke up to heavy rain, a tropical depression that churned into a tropical storm. So much rain fell, maybe a foot in a day. The road out of the villa washed out, a torrent of rushing brown water tossing white rocks and chunks of asphalt like a Colorado rapids. Angry rain and more rain and a howling wind all night. The bathroom flooded under the sideways falling water. How could the sky hold so much water? The generator was turned on, so we had lights when hardly anyone else on the hill did. No telephone, no DSL, no way out; the two of us at the edge of the world. Flights off the island were canceled; the road beyond the villa continued to wash away. The tree frogs croaked beneath the sound of wind and endless rain, maddeningly primitive. I kept getting up to see if any stars had appeared; it was crazy, there were no stars. The third morning it let up; pale yellow silt and sand filled the sea, washed from the earth, spreading like a virus, corrupting the Caribbean blue.

"There was a storm after the moon," I reminded Andre.

"There are always storms," he said.

"And we'll always have Montego," I said. I wouldn't waltz out of Andre Lucerne's life without some regret. I guessed at his plan: Get me under his directing and the rest would fall into place. I'd be naive to think he didn't want power over me. But he was mistaken if—

The three of us turned toward the door at the sound of someone rapping: two slow, three fast, pause, two slow. That would be Fits. Detective Collins went into gear. "Stay where you are," he told us. He walked soundlessly to the door, looked through the peephole and opened up. In walked Fits.

"You living here now, Detective?" Fits asked, without stopping for a reply. He walked toward Andre. "Any word?" he asked.

Andre stood up, pointed with his chin. Fits turned the corner. I stood up.

"Hey, darlin'." He came up to me, all open and warm, didn't hold back. "Whaddaya, cut yourself shaving?" He took me and pressed me to him, delicate toward my bruises. His was the most welcoming embrace, the only one without an agenda.

"I'm doing the part," I whispered into his ear. "And I've been shot, but only you know."

He pushed me back, lightly, to look into my eyes; was I on the level or had I lost my mind over the past missing days? "Tell me you're good."

"I'll be okay, Fits."

"Welcome home, baby."

He spun me once, and we slipped into a slow waltz. He whispered into my ear, "I know a doc with closed lips." Good old Fits.

Andre and Billy watched until Fits dipped me and our brief dance ended. Andre's expression was delight. This was what he lived for. Billy was not immune, but he poked at the scene: "Doesn't anyone around here ever ask what happened?" Fits, Andre, and I looked at the cop in our midst, Fits with his beefy arm still around my waist. "Yeah, guess not. I think I get it." He turned and headed for the door.

"Devin," I said, and he stopped. "Let me walk you to your car." I walked over to him and touched his back, letting go as we passed through the door. We were quiet until we reached the car. I felt as if a thousand eyes were on me from all over the hotel: Andre's crew, the maids, even the other guests; if White Shirt could see the parking lot his eyes would be on me too. I was performing for them all. But not for Billy. To think I thought I was invisible only few days ago. "So I'll come in tomorrow?"

"Whatever you want."

"I mean, you won't get into trouble?" He shot me a look—he'd already told me . . . I nodded. "I'll call you."

"Call the desk sergeant; arrange to make a statement."

"Won't you be there?"

"I'll file my report."

"Billy."

"You people don't operate in good faith."

I smiled. He was right, of course. "Worse than criminals?"

"You'll be all right here?"

I nodded. "I'll have to jump into Andre's movie with every-thing I've got, and I'm scared to death. I'll have no life once we start, but I'd like . . . *Can* I call you?"

"You have my number." He touched my hair, the lightest of gestures. "Have that arm looked at," he said, sounding the stern cop. He climbed into his car, backed out, and was gone. If he took a backward glance, I didn't see it.

I watched his car drive the sharp curve downhill that led out of the Hollywood Heights. A spasm of loneliness passed over me, utter and deep, but was quickly replaced by a spasm of excitement, the kind you get as a kid when it's not your birthday but feels as if it is; an unnamable sense—irrational joy, maybe—that something good was going to happen.

Andre always maintained I never really quit. Acting is what I do, and I happen to do it well. "The business end is just part of it; the liars and power creeps, the suck ups and phonies, the nasty, self-involved types are just something Osgood would have to live with for the rest of his life." That last line was from the one movie I did with Fits—I just wanted to try it out.

Anyway, no more hotel spying: no White Shirt or the kitty who befriended me or the old man at sunset with his ugly dog and jar of wine. I won't be wandering Hollywood Boulevard. I'm back in the acting game, where—for now—it looks like I belong: the good, the bad and the chronically make-believe. Funny, I was free to quit but not free to *un*quit until Andre started playing his dangerous games. I can hear Joe now saying, I told you so.

You just can't slam that Joe file all the way shut, can you, Ardennes; can't shake off the past. And there's my mother, telling me I would make things harder for myself than they had to be. Maybe so, Mom, but what's so good about everything coming easy? Maybe we have to fall on our faces a few times to catch on, to figure out how to make the pieces of our past fit together into some sort of whole.

I started back up the stairs and heard a door open and then a car start. The parrots suddenly squawked in the coral tree. I turned at the top of the stairs and saw Zaneda smile and wave to me from the unit across the way, where I'd seen the lovers that moonlit night. The Muse was coming back to life. Or was that me?

So here's the deal: I'll take Andre's movie all the way to the top, give Anne Dernier her voice, make her a character to remember, and then I'll see where I am.

For supporting me in this work I wish to thank Varley O'Connor, Traci Parks, Fred Ramey for "being the fellow," Marcy Rosewater, Karyn Parsons, and Tom Herman. I also thank Alex Rockwell for *Pete Smalls*, which brought me to Hollywood. Thanks to Brenda Heyob and Carol Davis for showing me L.A. and to Madge, Henry, Shereen, and Chisolm, my Jamaican family. With enduring appreciation, Peter, Jr., for his input, my sister Lorene, and the Col. Joseph Stefan and my mother for keeping the nightlight burning. And B., my secret weapon.